THE ODYSSEY

THE ODYSSEY

Homer

Translated into blank verse by William Cullen Bryant

*With an Introduction by
Louis Markos*

canonCLASSICS
MOSCOW, IDAHO | CANONPRESS.COM

Published by Canon Press
P.O. Box 8729, Moscow, Idaho 83843
800.488.2034 | www.canonpress.com

Homer, *The Odsssey*
Canon Classics Worldview edition copyright ©2020.
Introduction, copyright ©2020 by Louis Markos.
First published in the United States in 1872.
Translated by William Cullen Bryan.

Cover design by James Engerbretson
Cover illustration by Forrest Dickison
Interior design by Valerie Anne Bost and James Engerbretson
Printed in the United States of America.

Library of Congress Cataloging-in-Publication Data:

Homer, author. | Bryant, William Cullen, 1794-1878, translator. |
    Markos, Louis, writer of intoduction.
The Odyssey / Homer ; translated into blank verse by William Cullen
    Bryant ; with an introduction by Louis Markos.
Canon Classics Worldview edition. | Moscow, Idaho : Canon
    Press, [2020] | Series: Canon classics
LCCN 2019053148 | ISBN 9781944503642 (paperback)
LCSH: Odysseus, King of Ithaca (Mythological character)—Poetry.
    | Epic poetry, Greek—Translations into English.
Classification: LCC PA4025.A5 B7 2020 | DDC 883/.01—dc23
LC record available at https://lccn.loc.gov/2019053148

20 21 22 23 24 25 26   10 9 8 7 6 5 4 3 2 1

CONTENTS

INTRODUCTION

I f the *Iliad* is the first tragedy ever written, then the *Odyssey* is the first comedy. Whereas the first gives us man the warrior, seeking glory on the battlefield, the second gives us man the husband and father, seeking domestic bliss with his family. The first values strength and prowess; the second wit and perseverance. The first takes place in a world where the dividing line between good and evil is often hard to identify; the second in a world where virtue and vice are more defined.

The World Around

There was almost surely a real war fought between the Greeks and the Trojans, whose city of Troy was located on the northwest coast of modern day Turkey. And that war was most likely fought around 1200 BC, at the height of the Mycenaean Bronze Age.

When we speak of the Mycenaeans, we speak of a loosely federated group of individual city-states spread out across Greece, but mostly located in the Peloponnese. The chief of these city-states was Mycenae, but there were others at Argos, Sparta, Pylos, Salamis, Phthia, Thebes, and Athens, not to mention the islands of Crete and Ithaca. The leader of each city-state was a king in his own right, though they all looked to Agamemnon of Mycenae as their commander-in-chief.

Although the Mycenaeans defeated the Trojans, they did not set up any bases in Troy; instead, they returned home with their plunder. But their glory and power was not to last much longer. By 1100, Mycenaean civilization had collapsed, plunging Greece into a three-hundred-year Dark Age during which the art of writing was lost.

In the absence of writing, an oral tradition sprang up to preserve the memory of the Golden Age of Mycenae. That oral tradition was later carried across the Aegean to the coast of modern day Turkey, where it was systematized and perfected by a group of bards who learned the skill of reciting long tales from memory.

Although the *Odyssey* takes place in the same time period as the *Iliad*, it offers us a world and an ethos that reflect the Dark Ages rather than the Mycenaean Bronze Age.

About the Author

Though Homer was a Greek, he did not live in Greece but somewhere along the coast of Asia Minor (modern day Turkey). Seven cities competed for his birthplace, but he was most likely a resident of the island of Chios. Though we do not know for certain if Homer was blind, there is good reason to believe that he was—especially given the fact that he includes a blind bard in the *Odyssey* who may very well be a surrogate for himself.

The genius of Homer did not consist in his ability to "make up" stories out of his imagination, but to give shape to the oral tales of the homecomings (*nostoi* in Greek; root of our world nostalgia, which means "homecoming pain") of the Trojan warriors that had been handed down to him. It was most likely Homer who chose to center the *Odyssey* on Odysseus and his son Telemachus rather than on Agamemnon and Menelaus and their son/nephew Orestes.

Though he most likely lived near the end of the eighth century BC, at a time when Greece was reclaiming her written language from the Phoenicians, Homer was almost surely illiterate, the last in a long line of illiterate bards. The excessive use of repetition clearly identifies the epic as a product of oral composition.

If Homer did indeed write both the *Iliad* and *Odyssey*, and the full weight of ancient tradition says that he did, then he truly belongs in the category of Shakespeare. Whereas most great writers specialize in one specific genre and one defining mood, Homer, like Shakespeare, was equally adept at presenting tragedy (*Iliad*) and comedy (*Odyssey*) and at celebrating both war and peace, death and marriage.

What Other Notables Said

Traditionally, the *Iliad* is considered to be a greater, more epic work than the *Odyssey*. Written (probably) in the first century AD, Longinus's influential treatise "On the Sublime" expresses this view: the *Iliad* "was written at the height of [Homer's] inspiration, full of action and conflict, while the *Odyssey* for the most part consists of narrative, as is characteristic of old age. Accordingly, in the *Odyssey*, Homer may be likened to a sinking sun, whose grandeur remains without its intensity. He does not in the *Odyssey* maintain so high a pitch as in those poems of Ilium. His sublimities are not evenly sustained and free from the liability to sink; there is not the same profusion of accumulated passions, nor the supple and oratorical style, packed with images drawn from real life."[*]

Still, most readers today would give first place to the *Odyssey* on account of its masterful storytelling and its more memorable and relatable characters. Greco-Roman historian Michael Grant, partly playing off the Longinus quote above, lists the differences in the *Odyssey* that have made it the more popular of the two epics:

> The *Odyssey*, like the *Iliad*, is a display of courage, endurance
> and resourcefulness. But it is much more complex in struc-

* Longinus, *On the Sublime*, in *Critical Theory Since Plato*, rev. edition, ed. by Hazard Adams (New York: HBJ, 1992), 81.

ture—an epic changing into a novel ... Mind and character
now prevail over circumstances ... Love of wife and home
has started to take precedence over love of comrades and
honor, and courtliness over chivalry ... while there is less
deep and tragic feeling than in the *Iliad*, there is emphasis
on hospitality, friendship, acquired courtesy, and the forms
and formalities of decorum; the story of Telemachus is the
story of the education of a hero within this framework.[*]

The *Odyssey* has also had an even greater impact on popular culture
than its predecessor. The word "Odyssey" itself means a great adven-
ture (e.g., *2001: A Space Odyssey*) and it has been loosely adapted by
the Coen Brothers' film, *O Brother Where Art Thou*? James Joyce's *Ul-
ysses* teases its readers with constant allusions to the classic, and even
the children's story *Watership Down* borrows themes from it.

Plot Summary, Setting, and Characters

- *Setting: Various islands in the Mediterranean and then the
  island of Ithaca off the west coast of Greece, around 1200 BC.*
- *Odysseus:* Son of Laertes, King of Ithaca, Sacker of Cities,
  Master of Stratagems
- *Penelope:* Faithful wife of Odysseus who shares her hus-
  band's wit
- *Telemachus:* Son of Odysseus who proves to be both brave
  and courteous
- *Athena:* Daughter of Zeus and goddess of wisdom/war;
  patron of Odysseus
- *Hermes:* Son of Zeus and messenger of the gods who helps
  Odysseus
- *Poseidon:* God of the Sea; Odysseus's foe throughout the
  epic

[*] Michael Grant, *Myths of the Greeks and Romans* (New York: New American Library,
1962), 76-77.

- *Polyphemus:* Cyclops son of Poseidon; he prays to his father to curse Odysseus
- *Menelaus:* Brother of Agamemnon, King of Sparta, husband of Helen
- *Nestor:* King of Pylos whose son, Peisistratus, travels with Telemachus
- *Antinous* and *Eurymachus:* Two head suitors on Ithaca
- *Eumaeus* and *Eurycleia:* Faithful swineherd and nurse on Ithaca
- *Lotus Eaters:* Seemingly hospitable islanders who addict guests to their honey-sweet lotus, making them forget their homes
- *Aeolus:* God of the Wind who puts all the bad winds in a bag to help Odysseus
- *Laestrygonians:* Man-eating giants who destroy all but one of Odysseus's ships
- *Circe:* Enchantress who turns men to swine but is defeated by Odysseus
- *Tiresias:* Blind prophet whom Odysseus meets in the underworld
- *Agamemnon:* King of Mycenae who is killed by Aegisthus, the lover of his wife, Clytemnestra; his son, Orestes, later avenges him by killing Aegisthus
- *Achilles:* Greatest of the Greek warriors whom Odysseus meets in the underworld
- *Sirens:* Bird-women creatures who lure sailors to the rocks with their song
- *Scylla* and *Charybdis:* A beast with six heads and a giant whirlpool between which sailors have to navigate; whichever they choose, they risk much
- *Calypso:* Lovely goddess who offers to make Odysseus immortal

- *Nausicaa:* Princess of Phaeacia, takes in Odysseus when he washes up on shore
- *Alcinous* and *Arete:* King and Queen of Phaeacia, parents of Nausicaa

The *Odyssey* tells the story of Odysseus's ten-year journey from Troy back to his island home of Ithaca. It begins, like the *Iliad*, not at the beginning of the story but *in medias res* (Latin for "in the middle of things"), during the final year of his wanderings.

Books I–IV introduce Odysseus's son, Telemachus, as he waits disconsolately for the return of his father. Athena appears to rouse him to action, instructing him to visit Nestor and Menelaus to find out if his father is still alive. Meanwhile a group of evil suitors press Penelope to marry one of them.

Taking place simultaneously with Books I–IV, Books V–VIII reveal that Odysseus has been stranded on Calypso's island for seven years (*Calypso* is Greek for "hidden"). But Zeus sends Hermes to Calypso to tell her to release Odysseus. Odysseus leaves on a raft but is wrecked by Poseidon and washes ashore on Phaeacia, where Nausicaa helps him. The Phaeacians graciously agree to take Odysseus back to Ithaca, but first he tells them of his journeys.

Books IX–XII tell in flashback and in first person how Odysseus eluded the Lotus Eaters and defeated the cannibalistic Cyclops Polyphemus by getting him drunk and putting out his eye. Unfortunately, as Odysseus escaped, he boasted of his triumph, allowing Polyphemus, son of Poseidon, to curse him, causing him to arrive late in Ithaca having lost all his men and finding his home in turmoil.

The curse set in as members of Odysseus's crew 1) opened up a bag of wind that had been given him by the hospitable Aeolus, causing them to be blown off course; 2) got eaten by the giant Laestrygonians; and 3) were turned to swine by Circe the enchantress. Though Odysseus survived, he had to visit the underworld for information about how to avoid such monsters as the sirens and Scylla and Charybdis.

Finally, when his surviving men ate the forbidden Cattle of the Sun, they were all killed, leaving Odysseus alone and stranded on the island of Calypso.

After the sympathetic Phaeacians set him back home on Ithaca (Books XIII–XXIV), Odysseus reveals himself to Telemachus and the two plot together, first to test and then to kill the evil suitors. Husband and wife are reunited, and order is restored.

Worldview Analysis

The reader who moves from the *Iliad* to the *Odyssey* should notice immediately that the *Odyssey* takes place in a far more ethical world where the distinctions between good and evil are clearer for both the characters and the reader. Whereas we feel great remorse when Hector, the purported antagonist of the *Iliad*, dies, we feel no sorrow whatsoever when Odysseus kills the suitors.

In the last book of the *Iliad*, Achilles says that Zeus has two urns by his throne: one filled with blessings; the other with curses. When he showers on us the contents of the first, our lives are filled with joy; when the contents of the second rain down on us, our lives are destroyed by suffering and pain. How does Zeus choose which urn to draw from? No one can say; at least from Achilles' point of view, the choice is arbitrary.

In the first book of the *Odyssey*, Zeus himself rejects this point of view: "What a lamentable thing it is that men should blame the gods and regard *us* as the source of their troubles, when it is their own transgressions which bring them suffering that was not their destiny" (I.33–35).* Then, to prove his point, he tells the melodramatic story of how Agamemnon was killed by Aegisthus, the lover of his wife,

---

* All quotes from Homer are taken from *The Odyssey*, trans. by E. V. Rieu, rev. by D. C. H. Rieu (London: Penguin, 1991). References from this prose translation will be given in the text by book and line number.

Clytemnestra. Aegisthus was wrong to do this deed, asserts Zeus, and was justly killed by Agamemnon's son, Orestes.

It is safe to suggest that Homer here agrees with Zeus, for, in telling the story of the family of Agamemnon, he leaves out those parts that muddy the ethical waters. Thus, in the fuller version of the story—later dramatized by the Greek tragedian Aeschylus in his trilogy, the *Oresteia*—Agamemnon is killed by his wife (not by her lover), and Orestes follows his slaying of Aegisthus by doing the same to his mother. Matricide and wives-killing-husbands make for great tragic dilemmas, but that is not Homer's focus.

To drive home the ethical worldview around which his epic is constructed, Homer skillfully parallels the Agamemnon-Clytemnestra-Aegisthus-Orestes subplot with his central story of Odysseus, Penelope, the suitors, and Telemachus. The suitors, like Aegisthus, are simple villains, and no taboos are broken when Telemachus, like Orestes, avenges the indignities paid to his father. (Telemachus, in fact, consciously takes up Orestes as his role model.) That Penelope, *unlike* Clytemnestra, stays faithful to her absent husband only emphasizes further that our choices determine our fate.

Since the *Odyssey* takes place in a moral universe, it is vital that readers be provided with a key for distinguishing the good guys from the bad guys. In the Bible, the virtues of obedience, gratitude, faith, hope, and love separate saint from sinner, the righteous from the unrighteous. In the *Odyssey*, it is the good relationship between the guest and the host (*xenia* in Greek) that distinguishes the hero from the villain.

We immediately know Telemachus is a good person, for, when Athena comes to the palace in disguise, Telemachus alone takes her in and feeds her. While visiting Nestor and Menelaus, he further reveals his *xenia* by being a good and noble guest. The suitors, on the other hand, are bad guests who take advantage of Penelope's hospitality, just as the Lotus Eaters and Calypso are bad hosts who detain their guests against their will.

While on his journeys, Odysseus meets both good hosts (Aeolus, who freely gives him a bag of wind that will afford him safe passage home; the Phaeacians, who feed him royally and then escort him back to Ithaca) and bad hosts (Polyphemus, who, rather than feeding Odysseus's men, feeds *on* them; Circe, who turns his men to swine). In most cases, Odysseus is a good guest; however, in the cave of Polyphemus, Odysseus plays the role of a bad guest and pays for it by provoking the Cyclops' curse.

Though *xenia* is not as strong a theme in the Bible, hospitality is significant in the Old Testament—where the men of Sodom and Gomorrah are punished for treating the angels who visit their town with contempt and perverse lust (Genesis 19)—and in the New—where we are instructed to show hospitality because, by so doing, we may entertain angels unawares (Heb. 13:2). Whether in the Bible or in the *Odyssey*, the way one treats a guest or a host offers a window into that person's soul, revealing his inner character.

Though Odysseus is the protagonist of the epic, Homer unexpectedly devotes Books I–IV to Telemachus' maturation process. Like so many characters in literature (Orestes, Henry V, Huck Finn, Frodo Baggins) and the Bible (Samuel, David, Peter, Paul) Telemachus must go through a rite of passage that will test his mettle and enable him to come of age.

In Telemachus' case, he must discover whether he is the true son of his father. In the epic, it is Athena who calls upon the unsure, untested Telemachus to live up to his noble father: "You are no longer a child: you must put childish thoughts away.... You, my friend—and what a tall and splendid young man you have grown!—must be as brave as Orestes. Then future generations will sing your praises" (I.297–304; see 1 Cor. 13:11 for an interesting, though probably unconscious, echo by the classically educated Paul).

Whereas the typical teenager of today would balk at being told to live up to the deeds of some other young man, much less the deeds of his father, Telemachus eagerly accepts the challenge. Like a biblical hero, but unlike most modern heroes, Telemachus realizes that he lives and acts within a web of duties, responsibilities, and familial relationships which he cannot simply throw off. He is the son of Odysseus, not one of the *xenia*-despising suitors.

On the same day, somewhere on the other side of the Mediterranean, Odysseus, too, makes the choice to be true to his duties and familial identity. When Calypso, desperate to convince Odysseus to remain with her and accept her gift of immortality, expresses doubt that Penelope can exceed her in beauty, Odysseus freely admits that "my wise Penelope's looks and stature are insignificant compared with yours. For she is mortal, while you have immortality and unfading youth. Nevertheless I long to reach my home and see the day of my return. It is my never-failing wish" (V.216–221).

There is a wealth of wisdom and insight in that word "nevertheless" that cuts to the core of what it means to be human. If he is not the husband of Penelope, the son of Telemachus, and the King of Ithaca, then he is not really Odysseus. When most people today hear the name Odysseus, they think of someone with a wanderlust who wants to sail the seven seas (in great part because he is depicted that way in Alfred, Lord Tennyson's stirring Victorian poem, "Ulysses"), but that is not the Odysseus of Homer. His hero desires only one thing: to return home.

To say that Odysseus is a Greek Sinbad the Sailor is tantamount to saying that Paul traveled across the Mediterranean world because he was a tourist. Paul's travels had only one end: to spread the gospel. Just so, Odysseus travels only so that he may be reunited with his family. That is not to say he is a Christian hero. Like Jacob, he is not above being a deceiver and a trickster; like David, his sexual ethics are decidedly suspect. He also delays far longer than he should on the island of Circe, almost succumbing to the false homecoming that Circe tempts him with.

Nevertheless, he possesses an integrity that allows him to remain whole. Only in the cave of the Cyclops, when he misuses his identity and boastfully shouts out his name to Polyphemus, does he suffer a loss of that integrity—a loss that carries with it terrible consequences. After that slip, however, he grows increasingly in his self-understanding, and is even able to bear up under the numinous dread of visiting Hades and facing his own eventual death. Indeed, when he turns down Calypso's offer of immortality to return home to Penelope, he does so *after* he has seen how dreary the afterlife is. Still, he chooses to be mortal, for that is who and what he is.

Odysseus's moral growth, seen so powerfully in his refusal of immortality and of the suitor-like *luxuria* that Circe, Calypso, and Nausicaa offer, is also evidenced in Book IX, when he freely confesses to the Phaeacians his own guilt in provoking the Cyclops to wrath. Even though he must practice trickery on Ithaca to survive and exact his just revenge on the suitors, he has learned the value of honesty and that there are people, like the Phaeacians, who can and should be trusted.

In its moral-ethical outlook, the *Odyssey* overlaps with some key aspects of the Judeo-Christian worldview; however, it is in its overall narrative thrust that Homer's epic most closely parallels the story of scripture. Both the *Odyssey* and the Bible hinge upon the promised messianic coming of a good king who will restore justice by punishing the wicked and exalting the faithful. Our world, like Homer's Ithaca, is trapped in a state of futility from which it cannot free itself; it needs the intervention of a savior-judge who will arrive in the fullness of time and set things to right.

Although Books I–XII, which chronicle the dual journeys of Odysseus and his son, move swiftly, Books XIII–XXIV, during which Odysseus takes back his home, are often gruelingly slow-paced. But that slowness—which itself mimics the gradual unfolding of God's plan for human history—is used to draw out three themes that are also central to the Bible: recognition, endurance, and discernment.

Rather than announce his arrival the moment he lands on the beach of Ithaca, Odysseus, guided by Athena, only reveals himself to those he can trust. Not everyone on the island desires to see the return of the true king, and so he must be cautious, only revealing himself to those who have eyes to see and ears to hear.

In what may be the best known and most beloved moments in the epic, Odysseus, who wears a disguise throughout most of the second half of the epic, is only recognized by his faithful dog, Argus, who lifts his head at the approach of his master and then dies peacefully. Even so, when the Son of God came into the world as a mortal man, there were precious few who recognized him. To his own people the Messiah came, John sadly informs us in his prologue, but they neither knew nor accepted him (Jn. 1:10–11).

As the Son of God took the form of a poor servant from whom men turned their faces (see Is. 53:2–3), so Odysseus is disguised by Athena as an old and dirty beggar from whom most of the Ithacans turn in scorn. Of all his trials and tribulations, this proves to be the hardest for him, for he must bear up under humiliating indignities, even though he is the rightful king come home to his palace and his throne. He even has stools hurled at his head by the worst of the suitors. Still, as Christ will do over a thousand years later, he endures the scorn for the greater prize that awaits him (Heb. 12:2).

By suffering the suitor's insults, Odysseus is made a more perfect and obedient deliverer (see Heb. 5:7–10); but he also is empowered to do something of great importance. He is put in a position to test the suitors one by one so as to discern which of them is wholly evil and which can yet be redeemed. In a line that, like so many verses in the Bible, combines free will with the sovereign choice of God, Homer has Athena urge the disguised Odysseus "to go round collecting scraps from the Suitors and so learn to distinguish the good from the bad, though this did not mean that in the end she was to save a single one from destruction" (XVII.361–364).

Because of this careful sifting of the wheat from the chaff, when Odysseus brings down Armageddon on the evil suitors, both he and we are assured of the justice of his actions. In fact, when Eurycleia, Odysseus's faithful nurse, begins to gloat over the death of the suitors, Odysseus stops her, saying, "Restrain yourself, old woman, and gloat in silence. I'll have no cries of triumph here. It is an impious thing to exult over the slain. These men fell victims to the will of the gods and their own infamy. They paid respect to no one on earth who came near them—good or bad. And now their own transgressions have brought them to this ignominious death" (XXII.410–416).

~Louis Markos

21 Discussion Questions

Answers to discussion questions can be found in the back of the book.

1. Why does Homer choose to begin his epic in the final year of Odysseus's wanderings rather than with the fall of Troy?

2. How does the narrative structure of the *Odyssey* differ from that of the *Iliad*?

3. What did ancient critics say about Books I-IV?

4. Why does Telemachus have to visit Nestor and Menelaus?

5. How does Penelope hold off the suitors for so many years?

6. How exactly should the guest-host relationship (*xenia*) work?

7. Why does Athena, and other gods, appear in disguise most of the time?

8. What qualities does a hero need to survive and thrive in the world of the *Odyssey*?

9. Can you give an example of someone holding on through disguises to reach the truth?

10. *What are the two types of dangers Odysseus faces on his journeys?*

11. What is the lure of the Sirens that makes them so dangerous?

12. What does it mean to navigate between Scylla and Charybdis?

13. Why must Odysseus travel into the underworld?

14. Why does Homer give so prominent a role to Eumaeus the swineherd?

15. How does Penelope show her faithfulness in the *Odyssey*?

16. How does Odysseus differ from and resemble the heroes of the Bible?

17. Why does Homer build a friendship between Telemachus and Peisistratus?

18. How does Odysseus win back Penelope and why is that significant?

19. Why is Odysseus so cruel to the maids and serving women?

20. How is Odysseus able to convince Penelope that he has truly returned home?

21. In Book XXIV, Homer gives us a final glimpse of the underworld, where we hear Agamemnon describe the funeral of Achilles and the dead suitors tell of their death at the hands of Odysseus. Why does Homer include this seemingly anti-climactic scene?

BOOK I*

Tell me, O Muse, of that sagacious man   1
Who, having overthrown the sacred town
Of Ilium, wandered far and visited
The capitals of many nations, learned
The customs of their dwellers, and endured   5
Great suffering on the deep: his life was oft
In peril, as he labored to bring back
His comrades to their homes. He saved them not,
Though earnestly he strove; they perished all,
Through their own folly; for they banqueted,   10
Madmen! upon the oxen of the Sun—
The all-o'erlooking Sun, who cut them off
From their return. O goddess, virgin-child
Of Zeus, relate some part of this to me.
Now all the rest, as many as escaped is   15
The cruel doom of death, were at their homes
Safe from the perils of the war and sea,
While him alone, who pined to see his home

Invitation of Muse

* Note: this translation does not match the line numbering of the original Greek text.

1

And wife again, Calypso, queenly nymph,
Great among goddesses, detained within   20
Her spacious grot, in hope that he might yet
Become her husband. Even when the years
Brought round the time in which the gods decreed
That he should reach again his dwelling-place
In Ithaca, though he was with his friends,   25
His toils were not yet ended. Of the gods
All pitied him save Poseidon, who pursued
With wrath implacable the godlike chief,
Odysseus, even to his native land.
Among the Ethiopians was the god   30
Far off—the Ethiopians most remote
Of men. Two tribes there are: one dwells beneath
The rising, one beneath the setting sun.
He went to grace a hecatomb of beeves
And lambs, and sat delighted at the feast;   35
While in the palace of Olympian Zeus
The other gods assembled, and to them
The father of immortals and of men
Was speaking. To his mind arose the thought
Of that Aegisthus whom the famous son   40
Of Agamemnon, Prince Orestes, slew.
Of him he thought and thus bespake the gods:
"How strange it is that mortals blame the gods
And say that we inflict the ills they bear,
When they, by their own folly and against   45
The will of fate, bring sorrow on themselves!
As late Aegisthus, unconstrained by fate,
Married the queen of Atreus' son and slew
The husband just returned from war. Yet well
He knew the bitter penalty, for we   50

Warned him. We sent the herald Argicide,
Bidding him neither slay the chief nor woo
His queen, for that Orestes, when he came
To manhood and might claim his heritage,
Would take due vengeance for Atrides slain.   55
So Hermes said; his prudent words moved not
The purpose of Aegisthus? who now pays
The forfeit of his many crimes at once."
Pallas, the blue-eyed goddess, thus replied:
"O father, son of Cronus, king of kings!   60
Well he deserved his death. So perish all
Guilty of deeds like his! But I am grieved
For sage Odysseus, that most wretched man,
So long detained, repining, and afar
From those he loves, upon a distant isle   65
Girt by the waters of the central deep—
A forest isle, where dwells a deity
The daughter of wise Atlas, him who knows
The ocean to its utmost depths, and holds
Upright the lofty columns which divide   70
The earth from heaven. The daughter there detain
The unhappy chieftain, and with flattering words
Would win him to forget his Ithaca.
Meanwhile, impatient to behold the smokes
That rise from hearths in his own land, he pines   75
And willingly would die. Is not thy heart,
Olympius, touched by this? And did he not
Pay grateful sacrifice to thee beside
The Argive fleet in the broad realm of Troy?
Why then, O Zeus, art thou so wroth with him?"   80
Then answered cloud-compelling Zeus: "My child,
What words have passed thy lips? Can I forget

Godlike Odysseus, who in gifts of mind
Excels all other men, and who has brought
Large offerings to the gods that dwell in heaven?   85
Yet he who holds the earth in his embrace,
Poseidon, pursues him with perpetual hate
Because of Polypheme, the Cyclops, strong
Beyond all others of his giant race,
Whose eye Odysseus had put out. The nymph   90
Thoosa brought him forth—a daughter she
Of Phorcys, ruling in the barren deep—
And in the covert of o'erhanging rocks
She met with Poseidon. For this cause the god
Who shakes the shores, although he slay him not,   95
Sends forth Odysseus wandering far away
From his own country. Let us now consult
Together and provide for his return,
And Poseidon will lay by his wrath, for vain
It were for one like him to strive alone   100
Against the might of all the immortal gods."
And then the blue-eyed Pallas spake again:
"O father! son of Cronus, king of kings!
If such the pleasure of the blessed gods
That now the wise Odysseus shall return   105
To his own land, let us at once dispatch
Hermes, the Argicide, our messenger,
Down to Ogygia, to the bright-haired nymph,
And make our steadfast purpose known to bring
The sufferer Odysseus to his home,   110
And I will haste to Ithaca, and move
His son, that with a resolute heart he call
The long-haired Greeks together and forbid
The excesses of the suitor train, who slay

His flocks and slow-paced beeves with crooked horns.   115
To Sparta I will send him and the sands
Of Pylos, to inquire for the return
Of his dear father. So a glorious fame
Shall gather round him in the eyes of men."
She spake, and fastened underneath her feet   120
The fair, ambrosial golden sandals worn
To bear her over ocean like the wind,
And o'er the boundless land. In hand she took,
Well-tipped with trenchant brass, the mighty spear,
Heavy and huge and strong, with which she bears   125
Whole phalanxes of heroes to the earth,
When she, the daughter of a mighty sire,
Is angered. From the Olympian heights she plunged,
And stood among the men of Ithaca,
Just at the porch and threshold of their chief,   130
Odysseus. In her hand she bore the spear,
And seemed the stranger Mentes, he who led
The Taphians. There before the gate she found
The haughty suitors. Some beguiled the time
With draughts, while sitting on the hides of beeves   135
Which they had slaughtered. Heralds were with them,
And busy menials: some who in the bowls
Tempered the wine with water, some who cleansed
The tables with light sponges, and who set
The banquet forth and carved the meats for all.   140
Telemachus the godlike was the first
To see the goddess as he sat among
The crowd of suitors, sad at heart, and thought
Of his illustrious father, who might come
And scatter those who filled his palace halls,   145
And win new honor, and regain the rule

Over his own. As thus he sat and mused
Among the suitors, he beheld where stood
Pallas, and forth he sprang; he could not bear
To keep a stranger waiting at his door.   150
He came, and taking her right hand received
The brazen spear, and spake these winged words:
"Hail, stranger! thou art truly welcome here;
First come and share our feast and be refreshed,
Then say what thou requirest at our hands."   155
He spake and led the way, and in his steps
Pallas Athene followed. Entering then
The lofty halls, he set the spear upright
By a tall column, in the armory
With polished walls, where rested many a lance   160
Of the large-souled Odysseus. Then he placed
His guest upon a throne, o'er which he spread
A covering many-hued and beautiful,
And gave her feet a footstool. Near to her
He drew his party-colored seat, aloof   165
From where the suitors sat; that so his guest
Might not amid those haughty revelers
Be wearied with the tumult and enjoy
His meal the less, and that himself might ask
News of his absent father. In a bowl   170
Of silver, from a shapely ewer of gold,
A maid poured water for the hands, and set
A polished table near them. Then approached
A venerable matron bringing bread   180
And delicacies gathered from the board;   175
And he who served the feast before them placed
Chargers with various meats, and cups of gold;
While round the board a herald moved, and poured

Wine for the guests. The haughty suitors now
Came in, and took their places on the thrones   180
And couches; heralds poured upon their hands
The water; maidens heaped the canisters
With bread, and all put forth their hands to share
The banquet on the board, while to the brim
Boys filled the beakers. When the calls of thirst   185
And hunger were appeased, the suitors thought
Of other things that well become a feast—
Song and the dance. And then a herald brought
A shapely harp, and gave it to the hands
Of Phemius, who had only by constraint   190
Sung to the suitors. On the chords he struck
A prelude to his lay, while, as he played,
Telemachus, that others might not hear,
Leaned forward, and to blue-eyed Pallas spake:
"My friend and guest, wilt thou take no offence   195
At what I say? These revelers enjoy
The harp and song, for at no cost of theirs
They waste the substance of another man,
Whose white bones now are moldering in the rain
Upon some main-land, or are tossed about   200
By ocean billows. Should they see him once
In Ithaca, their prayers would rather rise
For swifter feet than richer stores of gold
And raiment. But an evil fate is his,
And he has perished. Even should we hear   205
From any of the dwellers upon earth
That he is near at hand, we could not hope.
For him is no return. But now, I pray,
Tell me, and frankly tell me, who thou art,
And of what race of men, and where thy home,   210

And who thy parents; how the mariners
Brought thee to Ithaca, and who they claim
To be, for well I deem thou couldst not come
Hither on foot. All this, I pray, relate
Truly, that I may know the whole. Art thou   215
For the first time arrived, or hast thou been
My father's guest? for many a stranger once
Resorted to our palace, and he knew
The way to win the kind regard of men."
Pallas, the blue-eyed goddess, answered thus: 220
"I will tell all and truly. I am named
Mentes; my father was the great in war
Anchialus. I rule a people skilled
To wield the oar, the Taphians, and I come
With ship and crew across the dark blue deep   225
To Temese, and to a race whose speech
Is different from my own, in quest of brass,
And bringing bright steel with me. I have left
Moored at the field behind the town my bark,
Within the bay of Reithrus, and beneath   230
The woods of Neius. We claim to be
Guests by descent, and from our fathers' time,
As thou wilt learn if thou shouldst meet and ask
Laertes, the old hero. It is said
He comes no more within the city walls,   235
But in the fields dwells sadly by himself,
Where an old handmaid sets upon his board
His food and drink when weariness unnerves
His limbs in creeping o'er the fertile soil
Of his rich vineyard. I am come because   240
I heard thy father had at last returned,
And now am certain that the gods delay

His journey hither; for the illustrious man
Cannot have died, but is detained alone
Somewhere upon the ocean, in some spot   245
Girt by the waters. There do cruel men
And savage keep him, pining to depart.
Now let me speak of what the gods reveal,
And what I deem will surely come to pass,
Although I am no seer and have no skill   250
In omens drawn from birds. Not long the chief
Will be an exile from his own dear land.
Though fettered to his place by links of steel;
For he has large invention, and will plan
A way for his escape. Now tell me this,   255
And truly; tall in stature as thou art,
Art thou in fact Odysseus' son? In face
And glorious eyes thou dost resemble him
Exceedingly; for he and I of yore
Were oftentimes companions, ere he sailed   260
For Ilium, whither also went the best
Among the Argives in their roomy ships,
Nor have we seen each other since that day."
Telemachus, the prudent, spake: "O guest,
True answer shalt thou have. My mother says   265
I am his son; I know not; never man
Knew his own father. Would I were the son
Of one whose happier lot it was to meet
Amidst his own estates the approach of age.
Now the most wretched of the sons of men   270
Is he to whom they say I owe my birth.
Thus is thy question answered." Then again
Spake blue-eyed Pallas: "Of a truth, the gods
Ordain not that thy race, in years to come,

Should be inglorious, since Penelope   275
Hath borne thee such as I behold thee now.
But frankly answer me—what feast is here,
And what is this assembly? What may be
The occasion? is a banquet given? is this
A wedding? A collation, where the guests   280
Furnish the meats, I think it cannot be,
So riotously goes the revel on
Throughout the palace. A well-judging man,
If he should come among them, would be moved
With anger at the shameful things they do."   285
Again Telemachus, the prudent, spake:
"Since thou dost ask me, stranger, know that once
Rich and illustrious might this house be called
While yet the chief was here. But now the gods
Have grown unkind and willed it otherwise,   290
They make his fate a mystery beyond
The fate of other men. I should not grieve
So deeply for his loss if he had fallen
With his companions on the field of Troy,
Or midst his kindred when the war was o'er.   295
Then all the Greeks had built his monument,
And he had left his son a heritage
Of glory. Now has he become the prey
Of Harpies, perishing ingloriously,
Unseen, his fate unheard of, and has left   300
Mourning and grief, my portion. Not for him
Alone I grieve; the. gods have cast on me
Yet other hardships. All the chiefs who rule
The isles, Dulichium, Samos, and the groves
That shade Zacynthus, and who bear the sway   305
In rugged Ithaca, have come to woo

My mother, and from day to day consume
My substance. She rejects not utterly
Their hateful suit, and yet she cannot bear
To end it by a marriage. Thus they waste 310
My heritage, and soon will seek my life."
Again in grief and anger Pallas spake:
"Yea, greatly dost thou need the absent chief
Odysseus here, that he might lay his hands
Upon these shameless suitors. Were he now 315
To come and stand before the palace gate
With helm and buckler and two spears, as first
I saw him in our house, when drinking wine
And feasting, just returned from Ephyre,
Where Ilus dwelt, the son of Mermerus— 320
For thither went Odysseus in a bark,
To seek a deadly drug with which to taint
His brazen arrows; Ilus gave it not;
He feared the immortal gods; my father gave
The poison, for exceedingly he loved 325
His guest—could now Odysseus, in such guise,
Once meet the suitors, short would be their lives
And bitter would the marriage banquet be.
Yet whether he return or not to take
Vengeance, in his own palace, on this crew 330
Of wassailers, rests only with the gods.
Now let me counsel thee to think betimes
How thou shalt thrust them from thy palace gates.
Observe me, and attend to what I say:
Tomorrow thou shalt call the Achaian chiefs 335
To an assembly; speak before them all,
And be the gods thy witnesses. Command
The suitors all to separate for their homes;

And if thy mother's mind be bent to wed,
Let her return to where her father dwells,   340
A mighty prince, and there they will appoint
Magnificent nuptials, and an ample dower
Such as should honor a beloved child.
And now, if thou wilt heed me, I will give
A counsel for thy good. Man thy best ship   345
With twenty rowers, and go forth to seek
News of thy absent father. Thou shalt hear
Haply of him from some one of the sons
Of men, or else some word of rumor sent
By Zeus, revealing what mankind should know.   350
First shape thy course for Pylos, and inquire
Of noble Nestor; then, at Sparta, ask
Of fair-haired Menelaus, for he came
Last of the mailed Achaeans to his home.'
And shouldst thou learn that yet thy father lives,   355
And will return, have patience yet a year,
However hard it seem. But shouldst thou find
That he is now no more, return forthwith
To thy own native land, and pile on high
His monument, and let the funeral rites   360
Be sumptuously performed as may become
The dead, and let thy mother wed again.
And when all this is fully brought to pass,
Take counsel with thy spirit and thy heart
How to destroy the suitor crew that haunt   365
Thy palace, whether by a secret snare
Or open force. No longer shouldst thou act
As if thou wert a boy; thou hast outgrown
The age of childish sports. Hast thou not heard
What honor the divine Orestes gained   370

With all men, when he slew the murderer,
The crafty wretch Aegisthus, by whose hand
The illustrious father of Orestes died?
And then, my friend, for I perceive that thou
Art of a manly and a stately growth—   375
Be also bold, that men hereafter born
May give thee praise. And now must I depart
To my good ship, and to my friends who wait,
Too anxiously perhaps, for my return.
Act wisely now, and bear my words in mind."   380
The prudent youth Telemachus rejoined:
"Well hast thou spoken, and with kind intent,
O stranger! like a father to a son;
And ne'er shall I forget what thou hast said.
Yet stay, I pray thee, though in haste, and bathe   335
And be refreshed, and take to thy good ship
Some gift with thee, such as may please thee well,
Precious and rare, which thou mayst ever keep
In memory of me—a gift like those
Which friendly hosts bestow upon their guests."   390
Then spake the blue-eyed Pallas: "Stay me not,
For now would I depart. Whatever gift
Thy heart may prompt thee to bestow, reserve
Till I come back, that I may bear it home,   394
And thou shalt take some precious thing in turn."
So spake the blue-eyed Pallas, and withdrew,
Ascending like a bird. She filled his heart
With strength and courage, waking vividly
His father's memory. Then the noble youth
Went forth among the suitors. Silent all   400
They sat and listened to the illustrious bard,
Who sang of the calamitous return

Of the Greek host from Troy, at the command
Of Pallas. From her chamber o'er the hall
The daughter of Icarius, the sage queen   405
Penelope, had heard the heavenly strain,
And knew its theme. Down by the lofty stairs
She came, but not alone; there followed her
Two maidens. When the glorious lady reached
The threshold of the strong-built hall, where sat   410
The suitors, holding up a delicate veil
Before her face, and with a gush of tears,
The queen bespake the sacred minstrel thus:
"Phemius! thou knowest many a pleasing theme—
The deeds of gods and heroes, such as bards   415
Are wont to celebrate. Take then thy place
And sing of one of these, and let the guests
In silence drink the wine; but cease this strain;
It is too sad; it cuts me to the heart,
And wakes a sorrow without bounds—such grief   420
I bear for him, my lord, of whom I think
Continually; whose glory is abroad
Through Hellas and through Argos, everywhere."
And then Telemachus, the prudent, spake:
"Why, O my mother! canst thou not endure   425
That thus the well-graced poet should delight
His hearers with a theme to which his mind
Is inly moved? The bards deserve no blame;
Zeus is the cause, for he at will inspires
The lay that each must sing. Reprove not, then,   430
The minstrel who relates the unhappy fate
Of the Greek warriors. All men most applaud
The song that has the newest theme; and thou—
Strengthen thy heart to hear it. Keep in mind

That not alone Odysseus is cut off   435
From his return, but that with him at Troy
Have many others perished. Now withdraw
Into thy chamber; ply thy household tasks,
The loom, the spindle; bid thy maidens speed
Their work. To say what words beseem a feast   440
Belongs to man, and most to me; for here
Within these walls the authority is mine."
The matron, wondering at his words, withdrew
To her own place, but in her heart laid up
Her son's wise sayings. When she now had reached,   445
With her attendant maids, the upper rooms,
She mourned Odysseus, her beloved spouse,
And wept, till blue-eyed Pallas closed her lids
In gentle slumbers. Noisily, meanwhile,
The suitors reveled in the shadowy halls;   450
And thus Telemachus, the prudent, spake:
"Ye suitors of my mother, insolent
And overbearing; cheerful be our feast,
Not riotous. It would become us well
To listen to the lay of such a bard,   455
So like the gods in voice. I bid you all
Meet in full council with the morrow morn,
That I may give you warning to depart
From out my palace, and to seek your feasts
Elsewhere at your own charge—haply to hold   460
Your daily banquets at each other's homes.
But if it seem to you the better way
To plunder one man's goods, go on to waste
My substance; I will call the immortal gods
To aid me, and if Zeus allow   465
Fit retribution for your deeds, ye die,

Within this very palace, unavenged."
He spake; the suitors bit their close-pressed lips,
Astonished at the youth's courageous words.
And thus Antinous, Eupeithes' son,   470
Made answer: "Most assuredly the gods,
Telemachus, have taught thee how to frame
Grand sentences and gallantly harangue.
Ne'er may the son of Cronus make thee king
Over the sea-girt Ithaca, whose isle   475
Is thy inheritance by claim of birth."
Telemachus, the prudent, thus rejoined:
"Wilt thou be angry at the word I speak,
Antinous? I would willingly accept
The kingly station if conferred by Zeus.   480
Dost thou indeed regard it as the worst
Of all conditions of mankind? Not so
For him who reigns; his house grows opulent,
And he the more is honored. Many kings
Within the bounds of sea-girt Ithaca   485
There are, both young and old, let any one
Bear rule, since great Odysseus is no more;
But I will be the lord of mine own house,
And o'er my servants whom the godlike chief,
Odysseus, brought from war, his share of spoil."   490
Eurymachus, the son of Polybus,
Addressed the youth in turn: "Assuredly,
What man hereafter, of the Achaean race,
Shall bear the rule o'er sea-girt Ithaca
Rests with the gods. But thou shalt keep thy wealth,   495
And may no son of violence come to make
A spoil of thy possessions while men dwell
In Ithaca. And now, my friend, I ask

Who was thy guest; whence came he, of what land
Claims he to be, where do his kindred dwell 500
And where his patrimonial acres lie?
With tidings of thy father's near return
Came he, or to receive a debt? How swift
Was his departure, waiting not for us
To know him! yet in aspect and in air 505
He seemed to be no man of vulgar note."
Telemachus, the prudent, answered thus:
"My father's coming, O Eurymachus,
Is to be hoped no more; nor can I trust
Tidings from whatsoever part they come, 510
Nor pay regard to oracles, although
My mother send to bring a soothsayer
Within the palace, and inquire of him.
But this man was my father's guest; he comes
From Taphos; Mentes is his name, a son 515
Of the brave chief Anchialus; he reigns
Over the Taphians, men who love the sea."
He spake, but in his secret heart he knew
The immortal goddess. Then the suitors turned.
Delighted, to the dance and cheerful song, 520
And waited for the evening. On their sports
The evening with its shadowy blackness came;
Then each to his own home withdrew to sleep,
While to his lofty chamber, in full view,
Built high in that magnificent palace home, 525
Telemachus went up, and sought his couch,
Intent on many thoughts. The chaste and sage
Dame Eurycleia by his side went up
With lighted torches—she a child of Ops,
Pisenor's son. Her, in her early bloom, 530

Laertes purchased for a hundred beeves,
And in his palace honored equally
With his chaste wife; yet never sought her bed.
He would not wrong his queen. 'Twas she who bore
The torches with Telemachus. She loved   535
Her young lord more than all the other maids,
And she had nursed him in his tender years.
He opened now the chamber door and sat
Upon the couch, put his soft tunic off
And placed it in the prudent matron's hands.   540
She folded it and smoothed it, hung it near
To that fair bed, and, going quickly forth,
Pulled at the silver ring to close the door,
And drew the thong that moved the fastening bolt.
He, lapped in the soft fleeces, all night long.   545
Thought of the voyage Pallas had ordained.

BOOK II

Now when the Morning, child of Dawn, appeared,   1
The dear son of Odysseus left his bed
And put his garments on. His trenchant sword
He hung upon his shoulders, and made fast
His shapely sandals to his shining feet,   5
And issued from his chamber like a god.
At once he bade the clear-voiced heralds call
The long-haired Greeks to council. They obeyed;
Quickly the chiefs assembled, and when all
Were at the appointed place, Telemachus   10
Went to the council, bearing in his hand
A brazen spear, yet went he not alone.
Two swift dogs followed him, while Pallas shed
A heavenly beauty over him, and all
Admired him as he came. He took the seat   15
Of his great father, and the aged men
Made way for him. And then Aegyptius spake,
A hero bowed with age, who much had seen
And known. His son, the warlike Antiphus,
Went with the great Odysseus in his fleet   20
To courser-breeding Troy, and afterward
horse

19

The cruel Cyclops, in the vaulted cave,
'Slew him for his last meal. Three other sons
There were, and one of these, Eurynomus,
Was of the suitor train; the others took   25
Charge of their father's acres. Never yet
Had he forgotten his lost son or ceased
To grieve for him, and as he spoke he wept.
"Hear, men of Ithaca, what I shall say. *Aegyptius*
No council, no assembly, have we held   30
Since great Odysseus in his roomy ships
Departed from our isle. Who now is he
That summons us? On which of our young men
Or elders presses this necessity?
Is it belike that one of you has heard   35
Of an approaching foe, and can declare
The tidings clearly? Or would he propose *news*
And urge some other matter which concerns
The public weal? A just and generous mind *valuable*
I deem is his, and 'tis my hope that Zeus   *judge*   40
Will bring to pass the good at which he aims."
As thus he spake Odysseus' son rejoiced
In his auspicious words, nor longer kept *happy*
His seat, but, yielding to an inward force,
Rose midst them all to speak, while in his hand   45
Pisenor, the sagacious counselor *wise*
And herald, placed the scepter. Then he turned
To the old man, Aegyptius, speaking thus:
"O aged man, not far from thee is he
Who called this council, as thou soon shalt know.   50
Mine chiefly is the trouble; I have brought
No news of an approaching foe, which I
Was first to hear, and would declare to all,

Nor urge I other matters which concern
The public weal; my own necessity—
The evil that has fallen on my house—
Constrains me; it is twofold. First, that I
Have lost an excellent father, who was king
Among you, and ruled o'er you with a sway
As gentle as a father's. Greater yet
Is the next evil, and will soon o'erthrow
My house and waste my substance utterly.
Suitors, the sons of those who, in our isle,
Hold the chief rank, importunately press
Round my unwilling mother. They disdain
To ask her of Icarius, that the king
Her father may endow her, and bestow
His daughter on the man who best may gain
His favor, but with every day they come
Into our palace, sacrificing here
Oxen and sheep and fatling goats, and hold
High festival, and drink the purple wine
Unstinted, with unbounded waste; for here
Is no man like Odysseus to repel
The mischief from my house. Not such are we
As he was, to resist the wrong. We pass
For weaklings, immature in valor, yet
If I had but the power, assuredly
I would resist, for by these men are done
Insufferable things, nor does my house
Perish with honor. Ye yourselves should feel
Shame at these doings; ye should dread reproach
From those who dwell around us, and should fear
The offended gods, lest they repay these crimes
With vengeance. I beseech you, O my friends,

55

60

65

70

75

80

85

Both by Olympian Zeus, and her by whom
Councils of men are summoned and dissolved—
The goddess Themis—that ye all refrain
And leave me to my grief alone, unless
Odysseus, my great father, may have done   90
Wrong in his anger to the gallant Greeks,
Which ye, by prompting men to acts like these,
Seek to avenge on me. Far better 'twere,
Should ye yourselves destroy our goods and slay
Our herds, since, were it so, there might in time   95
Be some requital. We, from street to street,
Would plead continually for recompense,
Till all should be restored. But now ye heap
Upon me wrongs for which is no redress."
Thus angrily he spake, and dashed to earth   100
The scepter, shedding tears. The people felt
Compassion; all were silent for a space,
And there was none who dared with railing words
Answer Telemachus, save one alone,
Antinous, who arose and thus replied: 105
"Telemachus, thou youth of braggart speech
And boundless in abuse, what hast thou said
To our dishonor? Thou wouldst fix on us
A brand of shame. The blame is not with us,
The Achaean suitors; 'tis thy mother's fault, no   110
Skilled as she is in crafty shifts. It is now
Already the third year, and soon will be
The fourth, since she began to cozen us.
She gives us all to hope, and sends fair words
To each by message, yet in her own mind   115
Has other purposes. This shrewd device
She planned; she laid upon the loom a web,

Delicate, wide, and vast in length, and said

Thus to us all: 'Young princes, who are come

To woo me, since Odysseus is no more—   120

My noble husband—urge me not, I pray,

To marriage, till I finish in the loom—

That so my threads may not be spun in vain—

A funeral vesture for the hero-chief

Laertes, when his fatal hour shall come   125

With death's long sleep. Else some Achaean dame

Might blame me, should I leave without a shroud

Him who in life possessed such ample wealth!'

Such were her words, and easily they wrought

Upon our generous minds. So went she on,   130

Weaving that ample web, and every night

Unraveled it by torchlight. Three full years

She practiced thus, and by the fraud deceived

The Grecian youths; but when the hours had brought

The fourth year round, a woman who knew all   135

Revealed the mystery, and we ourselves

Saw her unraveling the ample web.

Thenceforth, constrained, and with unwilling hands,

She finished it. Now let the suitors make

Their answer to thy words, that thou mayst know   140

Our purpose fully, and the Achaeans all

May know it likewise. Send thy mother hence,

Requiring that she wed the suitor whom

Her father chooses and herself prefers.

But if she still go on to treat the sons   145

Of Greece with such despite, too confident

In gifts which Pallas has bestowed on her

So richly, noble arts, and faculties

Of mind, and crafty shifts, beyond all those

Of whom we ever heard that lived of yore,   150
The bright-haired ladies of the Achaean race,
Tyro, Alcmena, and Mycene, famed
For glossy tresses, none of them endowed
As is Penelope, though this last shift
Be ill devised—so long will we consume   155
Thy substance and estate as she shall hold
Her present mood, the purpose which the gods
Have planted in her breast. She to herself
Gains great renown, but surely brings on thee
Loss of much goods. And now we go not hence   160
To our affairs nor elsewhere, till she wed
Whichever of the Greeks may please her most."
And then rejoined discreet Telemachus:
"Antinous, grievous wrong it were to send
Unwilling from this palace her who bore   165
And nursed me. Whether he be living yet
Or dead, my father is in distant lands;
And should I, of my own accord and will,
Dismiss my mother, I must make perforce
Icarius large amends, and that were hard.   170
And he would do me mischief, and the gods
Would send yet other evils on my head.
For then my mother, going forth, would call
On the grim Furies, and the general curse
Of all men would be on me. Think not I   175
Will ever speak that word. But if ye bear
A sense of injury for what is past,
Go from these halls; provide for other feasts,
Consuming what is yours, and visiting
Each other's homes in turn. But if it seem   180
To you the wiser and the better way

To plunder one man's goods, go on to waste
My substance. I shall call the eternal gods
To aid me, and, if Zeus allow
Fit retribution for your crimes, ye die   185
Within this very palace unavenged."
So spake Telemachus. The Thunderer, Zeus,
Sent flying from a lofty mountain-top
Two eagles. First they floated on the wind
Close to each other, and with wings outspread;   190
But as they came to where the murmuring crowd
Was gathered just beneath their flight, they turned
And clapped their heavy pinions, looking down
With deadly omen on the heads below,
And with their talons tore each other's cheeks   195
And necks, and then they darted to the right
Away through Ithaca among its roofs.
All who beheld the eagles were amazed,
And wondered what event was near at hand.
Among the rest an aged hero spake,   200
Named Halitherses, Master's son. He knew,
More truly than the others of his age,
To augur from the flight of birds, and read
The will of fate—and wisely thus he spake:
"Hear, men of Ithaca, what I shall say.   205
I speak of what most narrowly concerns
The suitors, over whom already hangs
Great peril, for Odysseus will not be
Long at a distance from his home and friends.
Even now he is not far, and meditates   210
Slaughter and death to all the suitor train;
And evil will ensue to many more
Of us, who dwell in sunny Ithaca.

Now let us think what measures may restrain
These men—or let them of their own accord   215
Desist—the soonest were for them the best.
For not as one untaught do I foretell
Events to come, but speak of what I know.
All things that I predicted to our chief,
What time the Argive troops embarked for Troy,   220
And sage Odysseus with them, are fulfilled;
I said that after many hardships borne,
And all his comrades lost, the twentieth year
Would bring him back, a stranger to us all—
And all that then I spake of comes to pass."   225
Eurymachus, the son of Polybus,
Answered the seer: "Go to thy house, old man,
And to thy boys, and prophesy to them,
Lest evil come upon them. I can act,
In matters such as these, a prophet's part   230
Better than thou. True, there are many birds
That fly about in sunshine, but not all
Are ominous. Odysseus far away
Has perished; well it would have been if thou
Hadst perished with him; then thou wouldst prate   235
Idly of things to come, nor wouidst thou stir
Telemachus to anger, in the hope
Of bearing to thy house some gift from him.
Now let me say, and be assured my words
Will be fulfilled: experienced as thou art,   240
If thou by treacherous speeches shalt inflame
A younger man than thou to violent deeds,
The sharper punishment shall first be his,
But we will lay on thee a penalty,
Old man, which thou shalt find it hard to bear,   245

And bitterly wilt thou repent. And now
Let me persuade Telemachus to send
His mother to her father. They will make
A marriage for her there, and give with her
A liberal dowry, such as may become   250
A favorite daughter on her wedding-day,
Else never will the sons of Greece renounce,
I think, the difficult suit. We do not fear
Telemachus himself, though glib of speech,
Nor care we for the empty oracle   255
Which thou, old man, dost utter, making thee
Only more hated. Still will his estate
Be wasted, nor will order e'er return
While she defers her marriage with some prince
Of the Achaeans. We shall urge our suit   260
For that most excellent of womankind
As rivals, nor withdraw to seek the hand
Of others, whom we fitly might espouse."
To this discreet Telemachus replied:
"Eurymachus, and ye, the illustrious train   265
Of suitors, I have nothing more to ask—
No more to say—for now the gods and all
The Achaeans know the truth. But let me have
A gallant bark, and twenty men to make
From coast to coast a voyage, visiting   270
Sparta and sandy Pylos, to inquire
For my long-absent father, and the chance
Of his return, if any of mankind
Can tell me aught, or if some rumor come
From Zeus, since thus are tidings often brought   275
To human knowledge. Should I learn that yet
He lives and may return, I then would wait

A twelvemonth, though impatient. Should I hear
That he no longer lives, I shall return
Homeward, and pile his monument on high   280
With funeral honors that become the dead,
And give my mother to a second spouse."
He spake and took his seat, and then arose
Mentor, once comrade of the excellent chief
Odysseus, who, departing with his fleet,   235
Consigned his household to the aged man,
That they should all obey him, and that he
Should safely keep his charge. He rose amid
The assembly, and addressed them wisely thus:
"Hear and attend, ye men of Ithaca,   290
To what I say. Let never sceptered king
Henceforth be gracious, mild, and merciful,
And righteous; rather be he deaf to prayer
And prone to deeds of wrong, since no one now
Remembers the divine Odysseus more,   295
Among the people over whom he ruled
Benignly like a father. Yet I bear
No envy to the haughty suitors here,
Moved as they are to deeds of violence
By evil counsels, since, in pillaging   300
The substance of Odysseus, who they say
Will nevermore return, they risk their lives.
But I am angry with the rest, with all
Of you who sit here mute, nor even with words
Of stern reproof restrain their violence,   305
Though ye so many are and they so few."
Leiocritus, Evenor's son, rejoined:
"Malicious Mentor, foolish man! what talk
Is this of holding us in check? 'twere hard

For numbers even greater than our own   310
To drive us from a feast. And should the prince
Of Ithaca, Odysseus, come himself,
Thinking to thrust the illustrious suitors forth
That banquet in these palace halls, his queen
Would have no cause for joy at his return,   315
Greatly as she desired it. He would draw
Sure death upon himself in strife with us
Who are so many. Thou hast spoken ill.
Now let the people who are gathered here
Disperse to their employments. We will leave   320
Mentor and Halitherses, who were both
His father's early comrades, to provide
For the youth's voyage. He will yet remain
A long time here, I think, to ask for news
In Ithaca, and never will set sail."   325
Thus having said, he instantly dismissed
The people; they departed to their homes;
The suitors sought the palace of the prince.
Then to the ocean-side, apart from all,
Went forth Telemachus, and washed his hands   330
In the gray surf, and prayed to Pallas thus:
"Hear me, thou deity who yesterday,
In visiting our palace, didst command
That I should traverse the black deep to learn
News of my absent father, and the chance   335
Of his return! The Greeks themselves withstand,
My purpose; the proud suitors most of all."
Such was his prayer, and straightway Pallas stood,
In form and voice like Mentor, by his side,
And thus accosted him with winged words: 340
"Telemachus, thou henceforth shalt not lack

Valor or wisdom. If with thee abides
Thy father's gallant spirit, as he was
In deed and word, thou wilt not vainly make
This voyage. But if thou be not in truth   345
The son of him and of Penelope
Then I rely not on thee to perform
What thou dost meditate. Few sons are like
Their fathers: most are worse, a very few
Excel their parents. Since thou wilt not lack   350
Valor and wisdom in the coming time,
Nor is thy father's shrewdness wanting quite
In thee, great hope there is that happily
This plan will be fulfilled. Regard not then
The suitor train, their purposes and plots.   355
Senseless are they, as little wise as just,
And have no thought of the black doom of death
Now drawing near to sweep them in a day
To their destruction. But thy enterprise
Must suffer no delay. So much am I   360
Thy father's friend and thine, that I will cause
A swift bark to be fitted out for sea,
And will myself attend thee. Go now hence
Among the suitors, and make ready there
The needful stores, and let them all be put   365
In vessels—wine in jars, and meal, the strength
Of man, in close thick skins—while I engage,
Among the people here, a willing crew.
Ships are there in our sea-girt Ithaca
Full many, new and old, and I will choose   370
The best of these, and see it well equipped.
Then will we drag it down to the broad sea."
Thus Pallas spake, the child of Zeus.

Telemachus obeyed the heavenly voice,
And stayed not; home he hastened, where he saw   375
Sadly the arrogant suitors in the hall,
Busily flaying goats and roasting swine.
Antinous, laughing, came to meet the youth,
And fastened on his hand, and thus he spake:
"Telemachus, thou youth of lofty speech   380
And boundless in abuse, let neither word
Nor deed that may displease thee vex thy heart,
But gaily eat and drink as thou wert wont.
The Achaeans generously will provide
Whatever thou requirest, ship and men—   385
All chosen rowers—that thou mayst arrive
Sooner at sacred Pylos, there to learn
Tidings of thy illustrious father's fate."
Then spake discreet Telemachus in turn:
"Antinous, never could I sit with you.   390
Arrogant ones! in silence nor enjoy
The feast in quiet. Is it not enough,
O suitors, that while I was yet a child
Ye wasted on your revelries my large
And rich possessions? Now that I am grown,   395
And, when I hear the words of other men,
Discern their meaning, now that every day
Strengthens my spirit, I will make the attempt
To bring the evil fates upon your heads,
Whether I go to Pylos or remain   400
Among this people. I shall surely make
This voyage, and it will not be in vain.
Although I go a passenger on board
Another's ship—since neither ship have I
Nor rowers—ye have judged that so were best."   405

He spake, and quickly from the suitor's hand
Withdrew his own. The others who prepared
Their banquet in the palace scoffed at him,
And flung at him their bitter taunts, and one
Among the insolent youths reviled him thus: 410
"Telemachus is certainly resolved
To butcher us. He goes to bring allies
From sandy Pylos or the Spartan coast,
He is so bent on slaughter. Or perhaps
He visits the rich land of Ephyre   415
In search of deadly poisons to be thrown
Into a cup and end us all at once."
Then said another of the haughty youths:
"Who knows but, wandering in his hollow bark,
He too may perish, far from all his friends,   420
Just as Odysseus perished? This would bring
Increase of labor; it would cast on us
The trouble to divide his goods, and give
His palace to his mother, and to him
Who takes the woman as his wedded wife."   425
So spake they, but Telemachus went down
To that high-vaulted room, his father's, where
Lay heaps of gold and brass, and garments store
In chests, and fragrant oils. And there stood casks
Of delicate old wine and pure, a drink   430
For gods, in rows against the wall, to wait
If ever, after many hardships borne,
Odysseus should return. Upon that room
Close-fitting double doors were shut, and there
Was one who night and day kept diligent watch,   435
A woman, Eurycleia, child of Ops,
Peisenor's son. Telemachus went in

And called her to him, and bespake her thus:
"Nurse, let sweet wine be drawn into my jars,
The finest next to that which thou dost keep   440
Expecting our unhappy lord, if yet
The nobly born Odysseus shall escape
The doom of death and come to us again.
Fill twelve, and fit the covers close, and pour
Meal into well-sewn skins, and let the tale   445
Be twenty measures of the flour of wheat.
This none but thou must know. Let all these things
Be brought together; then, as night shuts in,
When to her upper chamber, seeking rest,
My mother shall withdraw, I come and take   450
What thou providest for me. I am bound
For Sparta and for Pylos in the sands,
To gather news concerning the return
Of my dear father, if I haply may."
So spake the youth, and his beloved nurse   455
Sobbed, wept aloud, and spake these winged words:
"Why should there come, dear child, a thought like this
Into thy heart. Why wouldst thou wander forth
To distant regions—thou an only son
And dearly loved? Odysseus, nobly born,   460
Has perished, from his native land afar,
'Mid a strange race. These men, when thou art gone,
At once will lay their plots to take thy life,
And share thy wealth among them. Stay thou here
Among thy people; need is none that thou   465
Shouldst suffer, roaming o'er the barren deep."
Then spake discreet Telemachus again:
"Be of good cheer, O nurse, for my design
Is not without the sanction of a god;

But swear thou not to let my mother know   470
Of my intent until the eleventh day
Or twelfth shall pass, or till, in missing me,
She learn of my departure, lest she weep
And stain with tears the beauty of her face."
He spake; the ancient woman solemnly   475
Swore by the gods, and when the rite was o'er
Drew wine into the jars, and poured the <u>meal</u>
Into the well-sewn skins. Telemachus
Entered the hall and joined the suitor train.
Then did the blue-eyed goddess turn her thoughts   480
To other plans, and taking on herself
The semblance of Telemachus, she ranged
The city, speaking to each man in turn,
And bidding him at nightfall to repair
To where the good ship lay. That gallant ship   485
She begged of the renowned Noemon, son
Of Phronius, who with cheerful grace complied.
The sun went down, the city streets lay all
In shadow. Then she drew the good ship down
Into the sea, and brought and put on board   490
The appointments every well-built galley needs,
And <u>moored</u> her at the bottom of the port,
Where, in a throng, obedient to the word
Of Pallas, round her came her gallant crew.
With yet a new device the <u>blue-eyed maid</u>   495
Went to the palace of the godlike chief
Odysseus, where she poured a gentle sleep
Over the suitors. As they drank she made
Their senses wander, and their hands let fall
The goblets. Now no longer at the board   500
They sat, but sallied forth, and through the town

Went to their slumbers, for the power of sleep
Had fallen heavily upon their lids.
Then blue-eyed Pallas from those sumptuous halls
Summoned Telemachus. She took the form   505
And voice of Mentor, and bespake him thus:
"Telemachus, already at their oars
Sit thy well-armed companions and await
Thy coming; let us go without delay."
Thus having spoken, Pallas led the way   510
With rapid footsteps which he followed fast;
Till having reached the galley and the sea
They found their long-haired comrades at the beach,
And thus the gallant prince Telemachus
Bespake them: "Hither, comrades, let us bring   515
The sea-stores from the dwelling where they lie
My mother knows not of it, nor her maids;
The secret has been told to one alone."
He spake, and went before them. In his steps
They followed. To the gallant bark they brought   520
The stores, and, as the well-beloved son
Of King Odysseus bade, they laid them down
Within the hull. Telemachus went up
The vessel's side, but Pallas first embarked,
And at the stern sat down, while next to her   525
Telemachus was seated. Then the crew
Cast loose the fastenings and went all on board,
And took their places on the rowers' seats,
While blue-eyed Pallas sent a favoring breeze,
A fresh wind from the west, that murmuring swept   530
The dark-blue main. Telemachus gave forth
The word to wield the tackle; they obeyed,
And raised the fir-tree mast, and, fitting it

Into its socket, bound it fast with cords,
And drew and spread with firmly twisted ropes   535
The shining sails on high. The steady wind
Swelled out the canvas in the midst; the ship
Moved on, the dark sea roaring round her keel,
As swiftly through the waves she cleft her way.
And when the rigging of that swift black ship   540
Was firmly in its place, they filled their cups
With wine, and to the ever-living gods
Poured out libations, most of all to one,
Zeus's blue-eyed daughter. Thus through all that night
And all the ensuing morn they held their way.   545

BOOK III

Now from the fair broad bosom of the sea   1
Into the brazen vault of heaven the sun
Rose shining for the immortals and for men
Upon the foodfull earth. The voyagers
Arrived at Pylos, nobly built, the town   5
Of Neieus. There, upon the ocean-side,
They found the people offering coal-black steers
To dark-haired Poseidon. On nine seats they sat,
Five hundred on each seat; nine steers were slain
For each five hundred there. While they performed   10
The rite, and, tasting first the entrails, burned
The thighs to ocean's god, the Ithacans
Touched land, and, lifting up the good ship's sail,
Furled it and moored the keel, and then stepped out
Upon the shore. Forth from the galley came   15
Telemachus, the goddess guiding him,
And thus to him the blue-eyed Pallas said:
"Telemachus, there now is no excuse,
Not even the least, for shamefaced backwardness.
Thou hast come hither o'er the deep to ask   20
For tidings of thy father—what far land

Conceals him, what the fate that he has met.
Go then at once to Nestor, the renowned
In horsemanship, and we shall see what plan
He hath in mind for thee. Entreat him there   25
That frankly he declare it. He will speak
No word of falsehood; he is truly wise."
And thus discreet Telemachus replied:
"O Mentor, how shall I approach the chief,
And with what salutation? Little skill   30
Have I in courtly phrase, and shame becomes
A youth in questioning an aged man."
Pallas, the blue-eyed goddess, spake again:
"In part thy mind will prompt thy speech; in part
A god will put the words into thy mouth—   35
For well I deem that thou wert neither born
Nor trained without the favor of the gods."
Thus having said, the blue-eyed Pallas moved
With hasty pace before, and in her steps
He followed close, until they reached the seats   40
Of those assembled Pylians. Nestor there
Sat with his sons, while his companions stood
Around him and prepared the feast, and some
Roasted the flesh at fires, and some transfixed
The parts with spits. As they beheld the approach as   45
Of strangers they advanced, and took their hands,
And bade them sit. Pisistratus, a son
Of Nestor, came the first of all, and took
A hand of each, and placed them at the feast
On the soft hides that o'er the ocean sand so   50
Were spread beside his brother Thrasymede
And his own father; brought for their repast
Parts of the entrails, poured for them the wine

Into a golden goblet, held it forth
In his right hand, and with these words bespake   55
Pallas, the child of aegis-bearing Zeus:
"Pray, stranger, to King Poseidon. Ye have chanced
Upon his feast in coming to our coast.
And after thy libation poured, and prayer
Made to the god, give over to thy friend   60
The goblet of choice wine that he may make
Libation also; he, I question not,
Prays to the gods; we all have need of them.
A younger man is he than thou, and seems
In age to be my equal; therefore   65
Will give the golden goblet first to thee."
He spake, and in the hands of Pallas placed
The goblet of choice wine. Well pleased was she
With one so just and so discreet—well pleased
That first to her he reached the cup of gold,   70
And thus she prayed to Poseidon fervently:
"Hear, Poseidon, thou who dost embrace the earth,
And of thy grace disdain not to bestow
These blessings on thy suppliants. First of all
Vouchsafe to Nestor and his sons increase   75
Of glory; on the Pylian people next
Bestow, for this most sumptuous hecatomb,
Large recompense; and, lastly, grant to us—
Telemachus and me—a safe return
To our own country with the end attained so   80
Which brought us hither in our gallant bark."
Thus did she pray, while she fulfilled the prayer;
And then she handed to Telemachus
The fair round goblet, and in words like hers
The dear son of Odysseus prayed. Meanwhile   85

The Pylians, having roasted well the flesh
And drawn it from the spits, distributing
To each his portion, held high festival.
And when the calls of hunger and of thirst
Were silenced, Nestor, the Gerenian knight,   90
Began discourse, and thus bespake his guests:
"The fitting time is come to ask our guests
Who they may be, since now their feast is o'er.
Say then, O strangers, who ye are, and whence
Ye come along the pathway of the deep.   95
Have ye an errand here, or do ye roam
The seas at large, like pirates, braving death,
And visiting with ravage foreign states?"
And then discreet Telemachus replied
Boldly—for Pallas strengthened in that hour   100
His heart that he might confidently ask
News of his absent father, and so win
A worthy fame among, the sons of men:
"O Nestor, son of Neleus, pride of Greece!
Thou bid'st us tell thee whence we came, and I   105
Will faithfully declare it. We are come
From Ithaca, beneath the Neritus,
And private, and not general, is the cause
Of which I am to speak. I came to ask
Concerning my great father, the large souled no   110
And nobly-born Odysseus, who 'tis said
With thee, his friend in arms, laid waste the town
Of Ilium. We have heard where all the rest
Who warred against the Trojans were cut off,
And died sad deaths; his fate alone the son   115
Of Cronus hath not chosen to reveal—
Whether he fell on land by hostile hands,

Or while at sea was whelmed beneath the waves
Of Amphitrite. Wherefore to thy knees
I come, to ask that thou—if so thou wilt—   120
Relate the manner of his mournful death,
As thou didst see it with thine eyes, or else
As thou from other wanderers hast heard
Its history; for she who brought him forth
Bore him to be unhappy. Think thou not   125
To soften aught, through tenderness to me,
In thy recital, but in faithful words
Tell me the whole, whatever thou hast seen.
And I conjure thee, that if, in his life,
My father, great Odysseus, ever gave   130
Promise of word or deed for thee, and kept
His promise, in the realm of Troy, where ye
Achaeans bore such hardships, that thou now
Remember it and speak without disguise."
And Nestor the Gerenian knight replied: 135
"My friend, since thou recallest to my mind
The sufferings borne by us the sons of Greece,
Although of peerless valor, in that land,
Both when we ranged in ships the darkling sea
For booty wheresoe'er Achilles led,   140
And when around King Priam's populous town
We fought, where fell our bravest, know thou then
That there the valiant Ajax lies, and there
Achilles; there Patroclus, like the gods
In council; there my well-beloved son   145
Blameless and brave, Antilochus the swift
Of foot and warlike—many woes beside
We bore, and who of mortal birth could give
Their history? Nay, though thou shouldst remain

Five years or six, and ask of all the griefs   150
Endured by the brave Greeks, thou wouldst depart
Outwearied to thy home, ere thou hadst heard
The whole. Nine years in harassing the foe
We passed, beleaguering them and planning wiles
Innumerable. Cronus's son at last   155
With difficulty seemed to close the war.
Then was there none who might presume to vie
In wisdom with Odysseus; that great man
Excelled in every kind of stratagem—
Thy father—if indeed thou be his son.   160
I look on thee amazed; all thy discourse
Is just like his, and one would ne'er believe
A younger man could speak so much like him.
While we were there, Odysseus and myself
In council or assembly never spake   165
On different sides, but with a like intent
We thoughtfully consulted how to guide
The Achaeans in the way we deemed the best;
But after we had overthrown and spoiled
King Priam's lofty city, and set sail   170
For home, and by some heavenly power the Greeks
Were scattered, Zeus ordained for them
A sad return. For all were neither wise
Nor just, and many drew upon themselves
An evil doom—the fatal wrath of her,   175
The blue-eyed maid, who claims her birth from Zeus.
It was she who kindled strife between the sons
Of Atreus. They had called the Achaeans all
To an assembly, not with due regard
To order, at the setting of the sun,   180
And thither came the warriors overpowered

With wine. The brother kings set forth the cause
Of that assembly. Menelaus first
Bade all the Greeks prepare for their return
O'er the great deep. That counsel little pleased   185
King Agamemnon, who desired to keep
The people longer there, that he might soothe
By sacred hecatombs the fiery wrath
Of Pallas. Fool! who could not see how vain
Were such persuasion, for the eternal gods   190
Are not soon won to change their purposes.
They stood disputing thus, with bitter words,
Till wrangling noisily on different sides
Rose up the well-armed Greeks. The ensuing night
We rested, but we cherished in our breasts   195
A mutual hate; so for our punishment
Had Zeus ordained. With early morn we drew
Our ships to the great deep, and put our goods
And our deep-bosomed women all on board.
Yet half the host went not, but on the shore   200
Remained with Agamemnon, Atreus' son,
And shepherd of the people. All the rest
Embarked, weighed anchor, and sailed swiftly thence;
A deity made smooth the mighty deep,
And when we came to Tenedos we paid   205
Our offerings to the gods and longed for home—
Vainly; it pleased not unpropitious Zeus
To favor our return, and once again
He sent among us strife. A part of us
Led by Odysseus, that sagacious prince,   210
To please Atrides Agamemnon turned
Their well-oared galleys back. But I, with all
The vessels of the fleet that followed me,

Fled on my way, perceiving that some god
Was meditating evil. With us fled,   215
Encouraging his men, the warlike son
Of Tydeus. Fair-haired Menelaus came
Later to us in Lesbos, where we planned
For a long voyage, whether we should sail
Around the rugged Chios, toward the isle   220
Of Psyria, keeping that upon the left,
Or under Chios pass beside the steeps
Of windy Mimas. We besought the god
That he would show a sign, and he complied,
And bade us to Euboea cross the deep   225
Right in the midst, the sooner to escape
All danger. Then the wind blew strong and shrill,
And swiftly o'er the fishy gulfs our fleet
Flew on, and reached Geraestus in the night.
There, having passed the mighty deep, we made   230
To Poseidon offerings of many a thigh
Of beeves. The fourth day dawned, and now the men
Of Diomed, the mighty horseman, son
Of Tydeus, stopped at Argos with their fleet,
While I went on to Pylos with the wind,   235
Which never, from the moment that the god
First sent it o'er the waters, ceased to blow.
"So, my dear child, I reached my home, nor knew
Nor heard from others who among the Greeks
Was saved, or who had perished on the way.   240
Yet what I since have heard while here I sit
Within my palace thou shalt duly learn.
Nor is it what I ought to keep from thee.
'Tis said the Myrmidonian spearmen, led
By great Achilles' famous son, returned   245

Happily home; as happily the son
Of Paeas, Philoctetes the renowned.
Idomeneus brought also back to Crete
All his companions who survived the war;
The sea took none of them. But ye have heard,   250
Though far away, the fate of Atreus' son—
How he came home, and how Aegisthus laid
A plot to slay him, yet on his own head
Drew heavy punishment—so fortunate
It is when he who falls by murder leaves   255
A son; for 'twas the monarch's son who took
Vengeance upon the crafty murderer
Aegisthus, by whose hand Atrides died.
Thou too, my friend, for thou art large of frame,
And of a noble presence, be thou brave,   200
That men in time to come may give thee praise."
Then spake discreet Telemachus again:
"O Nestor, son of Neleus, pride of Greece,
Ample was his revenge, and far and wide
The Greeks will spread his fame to be the song   265
Of future times. O might the gods confer
On me an equal power to avenge myself
On that importunate, overbearing crew
Of suitors, who insult me, and devise
Evil against me! But the gods deny   270
Such fortune to my father and to me,
And all that now is left me is to bear."
Again spake Nestor the Gerenian knight:
"Since thou, my friend, hast spoken words which bring
What I have heard to mind—the rumor goes   275
That in thy palace many suitors wait
About thy mother, and in spite of thee

Do grievous wrong. Now tell me; dost thou yield
Willingly, or because the people, swayed
By oracles, regard thee as their foe?   280
Thy father yet may come again—who knows?—
Alone, or with the other Greeks, to take
The vengeance which these violent deeds deserve.
Should blue-eyed Pallas deign to favor thee,
As once she watched to guard the glorious chief   285
Odysseus in the realm of Troy, where we,
The Achaeans, bore such hardships—for I ne'er
Have seen the gods so openly befriend
A man as Pallas there befriended him—
Should she thus deign to favor thee and keep   290
Watch over thee, then haply some of these
Will never think of marriage rites again."
Then spake discreet Telemachus again:
"O aged man! I cannot think thy words
Will be fulfilled! for they import too much   295
And they amaze me. What thou sayst I wish
May come to pass, but know it cannot be,
Not even though the gods should will it so."
Then thus the blue-eyed goddess, Pallas, spake:
"Telemachus, what words have passed thy lips?   300
Easily can a god, whene'er he will,
In the most distant regions safely keep
A man; and I would rather reach my home
Securely, after many hardships borne,
Than perish suddenly on my return   305
As Agamemnon perished by the guile
Of base Aegisthus and the queen. And yet
The gods themselves have not the power to save
Whom most they cherish from the common doom

When cruel fate brings on the last long sleep." 310
Discreet Telemachus made answer thus:
"Let us, O Mentor, talk no more of this,
Though much we grieve; he never will return,
For his is the black doom of death ordained
By the great gods. Now suffer me to ask 315
Of Nestor further, since to him are known,"
Beyond all other men, the rules of right
And prudence. He has governed, so men say,
Three generations, and to me he seems
In aspect like the ever-living gods. 320
O Nestor, son of Neleus, truly say
How died the monarch over mighty realms,
Atrides Agamemnon? Where was then
His brother Menelaus? By what arts
Did treacherous Aegisthus plan his death, 325
And slay a braver warrior than himself?
Was not the brother in the Achaean town
Of Argos? or was he a wanderer
In other lands, which made the murderer bold?"
The knight, Gerenian Nestor, answered thus: 330
"I will tell all and truly. Thou hast guessed
Rightly and as it happened. Had the son
Of Atreus, fair-haired Menelaus, come
From Troy, and found Aegisthus yet alive
Within the palace, he had never flung 335
The loose earth on his corpse, but dogs and birds
Had preyed upon it, lying in the fields
Far from the city, and no woman's voice
Of all the Greeks had raised the wail for him.
Great was the crime he plotted. We were yet 340
Afar, enduring the hard toils of war,

While he, securely couched in his retreat
At Argos, famed for steeds, with flattering words
Corrupted Agamemnon's queen. At first
The noble Clytemnestra turned away   345
With horror from the crime; for yet her heart
Was right, and by her side there stood a bard
With whom Atrides, when he went to Troy,
Had left his wife with many an earnest charge.
But when the gods and fate had spread a net   350
For his destruction, then Aegisthus bore
The minstrel to a desert isle, and there
Left him to be devoured by birds of prey,
And led the queen, as willing as himself,
To his own palace. Many a victim's thigh   355
Upon the hallowed altars of the gods
He offered, many a gift of ornaments
Woven or wrought in gold he hung within
Their temples, since at length the mighty end
For which he hardly dared to hope was gained.   360
We sailed together from the coast of Troy,
Atrides, Menelaus, and myself,
Friends to each other. When the headland height
Of Athens, hallowed Sunium, met our eyes,
Apollo smote with his still shafts, and slew   365
Phrontis, Onetor's son, who steered the bark
Of Menelaus, holding in his hands
The rudder as the galley scudded on—
And skilled was he beyond all other men
To guide a vessel when the storm was high.   370
So there did Menelaus stay his course,
Though eager to go on, that he might lay
His friend in earth and pay the funeral rites.

But setting sail again with all his fleet
Upon the dark-blue sea, all-seeing Zeus   375
Decreed a perilous voyage. He sent forth
His shrill-voiced hurricane, and heaped on high
The mountain waves. There, scattering the barks
Far from each other, part he drove to Crete,
Where the Cydonians dwell, beside the stream   380
Of Jardanus. A smooth and pointed rock
Just on the bounds of Gortys stands amidst
The dark-blue deep. The south wind thitherward
Sweeps a great sea towards Phoestus, and against
The headland on the left, where that small rock   385
Meets and withstands the mighty wave. The ships
Were driven on this, and scarce the crews escaped
With life; the ships were dashed against the crags
And wrecked, save five, and these, with their black prows,
Were swept toward Egypt by the winds and waves.   390
Thus adding to his wealth and gathering gold
He roamed the ocean in his ships among
Men of strange speech. Aegisthus meantime planned
His guilty deeds at home; he slew the king
Atrides, and the people took his yoke.   395
Seven years in rich Mycenae he bore rule,
And on the eighth, to his destruction, came
The nobly-born Orestes, just returned
From Athens, and cut off that man of blood,
The crafty wretch Aegisthus, by whose hand   400
Fell his illustrious father. Then he bade
The Argives to the solemn burial-feast
Of his bad mother and the craven wretch
Aegisthus. Menelaus, that same day,
The great in war, arrived, and brought large wealth—   405

So large his galleys could contain no more.
"And thou, my friend, be thou not long away,
Wandering from home, thy rich possessions left,
And in thy palace-halls a lawless crew,
Lest they devour thy substance, and divide   410
Thy goods, and thou have crossed the sea in vain.
Yet must I counsel and enjoin on thee
To visit Menelaus, who has come
Just now from lands and nations of strange men,
Whence one could hardly hope for a return;   415
Whom once the tempest's violence had driven
Into that great wide sea o'er which the birds
Of heaven could scarce fly hither in a year,
Such is its fearful vastness. Go thou now,
Thou with thy ship and friends; or if thou choose   420
The way by land, a car and steeds are here,
And here my sons to guide thee to the town
Of hallowed Lacedaemon, there to find
The fair-haired Menelaus. Earnestly
Beseech of him that he declare the truth.   425
Falsely he will not speak, for he is wise."
He spake; the sun went down; the darkness crept
Over the earth, and blue-eyed Pallas said:
"Most wisely hast thou spoken, ancient man.
Now cut ye out the tongues, and mingle wine,   430
That we to Poseidon and the other gods
May pour libations, and then think of rest;
For now the hour is come; the light is gone,
Nor at a feast in honor of the gods
Should we long sit, but in good time withdraw."   435
Zeus's daughter spake; they hearkened to her words;
The heralds came to them, and on their hands

Poured water; boys began to fill the bowls
To the hard brim, and ministered to each
From left to right. Then threw they to the flames   440
The victims' tongues, and, rising, poured on earth
Wine to the gods; and when that rite was paid,
And when their thirst was satiate, Pallas rose
With nobly-born Telemachus to go
To their good ship, but Nestor still detained   445
The twain, and chidingly bespake them thus:
"Now Zeus and all the other gods forbid
That ye should go from me to your good ship,
As from some half-clad wretch, too poor to own
Mantles and blankets in whose soft warm folds   450
He and his guests might sleep; but I have both—
Mantles and blankets—beautifully wrought,
And never shall the son of that great man
Odysseus lie upon a galley's deck
While I am living. After me I hope   455
My sons, who dwell within my palace-halls,
Will duly welcome all who enter here."
And thus again the blue-eyed Pallas spake:
"Well hast thou said, my aged friend, and well
Doth it become Telemachus to heed   460
Thy words, for that were best. Let him remain
With thee and sleep in thine abode, while I
Repair to our black ship, encouraging
The crew, and setting them their proper tasks,
For I am eldest of them all; the rest   465
Are young men yet, and moved by friendship join
Our enterprise; the peers in age are they
Of the large-souled Telemachus. Tonight
I sleep within the hull of our black ship,

And sail with early morning for the land   470
Of the Cauconians, large of soul, from whom -
A debt is due me, neither new nor small.
Send meantime from thy palace in a car,
And with thy son, this youth, and be the steeds
The fleetest and the strongest in thy stalls."   475
The blue-eyed Pallas, having spoken thus,
Passed like an eagle out of sight, and all
Were seized with deep amazement as they saw.
The aged monarch, wondering at the sight,
Took by the hand Telemachus, and said: 480
"Of craven temper, and unapt for war,
O friend, thou canst not be, since thus the gods
Attend and guide thee in thy youth. And this,
Of all the gods whose dwelling is in heaven,
Can be no other than the spoiler-queen   485
Pallas, the child of Zeus, who also held
Thy father in such eminent esteem
Among the Grecians. Deign to favor us,
O queen! bestow on me and on my sons
And on my venerable spouse the mead   490
Of special glory. I will bring to thee
A sacrifice, a broad-horned yearling steer,
Which never man hath tamed or led beneath
The yoke. Her will I bring with gilded horns,
And lay an offering on thine altar-fires."   495
Such were his words, and Pallas heard the prayer,
And then Gerenian Nestor led the way,
And with his sons and sons-in-law approached
His glorious palace. When they came within
The monarch's sumptuous halls, each took his place   500
In order on the couches and the thrones.

The old man mingled for them as they came
A bowl of delicate wine, eleven years old,
Drawn by the damsel cupbearer, who took
Its cover from the jar. The aged chief   505
Mingled it in the bowl, and, pouring out
A part to Pallas, offered earnest prayer
To her, who sprang from aegis-bearing Zeus.
When due libations had been made, and all
Drank till they wished no more, most went away,   510
Each to his home to sleep; but Nestor made
Telemachus, the son of the great chief
Odysseus, rest upon a sumptuous couch
Within the echoing hall, and near to him
The chief of squadrons, skilled to wield the spear,   515
Peisistratus, who only of his sons
Abode in Nestor's halls unwedded yet;
While in an inner room of that tall pile
The monarch slumbered on a bed of state,
Decked for him by the labors of his queen.   520
Soon as the daughter of the dawn appeared,
The rosy-fingered Morning, Nestor left
His bed and went abroad, and took his seat
On smooth white stones before his lofty doors,
That glistened as with oil, on which before   525
Sat Neleus, wise in council as the gods.
But he had yielded to the will of fate,
And passed into the Underworld. Now sat
Gerenian Nestor in his father's place,
The guardian of the Greeks. Around his seat,   530
Just from the chambers of their rest, his sons
Echephron, Stratius, and Aretus came,
Perseus, and Thrasymedes; after these

Came brave Peisistratus, the sixth and last.
They led Telemachus, the godlike youth,   535
And placed him near them. The Gerenian knight
Nestor began, and thus bespake his sons:
"Do quickly what I ask, dear sons, and aid
To render Pallas, first of all the gods,
Propitious—Pallas, who has deigned to come,   540
And at a solemn feast to manifest
Herself to me. Let one of you go forth
Among the fields, and bring a heifer thence,
Led by the herdsman. To the dark-hulled ship
Of the large-souled Telemachus I bid   545
Another son repair, and bring the crew
Save only two; and let another call
Laerceus hither, skilled to work in gold,
That he may plate with gold the heifer's horns.
Let all the rest remain to bid the maids   550
Within prepare a sumptuous feast, and bring
Seats, wood, and limpid water from the fount."
He spake, and all were busy. From the field
The bullock came; from the swift-sailing bark
Came the companions of the gallant youth   555
Telemachus; with all his implements—
Hammer and anvil, and well-jointed tongs—
With which he wrought, the goldsmith also came,
And to be present at the sacred rites
Pallas came likewise. Nestor, aged knight,   560
Brought forth the gold; the artisan prepared
The metal, and about the bullock's horns
Wound it, that Pallas might with pleasure see
The victim so adorned. Then Stratius grasped
The horns, and, aided by Echephron, led   565

The bullock. From his room Aretus brought
A laver filled with water in one hand,
And in the other hand a canister
Of cakes, while Thrasymedes, great in war,
Stood near with a sharp ax, about to smite   570
The victim. Perseus held a vase to catch
The blood, while Nestor, aged horseman, took
Water and cakes, and offering first a part,
And flinging the shorn forelock to the flames,
Prayed to the goddess Pallas fervently.   575
And now, when they had prayed, and flung the cakes,
The large-souled Thrasymedes, Nestor's son,
Struck, where he stood, the blow; the bullock's strength
Gave way. At once the daughters of the king,
And his sons' wives, and queen Eurydice—   580
Nestor's chaste wife, and daughter eldest born
Of Clymenus, broke forth in shrilly cries.
From the great earth the sons then lifted up
And held the victim's head. Peisistratus,
The chief of squadrons, slew it. When the blood   535
Had ceased to flow, and life had left its limbs,
They quickly severed joint from joint; they hewed
The thighs away, and duly covered them
With caul, a double fold, on which they laid
Raw strips of flesh. The aged monarch burned   590
These over the cleft wood, and poured dark wine
Upon them, while beside him stood the youths
With five-pronged spits; and when the thighs were burned
And entrails tasted, all the rest they carved
Into small portions and transfixed with spits,   595
And roasted, holding the sharp spits in hand.
Meantime, fair Polycaste, youngest bora

Of Nestor's daughters, gave Telemachus
The bath; and after he had bathed she shed
A rich oil over him, and in a cloak   600
Of noble texture and a tunic robed
The prince, who, like a god in presence, left
The bath, and took his place where Nestor sat,
The shepherd of the people. When the youths
Had roasted well and from the spits withdrawn   605
The flesh, they took their places at the feast.
Then rose up chosen men, and poured the wine
Into the cups of gold; and when at length
The thirst and appetite were both allayed,
The knight, Gerenian Nestor, thus began: 610
"Rise now, my sons; join to the bright-haired steeds
My car, and let Telemachus depart."
He spake; they hearkened and obeyed, and straight
Yoked the swift horses to the car. Then came
The matron of the household, laying bread   615
And wine within the car, and dainties such
As make a prince's fare. Telemachus
Then climbed into the sumptuous seat. The son
Of Nestor and the chief of armed bands,
Peisistratus, climbed also, took his place   620
Beside him, grasped the reins, and with the lash
Urged on the coursers. Not unwillingly
They darted toward the plain, and left behind
The lofty Pylos. All that day they shook
The yoke on both their necks. The sun went down;   625
The highways lay in darkness when they came
To Pherae and the abode of Diocles,
Son of Orsilochus, who claimed to be
The offspring of Alpheius. They with him

Found welcome there, and there that night they slept.   630
And when the rosy-fingered Morn appeared,
They yoked the horses, climbed the shining car,
And issued from the palace gate beneath
The sounding portico. Peisistratus
Wielded the lash to urge the coursers on,   635
And not unwillingly they flew and reached
A land of harvests. Here the travelers found
Their journey's end, so swiftly those fleet steeds
Had borne them on. And now the sun went down,
And darkness gathered over all the ways.   640

BOOK IV

They came to Lacedaemon's valley, seamed   1
With dells, and to the palace of its king,
The glorious Menelaus, whom they found
Within, and at a wedding banquet, made
Both for his blameless daughter and his son,   5
And many guests. Her he must send away,
Bride of the son of that invincible chief,
Achilles. He betrothed her while in Troy,
And gave his kingly word, and now the gods
Fulfilled it by the marriage. He was now   10
Sending her forth, with steeds and cars, to reach
The noble city of the Myrmidons,
Where ruled her consort. From the Spartan coast
He brought Alector's daughter for his son,
The gallant Megapenthes, borne to him   15
By a handmaiden in his later years.
For not to Helen had the gods vouchsafed
Yet other offspring, after she had brought
A lovely daughter forth, Hermione,
Like golden Aphrodite both in face and form.   20
So banqueting the neighbors and the friends

Of glorious Menelaus sat beneath
The lofty ceiling of those spacious halls,
Delighted with the feast. A sacred bard
Amidst them touched the harp and sang to them   25
While, as the song began, two dancers sprang
Into the midst and trod the measure there
But they—the hero-youth Telemachus
And Nestor's eminent son—were at the gate,
And standing in the entrance with their steeds.   30
The worthy Eteoneus, coming forth—
The trusty servant of the glorious son
Of Atreus—saw, and hastening thence to tell
The shepherd of the people, through the hall
He came to him, and spake these winged words: 35
"O Menelaus, foster-child of Zeus,
Two strangers have arrived, two men who seem
Descended from almighty Zeus.
Shall we then loose the harness from their steeds,
Or bid them elsewhere seek a friendly host?"   40
The fair-haired king indignantly replied:
"Nay, Eteoneus, thou hast not been wont,
Son of Boethus, thus to play the fool.
Thou pratest idly, like a child. Ourselves
Have sat, as guests, at generous banquets given   45
By other men, when journeying hitherward
In hope that Zeus might grant a respite here
From our disasters. Hasten, then, to loose
The steeds, and bring the strangers to the feast."
He spake; the attendant hastened forth and called   50
The other trusty servitors, with charge
To follow. They unyoked the sweaty steeds,
And bound them to the stalls, and gave them oats,

With which they mingled the white barley-grains,
And close against the shining wall they placed   55
The car, and then they led the guests within
The sumptuous palace. Entering, these admired
The palace of the foster-child of Zeus,
For like the splendor of the sun and moon
Its glory was. They with delighted eyes   60
Gazed, and, descending to the polished baths,
They bathed. The attendant maids who at the bath
Had ministered, anointing them with oil,
Arrayed the stranger guests in fleecy cloaks
And tunics. Each sat down upon a throne   65
Near to Atrides. Now a handmaid brought
A beautiful ewer of gold, and laver wrought
Of silver, and poured water for their hands,
And spread a polished table near their seat;
The reverend matron of the household came   70
With bread, and set before them many a dish
Gathered from all the feast. The carver next
Brought chargers lifted high, and in them meats
Of every flavor, and before them placed
Beakers of gold. The fair-haired monarch gave   75
His hand to each, and then bespake them thus:
"Now taste our banquet and rejoice, and when
Ye are refreshed with food we will inquire
Who ye may be; for ye are not of those
Whose race degenerates, ye are surely born   80
Of sceptered kings, the favorites of Zeus.
Ignoble men have never sons like you."
Thus having said, and taking in his hands
A fading bullock's chine, which menials brought
Roasted, and placed beside the king in sign   85

Of honor, this he laid before his guests.
And they put forth their hands and banqueted;
And when the calls of hunger and of thirst
At length were stilled, Telemachus inclined
His head toward Nestor's son, that no one else   90
Might listen to his words, and thus he said:
"See, son of Nestor, my beloved friend,
In all these echoing rooms the sheen of brass,
Of gold, of amber, and of ivory;
Such is the palace of Olympian Zeus   95
Within its walls. How many things are here
Of priceless worth! I wonder as I gaze."
The fair-haired Menelaus heard him speak,
And thus accosted both with winged words:
"Dear sons, no mortal man may vie with Zeus,   100
Whose palace and possessions never know
Decay, but other men may vie or not
In wealth with me. 'Twas after suffering
And wandering long that in my fleet I brought
My wealth with me, and landed on this coast   105
In the eighth year. For I had roamed afar
To Cyprus and to Phoenice, and where
The Egyptians dwell, and Ethiopia's sons,
And the Sidonians, and the Erembian race,
And to the coast of Lybia, where the lambs   110
Are yeaned with budding horns. There do the ewes
Thrice in the circle of the year bring forth
Their young. There both the master of the herd
And herdsman know no lack of cheese, or flesh,
Or of sweet milk; for there the herds yield milk   115
The whole year round. While I was roaming thus,
And gathering store of wealth, another slew

My brother, unforewarned, and through the fraud
Of his own guilty consort. Therefore small
Is the content I find in bearing rule   120
O'er these possessions. Ye have doubtless heard
This from your parents, be they who they may;
For much have I endured, and I have lost
A palace, a most noble dwelling-place,
Full of things rare and precious. Even now   125
Would I possessed within my palace here
But the third part of these; and would that they
Were yet alive who perished on the plain
Of Troy afar from Argos and its steeds!
Yet while I grieve and while I mourn them all,   130
Here, sitting in my palace, I by turns
Indulge my heart in weeping, and by turns
I pause, for with continual sorrow comes
A weariness of spirit. Yet, in truth,
For none of all those warriors, though their fate   135
Afflicts me sorely, do I so much grieve
As for one hero. When I think of him,
The feast and couch are joyless, since, of all
The Achaean chiefs, none brought so much to pass
As did Odysseus, both in what he wrought   140
And what he suffered. Great calamities
Fell to his lot in life, and to my own
Grief for his sake that cannot be consoled.
Long has he been divided from his friends,
And whether he be living now or dead   145
We know not. Old Laertes, the sage queen
Penelope, and young Telemachus,
Whom, when he went to war he left new-born
At home, are sorrowing somewhere for his sake."

He spake, and woke anew the young man's grief   150
For his lost father. From his eyelids fell
Tears at the hearing of his father's name,
And with both hands he held before his eyes
The purple mantle. Menelaus saw
His tears, and pondered, doubting which were best—   155
To let the stranger of his own accord
Speak of his father, or to question him
At first, and then to tell him all he knew.
As thus he pondered, Helen, like in form
To Dian of the golden distaff, left   160
Her high-roofed chamber, where the air was sweet
With perfumes, and approached. Adrasta placed
A seat for her of costly workmanship;
Aicippe brought a mat of soft light wool,
And Phylo with a silver basket came,   165
Given by Alcandra, wife of Polybus,
Who dwelt at Thebes, in Egypt, and whose house
Was rich in things of price. Two silver baths
He gave to Menelaus, tripods two,
And talents ten of gold. His wife bestowed   170
Beautiful gifts on Helen—one of gold,
A distaff; one a silver basket edged
With gold and round in form. This Phylo brought
Heaped with spun yarn and placed before the queen;
Upon it lay the distaff, wrapped in wool   175
Of color like the violet. Helen there
Sat down, a footstool at her feet, and straight
Questioned with earnest words her husband thus:
"Say, Menelaus, foster-child of Zeus,
Is it yet known what lineage these men claim—   180
These visitants? And what I now shall say,

Will it be false or true? Yet must I speak.
Woman or man I think I never saw
So like another as this youth, on whom
I look with deep astonishment, is like   185
Telemachus, the son whom our great chief
Odysseus left at home a tender babe
When ye Achaeans for my guilty sake
Went forth to wage the bloody war with Troy."
And fair-haired Menelaus answered her: 190
"Yea, wife, so deem I as it seems to thee.
Such are his feet, his hands, the cast of the eye,
His head, the hair upon his brow. Just now,
In speaking of Odysseus, as I told
How he had toiled and suffered for my sake,   195
The stranger held the purple cloak before
His eyes, and from the lids dropped bitter tears.'
Peisistratus, the son of Nestor, spake
In answer: "Menelaus, foster-child
Of Zeus and son of Atreus! sovereign king!   200
He is, as thou hast said, that hero's son;
But he is modest, and he deems that ill
It would become him, on arriving here,
If he should venture in discourse while thou
Art present, in whose voice we take delight   205
As if it were the utterance of a god.
The knight Gerenian Nestor sent me forth
To guide him hither—for he earnestly
Desired to see thee, that thou mightest give
Counsel in what he yet should say or do.   210
For bitterly a son, who finds at home
No others to befriend him, must lament
The absence of a father. So it is

With young Telemachus; for far away
His father is, and in the land are none   215
Who have the power to shelter him from wrong."
The fair-haired Menelaus answered thus:
"O wonder! Then the son of one most dear,
Who for my sake so oft has braved and borne
The conflicts of the battle-field, hath come   220
Beneath my roof. I thought that I should greet
His father with a warmer welcome here
Than any other of the Argive race,
When Zeus the Olympian Thunderer should grant
A safe return to us across the deep   225
In our good ships. I would have founded here
For him a city in Argos, and have built
Dwellings, and would have brought from Ithaca
Him and his son, and all his wealth and all
His people. To this end I would have caused   230
Some neighboring district where my sway is owned
To be dispeopled. Dwelling here we oft
Should then have met each other, and no cause
Would e'er have parted us, two faithful friends
Delighting in each other, till at last   235
Came Death's black cloud to wrap us in its shade.
A god, no doubt, hath seen in this a good
Too great for us, and thus to him alone,
Unhappy man! denied a safe return."
He spake; his words awoke in every heart   240
Grief for the absent hero's sake. Then wept
The Argive Helen, child of Zeus; then wept
Telemachus; nor tearless were the eyes
Of Nestor's son, for to his mind arose
The memory of the good Antilochus,   245

Slain by the bright Aurora's eminent son;
Of him he thought, and spake these winged words:
"O son of Atreus! aged Nestor saith,
When in his palace we discourse of thee
And ask each other's thought, that thou art wise   250
Beyond all other men. Now, if thou mayst,
Indulge me, for not willingly I weep
Thus at the evening feast, and soon will Morn,
Child of the Dawn, appear. I do not blame
This sorrow for whoever meets his fate   255
And dies; the only honors we can pay
To those unhappy mortals is to shred
Our locks away, and wet our cheeks with tears.
I lost a brother, not the least in worth
Among the Argives, whom thou must have seen.   260
I knew him not: I never saw his face;
Yet is it said Antilochus excelled
The others; swift of foot, and brave in war."
The fair-haired Menelaus answered him:
"Since thou my friend hast spoken thus, as one   253
Discreet in word and deed, of riper years
Than thou, might speak and act—for thou art born
Of such a father, and thy words are wise—
And easy is it to discern the son
Of one on whom Cronus-son has bestowed   270
Both at the birth-hour and in wedded life
His blessing; as he gives to Nestor now
A calm old age that lapses pleasantly,
Within his palace-halls, from day to day,
And sons wise-minded, mighty with the spear—   275
Then let us lay aside this sudden grief
That has o'ertaken us, and only think

Of banqueting. Let water now be poured
Upon our hands; there will be time enough
Tomorrow for discourse; Telemachus   280
And I will then engage in mutual talk."
He spake, Asphalion, who with diligent heed
Served the great Menelaus, on their hands
Poured water, and they shared the meats that lay
Upon the board. But Helen, Zeus-born dame,   285
Had other thoughts, and with the wine they drank
Mingled a drug, an antidote to grief
And anger, bringing quick forgetfulness
Of all life's evils. Whoso drinks, when once
It is infused and in the cup, that day   290
Shall never wet his cheeks with tears, although
His father and his mother lie in death,
Nor though his brother or beloved son
Fall butchered by the sword before his eyes.
Such sovereign drugs she had, that child of Zeus,   295
Given her by Polydamna, wife of Thon,
A dame of Egypt, where the bounteous soil
Brings forth abundantly its potent herbs,
Of healing some and some of bane, and where
Dwell the physicians who excel in skill   300
All other men, for they are of the race
Of Paeon. Now when Helen in the cups
Had placed the drug, and bidden them to pour
The wine upon it, thus she spake again:
"Atrides Menelaus, reared by Zeus,   305
And ye the sons of heroes!—Zeus
The sovereign, gives, at pleasure, good and ill
To one or to another, for his power
Is infinite—now sitting in these halls,

Feast and enjoy free converse. I will speak   310
What suits the occasion. I could not relate,
I could not even name, the many toils
Borne by Odysseus, stout of heart I speak
Only of what that valiant warrior did
And suffered once in Troy, where ye of Greece   315
Endured such hardships. He had given himself
Unseemly stripes, and o'er his shoulders flung
Vile garments like a slave's, and entered thus
The enemy's town, and walked its spacious streets.
Another man he seemed in that disguise—   320
A beggar, though when at the Achaean fleet
So different was the semblance that he wore.
He entered Ilium thus transformed, and none
Knew who it was that passed, but I perceived,
And questioned him; he turned my quest aside   325
With crafty answers. After I had seen
The bath administered, anointed him
And clothed him, and had sworn a solemn oath
Not to reveal his visit to the men
Of Ilium till he reached again the tents   330
And galleys, then he opened to me all
The plans of the Achaeans. Leaving me,
On his return he slew with his long spear
Full many a Trojan, and in safety reached
The Argive camp with tidings for the host.   335
Then wept aloud the Trojan dames, but I
Was glad at heart, for I already longed
For my old home, and deeply I deplored
The evil fate that Aphrodite brought on me,
Who led me thither from my own dear land,   340
And from my daughter and my marriage-bower,

And from my lawful spouse, in whom I missed
No noble gift of person or of mind."
Then fair-haired Menelaus said to her:
"All thou hast spoken, woman, is most true.						345
Of many a valiant warrior I have known
The counsels and the purposes, and far
Have roamed in many lands, but never yet
My eyes have looked on such another man
As was Odysseus, of a heart so bold						350
And such endurance. Witness what he did
And bore, the heroic man, what time we sat,
The bravest of the Argives, pent within
The wooden horse, about to bring to Troy
Slaughter and death. Thou earnest to the place,					355
Moved, as it seemed, by some divinity
Who thought to give the glory of the day
To Troy. Deiphobus, the godlike chief,
Was with thee. Thrice about the hollow frame
That held the ambush thou didst walk and touch				360
Its sides, and call the Achaean chiefs by name,
And imitate the voices of the wives
Of all the Argives. Diomed and I
Sat with the great Odysseus in the midst,
And with him heard thy call, and rose at once					365
To sally forth or answer from within;
But he forbade, impatient as we were,
And so restrained us. All the Achaean chiefs
Kept silence save Anticlus, who alone
Began to speak, when, with his powerful hands,					370
Odysseus pressed together instantly
The opening lips, and saved us all, and thus
Held them till Pallas lured thee from the spot."

Then spake discreet Telemachus again:

"Atrides Menelaus, reared by Zeus,   375

Ruler of tribes! the harder was his lot,

Since even thus he could not shun the stroke

Of death, not though a heart of steel were his.

But now dismiss us to our beds, that there,

Couched softly, we may welcome balmy sleep."   380

He spake, and Argive Helen called her maids

To make up couches in the portico,

And throw fair purple blankets over them,

And tapestry above, and cover all

With shaggy cloaks. Forth from the palace halls   385

They went with torches, and made ready soon

The couches /thither heralds led the guests.

There in the vestibule Telemachus,

The hero, and with him the eminent son

Of Nestor, took their rest. Meanwhile the son   390

Of Atreus lay within an inner room

Of that magnificent pile, and near to him

The glorious lady, long-robed Helen, slept.

But when at length the daughter of the Dawn,

The rosy-fingered Morning, brought her light,   395

Then Menelaus, great in battle, rose,

Put on his garments, took his trenchant sword,

And, having hung it on his shoulder, laced

The shapely sandals to his shining feet,

And issued from his chamber like a god   400

In aspect. Near Telemachus he took

His seat, and calling him by name he spake:

"What urgent cause, my brave Telemachus,

Brings thee to sacred Lacedaemon o'er

The breast of the great ocean? Frankly say,   405

Is it a private or a public need?"
And thus discreet Telemachus replied:
"Atrides Menelaus, reared by Zeus,
Ruler of nations! I am come to ask
News of my father, if thou knowest aught.   410
My heritage is wasting; my rich fields
Are made a desolation. Enemies
Swarm in my palace, and from day to day
Slaughter my flocks and slow-paced horned herds
My mother's suitors they, and measureless   415
Their insolence. And therefore am I come
To clasp thy knees, and pray thee to relate
The manner of my father's sorrowful death
As thou hast seen it with thine eyes, or heard
Its story from some wandering man—for sure   420
His mother brought him forth to wretchedness
Beyond the common lot. I ask thee not
To soften aught in the sad history
Through tenderness to me, or kind regard,
But tell me plainly all that thou dost know;   425
And I beseech thee, if at any time
My father, good Odysseus, brought to pass
Aught that he undertook for thee in word
Or act while ye were in the realm of Troy,
Where the Greeks suffered sorely, bear it now   430
In mind, and let me have the naked truth."
Then Menelaus of the amber locks
Drew a deep sigh, and thus in answer said:
"Heavens! they would climb into a brave man's bed,
These craven weaklings. But as when a hart   435
Has hid her newborn suckling fawns within
The lair of some fierce lion, and gone forth

Herself to range the mountain-sides and feed
Among the grassy lawns, the lion comes
Back to the place and brings them sudden death,   440
So will Odysseus bring a bloody fate
Upon the suitor crew. O father Zeus,
And Pallas, and Apollo! I could wish
That now, with prowess such as once was his
When he, of yore, in Lesbos nobly built,   445
Rising to strive with Philomela's son,
In wrestling threw him heavily, and all
The Greeks rejoiced, Odysseus might engage
The suitors. Short were then their term of life,
And bitter would the nuptial banquet be.   450
Now for the questions thou hast put, and craved
From me a true reply, I will not seek
To pass them by with talk of other things,
Nor yet deceive thee, but of all that once
Was told me by the Ancient of the Deep,   455
Whose words are truth, I shall keep nothing back.
"In Egypt still, though longing to come home,
The gods detained me; for I had not paid
The sacrifice of chosen hecatombs,
And ever do the gods require of us   460
Remembrance of their laws. There is an isle
Within the billowy sea before you reach
The coast of Egypt—Pharos is its name—
At such a distance as a ship could pass
In one whole day with a shrill breeze astern.   465
A sheltered haven lies within that isle,
Whence the good ships go forth with fresh supplies
Of water. There the gods constrained my stay
For twenty days, and never in that time

Blew favoring winds across the waters, such   470
As bear the galley over the great deep.
Now would our stores of food have been consumed,
Now would the courage of my men have died,
Had not a goddess pitied me, and come
To my relief, by name Idothea, born   475
To the great Proteus, Ancient of the Deep.
For she was moved by my distress, and came
To me while I was wandering alone,
Apart from all the rest. They through the isle
Roamed everywhere from place to place, and, pinched   480
With hunger, threw the hook for fish. She came,
And, standing near, accosted me and said:
'Stranger, thou art an idiot, or at least
Of careless mood, or else art willingly
Neglectful, and art pleased with suffering,   485
That thou dost linger in this isle so long
And find no means to leave it, while the hearts
Of thy companions faint with the delay.'
She spake, and I replied: 'Whoe'er thou art,
goddess, let me say, not willingly   490
I linger here. I surely must have sinned
Against the immortal dwellers of high heaven;
But tell me—for the gods know all things—who
Of all the immortals holds me windbound here,
Hindering my voyage; tell me also how   495
To reach my home across the fishy deep.'
I ended, and the glorious goddess said
In answer: 'Stranger, I will truly speak;
The deathless Ancient of the Deep, whose words
Are ever true, Egyptian Proteus, oft   500
Here makes his haunt. To him are fully known—

For he is Poseidon's subject—all the depths
Of the great ocean. It is said I owe
To him my birth. If him thou canst ensnare
And seize, he will disclose to thee thy way   505
And all its distances, and tell thee how
To reach thy home across the fishy deep;
And further will reveal, if so he choose,
Foster-child of Zeus, whate'er of good
Or ill has in thy palace come to pass,   510
While thou wert wandering long and wearily.'
So said the goddess, and I spake again:
'Explain by what device to snare and hold
The aged deity, lest he foreknow
Or else suspect our purpose and escape.   515
'Twere hard for mortals to constrain a god.'
I ended, and the glorious goddess thus
Made answer: 'When the climbing sun has reached
The middle heaven, the Ancient of the Deep,
Who ne'er deceives, emerges from the waves,   520
And, covered with the dark scum of the sea,
Walks forth, and in a cavern vault lies down.
Thither fair Halosydna's progeny,
The sea-calves from the hoary ocean, throng,
Rank with the bitter odor of the brine,   525
And slumber near him. With the break of day
I will conduct thee thither and appoint
Thy place, but thou shalt choose to go with thee
Three of the bravest men in thy good ships.
And let me now relate the stratagems   530
Of the old prophet. He at first will count
The sea-calves, going o'er them all by fives;
And when he has beheld and numbered all,

Amidst them all will he lie down, as lies
A shepherd midst his flock. And then, as soon   535
As ye behold him stretched at length, exert
Your utmost strength to hold him there, although
He strive and struggle to escape your hands;
For he will try all stratagems, and take
The form of every reptile on the earth,   540
And turn to water and to raging flame—
Yet hold him firmly still, and all the more
Make fast the bands. When he again shall take
The form in which thou sawest him asleep,
Desist from force, and loose the bands that held   545
The ancient prophet. Ask of him what god
Afflicts thee thus, and by what means to cross
The fishy deep and find thy home again.'
Thus having said, the goddess straightway sprang
Into the billowy ocean, while I sought   550
The galleys, where they rested on the sand,
With an uneasy spirit. When I reached
The ship and shore we made our evening meal.
The hallowed night came down; we lay and slept
Upon the sea-beach. When the Morning came,   555
The rosy-fingered daughter of the Dawn,
Forth on the border of the mighty main
I went, and prayed the immortals fervently.
I led three comrades, whom I trusted most
In all adventures. Entering the depths   560
Of the great sea, the goddess brought us thence
Four skins of sea-calves newly flayed, that thus
We might deceive her father. Then she scooped
Beds for us in the sea-sand, and sat down
To wait his coming. We were near to her,   565

And there she laid us duly down, and threw
A skin o'er each. Now did our ambush seem
Beyond endurance, for the noisome smell
Of those sea-nourished creatures sickened us;
And who could bear to sleep beside a whale?   570
But she bethought her of an antidote,
A sovereign one, and so relieved us all.
To each she brought ambrosia, placing it
Beneath his nostrils, and the sweets it breathed
O'ercame the animal odor. All the morn   575
We waited patiently. The sea-calves came
From ocean in a throng, and laid themselves
In rows along the margin of the sea.
At noon emerged the aged seer, and found
His well-fed sea-calves. Going o'er them all   580
He counted them, ourselves among the rest,
With no misgiving of the fraud, and then
He laid him down to rest. We rushed with shouts
Upon him suddenly, and in our arms
Caught him; nor did the aged seer forget   585
His stratagems; and first he took the shape
Of a maned lion, of a serpent next.
Then of a panther, then of a huge boar,
Then turned to flowing water, then became
A tall tree full of leaves. With resolute hearts   590
We held him fast, until the aged seer
Was wearied out, in spite of all his wiles.
And questioned me in speech at last and said:
'O son of Atreus! who of all the gods
Hath taught thee how to take me in this snare,   595
Unwilling as I am? What wouldst thou have?'
He spake; I answered: 'Aged prophet, well

Thou knowest. Why deceitfully inquire?
It is that I am held a prisoner long
Within this isle, and vainly seek the means   600
Of my escape, and grief consumes my heart.
Now—since the gods know all things—tell me this,
What deity it is, that, hindering thus
My voyage, keeps me here, and tell me how
To cross the fishy deep and reach my home.'   605
Such were my words, and he in answer said:
'But thou to Zeus and to the other gods
Shouldst first have paid acceptable sacrifice,
And shouldst have then embarked to reach with speed
Thy native land across the dark-blue deep.   610
Now it is not thy fate to see again
Thy friends, thy stately palace, and the land
That saw thy birth, until thou stand once more
Beside the river that through Egypt flows
From Zeus, and offer sacred hecatombs   615
To the ever-living gods inhabiting
The boundless heaven, and they will speed thee forth
Upon the voyage thou dost long to make.'
He spake. My heart was broken as I heard
His bidding to recross the shadowy sea   620
To Egypt, for the way was difficult
And long; and yet I answered him and said:
'Duly will I perform, O aged seer,
What thou commandest. But I pray thee tell,
And truly, whether all the sons of Greece   625
Whom Nestor and myself, in setting sail
Left on the Trojan coast, have since returned
Safe with their galleys, or have any died
Untimely in their ships or in the arms

Of their companions since the war was closed?'   630
I spake; again he answered me and said:
'Why dost thou ask, Atrides, since to know
Thou needest not, nor is it well to explore
The secrets of my mind? Thou canst not, sure,
Refrain from tears when thou shalt know the whole.   635
Many are dead, and many left in Troy.
Two leaders only of the well-armed Greeks
Were slain returning; in that combat thou
Didst bear a part; one, living yet, is kept,
Far in the mighty main, from his return,   640
Amid his well-oared galleys Ajax died.
For Poseidon first had driven him on the rocks
Of Gyrae, yet had saved him from the sea;
And he, though Pallas hated him, had yet
Been rescued, but for uttering boastful words,   645
Which drew his fate upon him. He had said
That he, in spite of all the gods, would come
Safe from those mountain waves. When Poseidon heard
The boaster's challenge, instantly he laid
His strong hand on the trident, smote the rock   650
And cleft it to the base. Part stood erect,
Part fell into the deep. There Ajax sat,
And felt the shock, and with the falling mass
Was carried headlong to the billowy depths
Below, and drank the brine and perished there.   655
Thy brother in his roomy ships escaped
The danger, for imperial Hera's aid
Preserved him. But when near Meleia's heights
About to land, a tempest seized and swept
The hero thence across the fishy deep,   660
Lamenting his hard lot, to that far cape

Where once abode Thyestes, and where now
His son Aegisthus dwelt. But when the gods
Sent other winds, and safe at last appeared
The voyage, they returned, and reached their home.   665
With joy he stepped upon his native soil,
And kissed the earth that bore him, while his tears
At that most welcome sight flowed fast and warm.
Him from a lofty perch a spy beheld,
Whom treacherous Aegisthus planted there,   670
Bribed by two golden talents. He had watched
The whole year through, lest, coming unobserved,
The king might make his prowess felt. The spy
Flew to the royal palace with the news,
And instantly Aegisthus planned a snare.   675
He chose among the people twenty men,
The bravest, whom he stationed out of sight,
And gave command that others should prepare
A banquet. Then with chariots and with steeds,
And with a deadly purpose in his heart,   680
He went, and, meeting Agamemnon, bade
The shepherd of the people to the feast,
And slew him at the board as men might slay
A bullock at the crib. Of all who went
With Agamemnon thither, none survived,   685
And of the followers of Aegisthus none,
But all were slaughtered in the banquet-hall.'
He spake; my heart was breaking, and I wept,
While sitting on the sand, nor in my heart
Cared I to live, or longer to behold   690
The sweet light of the sun. But when there came
Respite from tears and writhing on the ground,
The Ancient of the Deep, who ne'er deceives,

Spake yet again: 'Atrides, lose no time
In tears; they profit nothing. Rather seek   695
The means by which thou mayst the soonest reach
Thy native land. There thou perchance mayst find
Aegisthus yet alive, or haply first
Orestes may have slain him, and thyself
Arrive to see the funeral rites performed.'   700
He spake, and though afflicted still, my heart
Was somewhat comforted; my spirit rose,
And thus I answered him with winged words:
'These men I know; name now the third, who still
Is kept from his return afar within   705
The mighty main—alive, perchance, or dead;
For, though I dread to hear, I long to know.'
I spake, and Proteus answered me again:
'It is Laertes' son, whose dwelling stands
In Ithaca. I saw him in an isle,   710
And in the cavern-palace of the nymph
Calypso, weeping bitterly, for she
Constrains his stay. He cannot leave the isle
For his own country; ship arrayed with oars
And seamen has he none to bear him o'er   715
The breast of the great ocean. But for thee,
It is not decreed that thou shalt meet thy fate
And die, most noble Menelaus, where
The steeds of Argos in her pastures graze.
The gods will send thee to the Elysian plain,   720
And to the end of earth, the dwelling-place
Of fair-haired Rhadamanthus. There do men
Lead easiest lives. No snow, no bitter cold,
No beating rains, are there; the ocean-deeps
With murmuring breezes from the West refresh   725

The dwellers. Thither shalt thou go; for thou
Art Helen's spouse, and son-in-law of Zeus.'
He spake, and plunged into the billowy deep.
I to the fleet returned in company
With my brave men, revolving, as I went,   730
A thousand projects in my thought. I reached
My galley by the sea, and we prepared
Our evening meal. The hallowed night came down,
And there upon the ocean-beach we slept.
But when the rosy-fingered Morn appeared,   735
The daughter of the Dawn, we drew our ships
To the great deep, and raised the masts and spread
The sails; the crews, all entering, took their seats
Upon the benches, ranged in order due,
And beat the foaming water with their oars.   740
Again to Egypt's coast I brought the fleet,
And to the river that descends from Zeus,
And there I offered chosen hecatombs;
And having thus appeased the gods, I reared
A tomb to Agamemnon, that his fame   745
Might never die. When this was done I sailed
For home; the gods bestowed a favoring wind.
But now remain thou till the eleventh day,
Or till the twelfth, beneath my roof, and then
Will I dismiss thee with munificent gifts—   750
Three steeds, a polished chariot, and a cup
Of price, with which to pour, from day to day,
Wine to the gods in memory of me."
Then spake discreet Telemachus again:
"Atrides, seek not to detain me long,   755
Though I could sit contentedly a year
Beside thee, never longing for my home,

Nor for my parents, such delight I find
In listening to thy words; but even now,
In hallowed Pylos, my companions grow   760
Weary, while thou delayest my return.
The gifts—whate'er thou choosest to bestow,
Let them be such as I can treasure up.
The steeds to Ithaca I may not take,
I leave them to adorn thy retinue;   765
For thou art ruler o'er a realm of plains,
Where grows much lotos, and sweet grasses spring,
And wheat and rye, and the luxuriant stalks
Of the white barley. But in Ithaca
Are no broad grounds for coursing, meadows none.   770
Goats graze amid its fields, a fairer land
Than those where horses feed. No isle that lies
Within the deep has either roads for steeds
Or meadows, least of all has Ithaca."
He spake; the valiant Menelaus smiled,   775
And kindly touched him with his hand and said:
"Dear son, thou comest of a generous stock;
Thy words declare it. I will change my gifts,
As well I may. Of all that in my house
Are treasured up, the choicest I will give,   730
And the most precious. I will give a cup
Wrought all of silver save its brim of gold.
It is the work of Hephaestus. Phaedimus
The hero, King of Sidon, gave it me,
When I was coming home, and underneath   785
His roof was sheltered. Now it shall be thine."
So talked they with each other. Meantime came
Those who prepared the banquet to the halls
Of the great monarch. Bringing sheep they came

And strengthening wine. Their wives, who on their brows   790
Wore showy fillets, brought the bread, and thus
Within the house of Menelaus all
Was bustle, setting forth the evening meal.
But in the well-paved court which lay before
The palace of Odysseus, where of late   795
Their insolence was shown, the suitor train
Amused themselves with casting quoits and spears,
While by themselves Antinous, and the youth
Of godlike mien, Eurymachus, who both
Were eminent above the others, sat.   800
To them Noemon, son of Phronius, went,
Drew near, bespake Antinous and inquired:
"Is it among us known, or is it not,
Antinous, when Telemachus returns
From sandy Pylos? Thither he is gone   805
And in my galley, which I need to cross
To spacious Elis. There I have twelve mares
And hardy mule-colts with them yet untamed,
And some I must subdue to take the yoke."
He spake, and they were both amazed; for they   810
Had never thought of him as visiting
Neleian Pylos, deeming that the youth
Was somewhere in his fields, among the flocks,
Or haply with the keeper of the swine.
Then did Antinous, Eupeithes' son,   815
Make answer: "Tell me truly when he sailed,
And what young men of Ithaca he chose
To go with him. Were they his slaves, or hired
To be his followers? Tell, for I would know
The whole. Took he thy ship against thy will?   820
Or didst thou yield it at his first request?"

Noemon, son of Phornius, thus replied:
"Most willingly I gave it, for what else
Would anyone have done when such a man
Desired it in his need? It would have been   825
Hard to deny it. For the band of youths
Who followed him, they are the bravest here
Of all our people; and I saw embark,
As their commander, Mentor, or some god
Like Mentor altogether. One thing moves   830
My wonder. Only yesterday, at dawn,
I met with Mentor here, whom I before
Had seen embarking for the Pylian coast."
Noemon spake, and to his father's house
Departed. Both were troubled at his words,   835
And all the suitors took at once their seats,
And ceased their pastimes. Then Antinous spake,
Son of Eupeithes, greatly vexed; his heart
Was darkened with blind rage; his eyes shot fire.
"Strange doings these! a great and proud exploit
Performed—this voyage of Telemachus,   840
Which we had called impossible! The boy,
In spite of us, has had his will and gone.
And carried off a ship, and for his crew
Chosen the bravest of the people here.
He yet will prove a pest. May Zeus   845
Crush him ere he can work us further harm!
Now give me a swift bark and twenty men
That I may lie in ambush and keep watch
For his return within the straits between   850
This isle and rugged Samos; then, I deem,
He will have sought his father to his cost."
He spake; they praised his words and bade him act,

And rose and left their places, entering
The palace of Odysseus. Brief the time   855
That passed before Penelope was warned
Of what the suitors treacherously planned.
The herald Medon told her all. He heard
In the outer court their counsels while within
They plotted, and he hastened through the house   860
To bring the tidings to Penelope.
Penelope perceived him as he stepped
Across the threshold, and bespake him thus:
"Why, herald, have the suitor princes sent
Thee hither? comest thou to bid the maids   865
Of great Odysseus leave their tasks and make
A banquet ready? Would their wooing here
And elsewhere were but ended, and this feast
Were their last feast on earth! Ye who in throngs
Come hither and so wastefully consume   870
The substance of the brave Telemachus,
Have ye not from your parents, while ye yet
Were children, heard how once Odysseus lived
Among them, never wronging any man
In all the realm by aught he did or said—   875
As mighty princes often do, through hate
Of some and love of others? Never man
Endured injustice at his hands, but you—
Your vile designs and acts are known; ye bear
No grateful memory of a good man's deeds."   880
And then, in turn, experienced Medon spake:
"O queen, I would this evil were the worst!
The suitors meditate a greater still,
And a more heinous far. May Zeus
Never permit the crime! Their purpose is   885

To meet Telemachus, on his return,
And slay him with the sword; for thou must know
That on a voyage to the Pylian coast
And noble Lacedaemon he has sailed,
To gather tidings of his father's fate."   890
He spake, and her knees failed her and her heart
Sank as she heard. Long time she could not speak;
Her eyes were filled with tears, and her clear voice
Was choked; yet, finding words at length, she said:
"O herald! wherefore should my son have gone?   895.
There was no need that he should trust himself
To the swift ships, those horses of the sea,
With which men traverse its unmeasured waste.
Was it that he might leave no name on earth? "
And then again experienced Medon spake: 900
"I know not whether prompted by some god
Or moved by his own heart thy son has sailed
For Pylos, hoping there to hear some news
Of his returning father, or his fate."
Thus having said, the herald, traversing   905
The palace of Odysseus, went his way,
While a keen anguish overpowered the queen,
Nor could she longer bear to keep her place
Upon her seat—and many seats were there—
But on the threshold of her gorgeous rooms   910
Lay piteously lamenting. Round her came
Her maidens wailing—all, both old and young,
Who formed her household. These Penelope,
Sobbing in her great sorrow, thus bespake:
"Hear me, my friends, the heavens have cast on me   915
Griefs heavier than on any others born
And reared with me—me, who had lost by death

Already a most gracious husband, one
Who bore a lion heart and who was graced
With every virtue, greatly eminent   920
Among the Greeks, and widely famed abroad
Through Hellas and all Argos. Now my son,
He whom I loved, is driven before the storms
From home, inglorious, and I was not told
Of his departure. Ye too, worthless crew!   925
Ye took no thought, not one of you, to call
Me from my sleep, although ye must have known
Full well when he embarked in his black ship.
And if it had been told me that he planned
This voyage, then, impatient as he was   930
To sail, he would have certainly remained,
Or else have left me in these halls a corpse.
And now let one of my attendants call
The aged Dolius, whom, when first I came
To this abode, my father gave to me   935
To be my servant, and who has in charge
My orchards. Let him haste and take his place
Beside Laertes, and to him declare
All that has happened, that he may devise
Some fitting remedy, or go among   940
The people, to deplore the dark designs
Of those who now are plotting to destroy
The heir of great Odysseus and his own."
Then Eurycleia, the beloved nurse,
Answered: "Dear lady, slay me with the sword,   945
Or leave me here alive; I will conceal
Nothing that has been done or said. I gave
All that he asked, both bread and delicate wine,
And took a solemn oath, which he required,

To tell thee naught of this till twelve days passed,   950
Or till thou shouldst thyself inquire and hear
Of his departure, that those lovely cheeks
Might not be stained with tears. Now bathe and put
Fresh garments on, and to the upper rooms
Ascending, with thy handmaids offer prayer   955
To Pallas, daughter of the god who bears
The aegis. She will then protect thy son,
Even from death. Grieve not the aged man,
Already much afflicted. Sure I am
The lineage of Arcesius has not lost   960
The favor of the gods, but some one yet
Surviving will possess its lofty halls
And its rich acres, stretching far away."
She spake; the queen repressed her grief, and held
Her eyes from tears. She took the bath and put   965
Fresh garments on, and, to the upper rooms
Ascending with her maidens, heaped with cakes
A canister, and prayed to Pallas thus:
"Daughter invincible of Zeus
The aegis-bearer, hear me. If within   970
Thy courts the wise Odysseus ever burned
Fat thighs of beeves or sheep, remember it,
And rescue my dear son, and bring to naught
The wicked plots of the proud suitor-crew."
She spake, and wept aloud. The goddess heard   975
Her prayer. Meantime the suitors filled with noise
The shadowy palace-halls, and there were some
Among that throng of arrogant youths who said:
"Truly the queen, whom we have wooed so long,
Prepares for marriage; little does she know   980
The bloody death we destine for her son."

So spake they, unaware of what was done
Elsewhere. Antinous then stood forth and said:
"Good friends, I warn you all that ye refrain
From boasts like these, lest someone should report   985
Your words within. Now let us silently
Rise up, and all conspire to put in act
The counsel all so heartily approve."
He spake, and chose a crew of twenty men,
The bravest. To the seaside and the ship   990
They went, and down to the deep water drew
The ship, and put the mast and sails on board,
And fitted duly to their leathern rings
The oars, and spread the white sail overhead.
Their nimble-handed servants brought them arms,   995
And there they moored the galley, went on board,
And supped and waited for the evening star.
Now in the upper chamber the chaste queen,
Penelope, lay fasting; food or wine
She had not tasted, and her thoughts were still   1000
Fixed on her blameless son. Would he escape
The threatened death, or perish by the hands
Of the insolent suitors? As a lion's thoughts,
When, midst a crowd of men, he sees with dread
The hostile circle slowly closing round,   1005
Such were her thoughts, when balmy sleep at length
Came creeping over her as on her couch
She lay reclined, her limbs relaxed in rest.
Now Pallas framed a new device; she called
A phantom up, in aspect like the dame   1010
Iphthima, whom Eumelus had espoused
In Pherae, daughter of the high-souled chief
Icarius. Her she sent into the halls

Of great Odysseus, that she might beguile
The sorrowful Penelope from tears   1015
And lamentations. By the thong that held
The bolt she slid into the royal bower
And standing by her head bespake the queen:
"Penelope, afflicted as thou art,
Art thou asleep? The ever-blessed gods   1020
Permit thee not to grieve and weep; thy son,
Who has not sinned against them, shall return."
And then discreet Penelope replied,
Still sweetly slumbering at the Gate of Dreams:
"Why, sister, art thou here, who ne'er before   1025
Hast come to me? The home is far away
In which thou dwellest. Thou exhortest me
To cease from grieving, and to lay aside
The painful thoughts that crowd into my mind,
And torture me who have already lost   1030
A noble-minded, lion-hearted spouse,
One eminent among Achaia's sons
For every virtue, and whose fame was spread
Through Hellas and through Argos. Now my son,
My best beloved, goes to sea—a boy,   1035
Unused to hardships, and unskilled to deal
With strangers. More I sorrow for his sake
Than for his father's. I am filled with fear,
And tremble lest he suffer wrong from those
Among whom he has gone, or on the deep,   1040
Where he has enemies who lie in wait
To slay him ere he reach his home again."
And then the shadowy image spake again:
"Be of good courage; let not fear o'ercome
Thy spirit, for there goes with him a guide   1045

Such as all others would desire to have
Beside them ever, trusting in her power—
Pallas Athene, and she looks on thee
With pity. From her presence I am sent,
Her messenger, declaring this to thee."   1050
Again discreet Penelope replied:
"If then thou be a goddess and hast heard
A goddess speak these words, declare, I pray,
Of that ill-fated one, if yet he live
And look upon the sun, or else have died   1055
And passed to the abodes beneath the earth."
Once more the shadowy image spake: "Of him
Will I say nothing, whether living yet
Or dead; no time is this for idle words."
She said, and from the chamber glided forth   1060
Beside the bolt, and mingled with the winds.
Then quickly from her couch of sleep arose
The daughter of Icarius, for her heart
Was glad, so plainly had the dream conveyed
Its message in the stillness of the night.   1065
Meanwhile the suitors on their ocean-path
Went in their galley, plotting cruelly
To slay Telemachus. A rocky isle
Far in the middle sea, between the coast
Of Ithaca and craggy Samos, lies,   1070
Named Asteris; of narrow bounds, yet there
A sheltered haven is to which two straits
Give entrance. There the Achaeans lay in wait.

BOOK V

Aurora, rising from her couch beside   1
The famed Tithonus, brought the light of day
To men and to immortals. Then the gods
Came to their seats in council. With them came
High-thundering Zeus, amongst them all   5
The mightiest. Pallas, mindful of the past,
Spake of Odysseus and his many woes,
Grieved that he still was with the island nymph:
"O father Zeus, and all ye blessed ones
Who live forever! let not sceptered king   10
Henceforth be gracious, mild, and merciful
And righteous; rather be he deaf to prayer
And prone to deeds of wrong, since no one now
Remembers the divine Odysseus more
Among the people over whom he ruled   15
Benignly, like a father. Still he lies,
Weighed down by many sorrows, in the isle
And dwelling of Calypso, who so long
Constrains his stay. To his dear native land
Depart he cannot; ship arrayed with oars   20
And seamen has he none, to bear him o'er

The breast of the broad ocean. Nay, even now,
Against his well-beloved son a plot
Is laid, to slay him as he journeys home
From Pylos the divine, and from the walls   25
Of famous Sparta, whither he had gone
To gather tidings of his father's fate."
Then answered her the Ruler of the storms:
"My child, what words are these that pass thy lips?
Was not thy long-determined counsel this—   30
That in good time Odysseus should return,
To be avenged? Guide, then, Telemachus
Wisely—for so thou canst—that, all unharmed,
He reach his native land, and, in their barks,
Homeward the suitor-train retrace their way.   35
He spake, and turned to Hermes, his dear son:
"Hermes—for thou in this my messenger
Art, as in all things—to the bright-haired nymph
Make known my steadfast purpose—the return
Of suffering Odysseus. Neither gods   40
Nor men shall guide his voyage. On a raft,
Made firm with bands, he shall depart and reach,
After long hardships, on the twentieth day,
The fertile shore of Scheria, on whose isle
Dwell the Phaeacians, kinsmen of the gods.   45
They like a god shall honor him, and thence
Send him to his loved country in a ship,
With ample gifts of brass and gold, and store
Of raiment—wealth like which he ne'er had brought
From conquered Ilion, had he reached his home   50
Safely, with all his portion of the spoil.
So is it preordained that he behold
His friends again, and stand once more within

His high-roofed palace, on his native soil."
He spake; the herald Argicide obeyed,   55
And hastily beneath his feet he bound
The fair, ambrosial golden sandals, worn
To bear him over ocean like the wind,
And o'er the boundless land. His wand he took,
Wherewith he softly seals the eyes of men,   60
And opens them at will from sleep. With this
In hand, the mighty Argus-queller flew,
And, lighting on Pieria, from the sky
Plunged downward to the deep, and skimmed its face
Like hovering seamew, that on the broad gulfs   65
Of the unfruitful ocean seeks her prey,
And often dips her pinions in the brine;
So Hermes flew along the waste of waves.
But when he reached that island, far away,
Forth from the dark-blue ocean-swell he stepped   70
Upon the sea-beach, walking till he came
To the vast cave in which the bright-haired nymph
Made her abode. He found the nymph within;
A fire blazed brightly on the hearth, and far
Was wafted o'er the isle the fragrant smoke   75
Of cloven cedar, burning in the flame,
And cypress-wood. Meanwhile, in her recess,
She, sweetly sang, as busily she threw
The golden shuttle through the web she wove.
And all about the grotto alders grew,   80
And poplars, and sweet-smelling cypresses.
In a green forest, high among whose boughs
Birds of broad wing, wood-owls, and falcons built
Their nests, and crows, with voices sounding far,
All haunting for their food the ocean-side.   85

A vine, with downy leaves and clustering grapes,
Crept over all the cavern rock. Four springs
Poured forth their glittering waters in a row,
And here and there went wandering side by side.
Around were meadows of soft green, o'ergrown   90
With violets and parsley. 'Twas a spot
Where even an immortal might awhile
Linger, and gaze with wonder and delight.
The herald Argus-queller stood, and saw,
And marveled; but as soon as he had viewed   95
The wonders of the place, he turned his steps,
Entering the broad-roofed cave. Calypso there,
The glorious goddess, saw him as he came,
And knew him; for the ever-living gods
Are to each other known, though one may dwell   100
Far from the rest. Odysseus, large of heart,
Was not within. Apart, upon the shore,
He sat and sorrowed, where he oft in tears
And sighs and vain repinings passed the hours,
Gazing with wet eyes on the barren deep.   105
Now, placing Hermes on a shining seat
Of state, Calypso, glorious goddess, said:
"Thou of the golden wand, revered and loved,
What, Hermes, brings thee hither? Passing few
Have been thy visits. Make thy pleasure known,   110
My heart enjoins me to obey, if aught
That thou commandest be within my power;
But first accept the offerings due a guest."
The goddess, speaking thus, before him placed
A table, where the heaped ambrosia lay,   115
And mingled the red nectar. Ate and drank
The herald Argus-queller, and, refreshed,

Answered the nymph, and made his message known:
"Art thou a goddess, and dost ask of me,
A god, why came I hither? Yet, since thou   120
Requirest, I will truly tell the cause.
I came unwillingly, at Zeus's command;
For who of choice would traverse the wide waste
Of the salt ocean, with no city near
Where men adore the gods with solemn rites   125
And chosen hecatombs. No god has power
To elude or to resist the purposes
Of aegis-bearing Zeus. With thee abides,
He bids me say, the most unhappy man
Of all who round the city of Priam waged   130
The battle through nine years, and, in the tenth,
Laying it waste, departed for their homes.
But in their voyage they provoked the wrath
Of Pallas, who called up the furious winds
And angry waves against them. By his side   135
Sank all his gallant comrades in the deep.
Him did the winds and waves drive hither. Him
Zeus bids thee send away with speed; for here
He must not perish, far from all he loves.
So is it preordained that he behold   140
His friends again, and stand once more within
His high-roofed palace, on his native soil."
He spake; Calypso, glorious goddess, heard,
And shuddered, and with winged words replied:
"Ye are unjust, ye gods, and, envious far   145
Beyond all other beings, cannot bear
That ever goddess openly should make
A mortal man her consort. Thus it was
When once Aurora, rosy-fingered, took

Orion for her husband; ye were stung,   150
Amid your blissful lives, with envious hate,
Till chaste Artemis, of the golden throne,
Smote him with silent arrows from her bow,
And slew him in Ortygia. Thus, again,
When bright-haired Ceres, swayed by her own heart,   155
In fields which bore three yearly harvests, met
Iasion as a lover, this was known
Erelong to Zeus, who flung from high
A flaming thunderbolt, and laid him dead.
And now ye envy me, that with me dwells   160
A mortal man. I saved him as he clung
Alone upon his floating keel; for Zeus
Had cloven with a bolt of fire from heaven
His galley in the midst of the black sea,
And all his gallant comrades perished there.   165
Him kindly I received; I cherished him,
And promised him a life that ne'er should know
Decay or death. But since no god has power
To elude or to withstand the purposes
Of aegis-bearing Zeus, let him depart—   170
If so the sovereign moves him and commands—
Over the barren deep. I send him not;
For neither ship arrayed with oars have I,
Nor seamen, o'er the boundless waste of waves
To bear him hence. My counsel I will give,   175
And nothing will I hide that he should know,
To place him safely on his native shore."
The herald Argus-queller answered her:
"Dismiss him thus, and bear in mind the wrath
Of Zeus, lest it be kindled against thee."   180
Thus having said, the mighty Argicide

Departed; and the nymph, who now had heard
The doom of Zeus, sought the great-hearted man
Odysseus. Him she found beside the deep,
Seated alone, with eyes from which the tears   185
Were never dried; for now no more the nymph
Delighted him; he wasted his sweet life
In yearning for his home. Night after night
He slept constrained within the hollow cave,
The unwilling by the fond; and day by day   190
He sat upon the rocks that edged the shore,
And in continual weeping and in sighs
And vain repinings wore the hours away,
Gazing through tears upon the barren deep.
The glorious goddess stood by him and spake: 195
"Unhappy! sit no longer sorrowing here,
Nor waste life thus. Lo! I most willingly
Dismiss thee hence. Rise, hew down trees, and bind
Their trunks with brazen clamps into a raft,
And fasten planks above, a lofty floor,   200
That it may bear thee o'er the dark-blue deep.
Bread will I put on board, water, and wine—
Red wine, that cheers the heart—and wrap thee well
In garments, and send after thee the wind,
That safely thou attain thy native shore,   205
If so the gods permit thee, who abide
In the broad heaven above, and better know
By far than I, and far more wisely judge."
Odysseus, the great sufferer, as she spake
Shuddered, and thus with winged words replied: 210
"Some other purpose than to send me home
Is in thy heart, O goddess, bidding me
To cross this frightful sea upon a raft—

This perilous sea, where never even ships
Pass with their rapid keels, though Zeus bestow   215
The wind that gladdens seaman. Nay, I climb
No raft, against thy wish, unless thou swear
The great oath of the gods that thou in this
Dost meditate no other harm to me."
He spake; Calypso, glorious goddess, smiled,   220
And smoothed his forehead with her hand, and said:
"Perverse, and slow to see where guile is not!
How could thy heart permit thee thus to speak?
Now bear me witness, Earth, and ye broad Heavens
Above us, and ye waters of the Styx   225
That flow beneath us, mightiest oath of all,
And most revered by all the blessed gods,
That I design no other harm to thee,
But that I plan for thee, and counsel thee
What I would do were I in need like thine.   230
I bear a juster mind; my bosom holds
A pitying heart, and not a heart of steel."
Thus having said, the glorious goddess moved
Away with hasty steps, and where she trod
He followed, till they reached the vaulted cave—   235
The goddess and the hero. There he took
The seat whence Hermes had just risen. The nymph
Brought forth whatever mortals eat and drink
To set before him. She right opposite
To that of great Odysseus took her seat.   240
Ambrosia there her maidens laid, and there
Poured nectar. Both put forth their hands, and took
The ready viands, till at length the calls
Of hunger and of thirst were satisfied;
Calypso, glorious goddess, then began: 245

"Son of Laertes, man of many wiles,
High-born Odysseus! thus wilt thou depart
Home to thy native country? Then farewell;
But, couldst thou know the sufferings Fate ordains
For thee ere yet thou landest on its shore,   250
Thou wouldst remain to keep this home with me
And be immortal, strong as is thy wish
To see thy wife—a wish that day by clay
Possesses thee. I cannot deem myself
In face or form less beautiful than she;   255
For never with immortals can the race
Of mortal dames in form or face compare."
Odysseus, the sagacious, answered her:
"Bear with me, gracious goddess; well I know
All thou couldst say. The sage Penelope   260
In feature and in stature comes not nigh
To thee, for she is mortal—deathless thou,
And ever young; yet day by day I long
To be at home once more, and pine to see
The hour of my return. Even though some god   265
Smite me on the black ocean, I shall bear
The stroke, for in my bosom dwells a mind
Patient of suffering; much have I endured,
And much survived, in tempests on the deep,
And in the battle; let this happen too."   270
He spake; the sun went down; the night came on;
And now the twain withdrew to a recess
Deep in the vaulted cave, where, side by side,
They took their rest. But when the child of Dawn,
Aurora, rosy-fingered, looked abroad,   275
Odysseus put his vest and mantle on;
The nymph too, in a robe of silver-white,

Ample, and delicate, and beautiful,
Arrayed herself, and round about her loins
Wound a fair golden girdle, drew a veil   280
Over her head, and planned to send away
Magnanimous Odysseus. She bestowed
A heavy ax, of steel and double-edged,
Well fitted to the hand, the handle wrought
Of olive-wood, firm set and beautiful.   285
A polished adze she gave him next, and led
The way to a far corner of the isle,
Where lofty trees, alders and poplars, stood,
And firs that reached the clouds, sapless and dry
Long since, and fitter thus to ride the waves.   290
Then, having shown where grew the tallest trees,
Calypso, glorious goddess, sought her home.
Trees then he felled, and soon the task was done.
Twenty in all he brought to earth, and squared
Their trunks with the sharp steel, and carefully   295
He smoothed their sides, and wrought them by a line.
Calypso, gracious goddess, having brought
Wimbles, he bored the beams, and, fitting them
Together, made them fast with nails and clamps.
As when some builder, skillful in his art,   300
Frames for a ship of burden the broad keel,
Such ample breadth Odysseus gave the raft.
Upon the massy beams he reared a deck,
And floored it with long planks from end to end.
On this a mast he raised, and to the mast   305
Fitted, a yard; he shaped a rudder next,
To guide the raft along her course, and round
With woven work of willow-boughs he fenced
Her sides against the dashings of the sea.

Calypso, gracious goddess, brought him store   310
Of canvas, which he fitly shaped to sails,
And, rigging her with cords and ropes and stays,
Heaved her with levers into the great deep.
'Twas the fourth day. His labors now were done,
And on the fifth the goddess from her isle   315
Dismissed him, newly from the bath, arrayed
In garments given by her, that shed perfumes.
A skin of dark red wine she put on board,
A larger one of water, and for food
A basket, stored with viands such as please   320
The appetite. A friendly wind and soft
She sent before. The great Odysseus spread
His canvas joyfully to catch the breeze,
And sat and guided with nice care the helm,
Gazing with fixed eye on the Pleiades,   325
Bootes setting late, and the Great Bear,
By others called the Wain, which, wheeling round,
Looks ever toward Orion, and alone
Dips not into the waters of the deep.
For so Calypso, glorious goddess, bade   330
That on his ocean journey he should keep
That constellation ever on his left.
Now seventeen days were in the voyage past,
And on the eighteenth shadowy heights appeared,
The nearest point of the Phaeacian land,   335
Lying on the dark ocean like a shield.
But mighty Poseidon, coming from among
The Ethiopians, saw him. Far away
He saw, from mountain-heights of Solyma,
The voyager, and burned with fiercer wrath,   340
And shook his head, and said within himself:

"Strange! now I see the gods have new designs
For this Odysseus, formed while I was yet
In Ethiopia. He draws near the land
Of the Phaeacians, where it is decreed   345
He shall o'erpass the boundary of his woes;
But first, I think, he will have much to bear."
He spake, and round about him called the clouds
And roused the ocean—wielding in his hand
The trident—summoned all the hurricanes   350
Of all the winds, and covered earth and sky
At once with mists, while from above the night
Fell suddenly. The east wind and the south
Pushed forth at once, with the strong-blowing west,
And the clear north rolled up his mighty waves.   355
Odysseus trembled in his knees and heart,
And thus to his great soul, lamenting, said:
"What will become of me? unhappy man!
I fear that all the goddess said was true,
Foretelling what disasters should o'ertake   360
My voyage ere I reach my native land.
Now are her words fulfilled. How Zeus
Wraps the great heaven in clouds and stirs the deep
To tumult! Wilder grow the hurricanes
Of all the winds, and now my fate is sure.   365
Thrice happy, four times happy, they who fell
On Troy's wide field, warring for Atreus' sons:
O, had I met my fate and perished there,
That very day on which the Trojan host,
Around the dead Achilles, hurled at me   370
Their brazen javelins, I had then received
Due burial, and great glory with the Greeks;
Now must I die a miserable death."

As thus he spake, upon him, from on high,
A huge and frightful billow broke; it whirled   375
The raft around, and far from it he fell.
His hands let go the rudder; a fierce rush
Of all the winds together snapped in twain
The mast; far off the yard and canvas flew
Into the deep; the billow held him long   330
Beneath the waters, and he strove in vain
Quickly to rise to air from that huge swell
Of ocean, for the garments weighed him down
Which fair Calypso gave him. But at length
Emerging, he rejected from his throat   335
The bitter brine that down his forehead streamed.
Even then, though hopeless with dismay, his thought
Was on the raft; and, struggling through the waves,
He seized it, sprang on board, and, seated there,
Escaped the threatened death. Still to and fro   390
The rolling billows drove it. As the wind
In autumn sweeps the thistles o'er the field,
Clinging together, so the blasts of heaven
Hither and thither drove it o'er the sea.
And now the south wind flung it to the north   395
To buffet; now the east wind to the west.
Ino Leucothea saw him clinging there—
The delicate-footed child of Cadmus, once
A mortal, speaking with a mortal voice,
Though now within the ocean gulfs she shares   400
The honors of the gods. With pity she
Beheld Odysseus struggling thus distressed,
And, rising from the abyss below, in form
A cormorant, the sea-nymph took her perch
On the well-banded raft, and thus she said: 405

"Ah, luckless man! how hast thou angered thus
Earth-shaking Poseidon, that he visits thee
With these disasters? Yet he cannot take,
Although he seek it earnestly, thy life.
Now do my bidding, for thou seemest wise.   410
Laying aside thy garments, let the raft
Drift with the winds, while thou, by strength of arm,
Makest thy way in swimming to the land
Of the Phaeacians, where thy safety lies.
Receive this veil, and bind its heavenly woof   415
Beneath thy breast, and have no further fear
Of hardship or of danger. But, as soon
As thou shalt touch the island, take it off,
And turn away thy face, and fling it far
From where thou standest into the black deep."   420
The goddess gave the veil as thus she spoke,
And to the tossing deep went down, in form
A cormorant; the black wave covered her.
But still Odysseus, mighty sufferer,
Pondered, and thus to his great soul he said: 425
"Ah me! perhaps some god is planning here
Some other fraud against me, bidding me
Forsake my raft. I will not yet obey,
For still far off I see the land in which
'Tis said my refuge lies. This will I do,   430
For this seems wisest. While the fastenings last
That hold these timbers, I will keep my place
And bide the tempest here; but when the waves
Shall dash my raft in pieces, I will swim,
For nothing better will remain to do."   435
As he revolved this purpose in his mind,
Earth-shaking Poseidon sent a mighty wave,

Florid and huge and high, and where he sat
It smote him. As a violent wind uplifts
The dry chaff heaped upon a threshing-floor,   440
And sends it scattered through the air abroad,
So did that wave fling loose the ponderous beams.
To one of these, Odysseus, clinging fast,
Bestrode it, like a horseman on his steed";
And now he took the garments off, bestowed   445
By fair Calypso, binding round his breast
The veil, and forward plunged into the deep,
With palms outspread, prepared to swim. Meanwhile
Poseidon beheld him—Poseidon, mighty king—
And shook his head, and said within himself: 450
"Go thus, and laden with mischances roam
The waters till thou come among the race
Cherished by Zeus, but well I deem
Thou wilt not find thy share of suffering light."
Thus having said he urged his coursers on,   455
With their fair-flowing manes, until he came
To Aegae, where his glorious palace stands.
But Pallas, child of Zeus, had other thoughts.
She stayed the course of every wind beside,
And bade them rest, and lulled them into sleep,   460
But summoned the swift north to break the waves,
That so Odysseus, the high-born, escaped
From death and from the fates, might be the guest
Of the Phaeacians—men who love the sea.
Two days and nights among the mighty waves   465
He floated, oft his heart foreboding death.
But when the bright-haired Eos had fulfilled
The third day's course, and all the winds were laid,
And calm was on the watery waste, he saw

That land was near, as, lifted on the crest   470
Of a huge swell, he looked with sharpened sight;
And as a father's life preserved makes glad
His children's hearts, when long time he has lain
Sick, wrung with pain, and wasting by the power
Of some malignant genius, till at length   475
The gracious gods bestow a welcome cure,
So welcome to Odysseus was the sight
Of woods and fields. By swimming on he thought
To climb and tread the shore; but when he drew
So near that one who shouted could be heard   480
From land, the sound of ocean on the rocks
Came to his ear—for there huge breakers roared
And spouted fearfully, and all around
Was covered with the sea-foam. Haven here
Was none for ships, nor sheltering creek, but shores   435
Beetling from high, and crags and walls of rock.
Odysseus trembled both in knees and heart,
And thus to his great soul, lamenting, said:
"Now woe is me! as soon as Zeus has shown
What I had little hoped to see, the land,   490
And I through all these waves have ploughed my way,
I find no issue from the hoary deep.
For sharp rocks border it, and all around
Roar the wild surges; slippery cliffs arise
Close to deep gulfs, and footing there is none   495
Where I might plant my steps and thus escape.
All effort now were fruitless to resist
The mighty billow hurrying me away
To dash me on the pointed rocks. If yet
I strive, by swimming further, to descry   500
Some sloping shore or harbor of the isle,

I fear the tempest, lest it hurl me back,
Heavily groaning, to the fishy deep;
Or huge sea-monster, from the multitude
Which sovereign Amphitrite feeds, be sent   505
Against me by some god—for well I know
The power who shakes the shores is wroth with me."
While he revolved these doubts within his mind,
A huge wave hurled him toward the rugged coast.
Then had his limbs been flayed, and all his bones   510
Broken at once, had not the blue-eyed maid,
Athena, prompted him. Borne toward the rock,
He clutched it instantly with both his hands,
And panting clung till that huge wave rolled by,
And so escaped its fury. Back it came,   515
And smote him once again, and flung him far
Seaward. As to the claws of Polypus,
Plucked from its bed, the pebbles thickly cling,
So flakes of skin, from off his powerful hands,
Were left upon the rock. The mighty surge   520
O'erwhelmed him; he had perished ere his time—
Hapless Odysseus!—but the blue-eyed maid,
Pallas, informed his mind with forecast. Straight
Emerging from the wave that shoreward rolled,
He swam along the coast and eyed it well,   525
In hope of sloping beach or sheltered creek.
But when, in swimming, he had reached the mouth
Of a soft-flowing river, here appeared
The spot he wished for, smooth, without a rock,
And here was shelter from the wind. He felt   530
The current's flow, and thus devoutly prayed:
"Hear me, O sovereign power, whoe'er thou art!
To thee, the long-desired, I come. I seek

Escape from Poseidon's threatenings on the sea.
The deathless gods respect the prayer of him   535
Who looks to them for help, a fugitive,
As I am now, when to thy stream I come,
And to thy knees, from many a hardship past.
Thou that here art ruler, I declare
Myself thy suppliant; be thou merciful."   540
He spoke: the river stayed his current, checked
The billows, smoothed them to a calm, and gave
The swimmer a safe landing at his mouth.
Then dropped his knees and sinewy arms at once,
Unstrung, for faint with struggling was his heart.   545
His body was, all swoll'n; the brine gushed forth
From mouth and nostrils; all unnerved he lay,
Breathless and speechless; utter weariness
O'ermastered him. But when he breathed again,
And his flown senses had returned, he loosed   550
The veil that Ino gave him from his breast,
And to the salt flood cast it. A great wave
Bore it far down the stream; the goddess there
In her own hands received it. He, meanwhile,
Withdrawing from the brink, lay down among   555
The reeds, and kissed the harvest-bearing earth,
And thus to his great soul, lamenting, said:
"Ah me! what must I suffer more? what yet
Will happen to me? If by the river's side
I pass the unfriendly watches of the night,   560
The cruel cold and dews that steep the bank
May, in this weakness, end me utterly,
For chilly blows this river-air at dawn;
But should I climb this hill, to sleep within
The shadowy wood, among thick shrubs, if cold   565

And weariness allow me, then I fear,
That, while the pleasant slumbers o'er me steal,
I may become the prey of savage beasts."
Yet, as he longer pondered, this seemed best.
He rose, and sought the wood, and found it near   570
The water, on a height, o'erlooking far
The region round. Between two shrubs that sprang
Both from one spot he entered—olive-trees,
One wild, one fruitful. The damp-blowing wind
Ne'er pierced their covert; never blazing sun   575
Darted his beams within, nor pelting shower
Beat through, so closely intertwined they grew.
Here entering, Odysseus heaped a bed
Of leaves with his own hands; he made it broad
And high, for thick the leaves had fallen around.   520
Two men and three, in that abundant store,
Might bide the winter storm, though keen the cold.
Odysseus, the great sufferer, on his couch
Looked and rejoiced, and placed himself within,
And heaped the leaves high o'er him and around,   535
As one who, dwelling in the distant fields.
Without a neighbor near him, hides a brand
In the dark ashes, keeping carefully
The seeds of fire alive, lest he, perforce,
To light his hearth must bring them from afar;   590

BOOK VI

So did Odysseus in that pile of leaves   1
Bury himself, while Pallas o'er his eyes
Poured sleep, and closed his lids, that he might take,
After his painful toils, the fitting rest.
Thus overcome with toil and weariness,   5
The noble sufferer Odysseus slept,
While Pallas hastened to the realm and town
Peopled by the Phaeacians, who of yore
Abode in spacious Hypereia, near
The insolent race of Cyclops, and endured   10
Wrong from their mightier hands. A godlike chief,
Nausithous, led them to a new abode,
And planted them in Scheria, far away
From plotting neighbors. With a wall he fenced
Their city, built them dwellings there, and reared   15
Fanes to the gods, and changed the plain to fields.
But he had bowed to death, and had gone down
To Hades, and Alcinous, whom the gods
Endowed with wisdom, governed in his stead.
Now to his palace, planning the return   20
Of the magnanimous Odysseus, came

The blue-eyed goddess Pallas, entering
The gorgeous chamber where a damsel slept—
Nausicaä, daughter of the large-souled king
Alcinous, beautiful in form and face   25
As one of the immortals. Near her lay,
And by the portal, one on either side,
Fair as the Graces, two attendant maids.
The shining doors were shut. But Pallas came
As comes a breath of air, and stood beside   30
The damsel's head and spake. In look she seemed
The daughter of the famous mariner
Dymas, a maiden whom Nausicaä loved,
The playmate of her girlhood. In her shape
The blue-eyed goddess stood, and thus she said: 35
"Nausicaä, has thy mother then brought forth
A careless housewife? Thy magnificent robes
Lie still neglected, though thy marriage day
Is near, when thou art to array thyself
In seemly garments, and bestow the like   40
On those who lead thee to the bridal rite;
For thus the praise of men is won, and thus
Thy father and thy gracious mother both
Will be rejoiced. Now with the early dawn
Let us all hasten to the washing-place.   45
I too would go with thee, and help thee there,
That thou mayst sooner end the task, for thou
Not long wilt be unwedded. Thou art wooed
Already by the noblest of the race
Of the Phaeacians, for thy birth, like theirs,   50
Is of the noblest. Make thy suit at morn
To thy illustrious father, that he bid
His mules and car be harnessed to convey

Thy girdles, robes, and mantles marvelous
In beauty. That were seemlier than to walk,   55
Since distant from the town the lavers lie."
Thus having said, the blue-eyed Pallas went
Back to Olympus, where the gods have made,
So saith tradition, their eternal seat.
The tempest shakes it not, nor is it drenched   60
By showers, and there the snow doth never fall.
The calm clear ether is without a cloud;
And in the golden light, that lies on all,
Days after day the blessed gods rejoice.
Thither the blue-eyed goddess, having given   65
Her message to the sleeping maid, withdrew.
Soon the bright morning came. Nausicaä rose,
Clad royally, as marveling at her dream
She hastened through the palace to declare
Her purpose to her father and the queen.   70
She found them both within. Her mother sat
Beside the hearth with her attendant maids,
And turned the distaff loaded with a fleece
Dyed in sea-purple. On the threshold stood
Her father, going forth to meet the chiefs   75
Of the Phaeacians in a council where
Their noblest asked his presence. Then the maid,
Approaching her beloved father, spake:
"I pray, dear father, give command to make
A chariot ready for me, with high sides   80
And sturdy wheels, to bear to the river-brink,
There to be cleansed, the costly robes that now
Lie soiled. Thee likewise it doth well beseem
At councils to appear in vestments fresh
And stainless. Thou hast also in these halls   85

Five sons, two wedded, three in boyhood's bloom,
And ever in the dance they need attire
New from the wash. All this must I provide."
She ended, for she shrank from saying aught
Of her own hopeful marriage. He perceived   90
Her thought and said: "Mules I deny thee not,
My daughter, nor aught else. Go then; my grooms
Shall make a carriage ready with high sides
And sturdy wheels, and a broad rack above."
He spake, and gave command. The grooms obeyed,   95
And, making ready in the outer court
The strong-wheeled chariot, led the harnessed mules
Under the yoke and made them fast; and then
Appeared the maiden, bringing from her bower
The shining garments. In the polished car   100
She piled them, while with many pleasant meats
And flavoring morsels for the day's repast
Her mother filled a hamper, and poured wine
Into a goatskin. As her daughter climbed to
The car, she gave into her hands a cruse   105
Of gold with smooth anointing oil for her
And her attendant maids. Nausicaä took
The scourge and showy reins, and struck the mules
To urge them onward. Onward with loud noise
They went, and with a speed that slackened not,   110
And bore the robes and her—yet not alone,
For with her went the maidens of her train.
Now when they reached the river's pleasant brink,
Where lavers had been hollowed out to last no
Perpetually, and freely through them flowed   115
Pure water that might cleanse the foulest stains,
They loosed the mules, and drove them from the wain

To browse the sweet grass by the eddying stream;
And took the garments out, and flung them down
In the dark water, and with hasty feet   120
Trampled them there in frolic rivalry.
And when the task was done, and all the stains
Were cleansed away, they spread the garments out
Along the beach and where the stream had washed
The gravel cleanest. Then they bathed, and gave   125
Their limbs the delicate oil, and took their meal
Upon the river's border—while the robes
Beneath the sun's warm rays were growing dry.
And now, when they were all refreshed by food,
Mistress and maidens laid their veils aside   130
And played at ball. Nausicaä the white-armed
Began a song. As when the archer-queen
Artemis, going forth among the hills—
The sides of high Taygetus or slopes
Of Erymanthus—chases joyously   135
Boars and fleet stags, and round her in a throng
Frolic the rural nymphs, Latona's heart
Is glad, for over all the rest are seen
Her daughter's head and brow, and she at once
Is known among them, though they all are fair,   140
Such was this spotless virgin midst her maids.
Now when they were about to move for home
With harnessed mules and with the shining robes
Carefully folded, then the blue-eyed maid,
Pallas, bethought herself of this—to rouse   145
Odysseus and to bring him to behold
The bright-eyed maiden, that she might direct
The stranger's way to the Phaeacian town.
The royal damsel at a handmaid cast

The ball; it missed, and fell into the stream   150
Where a deep eddy whirled. All shrieked aloud.
The great Odysseus started from his sleep
And sat upright, discoursing to himself:
"Ah me! upon what region am I thrown?
What men are here—wild, savage, and unjust,   155
Or hospitable, and who hold the gods
In reverence? There are voices in the air,
Womanly voices, as of nymphs that haunt
The mountain summits, and the river-founts,
And the moist grassy meadows. Or perchance   160
Am I near men who have the power of speech?
Nay, let me then go forth at once and learn."
Thus having said, the great Odysseus left
The thicket. From the close-grown wood he rent,
With his strong hand, a branch well set with leaves,   165
And wound it as a covering round his waist.
Then like a mountain lion he went forth,
That walks abroad, confiding in his strength,
In rain and wind; his eyes shoot fire; he falls
On oxen, or on sheep, or forest-deer,   170
For hunger prompts him even to attack
The flock within its closely guarded fold.
Such seemed Odysseus when about to meet
Those fair-haired maidens, naked as he was,
But forced by strong necessity. To them   175
His look was frightful, for his limbs were foul
With sea-foam yet. To right and left they fled
Along the jutting river-banks. Alone
The daughter of Alcinous kept her place,
For Pallas gave her courage and forbade   180
Her limbs to tremble. So she waited there.

Odysseus pondered whether to approach
The bright-eyed damsel and embrace her knees
And supplicate, or, keeping yet aloof,
Pray her with soothing words to show the way   185
Townward and give him garments. Musing thus,
It seemed the best to keep at distance still,
And use soft words, lest, should he clasp her knees,
The maid might be displeased. With gentle words is
Skillfully ordered thus Odysseus spake: 190
"O queen, I am thy suppliant, whether thou
Be mortal or a goddess. If perchance
Thou art of that immortal race who dwell
In the broad heaven, thou art, I deem, most like
To Dian, daughter of imperial Zeus,   195
In shape, in stature, and in noble air.
If mortal and a dweller of the earth,
Thrice happy are thy father and his queen.
Thrice happy are thy brothers; and their hearts
Must overflow with gladness for thy sake,   200
Beholding such a scion of their house
Enter the choral dance. But happiest he
Beyond them all, who, bringing princely gifts,
Shall bear thee to his home a bride; for sure
I never looked on one of mortal race,   205
Woman or man, like thee, and as I gaze
I wonder. Like to thee I saw of late,
In Delos, a young palm-tree growing up
Beside Apollo's altar; for I sailed
To Delos, with much people following me,   210
On a disastrous voyage. Long I gazed
Upon it wonder-struck, as I am now—
For never from the earth so fair a tree

Had sprung. So marvel I, and am amazed
At thee, O lady, and in awe forbear   215
To clasp thy knees. Yet much have I endured.
It was but yestereve that I escaped
From the black sea, upon the twentieth day,
So long the billows and the rushing gales
Farther and farther from Ogygia's isle   220
Had borne me. Now upon this shore some god
Casts me, perchance to meet new sufferings here;
For yet the end is not, and many things
The gods must first accomplish. But do thou,
queen, have pity on me, since to thee   225
I come the first of all. I do not know
A single dweller of the land beside.
Show me, I pray, thy city; and bestow
Some poor old robe to wrap me—if, indeed,
In coming hither, thou hast brought with thee   230
Aught poor or coarse. And may the gods vouchsafe
To thee whatever blessing thou canst wish,
Husband and home and wedded harmony.
There is no better, no more blessed state,
Than when the wife and husband in accord   235
Order their household lovingly. Then those
Repine who hate them, those who wish them well
Rejoice, and they themselves the most of all."
And then the white-armed maid Nausicaä said:
"Since then, O stranger, thou art not malign   240
Of purpose nor weak-minded—yet, in truth,
Olympian Zeus bestows the goods
Of fortune on the noble and the base
To each one at his pleasure; and thy griefs
Are doubtless sent by him, and it is fit   245

That thou submit in patience—now that thou
Hast reached our lands, and art within our realm,
Thou shalt not lack for garments nor for aught
Due to a suppliant stranger in his need.
The city I will show thee, and will name   250
Its dwellers—the Phaeacians—they possess
The city; all the region lying round
Is theirs, and I am daughter of the prince
Alcinous, large of soul, to whom are given
The rule of the Phaeacians and their power."   255
So spake the damsel, and commanded thus
Her fair-haired maids: "Stay! whither do ye flee,
My handmaids, when a man appears in sight?
Ye think, perhaps, he is some enemy.
Nay, there is no man living now, nor yet   260
Will live, to enter, bringing war, the land
Of the Phaeacians. Very dear are they
To the great gods. We dwell apart, afar
Within the unmeasured deep, amid its waves
The most remote of men; no other race   265
Hath commerce with us. This man comes to us
A wanderer and unhappy, and to him
Our cares are due. The stranger and the poor
Are sent by Zeus, and slight regards to them
Are grateful. Maidens, give the stranger food   270
And drink, and take him to the river-side
To bathe where there is shelter from the wind."
So spake the mistress; and they stayed their flight
And bade each other stand, and led the chief
Under a shelter as the royal maid,   275
Daughter of stout Alcinous, gave command,
And laid a cloak and tunic near the spot

To be his raiment, and a golden cruse
Of limpid oil. Then, as they bade him bathe
In the fresh stream, the noble chieftain said: 280
"Withdraw, ye maidens, hence, while I prepare
To cleanse my shoulders from the bitter brine,
And to anoint them; long have these my limbs
Been unrefreshed by oil. I will not bathe
Before you. I should be ashamed to stand   285
Unclothed in presence of these bright-haired maids."
He spake; they hearkened and withdrew, and told
The damsel what he said. Odysseus then
Washed the salt spray of ocean from his back
And his broad shoulders in the flowing stream,   290
And wiped away the sea-froth from his brows.
And when the bath was over, and his limbs
Had been anointed, and he had put on
The garments sent him by the spotless maid,
Zeus's daughter, Pallas, caused him to appear   295
Of statelier size and more majestic mien,
And bade the locks that crowned his head flow down,
Curling like blossoms of the hyacinth.
As when some skillful workman trained and taught
By Hephaestus and Athena in his art   300
Binds the bright silver with a verge of gold,
And graceful is his handiwork, such grace
Did Pallas shed upon the hero's brow
And shoulders, as he passed along the beach,
And, glorious in his beauty and the pride   305
Of noble bearing, sat aloof. The maid
Admired, and to her bright-haired women spake:
"Listen to me, my maidens, while I speak.
This man comes not among the godlike sons

Of the Phaeacian stock against the will   310
Of all the gods of heaven. I thought him late
Of an unseemly aspect; now he bears
A likeness to the immortal ones whose home
Is the broad heaven. I would that I might call
A man like him my husband, dwelling here,   315
And here content to dwell. Now hasten, maids,
And set before the stranger food and wine."
She spake; they heard and cheerfully obeyed,
And set before Odysseus food and wine.
The patient chief Odysseus ate and drank   320
Full eagerly, for he had fasted long.
White-armed Nausicaä then had other cares.
She placed the smoothly folded robes within
The sumptuous chariot, yoked the firm-hoofed mules,
And mounted to her place, and from the seat   325
Spake kindly, counseling Odysseus thus:
"Now, stranger, rise and follow to the town,
And to my royal father's palace I
Will be thy guide, where, doubt not, thou wilt meet
The noblest men of our Phaeacian race.   330
But do as I advise—for not inapt
I deem thee. While we traverse yet the fields
Among the tilth, keep thou among my train
Of maidens, following fast behind the mules
And chariot. I will lead thee in the way.   335
But when our train goes upward toward the town,
Fenced with its towery wall, and on each side
Embraced by a fair haven, with a strait
Of narrow entrance, where our well-oared barks
Have each a mooring-place along the road.   340
And there round Poseidon's glorious fane extends

A market-place, surrounded by huge stones,
Dragged from the quarry hither, where is kept
The rigging of the barks—sail-cloth and ropes—
And oars are polished there—for little reck   345
Phaeacians of the quiver and the bow,
And give most heed to masts and shrouds and ships
Well poised, in which it is their pride to cross
The foamy deep—when there I would not bring
Rude taunts upon myself, for in the crowd   350
Are brutal men. One of the baser sort
Perchance might say, on meeting us: "What man,
Handsome and lusty-limbed, is he who thus
Follows Nausicaä? where was it her luck
To find him? will he be her husband yet?   355
Perhaps she brings some wanderer from his ship,
A stranger from strange lands, for we have here
No neighbors; or, perhaps, it is a god
Called down by fervent prayer from heaven to dwell
Henceforth with her. 'Tis well if she have found   360
A husband elsewhere, since at home she meets
Her many noble wooers with disdain;
They are Phaeacians.' Thus the crowd would say,
And it would bring reproach upon my name.
I too would blame another who should do   365
The like, and, while her parents were alive,
Without their knowledge should consort with men
Before her marriage. Stranger, now observe
My words, and thou shalt speedily obtain
Safe-conduct from my father, and be sent   370
Upon thy voyage homeward. We shall reach
A beautiful grove of poplars by the way,
Sacred to Pallas; from it flows a brook,

And round it lies a meadow. In this spot
My father has his country-grounds, and here   375
His garden flourishes, as far from town
As one could hear a shout. There sit thou down
And wait till we are in the city's streets
And at my father's house. When it shall seem
That we are there, arise and onward fare   380
To the Phaeacian city, and inquire
Where dwells Alcinous the large-souled king,
My father; 'tis not hard to find; a child
Might lead thee thither. Of the houses reared
By the Phaeacians there is none like that   385
In which Alcinous the hero dwells.
When thou art once within the court and hall,
Go quickly through the palace till thou find
My mother where she sits beside the hearth,
Leaning against a column in its blaze,   390
And twisting threads, a marvel to behold,
Of bright sea-purple, while her maidens sit
Behind her. Near her is my father's throne,
On which he sits at feasts, and drinks the wine
Like one of the immortals. Pass it by   395
And clasp my mother's knees; so mayst thou see
Soon and with joy the day of thy return,
Although thy home be far. For if her mood
Be kindly toward thee, thou mayst hope to greet
Thy friends once more, and enter yet again   400
Thy own fair palace in thy native land."
Thus having said, she raised the shining scourge
And struck the mules, that quickly left behind
The river. On they went with easy pace
And even steps. The damsel wielded well   405

The reins, and used the lash with gentle hand,
So that Odysseus and her train of maids
On foot could follow close. And now the sun
Was sinking when they came to that fair grove
Sacred to Pallas. There the noble chief   410
Odysseus sat him down, and instantly
Prayed to the daughter of imperial Zeus:
"O thou unconquerable child of Zeus
The aegis-bearer! harken to me now,
Since late thou wouldst not listen to my prayer,   415
What time the mighty shaker of the shores
Pursued and wrecked me! Grant me to receive
Pity and kindness from Phaeacia's sons."
So prayed he, supplicating. Pallas heard
The prayer, but came not to him openly.   420
Awe of her father's brother held her back;
For he would still pursue with violent hate
Odysseus, till he reached his native land.

BOOK VII

So prayed Odysseus the great sufferer.   1
The strong mules bore the damsel toward the town,
And when she reached her father's stately halls
She stopped beneath the porch. Her brothers came
Around her, like in aspect to the gods,   5
And loosed the mules, and bore the garments in.
She sought her chamber, where an aged dame
Attendant there, an Epirote, and named
Eurymedusa, lighted her a fire.
She by the well-oared galleys had been brought   10
Beforetime from Epirus, and was given
To king Alcinous, ruler over all
Phaeacia's sons, who hearkened to his voice
As if he were a god. 'Twas she who reared
White-armed Nausicaä in the royal halls,   15
Tended her hearth, and dressed her evening meal.
Now rose Odysseus up, and townward turned
His steps, while friendly Pallas wrapt his way
In darkness, lest someone among the sons
Of the Phaeacians with unmannerly words   20
Might call to him or ask him who he was.

And just as he was entering that fair town
The blue-eyed Pallas met him, in the form
Of a young virgin with an urn. She stood
Before him, and Odysseus thus inquired: 25
"Wilt thou, my daughter, guide me to the house
Where dwells Alcinous, he who rules this land?
I am a stranger, who have come from far
After long hardships, and of all who dwell
Within this realm I know not even one."   30
Pallas, the blue-eyed goddess, thus replied:
"Father and stranger, I will show the house;
The dwelling of my own good father stands
Close by it. Follow silently, I pray,
And I will lead. Look not on any man   35
Nor ask a question; for the people here
Affect not strangers, nor do oft receive
With kindly welcome him who comes from far.,
They trust in their swift barks, which to and fro,
By Poseidon's favor, cross the mighty deep.   40
Their galleys have the speed of wings or thought.'
Thus Pallas spake, and quickly led the way.
He followed in her steps. They saw him not—
Those trained Phaeacian seamen—for the power
That led him, Pallas of the amber hair,   45
Forbade the sight, and threw a friendly veil
Of darkness over him. Odysseus saw,
Wondering, the haven and the gallant ships,
The market-place where heroes thronged, the walls
Long, lofty, and beset with palisades,   50
A marvel to the sight. But when they came
To the king's stately palace, thus began
The blue-eyed goddess, speaking to the chief:'

"Father and stranger, here thou seest the house
Which thou hast bid me show thee. Thou wilt find   55
The princes, nurslings of the gods, within,
Royally feasting. Enter, and fear not;
The bold man ever is the better man,
Although he come from far. Thou first of all
Wilt see the queen. Arete is the name   60
The people give her. She is of a stock
The very same from which Alcinous
The king derives his lineage. For long since
Nausithous, its founder, was brought forth
To Poseidon, the great Shaker of the shores,   65
By Peribaea, fairest of her sex,
And youngest daughter of Eurymedon,
The large of soul, who ruled the arrogant brood
Of giants, and beheld that guilty race
Cut off, and perished by a fate like theirs.   70
Her Poseidon wooed; she bore to him a son,
Large-souled Nausithous, whom Phaeacia owned
Its sovereign. To Nausithous were born
Rhexenor and Alcinous. He who bears
The silver bow, Apollo, smote to death   75
Rhexenor, newly wedded, in his home.
He left no son, and but one daughter, named
Arete; her Alcinous made his wife,
And honored her as nowhere else on earth
Is any woman honored who bears charge so   80
Over a husband's household. From their hearts
Her children pay her reverence, and the king
And all the people, for they look on her
As if she were a goddess. When she goes
Abroad into the streets, all welcome her   85

With acclamations. Never does she fail
In wise discernment, but decides disputes
Kindly and justly between man and man.
And if thou gain her favor, there is hope
That thou mayst see thy friends once more, and stand   90
In thy tall palace on thy native soil."
The blue-eyed Pallas, having spoken thus,
Departed o'er the barren deep. She left
The pleasant isle of Scheria, and repaired
To Marathon and to the spacious streets   95
Of Athens, entering there the massive halls
Where dwelt Erectheus, while Odysseus toward
The gorgeous palace of Alcinous turned
His steps, yet stopped and pondered ere he crossed
The threshold. For on every side beneath   100
The lofty roof of that magnanimous king
A glory shone as of the sun or moon.
There from the threshold, on each side, were walls
Of brass that led towards the inner rooms,
With blue steel cornices. The doors within   105
The massive building were of gold, and posts
Of silver on the brazen threshold stood,
And silver was the lintel, and above
Its architrave was gold; and on each side
Stood gold and silver mastiffs, the rare work   110
Of Hephaestus's practiced skill, placed there to guard
The house of great Alcinous, and endowed
With deathless life, that knows no touch of age.
Along the walls within, on either side,
And from the threshold to the inner rooms,   115
Were firmly planted thrones on which were laid
Delicate mantles, woven by the hands

Of women. The Phaeacian princes here
Were seated; here they ate and drank, and held
Perpetual banquet. Slender forms of boys   120
In gold upon the shapely altars stood,
With blazing torches in their hands to light
At eve the palace guests; while fifty maids
Waited within the halls, where some in querns
Ground small the yellow grain; some wove the web   125
Or twirled the spindle, sitting, with a quick
Light motion, like the aspen's glancing leaves.
The well- wrought tissues glistened as with oil.
As far as the Phaeacian race excel
In guiding their swift galleys o'er the deep,   130
So far the women in their woven work
Surpass all others. Pallas gives them skill
In handiwork and beautiful design.
Without the palace-court, and near the gate,
A spacious garden of four acres lay.   135
A hedge enclosed it round, and lofty trees
Flourished in generous growth within—the pear
And the pomegranate, and the apple-tree
With its fair fruitage, and the luscious fig
And olive always green. The fruit they bear   140
Falls not, nor ever fails in winter time
Nor summer, but is yielded all the year.
The ever-blowing west-wind causes some
To swell and some to ripen; pear succeeds
To pear; to apple, apple; grape to grape;   145
Fig ripens after fig. A fruitful field
Of vines was planted near; in part it lay
Open and basking in the sun, which dried
The soil, and here men gathered in the grapes,

And there they trod the wine-press. Farther on   150
Were grapes unripened yet, which just had cast
The flower, and others still which just began
To redden. At the garden's furthest bound
Were beds of many plants that all the year
Bore flowers. There gushed two fountains: one of them   153
Ran wandering through the field; the other flowed
Beneath the threshold to the palace-court,
And all the people filled their vessels there.
Such were the blessings which the gracious gods
Bestowed on King Alcinous and his house.   160
Odysseus, the great sufferer, standing there,
Admired the sight; and when he had beheld
The whole in silent wonderment, he crossed
The threshold quickly, entering the hall
Where the Phaeacian peers and princes poured   165
Wine from their goblets to the sleepless one,
The Argus-queller, to whose deity
They made the last libations when they thought
Of slumber. The great sufferer, concealed
In a thick mist, which Pallas raised and cast   170
Around him, hastened through the hall and came
Close to Arete and Alcinous,
The royal pair. Then did Odysseus clasp
Arete's knees, when suddenly the cloud
Raised by the goddess vanished. All within   175
The palace were struck mute as they beheld
The man before them. Thus Odysseus prayed:
"Arete, daughter of the godlike chief
Rhexenor! to thy husband I am come
And to thy knees, from many hardships borne,   180
And to these guests, to whom may the good gods

Grant to live happily, and to hand down,
Each one to his own children, in his home,
The wealth and honors which the people's love
Bestowed upon him. Grant me, I entreat,   185
An escort, that I may behold again
And soon my own dear country. I have passed
Long years in sorrow, far from all I love."
He ended, and sat down upon the hearth
Among the ashes, near the fire, and all   190
Were silent utterly. At length outspake
Echeneus, oldest and most eloquent chief
Of the Phaeacians; large his knowledge was
Of things long past. With generous intent,
And speaking to the assembly, he began: 195
"Alcinous, this is not a seemly sight—
A stranger sitting on the hearth among
The cinders. All the others here await
Thy order, and move not. I pray thee, raise
The stranger up, and seat him on a throne   200
Studded with silver. Be thy heralds called,
And bid them mingle wine, which we may pour
To Zeus, the god of thunders, who attends
And honors every suppliant. Let the dame
Who oversees the palace feast provide   205
Our guest a banquet from the stores within."
This when the reverend king Alcinous heard,
Forthwith he took Odysseus by the hand—
"That man of wise devices—raised him up
And seated him upon a shining throne,   210
From which he bade Laodamas arise,
His manly son, whose seat was next to his.
"Now mingle wine, Protonous, in a vase,

For all within the palace, to be poured
To Zeus, the god of thunders, who attends   215
And honors every suppliant." As he spake
Protonous mingled the delicious wines,
And passed from right to left, distributing
The cups to all; and when they all had poured
A part to Zeus, and all had drunk their fill,   220
Alcinous took the word, and thus he said:
"Princes and chiefs of the Phaeacians, hear.
I speak as my heart bids me. Since the feast
Is over, take your rest within your homes.
Tomorrow shall the Senators be called   225
In larger concourse. We will pay our guest
Due honor in the palace, worshiping
The gods with solemn sacrifice. And then
Will we bethink us how to send him home, ,
That with no hindrance and no hardship borne   230
Under our escort he may come again
Gladly and quickly to his native land,
Though far away it lie, and that no wrong
Or loss may happen to him ere he set
Foot on its soil; and there must he endure   235
Whatever, when his mother brought him forth,
Fate and the unrelenting Sisters spun
For the newborn. But should he prove to be
One of the immortals who has come from heaven
Then have the gods a different design.   240
For hitherto the gods have shown themselves
Visibly at our solemn hecatombs,
And sat with us, and feasted like ourselves,
And when the traveler meets with them alone,
They never hide themselves; for we to them   245

Are near of kin, as near as is the race
Of Cyclops and the savage giant brood."
Odysseus the sagacious answered him:
"Nay, think not so, Alcinous. I am not
In form or aspect as the immortals are,   250
Whose habitation is the ample heaven.
But I am like whomever thou mayst know,
Among mankind, inured to suffering;
To them shouldst thou compare me. I could tell
Of bitterer sorrows yet, which I have borne;   255
Such was the pleasure of the gods. But now
Leave me, whatever have my hardships been,
To take the meal before me. Naught exceeds
The impatient stomach's importunity
When even the afflicted and the sorrowful   260
Are forced to heed its call. So even now,
Midst all the sorrow that is in my heart,
It bids me eat and drink, and put aside
The thought of my misfortunes till itself
Be satiate. But, ye princes, with the dawn   265
Provide for me, in my calamity,
The means to reach again my native land.
For, after all my hardships, I would die
Willingly, could I look on my estates,
My servants, and my lofty halls once more."   270
He ended; they approved his words, and bade
Set forward on his homeward way the guest
Who spake so wisely. When they all had made
Libations and had drunk, they each withdrew
To sleep at home, and left the noble chief   275
Odysseus in the palace, where with him
Arete and her godlike husband sat,

While from the feast the maidens bore away
The chargers. The white-armed Arete then
Began to speak; for when she cast her eyes   280
On the fair garments which Odysseus wore,
She knew the mantle and the tunic well,
Wrought by herself and her attendant maids,
And thus with winged words bespake the chief:
"Stranger, I first must ask thee who thou art,   285
And of what race of men. From whom hast thou
Received those garments? Sure thou dost not say
That thou art come from wandering o'er the sea."
Odysseus, the sagacious, answered thus:
"'Twere hard, O sovereign lady, to relate   290
In order all my sufferings, for the gods
Of heaven have made them many; yet will I
Tell all thou askest of me, and obey
Thy bidding. Far within the ocean lies
An island named Ogygia, where abides   295
Calypso, artful goddess, with bright locks,
Daughter of Atlas, and of dreaded power.
No god consorts with her, nor any one
Of mortal birth. But me in my distress
Some god conveyed alone to her abode,   300
When, launching his white lightning, Zeus
Had cloven in the midst of the black sea
My galley. There my gallant comrades all
Perished, but I in both my arms held fast
The keel of my good ship, and floated on   305
Nine days till, on the tenth, in the dark night,
The gods had brought me to Ogygia's isle,
Where dwells Calypso of the radiant hair
And dreaded might, who kindly welcomed me,

And cherished me, and would have made my life   310
Immortal, and beyond the power of age
In all the coming time. And there I wore
Seven years away, still moistening with my tears
The ambrosial raiment which the goddess gave.
But when the eighth year had begun its round   315
She counseled my departure, whether Zeus
Had so required, or she herself had changed
Her purpose. On a raft made strong with clamps
She placed me, sent on board an ample store
Of bread and pleasant wine, and made me put   320
Ambrosial garments on, and gave a soft
And favorable wind. For seventeen days
I held my steady course across the deep,
And on the eighteenth day the shadowy heights
Of your own isle appeared, and then my heart,   325
Ill-fated as I was, rejoiced. Yet still
Was I to struggle with calamities
Sent by earth-shaking Poseidon, who called up
The winds against me, and withstood my way,
And stirred the boundless ocean to its depths.   330
Nor did the billows suffer me to keep
My place, but swept me, groaning, from the raft,
Whose planks they scattered. Still I labored through
The billowy depth, and swam, till wind and wave
Drove me against your coast. As there I sought   335
To land, I found the surges hurrying me
Against huge rocks that lined the frightful shore;
But, turning back, I swam again and reached
A river and the landing-place I wished,
Smooth, without rocks, and sheltered from the wind.   340
I swooned, but soon revived. Ambrosial night

Came on. I left the Zeus-descended stream
And slept among the thickets, drawing round
My limbs the withered leaves, while on my lids
A deity poured bounteously the balm   345
Of slumber. All night long, among the leaves,
I slept, with all that sorrow in my heart,
Till morn, till noon. Then as the sun went down
The balmy slumber left me, and I saw
Thy daughter's handmaids sporting on the shore,   350
And her among them, goddess-like. To her
I came a suppliant, nor did she receive
My suit unkindly as a maid so young
Might do, for youth is foolish. She bestowed
Food and red wine abundantly, and gave,   355
When I had bathed, the garments I have on.
Thus is my tale of suffering truly told."
And then Alcinous answered him and said:
"Stranger, one duty hath my child o'erlooked—
To bid thee follow hither with her maids,   360
Since thou didst sue to her the first of all."
Odysseus, the sagacious, thus replied:
"Blame not for that, O hero, I entreat,
Thy faultless daughter. She commanded me
To follow with her maids, but I refrained   365
For fear and awe of thee, lest, at the sight,
Thou mightest be displeased; for we are prone
To dark misgivings—we, the sons of men."
Again Alcinous spake: "The heart that beats
Within my bosom is not rashly moved   370
To wrath, and better is the temperate mood.
This must I say, O Father Zeus,
And Pallas and Apollo! I could wish

That, being as thou art, and of like mind
With me, thou wouldst receive to be thy bride   375
My daughter, and be called my son-in-law,
And here abide. A palace I would give,
And riches, shouldst thou willingly remain.
Against thy will let no Phaeacian dare
To keep thee here. May Father Zeus forbid!   380
And that thou mayst be sure of my intent,
I name tomorrow for thy voyage home.
Sleep in thy bed till then; and they shall row
O'er the calm sea thy galley, till thou come
To thine own land and home, or wheresoever   385
Thou wilt, though further off the coast should be
Than far Euboea, most remote of lands—
So do the people of our isle declare,
Who saw it when they over sea conveyed
The fair-haired Rhadamanthus, on his way   390
To visit Tityus, son of Earth. They went
Thither, accomplishing with little toil
Their voyage in the compass of a day,
And brought the hero to our isle again.
Now shalt thou learn, and in thy heart confess,   395
How much our galleys and our youths excel
With bladed oars to stir the whirling brine."
So spake the king, and the great sufferer
Odysseus heard with gladness, and preferred
A prayer, and called on Zeus and said: 400
"Grant, Father Zeus, that all the king has said
May be fulfilled! so shall his praise go forth
Over the foodful earth, and never die,
And I shall see my native land again."
So they conferred. White-armed Arete spake,   405

And bade her maidens in the portico
Place couches, and upon them lay fair rugs
Of purple dye, and tapestry on these,
And for the outer, covering shaggy cloaks.
Forth from the hall they issued, torch in hand;   410
And when with speed the ample bed was made,
They came and summoned thus the chief to rest:
"Rise, stranger, go to rest; thy bed is made."
Thus spake the maidens, and the thought of sleep
Was welcome to Odysseus. So that night   415
On his deep couch the noble sufferer
Slumbered beneath the sounding portico.
Alcinous laid him down in a recess
Within his lofty palace, near to whom
The queen his consort graced the marriage-bed.   420

BOOK VIII

When Morn appeared, the rosy-fingered child   1
Of Dawn, Alcinous, mighty and revered,
Rose from his bed. Odysseus, noble chief,
Spoiler of cities, also left his couch.
Alcinous, mighty and revered, went forth   5
Before, and led him to the market-place
Of the Phaeacians, built beside the fleet,
And there on polished stones they took their seats
Near to each other. Pallas, who now seemed
A herald of the wise Alcinous, went   10
Through all the city, planning how to send
Magnanimous Odysseus to his home,
And came and stood by every chief and said:
"Leaders and chiefs of the Phaeacians, come
Speedily to the market-place, and there   15
Hear of the stranger who from wandering o'er
The deep has come where wise Alcinous holds
His court; in aspect he is like the gods."
She spake, and every mind and heart was moved,
And all the market-place and all its seats   20
Were quickly filled with people. Many gazed,

139

Admiring, on Laertes' well-graced son;
For on his face and form had Pallas shed
A glory, and had made him seem more tall
And of an ampler bulk, that he might find   25
Favor with the Phaeacians, and be deemed
Worthy of awe and able to achieve
The many feats which the Phaeacian chiefs,
To try the stranger's prowess, might propose.
And now when all the summoned had arrived,   30
Alcinous to the full assembly spake:
"Princes and chiefs of the Phaeacians, hear:
I speak the promptings of my heart. This guest
I know him not—has come to my abode,
A wanderer—haply from the tribes who dwell   35
In the far East, or haply from the West—
And asked an escort and safe-conduct home;
And let us make them ready, as our wont
Has ever been. No stranger ever comes
Across my threshold who is suffered long   40
To pine for his departure. Let us draw
A dark-hulled ship down to the holy sea
On her first voyage. Let us choose her crew
Among the people, two-and-fifty youths
Of our best seamen. Then make fast the oars   45
Beside the benches, leave them there, and come
Into our palace and partake in haste
A feast which I will liberally spread
For all of you. This I command the youths;
But you, ye sceptered princes, come at once   50
To my fair palace, that we there may pay
The honors due our guest; let none refuse.
Call also the divine Demodocus,

The bard, on whom a deity bestowed
In ample measure the sweet gift of song,   55
Delightful when the spirit prompts the lay."
He spake, and led the way; the sceptered train
Of princes followed him. The herald sought
Meantime the sacred bard. The chosen youths
Fifty-and-two betook them to the marge   60
Of the unfruitful sea; and when they reached
The ship and beach they drew the dark hull down
To the deep water, put the mast on board
And the ship's sails, and fitted well the oars
Into the leathern rings, and, having moored   65
Their bark in the deep water, went with speed
To their wise monarch in his spacious halls.
There portico and court and hall were thronged
With people, young and old in multitude;
And there Alcinous sacrificed twelve sheep,   70
Eight white-toothed swine, and two splay-footed beeves.
And these they flayed, and duly dressed, and made
A noble banquet ready. Then appeared
The herald, leading the sweet singer in,
Him whom the Muse with an exceeding love   75
Had cherished, and had visited with good
And evil, quenched his eyesight and bestowed
Sweetness of song. Pontonous mid the guests
Placed for the bard a silver-studded throne,
Against a lofty column hung his harp   75
Above his head, and taught him how to find
And take it down. Near him the herald set
A basket and fair table, and a cup
Of wine, that he might drink when he desired;
Then all put forth their hands and shared the feast.   80

And when their thirst and hunger were allayed.

The Muse inspired the bard to sing the praise

Of heroes; 'twas a song whose fame had reached

To the high heaven, a story of the strife

Between Odysseus and Achilles, son   90

Of Peleus, wrangling at a solemn feast

Made for the gods. They strove with angry words,

And Agamemnon, king of men, rejoiced

To hear the noblest of the Achaean host

Contending; for all this had been foretold   95

To him in sacred Pythia by the voice

Of Phoebus, when the monarch to inquire

At the oracle had crossed the rock which formed

Its threshold. Then began the train of woes

Which at the will of sovereign Zeus   100

Befell the sons of Ilium and of Greece.

So sang renowned Demodocus. Meanwhile

Odysseus took into his brawny hands

An ample veil of purple, drawing it

Around his head to hide his noble face,   105

Ashamed that the Phaeacians should behold

The tears that flowed so freely from his lids.

But when the sacred bard had ceased his song,

He wiped the tears away and laid the veil

Aside, and took a double beaker filled   110

With wine, and poured libations to the gods.

Yet when again the minstrel sang, and all

The chiefs of the Phaeacian people, charmed

To hear his music, bade the strain proceed,

Again Odysseus hid his face and wept us   115

No other eye beheld the tears he shed.

Alcinous only watched him, and perceived

His grief, and heard the sighs he drew, and spake
To the Phaeacians, lovers of the sea:
"Now that we all, to our content, have shared   120
The feast and heard the harp, whose notes so well
Suit with a liberal banquet, let us forth
And try our skill in games, that this our guest,
Returning to his country, may relate
How in the boxing and the wrestling match,   125
In leaping and in running, we excel."
He spake, and went before; they followed him.
Then did the herald hang the clear-toned harp
Again on high, and taking by the hand
Demodocus, he led him from the place,   130
Guiding him in the way which just before
The princes of Phaeacia trod to see
The public games. Into the market-place
They went; a vast innumerable crowd
Pressed after. Then did many a valiant youth   135
Arise—Acroneus and Ocyalus,
Elatreus, Nauteus, Prymneus, after whom
Up stood Anchialus, and by his side
Eretmeus, Ponteus, Proreus, Thoon, rose;
Anabasineus and Amphialus,   140
A son of Polyneius, Tecton's son;
Then rose the son of Naubolus, like Ares
In warlike port, Euryalus by name,
And goodliest both in feature and in form
Of all Phaeacia's sons save one alone,   145
Laodamas the faultless. Next three sons
Of King Alcinous rose: Laodamas,
Halms, and Clytoneius, like a god
In aspect. Some of these began the games,

Contending in the race. For them a course   150
Was marked from goal to goal. They darted forth
At once and swiftly, raising, as they ran,
The dust along the plain. The swiftest there
Was Clytoneius in the race. As far
As mules, in furrowing the fallow ground,   155
Gain on the steers, he ran before the rest,
And reached the crowd, and left them all behind.
Others in wrestling strove laboriously—
And here Euryalus excelled them all;
But in the leap Amphialus was first;   160
Elatreus flung the quoit with firmest hand;
And in the boxer's art Laodamas,
The monarch's valiant son, was conqueror.
This when the admiring multitude had seen,
Thus spake the monarch's son, Laodamas: 165
"And now, my friends, inquire we of our guest
If he has learned and practiced feats like these.
For he is not ill-made in legs and thighs
And in both arms, in firmly planted neck
And strong-built frame; nor does he seem to lack   170
A certain youthful vigor, though impaired
By many hardships—for I know of naught
That more severely tries the strongest man,
And breaks him down, than perils of the sea."
Euryalus replied: "Laodamas,   175
Well hast thou said, and rightly: go thou now
And speak to him thyself, and challenge him."
The son of King Alcinous, as he heard,
Came forward, and bespake Odysseus thus:
"Thou also, guest and father, try these feats,   180
If thou perchance wert trained to them. I think

Thou must be skilled in games, since there is not
A greater glory for a man while yet
He lives on earth than what he hath wrought out,
By strenuous effort, with his feet and hands.   185
Try, then, thy skill, and give no place to grief.
Not long will thy departure be delayed;
Thy bark is launched; the crew are ready here."
Odysseus, the sagacious, answered thus:
"Why press me, O Laodamas! to try   190
These feats, when all my thoughts are of my woes,
And not of games? I, who have borne so much
Of pain and toil, sit pining for my home
In your assembly, supplicating here
Your king and all the people of your land."   195
Then spake Euryalus with chiding words:
"Stranger, I well perceive thou canst not boast,
As many others can, of skill in games;
But thou art one of those who dwell in ships
With many benches, rulers o'er a crew   200
Of sailors—a mere trader looking out
For freight, and watching o'er the wares that form
The cargo. Thou hast doubtless gathered wealth
By rapine, and art surely no athlete."
Odysseus, the sagacious, frowned and said: 205
"Stranger, thou speakest not becomingly,
But like a man who recks not what he says.
The gods bestow not equally on all
The gifts that men desire—the grace of form,
The mind, the eloquence. One man to sight   210
Is undistinguished, but on him the gods
Bestow the power of words. All look on him
Gladly; he knows whereof he speaks; his speech

Is mild and modest; he is eminent
In all assemblies, and, whene'er he walks   215
The city, men regard him as a god.
Another in the form he wears is like
The immortals, yet has he no power to speak
Becoming words. So thou hast comely looks—
A god would not have shaped thee otherwise   220
Than we behold thee—yet thy wit is small,
And thy unmannerly words have angered me
Even to the heart. Not quite unskilled am I
In games, as thou dost idly talk, and once,
When I could trust my youth and my strong arms,   225
I think that in these contests I was deemed
Among the first. But I am now pressed down
With toil and sorrow; much have I endured
In wars with heroes and on stormy seas.
Yet even thus, a sufferer as I am,   230
Will I essay these feats; for sharp have been
Thy words, and they provoke me to the proof."
He spake, and rising with his mantle on
He seized a broader, thicker, heavier quoit,
By no small odds, than the Phaeacians used,   235
And swinging it around with vigorous arm
He sent it forth; it sounded as it went;
And the Phaeacians, skillful with the oar
And sail, bent low as o'er them, from his hand,
Flew the swift stone beyond the other marks.   240
And Pallas, in a human form, set up
A mark where it descended, and exclaimed:
"Stranger! a blind man, groping here, could find
Thy mark full easily, since it is not
Among the many, but beyond them all.   245

Then fear thou nothing in this game at least;
For no Phaeacian here can throw the quoit
As far as thou, much less exceed thy cast."
She spake; Odysseus the great sufferer
Heard, and rejoiced to know he had a friend   250
In that great circle. With a lighter heart
Thus said the chief to the Phaeacian crowd:
"Follow that cast, young men, and I will send
Another stone, at once, as far, perchance,
Or further still. If there are others yet   255
Who feel the wish, let them come forward here—
For much your words have chafed me—let them try
With me the boxing or the wrestling match,
Or foot-race; there is naught that I refuse—
Any of the Phaeacians. I except   260
Laodamas; he is my host, and who
Would enter such a contest with a friend?
A senseless, worthless man is he who seeks
A strife like this with one who shelters him
In a strange land; he mars the welcome given.   265
As for the rest, there is no rival here
Whom I reject or scorn; for I would know
Their prowess, and would try my own with theirs
Before you all. At any of the games
Practiced among mankind I am not ill,   270
Whatever they may be. The polished bow
I well know how to handle. I should be
The first to strike a foe by arrows sent
Among a hostile squadron, though there stood
A crowd of fellow-warriors by my side   275
And also aimed their shafts. The only one
Whose skill in archery excelled my own,

When we Achaeans drew the bow at Troy,
Was Philoctetes; to all other men
On earth that live by bread I hold myself   280
Superior. Yet I claim no rivalry
With men of ancient times—with Hercules
And Eurytus the Oechalian, who defied
The immortals to a contest with the bow.
Therefore was mighty Eurytus cut off.   285
Apollo, angry to be challenged, slew
The hero. I can hurl a spear beyond
Where others send an arrow. All my fear
Is for my feet, so weakened have I been
Among the stormy waves with want of food   290
At sea, and thus my limbs have lost their strength."
He ended here, and all the assembly sat
In silence; King Alcinous only spake:
"Stranger, since thou dost speak without offence,
And but to assert the prowess of thine arm,   295
Indignant that amid the public games
This man should rail ,at thee, and since thy wish
Is only that all others who can speak
Becomingly may not in time to come
Dispraise that prowess, now, then, heed my words,   300
And speak of them within thy palace halls
To other heroes when thou banquetest
Beside thy wife and children, and dost think
Of things that we excel in—arts which Zeus
Gives us, transmitted from our ancestors.   305
In boxing and in wrestling small renown
Have we, but we are swift of foot; we guide
Our galleys bravely o'er the deep; we take
Delight in feasts; we love the harp, the dance,

And change of raiment, the warm bath and bed.   310
Rise, then, Phaeacian masters of the dance,
And tread your measures, that our guest may tell
His friends at home how greatly we surpass
All other men in seamanship, the race,
The dance, the art of song. Go, one of you,   315
And bring Demodocus his clear-toned harp,
That somewhere in our palace has been left."
Thus spake the godlike king. The herald rose
To bring the sweet harp from the royal house.
Then the nine umpires also rose, who ruled   320
The games; they smoothed the floor, and made the ring
Of gazers wider. Next the herald came,
And brought Demodocus the clear-toned harp.
The minstrel went into the midst, and there
Gathered the graceful dancers; they were youths   325
In life's first bloom. With even steps they smote
The sacred floor. Odysseus, gazing, saw
The twinkle of their feet and was amazed.
The minstrel struck the chords and gracefully
Began the lay: he sang the loves of Ares   330
And Aphrodite of the glittering crown, who first
Had met each other stealthily beneath
The roof of Hephaestus. Ares with many gifts
Won her, and wronged her spouse, the King of Fire;
But from the Sun, who saw their guilt, there came   335
A messenger to Hephaestus. When he heard
The unwelcome tidings, planning his revenge,
He hastened to his smithy, where he forged
Chains that no power might loosen or might break,
Made to hold fast forever. When the snare   340
In all its parts was finished, he repaired,

Angry with Ares, to where the marriage-bed
Stood in his chamber. To the posts he tied
The encircling chains on every side, and made
Fast to the ceiling many, like the threads   345
Spun by the spider, which no eye could see,
Not even of the gods, so artfully
He wrought them. Then, as soon as he had wrapped
The snare about the bed, he feigned to go
To Lemnos nobly built, most dear to him   350
Of all the lands. But Ares, the god who holds
The shining reins, had kept no careless watch,
And when he saw the great artificer
Depart he went with speed to Hephaestus's house,
Drawn thither by the love of her who wears   355
The glittering crown. There Cytherea sat,
Arrived that moment from a visit paid.
Entering, he took her by the hand and said:
"Come, my beloved, let us to the couch.
Hephaestus is here no longer; he is gone,   360
And is among the Sintians, men who speak
A barbarous tongue, in Lemnos far away."
He spake, and she approved his words, and both
Lay down upon the bed, when suddenly
The network, wrought by Hephaestus's skillful hand,   365
Caught them, and clasped them round, nor could they lift
Or move a limb, and saw that no escape
Was possible. And now approached the King
Of Fire, returning ere he reached the isle
Of Lemnos, for the Sun in his behalf   370
Kept watch and told him all. He hastened home
In bitterness of heart, but when he reached
The threshold stopped. A fury without bounds

Possessed him, and he shouted terribly,
And called aloud on all the gods of heaven: 375
"O Father Zeus, and all ye blessed ones,
And deathless! Come, for here is what will move
Your laughter, yet is not to be endured.
Zeus's daughter, Aphrodite, thus dishonors me,
Lame as I am, and loves the butcher Ares;   380
For he is well to look at, and is sound
Of foot, while I am weakly—but for this
Are none but my two parents to be blamed,
Who never should have given me birth. Behold
Where lie embraced the lovers in my bed—   385
A hateful sight. Yet they will hardly take
Even a short slumber there, though side by side,
Enamored as they are; nor will they both
Be drowsy very soon. The net and chains
Will hold them till her father shall restore   390
All the large gifts which, on our marriage-day,
I gave him to possess the impudent minx
His daughter, who is fair, indeed, but false."
He spake, and to the brazen palace flocked
The gods; there Poseidon came, who shakes the earth;   395
There came beneficent Hermes; there too came
Apollo, archer-god; the goddesses,
Through womanly reserve, remained at home.
Meantime the gods, the givers of all good,
Stood in the entrance; and as they beheld   400
The cunning snare of Hephaestus, there arose
Infinite laughter from the blessed ones,
And one of them bespake his neighbor thus:
"Wrong prospers not; the slow o'ertakes the swift.
Hephaestus the slow has trapped the fleetest god   405

Upon Olympus, Ares; though lame himself,
His net has taken the adulterer,
Who now must pay the forfeit of his crime."
So talked they with each other. Then the son
Of Zeus, Apollo, thus to Hermes said: 410
"Hermes, thou son and messenger of Zeus,
And bountiful of gifts, couldst thou endure,
Fettered with such strong chains as these, to lie
Upon a couch with Aphrodite at thy side? "
The herald-god, the Argus-queller, thus   415
Made answer: "Nay, I would that it were so,
O archer-king, Apollo; I could bear
Chains thrice as many, and of infinite strength,
And all the gods and all the goddesses
Might come to look upon me, I would keep   420
My place with golden Aphrodite at my side."
He spake, and all the immortals laughed to hear.
Poseidon alone laughed not, but earnestly
Prayed Hephaestus, the renowned artificer,
To set Ares free, and spake these winged words: 425
"Release thy prisoner. What thou dost require
I promise here—that he shall make to thee
Due recompense in presence of the gods."
Illustrious Hephaestus answered: "Do not lay,
Earth-shaking Poseidon, this command on me,
Since little is the worth of pledges given   430
For worthless debtors. How could I demand
My right from thee among the assembled gods,
If Ares, set free, escape from debt and chains?"
Again the god who shakes the earth replied: 435
"Hephaestus, though Ares deny the forfeit due,
And take to flight, it shall be paid by me."

Again illustrious Hephaestus said: "Thy word
I ought not and I seek not to decline."
He spake, and then the might of Hephaestus loosed   440
The net, and, freed from those strong fetters, both
The prisoners sprang away. Ares flew to Thrace,
And laughter-loving Aphrodite to the isle
Of Cyprus, where at Paphos stand her grove
And perfumed altar. Here the Graces gave   445
The bath, anointed with ambrosial oil
Her limbs—such oil as to the eternal gods
Lends a fresh beauty, and arrayed her last
In graceful robes, a marvel to behold.
So sang the famous bard, while inly pleased   450
Odysseus heard, and pleased were all the rest,
Phaeacia's sons, expert with oar and sail.
Alcinous called his sons Laodamas
And Halius forth, and bade them dance alone,
For none of all the others equalled them.   455
Then taking a fair purple ball, the work
Of skillful Polybus, and, bending back,
One flung it toward the shadowy clouds on high,
The other springing upward easily
Grasped it before he touched the ground again.   450
And when they thus had tossed the ball awhile,
They danced upon the nourishing earth, and oft
Changed places with each other, while the youths,
That stood within the circle filled the air
With their applauses; mighty was the din.   465
Then great Odysseus to Alcinous said:
"O King Alcinous! mightiest of the race
For whom thou hast engaged that they excel
All others in the dance, what thou hast said

Is amply proved. I look and am amazed."   470
Well pleased Alcinous the mighty heard,
And thus to his seafaring people spake:
"Leaders and chiefs of the Phaeacians, hear!
Wise seems the stranger. Haste we to bestow
Gifts that may well beseem his liberal hests.   475
Twelve honored princes in our land bear sway,
The thirteenth prince am I. Let each one bring
A well-bleached cloak, a tunic, and beside
Of precious gold a talent Let them all
Be brought at once, that, having seen them here,   430
Our guest may with a cheerful heart partake
The evening meal. And let Euryalus,
Who spake but now so unbecomingly,
Appease him both with words and with a gift."
He spake; they all approved, and each one sent   485
His herald with a charge to bring the gifts,
And thus Euryalus addressed the king:
"O King Alcinous, mightiest of our race,
I will obey thee, and will seek to appease
Our guest. This sword of brass will I bestow,   490
With hilt of silver, and an ivory sheath
New wrought, which he may deem a gift of price."
He spake, and gave the silver-studded sword
Into his hand, and spake these winged words:
"Stranger and father, hail! If any word   495
That hath been uttered gave offence, may storms
Sweep it away forever. May the gods
Give thee to see thy wife again, and reach
Thy native land, where all thy sufferings
And this long absence from thy friends shall end!"   500
Odysseus, the sagacious, thus replied:

"Hail also, friend! and may the gods confer
On thee all happiness, and may the time
Never arrive when thou shalt miss the sword
Placed in my hands with reconciling words!"   505
He spake, and slung the silver-studded sword
Upon his shoulders. Now the sun went down,
And the rich presents were already brought.
The noble heralds came and carried them
Into the palace of Alcinous, where   510
His blameless sons received and ranged them all
In fair array before the queenly dame
Their mother. Meantime had the mighty king
Alcinous to his palace led the way,
Where they who followed took the lofty seats,   515
And thus Alcinous to Arete said:
"Bring now a coffer hither, fairly shaped,
The best we have, and lay a well-bleached cloak
And tunic in it; set upon the fire
A brazen cauldron for our guest, to warm   520
The water of his bath, that having bathed
And viewed the gifts which the Phaeacian chiefs
Have brought him, ranged in order, he may sit
Delighted at the banquet and enjoy
The music. I will give this beautiful cup   525
Of gold, that he, in memory of me,
May daily in his palace pour to Zeus
Libations, and to all the other gods."
He spake; Arete bade her maidens haste
To place an ample tripod on the fire.   530
Forthwith upon the blazing fire they set
A laver with three feet, and in it poured
Water, and heaped fresh fuel on the flames.

The flames crept up the vessel's swelling sides,
And warmed the water. Meantime from her room   535
Arete brought a beautiful chest, in which
She laid the presents destined for her guest—
Garments and gold which the Phaeacians gave—
And laid the cloak and tunic with the rest,
And thus in winged words addressed the chief: 540
"Look to the lid thyself, and cast a cord
Around it, lest, upon thy voyage home,
Thou suffer loss, when haply thou shalt take
A pleasant slumber in the dark-hulled ship."
Odysseus, the sagacious, heard, and straight   545
He fitted to its place the lid, and wound
And knotted artfully around the chest
A cord, as queenly Circe long before
Had taught him. Then to call him to the bath
The housewife of the palace came. He saw   550
Gladly the steaming laver, for not oft
Had he been cared for thus, since he had left
The dwelling of the nymph with amber hair,
Calypso, though attended while with her
As if he were a god. Now when the maids   555
Had seen him bathed, and had anointed him
With oil, and put his sumptuous mantle on,
And tunic, forth he issued from the bath,
And came to those who sat before their wine.
Nausicaä, goddess-like in beauty, stood   560
Beside a pillar of that noble roof,
And looking on Odysseus as he passed,
Admired, and said to him in winged words:
"Stranger, farewell, and in thy native land
Remember thou hast owed thy life to me."   565

Odysseus, the sagacious, answering said:
"Nausicaä, daughter of the large-souled king
Alcinous! so may Zeus, the Thunderer,
Husband of Hera, grant that I behold
My home, returning safe, as I will make   570
To thee as to a goddess day by day
My prayer; for, lady, thou hast saved my life."
He spake, and near Alcinous took his place
Upon a throne. And now they served the feast
To each, and mingled wine. A herald led   575
Thither the gentle bard Demodocus,
Whom all the people honored. Him they placed
Amidst the assembly, where he leaned against
A lofty column. Sage Odysseus then
Carved from the broad loin of a white-tusked boar   580
A part, where yet a mass of flesh remained
Bordered with fat, and to the herald said:
"Bear this, O herald, to Demodocus,
That he may eat. Him, even in my grief,
Will I embrace, for worthily the bards   585
Are honored and revered o'er all the earth
By every race of men. The Muse herself
Hath taught them song; she loves the minstrel tribe."
He spake; the herald laid the flesh before
Demodocus the hero, who received   590
The gift well pleased. Then all the guests put forth
Their hands and shared the viands on the board;
And when their thirst and hunger were allayed,
Thus to the' minstrel sage Odysseus spake:
"Demodocus, above all other men   595
I give thee praise, for either has the Muse,
Zeus's daughter, or Apollo, visited

And taught thee. Truly hast thou sung the fate
Of the Achaean warriors—what they did
And suffered—all their labors as if thou   600
Hadst been among them, or hadst heard the tale
From an eye-witness. Now, I pray, proceed,
And sing the invention of the wooden horse
Made by Epeius with Athena's aid,
And by the chief Odysseus artfully   605
Conveyed into the Trojan citadel,
With armed warriors in its womb to lay
The city waste. And I, if thou relate
The story rightly, will at once declare
To all that largely hath some bounteous god   610
Bestowed on thee the holy gift of song."
He spake; the poet felt the inspiring god,
And sang, beginning where the Argives hurled
Firebrands among their tents, and sailed away
In their good galleys, save the band that sat   615
Beside renowned Odysseus in the horse,
Concealed from sight, amid the Trojan crowd,
Who now had drawn it to the citadel.
So there it stood, while, sitting round it, talked
The men of Troy, and wist not what to do.   620
By turns three counsels pleased them—to hew down
The hollow trunk with the remorseless steel;
Or drag it to a height, and cast it thence
Headlong among the rocks; or, lastly, leave
The enormous image standing and unharmed,   625
An offering to appease the gods. And this
At last was done; for so had fate decreed
That they should be destroyed whene'er their town
Should hold within its walls the horse of wood,

In which the mightiest of the Argives came   630
Among the sons of Troy to smite and slay.
Then sang the bard how, issuing from the womb
Of that deceitful horse, the sons of Greece
Laid Ilium waste; how each in different ways
Ravaged the town, while, terrible as Ares,   633
Odysseus, joined with Menelaus, sought
The palace of Deiphobus, and there
Maintained a desperate battle, till the aid
Of mighty Pallas made the victory his.
So sang renowned Demodocus; the strain   640
Melted to tears Odysseus, from whose lids
They dropped and wet his cheeks. As when a wife
Weeps her beloved husband, slain before
His town and people, fighting to defend
Them and his own dear babes from deadly harm,   645
She sees him gasp and die, and at the sight
She falls with piercing cries upon his corpse,
Meantime the victors beat her on the back
And shoulders with their spears, and bear her off
To toil and grieve in slavery, where her cheeks   650
In that long bitter sorrow lose their bloom;
So from the eyelids of Odysseus fell
The tears, yet fell unnoticed by them all
Save that Alcinous, sitting at his side,
Saw them, and heard his heavy sighs, and thus   655
Bespake his people, masters of the oar:
"Princes and chiefs of the Phaeacian race,
Give ear. Let now Demodocus lay by
His clear-toned harp. The matter of his song
Delights not all alike. Since first we sat   660
At meat, and since our noble bard began

His lay, our guest has never ceased to grieve;
Some mighty sorrow weighs upon his heart
Now let the bard refrain, that we may all
Enjoy the banquet, both our guest and we   665
Who welcome him, for it is fitting thus.
And now are all things for our worthy guest
Made ready, both the escort and these gifts,
The pledges of our kind regard. A guest,
A suppliant, is a brother, even to him   670
Who bears a heart not easy to be moved.
No longer, then, keep back with studied art
What I shall ask; 'twere better far to speak
With freedom. Tell the name thy mother gave,
Thy father, and all those who dwell within,   675
And round thy city. For no living man
Is nameless from the time that he is born.
Humble or high in station, at their birth
The parents give them names. Declare thy land,
Thy people, and thy city, that our ships   680
May learn, and bear thee to the place; for here
In our Phaeacian ships no pilots are,
Nor rudders, as in ships of other lands.
Ours know the thoughts and the intents of men.
To them all cities and all fertile coasts   685
Inhabited by men are known; they cross
The great sea scudding fast, involved in mist
And darkness, with no fear of perishing
Or meeting harm. I heard Nausithous,
My father, say that Poseidon was displeased   690
With us for safely bearing to their homes
So many men, and that he would destroy
In after time some good Phaeacian ship,

Returning from a convoy, in the waves
Of the dark sea, and leave her planted there,   695
A mountain huge and high, before our town.
So did the aged chieftain prophesy;
The god, as best may please him, will fulfill
My father's words, or leave them unfulfilled.
Now tell me truly whither thou hast roamed,   700
And what the tribes of men that thou hast seen;
Tell which of them are savage, rude, unjust,
And which are hospitable and revere
The blessed gods. Declare why thou didst weep
And sigh when hearing what unhappy fate   705
Befell the Argive and Achaean host
And town of Troy. The gods decreed it; they
Ordain destruction to the sons of men,
A theme of song thereafter. Hadst thou not
Some valiant kinsman who was slain at Troy?   710
A son-in-law? the father of thy wife?
Nearest of all are they to us, save those
Of our own blood. Or haply might it be
Some bosom-friend, one eminently graced
With all that wins our love; for not less dear   715
Than if he were a brother should we hold
The wise and gentle man who is our friend."

BOOK IX

Odysseus, the sagacious, answered thus: 1
"O King Alcinous, most renowned of men
A pleasant thing it is to hear a bard
Like this, endowed with such a voice, so like
The voices of the gods. Nor can I deem   5
Aught more delightful than the general joy
Of a whole people when the assembled guests
Seated in order in the royal halls
Are listening to the minstrel, while the board
Is spread with bread and meats, and from the jars   10
The cupbearer draws wine and fills the cups.
To me there is no more delightful sight.
"But now thy mind is moved to ask of me
The story of the sufferings I have borne,
And that will wake my grief anew. What first,   15
What next, shall I relate? what last of all?
For manifold are the misfortunes cast
Upon me by the immortals. Let me first
Declare my name, that ye may know, and I
Perchance, before my day of death shall come,   20
May be your host, though dwelling far away.

I am Odysseus, and my father's name
Laertes; widely am I known to men
As quick in shrewd devices, and my fame
Hath reached to heaven. In sunny Ithaca   25
I dwell, where high Neritus, seen afar
Rustles with woods. Around are many isles,
Well peopled, near each other. Samos there
Lies, with Dulichium, and Zacynthus dark
With forests. Ithaca, with its low shores,   30
Lies highest toward the setting sun; the rest
Are on the side where first the morning breaks.
A rugged region 'tis, but nourishes
Nobly its youths, nor have I ever seen
A sweeter spot on earth. Calypso late,   35
That glorious goddess, in her grotto long
Detained me from it, and desired that I
Should be her husband; in her royal home
Aeean Circe, mistress of strange arts,
Detained me also, and desired that I   40
Should be her husband—yet they could not move
The purpose of my heart. For there is naught
More sweet and dear than our own native land
And parents, though perchance our lot be cast
In a rich home, yet far from our own kin   45
And in a foreign land. Now let me speak
Of the calamitous voyage which the will
Of Zeus ordained on my return from Troy.
"The wind that blew me from the Trojan shore
Bore me to the Ciconians, who abode   50
In Ismarus. I laid the city waste
And slew its dwellers, carried off their wives
And all their wealth and parted them among

My men, that none might want an equal share.
And then I warned them with all haste to leave   55
The region. Madmen! they obeyed me not.
"And there they drank much wine, and on the beach
Slew many sheep and many slow-paced steers
With crumpled horns. Then the Ciconians called
To their Ciconian neighbors, braver men   60
Than they, and more in number, whose abode
Was on the mainland, trained to fight from steeds,
Or, if need were, on foot. In swarms they came,
Thick as new leaves or morning flowers in spring.
Then fell on our unhappy company   65
An evil fate from Zeus, and many griefs.
They formed their lines, and fought at our good ships,
Where man encountered man with brazen spears.
While yet 'twas morning, and the holy light
Of day waxed brighter, we withstood the assault   70
And kept our ground, although more numerous they.
But when the sun was sloping toward the west
The enemy prevailed; the Achaean band
Was routed, and was made to flee. That day
There perished from each galley of our fleet   75
Six valiant men; the rest escaped with life.
"Onward we sailed, lamenting bitterly
Our comrades slain, yet happy to escape
From death ourselves. Nor did we put to sea
In our good ships until we thrice had called   80
Aloud by name each one of our poor friends
Who fell in battle by Ciconian hands.
The Cloud-compeller, Zeus, against us sent
The north-wind in a hurricane, and wrapped
The earth and heaven in clouds, and from the skies   85

Fell suddenly the night. With stooping masts
Our galleys scudded; the strong tempest split
And tore the sails; we drew and laid them down
Within the ships, in fear of utter wreck,
And toward the mainland eagerly we turned   90
The rudders. There we lay two days and nights,
Worn out with grief and hardship. When at length
The fair-haired Morning brought the third day round,
We raised the masts, and, spreading the white sails
To take the wind, we sat us down. The wind   95
Carried us forward with the pilot's aid:
And then should I have reached my native land
Safely, had not the currents and the waves
Of ocean and the north-wind driven me back,
What time I strove to pass Maleia's cape,   100
And swept me to Cytherae from my course.
"Still onward driven before those baleful winds
Across the fishy deep for nine whole days,
On the tenth day we reached the land where dwell
The Lotus-eaters, men whose food is flowers.   105
We landed on the mainland, and our crews
Near the fleet galleys took their evening meal.
And when we all had eaten and had drunk
I sent explorers forth—two chosen men,
A herald was the third—to learn what race   110
Of mortals nourished by the fruits of earth
Possessed the land. They went and found themselves
Among the Lotus-eaters soon, who used
No violence against their lives, but gave
Into their hands the lotus plant to taste.   115
Whoever tasted once of that sweet food
Wished not to see his native country more,

Nor give his friends the knowledge of his fate.
And then my messengers desired to dwell
Among the Lotus-eaters, and to feed   120
Upon the lotus, never to return.
By force I led them weeping to the fleet,
And bound them in the hollow ships beneath
The benches. Then I ordered all the rest
Of my beloved comrades to embark   125
In haste, lest, tasting of the lotus, they
Should think no more of home. All straightway went
On board, and on the benches took their place,
And smote the hoary ocean with their oars.
"Onward we sailed with sorrowing hearts, and reached   130
The country of the Cyclops, an untamed
And lawless race, who, trusting to the gods,
Plant not, nor plough the fields, but all things spring
For them untended—barley, wheat, and vines
Yielding large clusters filled with wine, and nursed   135
By showers from Zeus. No laws have they; they hold
No councils. On the mountain heights they dwell
In vaulted caves, where each one rules his wives
And children as he pleases; none give heed
To what the others do. Before the port   140
Of that Cyclopean land there is an isle,
Low-lying, neither near nor yet remote—
A woodland region, where the wild goats breed
Innumerable; for the foot of man
Disturbs them not, and huntsmen toiling through   145
Thick woods, or wandering over mountain heights,
Enter not here. The fields are never grazed
By sheep, nor furrowed by the plough, but lie
Untilled, unsown, and uninhabited

By man, and only feed the bleating goats.   150
The Cyclops have no barks with crimson prows,
Nor shipwrights skilled to frame a galley's deck
With benches for the rowers, and equipped
For any service, voyaging by turns
To all the cities, as is often done   155
By men who cross the deep from place to place,
And make a prosperous region of an isle.
No meager soil is there; it well might bear
All fruits in their due time. Along the shore
Of the gray deep are meadows smooth and moist.   160
The vine would flourish long; the ploughman's task
Is easy, and the husbandman would reap
Large harvests, for the mold is rich below.
And there is a safe haven, where no need
Of cable is; no anchor there is cast,   165
Nor hawsers fastened to the strand, but they
Who enter there remain until it please
The mariners, with favorable wind,
To put to sea again. A limpid stream
Flows from a fount beneath a hollow rock   170
Into that harbor at its further end,
And poplars grow around it. Thither went
Our fleet; some deity had guided us
Through the dark night, for nothing had we seen.
Thick was the gloom around our barks the moon   175
Shone not in heaven, the clouds had quenched her light.
No eye discerned the isle, nor the long waves
That rolled against the shore, till our good ships
Touched land, and, disembarking there, we gave
Ourselves to sleep upon the water-side   180
And waited for the holy Morn to rise.

"And when at length the daughter of the Dawn,
The rosy-fingered Morn, appeared, we walked
Around the isle, admiring as we went
Meanwhile the nymphs, the daughters of the God   185
Who bears the aegis, roused the mountain goats,
That so our crews might make their morning meal.
And straightway from our ships we took in hand
Our crooked bows and our long-bladed spears.
"Let all the rest of my beloved friends   190
Remain, while I, with my own bark and crew.
Go forth to learn what race of men are these,
Whether ill-mannered, savage, and unjust,
Or kind to guests and reverent toward the gods.'
I spake, and, having ordered all my crew   195
To go on board and cast the hawsers loose,
Embarked on my own ship. They all obeyed,
And manned the benches, sitting there in rows,
And smote the hoary ocean with their oars.
But when we came upon that neighboring coast,   200
We saw upon its verge beside the sea
A cave high vaulted, overbrowed with shrubs
Of laurel. There much cattle lay at rest,
Both sheep and goats. Around it was a court,
A high enclosure of hewn stone, and pines   205
Tall stemmed, and towering oaks. Here dwelt a man
Of giant bulk, who by himself, alone,
Was wont to tend his flocks. He never held
Converse with others, but devised apart
His wicked deeds. A frightful prodigy   210
Was he, and like no man who lives by bread,
But more like a huge mountain summit, rough
With woods, that towers alone above the rest.

"Then, bidding all the others stay and guard
The ship, I chose among my bravest men   215
Twelve whom I took with me. I had on board
A goatskin of dark wine—a pleasant sort,
Which Maron late, Evanthes' son, a priest
Of Phoebus, guardian god of Ismarus,
Gave me, when, moved with reverence, we saved   220
Him and his children and his wife from death.
For his abode was in the thick-grown grove
Of Phoebus. Costly were the gifts he gave—
Seven talents of wrought gold; a chalice all
Of silver; and he drew for me, besides,   225
Into twelve jars, a choice rich wine, unspoiled
By mixtures, and a beverage for gods.
No one within his dwellings, maids or men,
Knew of it, save the master and his wife,
And matron of the household. Whensoe'er   230
They drank this rich red wine, he only filled
A single cup with wine, and tempered that
With twenty more of water. From the cup
Arose a fragrance that might please the gods,
And hard it was to put the draught aside.   235
Of this I took a skin well filled, besides
Food in a hamper—for my thoughtful mind
Misgave me, lest I should encounter one
Of formidable strength and savage mood,
And with no sense of justice or of right.   240
Soon were we at the cave, but found not him
Within it; he was in the fertile meads,
Tending his flocks. We entered, wondering much
At all we saw. Around were baskets heaped
With cheeses; pens were thronged with lambs and kids,   245

Each in a separate fold; the elder ones,
The younger, and the newly yeaned, had each
Their place apart. The vessels swam with whey—
Pails smoothly wrought, and buckets into which
He milked the cattle. My companions then   250
Begged me with many pressing words to take
Part of the cheeses, and, returning, drive
With speed to our good galley lambs and kids
From where they stabled, and set sail again
On the salt sea. I granted not their wish;   255
Far better if I had. 'Twas my intent
To see the owner of the flocks and prove
His hospitality. No pleasant sight
Was that to be for those with whom I came.
"And then we lit a fire, and sacrificed,   260
And ate the cheeses, and within the cave
Sat waiting, till from pasturing his flocks
He came; a heavy load of well-dried wood
He bore, to make a blaze at supper-time.
Without the den he flung his burden down   265
With such a crash that we in terror slunk
Into a corner of the cave. He drove
His well-fed flock, all those whose milk he drew,
Under that spacious vault of rock, but left
The males, both goats and rams, without the court.   270
And then he lifted a huge barrier up,
A mighty weight; not two-and-twenty wains,
Four-wheeled and strong, could move it from the ground:
Such was the enormous rock he raised, and placed
Against the entrance. Then he sat and milked   275
The ewes and bleating goats, each one in turn,
And gave to each its young. Next, half the milk

He caused to curdle, and disposed the curd
In woven baskets; and the other half
He kept in bowls to be his evening drink.   280
His tasks all ended thus, he lit a fire,
And saw us where we lurked, and questioned us:
'Who are ye, strangers? Tell me whence ye came
Across the ocean. Are ye men of trade,
Or wanderers at will, like those who roam   285
The sea for plunder, and, with their own lives
In peril, carry death to distant shores?'
He spake, and we who heard with sinking hearts
Trembled at that deep voice and frightful form,
And thus I answered: 'We are Greeks who come   290
From Ilium, driven across the mighty deep
By changing winds, and while we sought our home
Have made a different voyage, and been forced
Upon another course; such was the will
Of Zeus. We boast ourselves to be   295
Soldiers of Agamemnon, Atreus' son,
Whose fame is now the greatest under heaven,
So mighty was the city which he sacked,
So many were the warriors whom he slew;
And now we come as suppliants to thy knees,   300
And ask thee to receive us as thy guests,
Or else bestow the gifts which custom makes
The stranger's due. Great as thou art, revere
The gods; for suitors to thy grace are we,
And hospitable Zeus, whose presence goes   305
With every worthy stranger, will avenge
Suppliants and strangers when they suffer wrong.'
I spake, and savagely he answered me:
'Thou art a fool, O stranger, or art come

From some far country—thou who biddest me   310
Fear or regard the gods. We little care—
We Cyclops—for the aegis-bearer, Zeus,
Or any other of the blessed gods;
We are their betters. Think not I would spare
Thee or thy comrades to avoid the wrath   315
Of Zeus, unless it were my choice;
But say—for I would know—where hast thou left
Thy gallant bark in landing? was it near,
Or in some distant corner of the isle?'
He spake to tempt me, but I well perceived   320
His craft, and answered with dissembling words:
'Poseidon, who shakes the shores, hath wrecked my bark
On rocks that edge thine island, hurling it
Against the headland. From the open sea
The tempest swept it hitherward, and I,   325
With these, escaped the bitter doom of death.'
I spake; the savage answered not, but sprang,
And, laying hands on my companions, seized
Two, whom he dashed like whelps against the ground.
Their brains flowed out, and weltered where they fell.   330
He hewed them limb from limb for his repast,
And, like a lion of the mountain wilds,
Devoured them as they were, and left no part—
Entrails nor flesh nor marrowy bones. We wept
To see his cruelties, and raised our hands   335
To Zeus, and hopeless misery filled our hearts.
And when the Cyclops now had filled himself,
Devouring human flesh, and drinking milk
Unmingled, in his cave he laid him down,
Stretched out amid his flocks. The thought arose   340
In my courageous heart to go to him,

And draw the trenchant sword upon my thigh,
And where the midriff joins the liver deal
A stroke to pierce his breast. A second thought
Restrained me—that a miserable death   345
Would overtake us, since we had no power
To move the mighty rock which he had laid
At the high opening. So all night we grieved,
Waiting the holy Morn; and when at length
That rosy-fingered daughter of the Dawn   350
Appeared, the Cyclops lit a fire, and milked
His fair flock one by one, and brought their young
Each to its mother's side. When he had thus
Performed his household tasks, he seized again
Two of our number for his morning meal.   355
These he devoured, and then he moved away
With ease the massive rock that closed the cave,
And, driving forth his well-fed flock, he laid
The massive barrier back, as one would fit
The lid upon a quiver. With loud noise   360
The Cyclops drove that well-fed flock afield,
While I was left to think of many a plan
To do him mischief and avenge our wrongs,
If haply Pallas should confer on me
That glory. To my mind, as I revolved   365
The plans, this seemed the wisest of them all.
"Beside the stalls there lay a massive club
Of olive-wood, yet green, which from its stock
The Cyclops hewed, that he might carry it
When seasoned. As it lay it seemed to us   370
The mast of some black galley, broad of beam,
With twenty oarsmen, built to carry freight
Across the mighty deep—such was its length

And thickness. Standing by it, I cut off
A fathom's length, and gave it to my men,   375
And bade them smooth its sides, and they obeyed
While I made sharp the smaller end, and brought
The point to hardness in the glowing fire;
And then I hid the weapon in a heap
Of litter, which lay thick about the cave.   380
I bade my comrades now decide by lot
Which of them all should dare, along with me,
To lift the stake, and with its point bore out
Our enemy's eye, when softly wrapped in sleep.
The lot was cast, and fell on those whom most   385
I wished with me—four men, and I the fifth.
"At eve the keeper of these fair-woolled flocks
Returned, and brought his well-fed sheep and goats
Into the spacious cavern, leaving none
Without it, whether through some doubt of us   390
Or through the ordering of some god. He raised
The massive rock again, and laid it close
Against the opening. Then he sat and milked
The ewes and bleating goats, each one in turn,
And gave to each her young. When he had thus   395
Performed his household tasks, he seized again
Two of our number for his evening meal.
Then drew I near, and bearing in my hand
A wooden cup of dark red wine I said:
'Take this, O Cyclops, after thy repast   400
Of human flesh, and drink, that thou mayst know
What liquor was concealed within our ship.
I brought it as an offering to thee,
For I had hope that thou wouldst pity us,
And send us home. Yet are thy cruelties   405

Beyond all limit. Wicked as thou art,
Hereafter who, of all the human race,
Will dare approach thee, guilty of such wrong?'
As thus I spake, he took the cup and drank.
The luscious wine delighted mightily   410
His palate, and he asked a second draught.
'Give me to drink again, and generously,
And tell thy name, that I may make a gift
Such as becomes a host. The fertile land
In which the Cyclops dwell yields wine, 'tis true,   415
And the large grapes are nursed by rains from Zeus,
But nectar and ambrosia are in this.'
He spake; I gave him of the generous juice
Again, and thrice I filled and brought the cup,
And thrice the Cyclops in his folly drank.   420
But when I saw the wine begin to cloud
His senses, I bespake him sweetly thus:
'Thou hast inquired, O Cyclops, by what name
Men know me. I will tell thee, but do thou
Bestow in turn some hospitable gift,   425
As thou hast promised. Noman is my name,
My father and my mother gave it me,
And Noman am I called by all my friends.'
I ended, and he answered savagely:
'Noman shall be the last of all his band   430
Whom I will eat, the rest will I devour
Before him. Let that respite be my gift.'
He spake, and, sinking backward at full length,
Lay on the ground, with his huge neck aside;
All-powerful sleep had overtaken him.   435
Then from his mouth came bits of human flesh
Mingled with wine, and from his drunken throat

Rejected noisily. I put the stake
Among the glowing coals to gather heat,
And uttered cheerful words, encouraging   440
My men, that none might fail me through their fears.
And when the olive-wood began to blaze—
For though yet green it freely took the fire—
I drew it from the embers. Round me stood
My comrades, whom some deity inspired   445
With calm, high courage. In their hands they took
And thrust into his eye the pointed bar,
While perched upon a higher stand than they
I twirled it round. As when a workman bores
Some timber of a ship, the men who stand   450
Below him with a strap, on either side
Twirl it, and round it spins unceasingly,
So, thrusting in his eye that pointed bar,
We made it turn. The blood came streaming forth
On the hot wood; the eyelids and the brow   455
Were scalded by the vapor, and the roots
Of the scorched eyeball crackled with the fire.
As when a smith, in forging ax or adze,
Plunges, to temper it, the hissing blade
Into cold water, strengthening thus the steel,   460
So hissed the eyeball of the Cyclops round
That olive stake. He raised a fearful howl;
The rocks rang with it, and we fled from him
In terror. Plucking from his eye the stake
All foul and dripping with the abundant blood,   465
He flung it madly from him with both hands.
Then called he to the Cyclops who in grots
Dwelt on that breezy height. They heard his voice
And came by various ways, and stood beside

The cave, and asked the occasion of his grief.   470
"What hurts thee, Polyphemus, that thou thus
Dost break our slumbers in the ambrosial night
With cries? Hath any of the sons of men
Driven off thy flocks in spite of thee, or tried
By treachery or force to take thy life?'   475
Huge Polyphemus answered from his den:
O friends! 'tis Noman who is killing me;
By treachery Noman kills me; none by force.'
Then thus with winged words they spake again:
'If no man does thee violence, and thou   480
Art quite alone, reflect that none escape
Diseases; they are sent by Zeus. But make
Thy prayer to Father Poseidon, ocean's king.'
So spake they and departed. In my heart
I laughed to think that by the name I took,   485
And by my shrewd device, I had deceived
The Cyclops. Meantime, groaning and in pain,
And groping with his hands, he moved away
The rock that barred the entrance. There he sat,
With arms outstretched, to seize whoever sought   490
To issue from the cavern with the flock,
So dull of thought he deemed me. Then I planned
How best to save my comrades and myself
From death. I framed a thousand stratagems
And arts—for here was life at stake, and great   495
The danger was. At last I fixed on this:
The rams were plump and beautiful, and large
With thick dark fleeces. These I silently
Bound to each other, three and three, with twigs
Of which that prodigy of lawless guilt,   500
The Cyclops, made his bed. The middle ram

Of every three conveyed a man; the two,
One on each side, were there to make him safe.
Thus each of us was borne by three; but I
Chose for myself the finest one of all,   505
And seized him by the back, and, slipping down
Beneath his shaggy belly, stretched myself
At length, and clung with resolute heart, and hands
That firmly clenched the rich abundant fleece.
Then sighed we for the holy Morn to rise.   510
And when again the daughter of the Dawn,
The rosy-fingered Morn, looked forth, the males
Went forth to pasture, while the ewes remained
Within the stables, bleating, yet un milked,
For heavy were their udders. Carefully   515
The master handled, though in grievous pain,
The back of every one that rose and passed,
Yet, slow of thought, perceived not that my men
Were clinging hid beneath their woolly breasts.
As the last ram of all the flock went out,   520
His thick fleece heavy with my weight, and I
In agitated thought, he felt his back,
And thus the giant Polyphemus spake:
'My favorite ram, how art thou now the last
To leave the cave? It hath not been thy wont   525
To let the sheep go first, but thou didst come
Earliest to feed among the flowery grass,
Walking with stately strides, and thou wert first
At the fresh stream, and first at eve to seek
The stable; now thou art the last of all.   530
Grievest thou for thy master, who has lost
His eye, put out by a deceitful wretch
And his vile crew, who stupefied me first

With wine—this Noman—who, if right I deem,
Has not escaped from death. O, didst thou think   535
As I do, and hadst but the power of speech
To tell me where he hides from my strong arm,
Then should his brains, dashed out against the ground,
Be scattered here and there; then should my heart
Be somewhat lighter, even amid the woes   540
Which Noman, worthless wretch, has brought on me!'
He spake, and sent him forth among the rest;
And when we were a little way beyond
The cavern and the court, I loosed my hold
Upon the animal and unbound my men.   545
Then quickly we surrounded and drove off,
Fat sheep and stately paced, a numerous flock,
And brought them to our ship, where joyfully
Our friends received us, though with grief and tears
For those who perished. Yet I suffered not   550
That they should weep, but, frowning, gave command
By signs to lift with speed the fair-woolled sheep
On board, and launch our ship on the salt sea.
They went on board, where each one took his place
Upon the benches, and with diligent oars   555
Smote the gray deep; and when we were as far
As one upon the shore could hear a shout,
Thus to the Cyclops tauntingly I called:
'Ha! Cyclops! those whom in thy rocky cave
Thou, in thy brutal fury, hast devoured,   560
Were friends of one not unexpert in war;
Amply have thy own guilty deeds returned
Upon thee. Cruel one! who didst not fear
To eat the strangers sheltered by thy roof,
Zeus and the other gods avenge them thus.'   565

I spake the anger in his bosom raged
More fiercely. From a mountain peak he wrenched
Its summit, hurling it to fall beside
Our galley, where it almost touched the helm.
The rock dashed high the water where it fell,   570
And the returning billow swept us back
And toward the shore. I seized a long-stemmed pike
And pushed it from the shore, encouraging
The men to bend with vigor to their oars
And so escape. With nods I gave the sign.   575
Forward to vigorous strokes the oarsmen leaned
Till we were out at sea as far from land
As when I spake before, and then again
I shouted to the Cyclops, though my crew
Strove to prevent it with beseeching words,   580
And one man first and then another said:
'O most unwise! why chafe that savage man
To fury—him who just has cast his bolt
Into the sea, and forced us toward the land
Where we had wellnigh perished? Should he hear   585
A cry from us, or even a word of speech,
Then would he fling a rock to crush our heads
And wreck our ship, so fatal is his cast.'
He spake, but moved not my courageous heart;
And then I spake again, and angrily: 590
'Cyclops, if any man of mortal birth
Note thine unseemly blindness, and inquire
The occasion, tell him that Laertes' son,
Odysseus, the destroyer of walled towns,
Whose home is Ithaca, put out thine eye.'   595
I spake; he answered with a wailing voice:
'Now, woe is me! the ancient oracles

Concerning me have come to pass. Here dwelt
A seer named Telemus Eurymides,
Great, good, and eminent in prophecy,   600
And prophesying he grew old among
The Cyclops. He foretold my coming fate—
That I should lose my sight, and by the hand
And cunning of Odysseus. Yet I looked
For one of noble presence, mighty strength,   605
And giant stature landing on our coast.
Now a mere weakling, insignificant
And small of stature, has put out my eye,
First stupefying me with wine. Yet come
Hither, I pray, Odysseus, and receive   610
The hospitable gifts which are thy due;
And I will pray to Poseidon, and entreat
The mighty god to guide thee safely home.
His son am I, and he declares himself
My father. He can heal me if he will,   615
And no one else of all the immortal gods
Or mortal men can give me back my sight.'
He spake; I answered: 'Rather would I take
Thy life and breath, and send thee to the abode
Of Hades, where thou wouldst be past the power   620
Of even Poseidon to restore thine eye.'
As thus I said, the Cyclops raised his hands,
And spread them toward the starry heaven, and thus
Prayed to the deity who rules the deep:
'Hear, dark-haired Poseidon, who dost swathe the earth!   625
If I am thine, and thou dost own thyself
My father, grant that this Odysseus ne'er
May reach his native land! But if it be
The will of fate that he behold again

His friends, and enter his own palace-halls   630
In his own country, late and sorrowful
Be his return, with all his comrades lost,
And in a borrowed ship, and may he find
In his own home new griefs awaiting him.'
He prayed, and Poseidon hearkened to his prayer.   635
And then the Cyclops seized another stone,
Far larger than the last, and swung it round,
And cast it with vast strength. It fell behind
Our black-prowed galley, where it almost struck
The rudder's end. The sea was dashed on high   640
Beneath the falling rock, and bore our ship
On toward the shore we sought. When we reached
The island where together, in a fleet
Our other galleys lay, we found our friends
Sitting where they had waited long in grief.   645
We touched the shore and drew our galley up
On the smooth sand, and stepped upon the beach;
And taking from on board the sheep that formed
Part of the Cyclops' flock, divided them,
That none might be without an equal share.   650
When all the rest were shared, my warrior friends
Decreed the ram to me. Of him I made
Upon the beach a sacrifice to Zeus
The Cloud-compeller, son of Cronus, whose rule
Is over all; to him I burned the thighs.   655
He heeded not the offering; even then
He planned the wreck of all my gallant ships,
And death of my dear comrades. All that day
Till set of sun we sat and feasted high
Upon the abundant meats and delicate wine.   660
But when the sun went down, and darkness crept

Over the earth, we slumbered on the shore;
And when again the daughter of the Dawn,
The rosy-fingered Morn, looked forth, I called
My men with cheerful words to climb the decks 665
And cast the hawsers loose. With speed they went
On board and manned the benches, took in hand
The oars and smote with them the hoary deep.
Onward in sadness, glad to have escaped,
We sailed, yet sorrowing for our comrades lost." 670

BOOK X

"We reached the Aeolian isle, where Aeolus,   1
Dear to the gods, a son of Hippotas,
Made his abode. It was a floating isle;
A wall of brass enclosed it, and smooth rocks
Edged it around. Twelve children in his halls   5
Were born, six daughters and six blooming sons;
He gave his daughters to his sons for wives.
And they with their dear father and his queen
Banquet from day to day, with endless change
Of meats before them. In his halls all day   10
The sound of pipes is in the perfumed air;
At night the youths beside their modest wives
Sleep on fair couches spread with tapestry.
So coming to his town and fair abode,
I found a friendly welcome. One full month   15
The monarch kept me with him, and inquired
Of all that might concern the fate of Troy,
The Argive fleet, and the return to Greece,
And just as it befell I told him all.
And when I spake to him of going thence,   20
And prayed him to dismiss me, he complied,

184

And helped to make us ready for the sea.
The bladder of a bullock nine years old
He gave, in which he had compressed and bound
The stormy winds of air; for Cronus's son   25
Had given him empire o'er the winds, with power
To calm them or to rouse them at his will.
This in our roomy galley he made fast
With a bright chain of silver, that no breath
Of ruder air might blow. He only left   30
The west wind free to waft our ships and us
Upon our way. But that was not to be;
We perished by a folly of our own.
"Nine days we held our way, both day and night;
And now appeared in sight our native fields   35
On the tenth night, where on the shore we saw
Men kindling fires. Meantime a pleasant sleep
Had overcome my weary limbs, for long
Had I been guiding with incessant toil
The rudder, nor would trust it to the hand   40
Of any other, such was my desire
To reach our country by the shortest way.
Then talked my crew among themselves, and said
That I had brought with me from Aeolus,
The large-souled son of Hippotas, rich gifts   45
Of gold and silver. Standing side by side
And looking at each other, thus they said:
"How wonderfully is our chief revered
And loved by all men, wander where he will
Into what realm soever! From the coast   50
Of Troy he sailed with many precious things,
His share of spoil, while we, who with him went
And with him came, are empty-handed yet;

And now hath Aeolus, to show how much
He prizes him, bestowed the treasures here.   55
Come, let us see them; let us know how much
Of gold and silver is concealed in this.'
Thus speaking to each other, they obeyed
The evil counsel. They untied the sack,
And straight the winds rushed forth and seized the ship,   60
And swept the crews, lamenting bitterly.
Far from their country out upon the deep;
And then I woke, and in my noble mind
Bethought me whether I should drop at once
Into the deep and perish, or remain   65
And silently endure and keep my place
Among the living. I remained, endured,
And covered with my mantle lay within
My galley, while the furious whirlwind bore
Back to the Aeolian isle our groaning crews.   70
We landed on the coast, and to our barks
Brought water. Then my men prepared a meal
Beside the fleet; and having tasted food
And wine, I took a herald and a friend,
And, hastening to the sumptuous palace-halls   75
Of Aeolus, I found him with his wife
And children banqueting. We sat us down
Upon the threshold at the palace-doors,
And they were all astonished, and inquired:
'Why art thou here? What god thine enemy   80
Pursues thee, O Odysseus! whom we sent
So well prepared to reach thy native land,
Thy home, or any place that pleased thee most?
They spake, and sorrowfully I replied:
The fault is all with my unthinking crew   85

And my own luckless slumber. Yet, my friends,
Repair the mischief, for ye have the power.'
Thus with submissive words I spake, but they
Sat mute, the father only answered me:
'Hence with thee! Leave our island instantly,   90
Vilest of living men! It may not be
That I receive or aid as he departs
One who is hated by the blessed gods—
And thou art hated by the gods. Away!'
He spake, and sent us from the palace-door   95
Lamenting. Sorrowfully went we on.
And now with rowing hard and long—the fruit
Of our own folly—all our crews lost heart,
And every hope of safe return was gone.
Six days and nights we sailed; the seventh we came   100
To lofty Laestrigoni with wide gates,
The city of Lamos, where, on going forth,
The shepherd calls to shepherd entering in.
There might a man who never yields to sleep
Earn double wages, first in pasturing herds,   105
And then in tending sheep; for there the fields
Grazed in the daytime are by others grazed
At night. We reached its noble haven, girt
By towering rocks that rise on every side,
And the bold shores run out to form its mouth—   110
A narrow entrance. There the other crews
Stationed their barks, and moored them close beside
Each other, in that hill-encircled port.
No billow, even the smallest, rises there;
The water glimmers with perpetual calm.   115
I only kept my dark-hulled ship without,
And bound its cable to a jutting rock.

I climbed a rugged headland, and looked forth.
No marks of tilth appeared, the work of men
Or oxen, only smokes that from below   120
Rose in the air. And then I sent forth scouts
To learn what race of men who live by bread
Inhabited the land. Two chosen men
I sent, a herald made the third; and these
Went inland by a level path, on which   125
The wains brought fuel from the woody heights
Into the city. On their way they met,
Before the town, a damsel with a ewer—
The stately daughter of Antiphates,
The Laestrigonian, who was coming down;   130
To where Artacia's smoothly flowing fount
Gave water for the city. They drew near
And spake, and asked her who was sovereign there,
And who his people. Straight she pointed out
A lofty pile in which her father dwelt.   135
They entered that proud palace, and beheld,
Tall as a mountain peak, the monarch's wife,
And shuddered at the sight. With eager haste
She called her husband, King Antiphates,
From council. With a murderous intent   140
He came, and, seizing one of my poor friends,
Devoured him, while the other two betook
Themselves to sudden flight and reached the ships.
And then he raised a fearful yell that rang
Through all the city. The strong Laestrigons   145
Rushed forth by thousands from all sides, more like
To giants than to common men. They hurled
Stones of enormous weight from cliffs above,
And cries of those who perished and the crash

Of shattered galleys rose. They speared our friends   150
Like fishes for their horrid feasts, and thus
Bore them away. While those within the port
Were slaughtered, drawing my good sword I cut
The hawsers fastened to my ship's blue prow,
And cheered my men, and bade them fling themselves   155
Upon the oars, that so we might escape
Our threatened fate. They heard, and plied their oars
Like men who rowed for life. The galley shot
Forth from these beetling rocks into the sea
Full gladly; all the others perished there.   160
Onward we sailed, with sorrow in our hearts
For our lost friends, though glad to be reprieved
From death. And now we landed at an isle—
Aeaea, where the fair-haired Circe dwelt,
A goddess high in rank and skilled in song,   165
Own sister of the wise Aesetes. Both
Were children of the source of light, the Sun,
And Perse, Ocean's daughter, brought them forth.
We found a haven here, where ships might lie;
And guided by some deity we brought   170
Our galley silently against the shore,
And disembarked, and gave two days and nights
To rest, unmanned with hardship and with grief.
When bright-haired Morning brought the third day round,
I took my spear and my good sword, and left   175
The ship, and climbed a height, in hope to spy
Some trace of human toil, or hear some voice.
On a steep precipice I stood, and saw
From the broad earth below a rising smoke,
Where midst the thickets and the forest-ground   180
Stood Circe's palace. Seeing that dark smoke,

The thought arose within my mind that there
I should inquire. I pondered till at last
This seemed the wisest—to return at once
To my good ship upon the ocean-side,   185
And give my crew their meal, and send them forth
To view the region. Coming to the spot
Where lay my well-oared bark, some pitying god
Beneath whose eye I wandered forth alone
Sent a huge stag into my very path,   190
High-horned, which from his pasture in the wood
Descended to the river-side to drink,
For grievously he felt the hot sun's power.
Him as he ran I smote; the weapon pierced,
Just at the spine, the middle of his back.   195
The brazen blade passed through, and with a moan
He fell amid the dust, and yielded up
His life. I went to him, and set my foot
Against him, and plucked forth the brazen spear,
And left it leaning there. And then I broke   200
Lithe osiers from the shrubs, and twined of these
A rope, which, doubled, was an ell in length.
With that I tied the enormous creature's feet,
And slung him on my neck, and brought him thus
To my black ship. I used the spear to prop   205
My steps, since he no longer could be borne
Upon the shoulder, aided by the hand,
Such was the animal's bulk. I flung him down
Before the ship, encouraging my men
With cheerful words, and thus I said to each: 210
'My friends, we will not, wretched as we are,
Go down to Hades' realm before our time.
While food and wine are yet within the hold

Of our good galley, let us not forget
Our daily meals, and famine-stricken pine.'   215
"I spake; they all obeyed, and at my word
Came forth, and standing by the barren deep
Admired the stag, for he was huge of bulk;
And when their eyes were tired with wondering,
My people washed their hands, and soon had made   220
A noble banquet ready. All that day
Till set of sun we sat and feasted there
Upon the abundant meat and delicate wine;
And when the sun went down, and darkness came,
We slept upon the shore. But when the Morn,   225
The rosy-fingered child of Dawn, looked forth,
I called a council of my men and spake:
'Give ear, my friends, amid your sufferings,
To words that I shall say. We cannot here
Know which way lies the west, nor where the east,   230
Nor where the sun, that shines for all mankind,
Descends below the earth, nor where again
He rises from it. Yet will we consult,
If room there be for counsel—which I doubt,
For when I climbed that height I overlooked   235
An isle surrounded by the boundless deep—
An isle low lying. In the midst I saw
Smoke rising from a thicket of the wood.'
I spake; their courage died within their hearts
As they remembered what Antiphates,   240
The Laestrigon, had done, and what foul deeds
The cannibal Cyclops, and they wept aloud.
Tears flowed abundantly, but tears were now
Of no avail to our unhappy band.
Numbering my well-armed men, I made of them   245

Two equal parties, giving each its chief.
Myself commanded one; Eurylochus,
The hero, took the other in his charge.
Then in a brazen helm we shook the lots;
The lot of brave Eurylochus leaped forth,   250
And he with two-and-twenty of our men
Went forward with quick steps, and yet in tears,
While we as sorrowful were left behind.
They found the fair abode where Circe dwelt,
A palace of hewn stone within the vale,   255
Yet nobly seated. There were mountain wolves
And lions round it, which herself had tamed
With powerful drugs; yet these assaulted not
The visitors, but, wagging their long tails,
Stood on their hinder feet, and fawned on them,   260
Like mastiffs on their master when he comes
From banqueting and brings them food. So fawned
The strong-clawed wolves and lions on my men.
With fear my men beheld those beasts of prey,
Yet went, and, standing in the portico   265
Of the bright-haired divinity, they heard
Her sweet voice singing, as within she threw
The shuttle through the wide immortal web,
Such as is woven by the goddesses—
Delicate, bright of hue, and beautiful.   270
Polites then, a chief the most beloved
And most discreet of all my comrades, spake:
'Someone is here, my friends, who sweetly sings,
Weaving an ample web, and all the floor
Rings to her voice. Whoever she may be,   275
Woman or goddess, let us call to her.'
He spake; aloud they called, and forth she came

And threw at once the shining doors apart,
And bade my comrades enter. Without thought
They followed her. Eurylochus alone   280
Remained without, for he suspected guile.
She led them in and seated them on thrones.
Then mingling for them Pramnian wine with cheese,
Meal, and fresh honey, and infusing drugs
Into the mixture—drugs which made them lose   285
The memory of their home—she handed them
The beverage and they drank. Then instantly
She touched them with a wand, and shut them up
In sties, transformed to swine in head and voice,
Bristles and shape, though still the human mind   290
Remained to them. Thus sorrowing they were driven
Into their cells, where Circe flung to them
Acorns of oak and ilex, and the fruit
Of cornel, such as nourish wallowing swine.
"Back came Eurylochus to our good ship   295
With news of our poor comrades and their fate,
He strove to speak, but could not; he was stunned
By that calamity; his eyes were filled
With tears, and his whole soul was given to grief.
We marveled greatly; long we questioned him,   300
And thus he spake of our lost friends at last:
'Through yonder thickets, as thou gav'st command,
Illustrious chief! we went, until we reached
A stately palace of hewn stones, within
A vale, yet nobly seated. Someone there,   305
Goddess or woman, weaving busily
An ample web, sang sweetly as she wrought.
My comrades called aloud, and forth she came,
And threw at once the shining doors apart,

And bade us enter. Without thought the rest   310
Followed, while I alone, suspecting guile,
Remained without. My comrades, from that hour,
Were seen no more; not one of them again
Came forth, though long I sat and watched for them.'
He spake; I slung my silver-studded sword   315
Upon my shoulders—a huge blade of brass—
And my bow with it, and commanded him
To lead the way. He seized and clasped my knees
With both his hands in attitude of prayer,
And sorrowfully said these winged words: 320
'Take me not thither; force me not to go,
O foster-child of Zeus! but leave me here;
For thou wilt not return, I know, nor yet
Deliver one of our lost friends. Our part
Is to betake ourselves to instant flight   325
With these who yet remain, and so escape.'
He spake, and I replied: 'Eurylochus,
Remain thou here, beside our roomy ship,
Eating and drinking. I shall surely go.
A strong necessity is laid on me.'   330
I spake, and from the ship and shore went up
Into the isle and when I found myself
Within that awful valley, and not far
From the great palace in which Circe dwelt,
The sorceress, there met me on my way   335
A youth; he seemed in manhood's early prime,
When youth has most of grace. He took my hand
And held it, and, accosting me, began:
'Rash mortal! whither art thou wandering thus
Alone among the hills, where every place   340
Is strange to thee? Thy comrades are shut up

In Circe's palace in close cells like swine.
Com'st thou to set them free? Nay, thou like them
Wilt rather find thyself constrained to stay.
Let me bestow the means to make thee safe   345
Against that mischief. Take this potent herb,
And bear it with thee to the palace-halls
Of Circe, and it shall avert from thee
The threatened evil. I will now reveal
The treacherous arts of Circe. She will bring   350
A mingled draught to thee, and drug the bowl,
But will not harm thee thus; the virtuous plant
I gave thee will prevent it. Hear yet more:
When she shall smite thee with her wand, draw forth
Thy good sword from thy thigh and rush at her   355
As if to take her life, and she will crouch
In fear, and will solicit thine embrace.
Refuse her not, that so she may release
Thy comrades, and may send thee also back
To thine own land; but first exact of her   360
The solemn oath which binds the blessed gods,
That she will meditate no other harm
To thee, nor strip thee of thy manly strength.'
The Argus-queller spake, and plucked from earth
The potent plant and handed it to me,   365
And taught me all its powers. The root is black,
The blossom white as milk. Among the gods
Its name is Moly; hard it is for men
To dig it up; the gods find nothing hard.'
Back through the woody island Hermes went   370
Toward high Olympus, while I took my way
To Circe's halls, yet with a beating heart.
There, as I stood beneath the portico

Of that bright-haired divinity, I called
Aloud; the goddess heard my voice and came,   375
And threw at once the shining doors apart,
And prayed me to come in. I followed her,
Yet grieving still. She led me in and gave
A seat upon a silver-studded throne,
Beautiful, nobly wrought, and placed beneath   380
A footstool, and prepared a mingled draught
Within a golden chalice, and infused
A drug with mischievous intent. She gave
The cup; I drank it off; the charm wrought not,
And then she smote me with her wand and said: 385
'Go to the sty, and with thy fellows sprawl.'
She spake; but drawing forth the trusty sword
Upon my thigh, I rushed at her as if
To take her life. She shrieked and, stooping low,
Ran underneath my arm and clasped my knees,   390
And uttered piteously these winged words:
'Who art thou? of what race and of what land,
And who thy parents? I am wonder-struck
To see that thou couldst drink that magic juice
And yield not to its power. No living man,   395
Whoever he might be, that tasted once
Those drugs, or passed them o'er his lips, has yet
Withstood them. In thy breast a spirit dwells
Not to be thus subdued. Art thou not then
Odysseus, master of wise stratagems,   400
Whose coming hither, on his way from Troy,
In his black galley, oft has been foretold
By Hermes of the golden wand? But sheathe
Thy sword and share my couch, that, joined in love,
Each may hereafter trust the other's faith.'   405

She spake, and I replied: 'How canst thou ask,
Circe, that I gently deal with thee,
Since thou, in thine own palace, hast transformed
My friends to swine, and plottest even now
To keep me with thee, luring me to pass   410
Into thy chamber and to share thy couch,
That thou mayst strip me of my manly strength
I come not to thy couch till thou engage,
O goddess, by a solemn oath, that thou
Wilt never seek to do me further harm.'   415
I spake; she straightway took the oath required,
And, after it was uttered and confirmed,
Up to her sumptuous couch I went. Meanwhile
Four diligent maidens ministered within
The palace—servants of the household they,   420
Who had their birth from fountains and from groves,
And sacred rivers flowing to the sea.
One spread the thrones with gorgeous coverings;
Above was purple arras, and beneath
Were linen webs; another, setting forth   425
The silver tables just before the thrones,
Placed on them canisters of gold; a third
Mingled the rich wines in a silver bowl,
And placed the golden cups; and, last, the fourth
Brought water from the fountain, and beneath   430
A massive tripod kindled a great fire
And warmed the water. When it boiled within
The shining brass, she led me to the bath,
And washed me from the tripod. On my head
And shoulders pleasantly she shed the streams   435
That from my members took away the sense
Of weariness, unmanning body and mind.

And when she thus had bathed me and with oil
Anointed me, she put a princely cloak
And tunic on me, led me in, and showed   440
My seat—a stately silver-studded throne,
High-wrought—and placed a footstool for my feet.
Then came a handmaid with a golden ewer,
And from it poured pure water for my hands
Into a silver laver. Next she placed   445
A polished table near to me, on which
The matron of the palace laid the feast,
With many delicacies from her store,
And bade me eat. The banquet pleased me not.
My thoughts were elsewhere; dark imaginings   450
Were in my mind. When Circe marked my mood,
As in a gloomy revery I sat,
And put not forth my hands to touch the feast,
She came to me and spake these winged words:
'Why sittest thou like one who has no power   455
Of speech, Odysseus, wrapt in thoughts that gnaw
Thy heart, and tasting neither food nor wine?
Still dost thou dream of fraud? It is not well
That thou shouldst fear it longer, since I pledged
Myself against it with a mighty oath.'   460
She spake, and I replied: 'What man whose heart
Is faithful could endure to taste of food
Or wine till he should see his captive friends
Once more at large? If with a kind intent
Thou bidst me eat and drink, let me behold   465
With mine own eyes my dear companions free.'
I spake; and Circe took her wand and went
Forth from her halls, and, opening the gate
That closed the sty, drove forth what seemed a herd

Of swine in their ninth year. They ranged themselves 470
Before her, and she went from each to each
And shed on them another drug. Forthwith
Fell from their limbs the bristles which had grown
All over them, when mighty Circe gave
At first the baleful potion. Now again 475
My friends were men, and younger than before,
And of a nobler mien and statelier growth.
They knew me all; and each one pressed my hand
In his, and there were tears and sobs of joy
That sounded through the palace. Circe too 480
Was moved, the mighty goddess; she drew near
And stood by me, and spake these winged words:
'Son of Laertes, nobly born and wise,
Odysseus! go to thy good ship beside
The sea and draw it up the beach, and hide 485
The goods and weapons in the caverns there,
And come thou back and bring with thee thy friends.'
She spake, and easily my generous mind
Was moved by what she said. Forthwith I went
To my good ship beside the sea, and found 490
My friends in tears, lamenting bitterly.
As in some grange the calves come leaping round
A herd of kine returning to the stall
From grassy fields where they have grazed their fill,
Nor can the stall contain the young which spring 495
Around their mothers with continual bleat;
So when my comrades saw me through their tears,
They sprang to meet me, and their joy was such
As if they were in their own native land
And their own city, on the rugged coast 500
Of Ithaca, where they were born and reared;

And as they wept they spake these winged words:
'O foster-child of Zeus! we welcome thee
On thy return with a delight as great
As if we all had reached again the land   505
That gave us birth, our Ithaca. And now
Tell by what death our other friends have died.'
They spake; I answered with consoling words:
'First draw our galley up the beach, and hide
Our goods and all our weapons in the caves,   510
And then let all make haste to follow me,
And see our friends in Circe's sacred halls,
Eating and drinking at the plenteous board.'
I spake; and cheerfully my men obeyed,
Save that Eurylochus alone essayed   515
To hold them back, and spake these winged words:
'Ah, whither are we going, wretched ones?
Are ye so eager for an evil fate,
That ye must go where Circe dwells, who waits
To turn us into lions, swine, or wolves,   520
Forced to remain and guard her spacious house?
So was it with the Cyclops, when our friends
Went with this daring chief to his abode,
And perished there through his foolhardiness.'
He spake; and then I thought to draw my sword   525
From my stout thigh, and with the trenchant blade
Strike off his head and let it fall to earth,
Though he were my near kinsman; yet the rest
Restrained me, each one speaking kindly words:
'Nay, foster-child of Zeus! if thou consent,   530
This man shall stay behind and with the ship,
And he shall guard the ship, but lead us thou
To where the sacred halls of Circe stand.'

They spake, and from the ship and shore went up
Into the land, nor was Eurylochus   535
Left with the ship; he followed, for he feared
My terrible threat Meantime had Circe bathed
My comrades at the palace, and with oil
Anointed them, and robed them in fair cloaks
And tunics. There we found them banqueting.   540
When they and those who came with me beheld
Each other, and the memory of the past
And all the palace echoed with their sobs.
And then the mighty goddess came and said: 545
'Son of Laertes, nobly born and wise,
Prolong thou not these sorrows. Well I know
What ye have suffered on the fishy deep,
And all the evil that malignant men
Have done to you on land. Now take the food   550
Before you, drink the wine, till ye receive
Into your hearts the courage that was yours
When long ago ye left your fatherland,
The rugged Ithaca. Ye are unnerved
And spiritless with thinking constantly   555
On your long wanderings, and your minds allow
No space for mirth, for ye have suffered much.'
She spake; her words persuaded easily
Our generous minds, and there from day to day
We lingered a full year, and banqueted   560
Nobly on plenteous meats and delicate wines.
But when the year was ended, and the hours
Renewed their circle, my beloved friends
From Circe's palace called me forth and said:
'Good chief, do not forget thy native land,   565
If fate indeed permit that ever thou

Return in safety to that lofty pile
Thy palace in the country of thy birth.
So spake they, and my generous mind was moved.
All that day long until the set of sun   570
We sat and feasted on the abundant meats
And delicate wines; and when the sun went down
They took their rest within the darkened halls,
While I to Circe's sumptuous couch went up,
A suppliant at her knees. The goddess heard   575
My prayer, as thus in winged words I said:
'O Circe! make, I pray, the promise good
Which thou hast given, to send me to my home.
My heart is pining for it, and the hearts
Of all my friends, who weary out my life   580
Lamenting round me when thou art not nigh.'
I spake; the mighty goddess thus replied:
'Son of Laertes, nobly born and wise,
Odysseus! ye must not remain with me
Unwillingly; but ye have yet to make   585
Another voyage, and must visit first
The abode of Hades, and of Proserpine
His dreaded queen, and there consult the soul
Of the blind seer Tiresias—him of Thebes—
Whose intellect was spared; for Proserpine   590
Gave back to him in death the power of mind,
That only he might know of things to come.
The rest are shades that flit from place to place.'
Thus spake the goddess; and my heart was wrung
With sorrow, and I sat upon the couch   595
And wept, nor could I longer wish to live
And see the light of day. But when my grief,
With shedding tears and tossing where I sat,

Was somewhat spent, I spake to Circe thus:
'O Circe, who will guide me when I make   600
This voyage? for no galley built by man
Has ever yet arrived at Hades' realm.'
I spake: the mighty goddess answered me:
'Son of Laertes, nobly born and wise,
Take thou no thought of who shall guide thy bark,   605
But raise the mast and spread the glimmering sail,
And seat thyself, and let the north-wind waft
Thy galley on. As soon as thou shalt cross
Oceanus, and come to the low shore
And groves of Proserpine, the lofty groups   610
Of poplars, and the willows that let fall
Their withered fruit, moor thou thy galley there
In the deep eddies of Oceanus,
And pass to Hades' comfortless abode.
There into Acheron are poured the streams   615
Of Pyriphlegethon, and of that arm
Of Styx, Cocytus. At the place where meet
The ever-roaring waters stands a rock;
Draw near to that, and there I bid thee scoop
In earth a trench, a cubit long and wide.   620
And round about it pour to all the dead
Libations—milk and honey first, and next
Rich wine, and lastly water, scattering
White meal upon them. Offer there thy prayer
Fervently to that troop of airy forms,   625
And make the vow that thou wilt sacrifice,
When thou at last shalt come to Ithaca,
A heifer without blemish, barren yet,
In thine own courts, and heap the altar-pyre
With things of price; and to the seer alone,   630

Tiresias, by himself, a ram whose fleece
Is wholly black, the best of all thy flocks.
And after thou hast duly offered prayer
To all the illustrious nations of the dead,
Then sacrifice a ram and a black ewe,   635
Their faces turned toward Erebus, but thine
The other way and toward the river streams.
Thither the souls of those who died will flock
In multitudes. Then call thy friends, and give
Command to flay in haste the sheep that lie   640
Slain by the cruel brass, and, burning there
The carcasses, pay worship to the gods—
The powerful Hades and dread Proserpine.
Draw then the sword upon thy thigh, and sit,
And suffer none of all those airy forms   645
To touch the blood until thou first bespeak
Tiresias. He will come, and speedily—
The leader of the people—and will tell
What voyage thou must make, what length of way
Thou yet must measure, and will show thee how   650
Thou mayst return across the fishy deep.'
She spake; and while she spake the Morn looked forth
Upon her golden throne. The Nymph bestowed
On me a cloak and tunic, and arrayed
Herself in a white robe with ample folds—   655
A delicate web and graceful. Round her loins
She clasped a shining zone of gold, and hung
A veil upon her forehead. Forth I went
Throughout the palace and aroused my friends,
And thus I said in cheerful tones to each: 660
'No longer give yourselves to idle rest
And pleasant slumber; we are to depart.

The gracious Circe counsels us to go.'
I spake, and easily their generous minds
Inclined to me. Yet brought I not away   665
All my companions safely from the isle.
Elpenor was the youngest of our band,
Not brave in war was he, nor wise in thought.
He, overcome with wine, and for the sake
Of coolness, had lain down to sleep, apart   670
From all the rest, in Circe's sacred house;
And as my friends bestirred themselves, the noise
And tumult roused him; he forgot to come
By the long staircase; headlong from the roof
He plunged; his neck was broken at the spine,   675
And his soul went to the abode of death.
My friends came round me, and I said to them:
'Haply your thought may be that you are bound
For the dear country of your birth; but know
That Circe sends us elsewhere, to consult   680
The Theban seer, Tiresias, in the abode
Of Hades and the dreaded Proserpine.'
I spake, and their hearts failed them as they heard;
They sat them down, and wept, and tore their hair,
But fruitless were their sorrow and their tears.   685
Thus as we sadly moved to our good ship
Upon the sea-shore, weeping all the while,
Circe, meantime, had visited its deck,
And there had bound a ram and a black ewe
By means we saw not; for what eye discerns   690
The presence of a deity, who moves
From place to place, and wills not to be seen?"

BOOK XI

Now, when we reached our galley by the shore,   1
We drew it first into the mighty deep,
And set the mast and sails, and led on board
The sheep, and sorrowfully and in tears
Embarked ourselves. The fair-haired and august   5
Circe, expert in music, sent with us
A kindly fellow-voyager—a wind
That breathed behind the dark-prowed bark, and swelled
The sails; and now, with all things in their place
Throughout the ship, we sat us down—the breeze   10
And helmsman guiding us upon our way.
All day our sails were stretched, as o'er the deep
Our vessel ran; the sun went down; the paths
Of the great sea were darkened, and our bark
Reached the far confines of Oceanus.   15
There lies the land, and there the people dwell
Of the Cimmerians, in eternal cloud
And darkness. Never does the glorious sun
Look on them with his rays, when he goes up
Into the starry sky, nor when again   20
He sinks from heaven to earth. Unwholesome night

O'erhangs the wretched race. We touched the land,
And, drawing up our galley on the beach,
Took from on board the sheep, and followed
Beside the ocean-stream until we reached   25
The place of which the goddess Circe spake.
"Here Perimedes and Eurylochus
Held in their grasp the victims, while I drew
The trusty sword upon my thigh, and scooped
A trench in earth, a cubit long and wide,   30
Round which we stood, and poured to all the dead
Libations—milk and honey first, and next
Rich wine, and lastly water, scattering
White meal upon them. Then I offered prayer
Fervently to that troop of airy forms,   35
And made a vow that I would sacrifice,
When I at last should come to Ithaca,
A heifer without blemish, barren yet,
In my own courts, and heap the altar-pyre
With things of price, and to the seer alone,   40
Tiresias, by himself, a ram whose fleece
Was wholly black, the best of all my flocks.
When I had worshiped thus with prayer and vows
The nations of the dead, I took the sheep
And pierced their throats above the hollow trench.   45
The blood flowed dark; and thronging round me came
Souls of the dead from Erebus—young wives
And maids unwedded, men worn out with years
And toil, and virgins of a tender age
In their new grief, and many a warrior slain   50
In battle, mangled by the spear, and clad
In bloody armor, who about the trench
Flitted on every side, now here, now there,

With gibbering cries, and I grew pale with fear.
Then calling to my friends, I bade them flay   55
The victims lying slaughtered by the knife,
And, burning them with fire, invoke the gods—
The mighty Hades and dread Proserpine.
Then from my thigh I drew the trusty sword,
And sat me down, and suffered none of all   60
Those airy phantoms to approach the blood
Until I should bespeak the Theban seer.
And first the soul of my companion came,
Elpenor, for he was not buried yet
In earth's broad bosom. We had left him dead   65
In Circe's halls, unwept and unentombed.
We had another task. But when I now
Beheld I pitied him, and, shedding tears,
I said these winged words: 'How earnest thou,
Elpenor, hither into these abodes   70
Of night and darkness? Thou hast made more speed,
Although on foot, than I in my good ship.'
I spake; the phantom sobbed and answered me:
'Son of Laertes, nobly born and wise,
Odysseus! 'twas the evil doom decreed   75
By some divinity, and too much wine,
That wrought my death. I laid myself to sleep
In Circe's palace, and, remembering not
The way to the long stairs that led below,
Fell from the roof, and by the fall my neck   80
Was broken at the spine; my soul went down
To Hades. I conjure thee now, by those
Whom thou hast left behind and far away,
Thy consort and thy father—him by whom
Thou when a boy wert reared—and by thy son   85

Telemachus, who in thy palace-halls
Is left alone—for well I know that thou,
In going hence from Hades' realm, wilt moor
Thy gallant vessel in the Aeaean isle—
That there, O king, thou wilt remember me,   90
And leave me not when thou departest thence
Unwept, unburied, lest I bring on thee
The anger of the gods. But burn me there
With all the armor that I wore, and pile,
Close to the hoary deep, a mound for me—   95
A hapless man of whom posterity
Shall hear. Do this for me, and plant upright
Upon my tomb the oar with which I rowed,
While yet a living man, among thy friends.'
He spake and I replied: 'Unhappy youth,   100
All this I duly will perform for thee.'
And then the soul of Anticleia came—
My own dead mother, daughter of the king
Autolycus, large-minded. Her I left
Alive, what time I sailed for Troy, and now   105
I wept to see her there, and pitied her,
And yet forbade her, though with grief, to come
Near to the blood till I should first accost
Tiresias. He too came, the Theban seer,
Tiresias, bearing in his hand a wand   110
Of gold; he knew me and bespake me thus:
'Why, O unhappy mortal, hast thou left
The light of day to come among the dead
And to this joyless land? Go from the trench
And turn thy sword away, that I may drink us   115
The blood, and speak the word of prophecy.'
He spake; withdrawing from the trench, I thrust

Into its sheath my silver-studded sword,
And after drinking of the dark red blood
The blameless prophet turned to me and said: 120
'Illustrious chief Odysseus, thy desire
Is for a happy passage to thy home,
Yet will a god withstand thee. Not unmarked
By Poseidon shalt thou, as I deem, proceed
Upon thy voyage. He hath laid up wrath   125
Against thee in his heart, for that thy hand
Deprived his son of sight. Yet may ye still
Return, though after many hardships borne,
If thou but hold thy appetite in check,
And that of thy companions, when thou bring   130
Thy gallant bark to the Trinacrian isle,
Safe from the gloomy deep. There will ye find
The beeves and fatling wethers of the Sun—
The all-beholding and all-hearing Sun.
If these ye leave unharmed, and keep in mind   135
The thought of your return, ye may go back,
Though sufferers, to your home in Ithaca;
But if thou do them harm, the event will be
Destruction to thy ship and to its crew;
And thou, if thou escape it, wilt return   140
Late to thy country, all thy comrades lost,
And in a foreign bark, and thou shalt find
Wrong in thy household—arrogant men who waste
Thy substance, wooers of thy noble wife,
And offering bridal gifts. On thy return   145
Thou shalt avenge thee of their violent deeds;
And when thou shalt have slain them in thy halls,
Whether by stratagem or by the sword
In open fight, then take a shapely oar

And journey on, until thou meet with men   150
Who have not known the sea nor eaten food
Seasoned with salt, nor ever have beheld
Galleys with crimson prows, nor shapely oars,
Which are the wings of ships. I will declare
A sign by which to know them, nor canst thou   155
Mistake it. When a traveler, meeting thee,
Shalt say that thou dost bear a winnowing-fan
Upon thy sturdy shoulder, stop and plant
Thy shapely oar upright in earth, and there
Pay to King Poseidon solemn sacrifice—   160
A ram, a bull, and from his herd of swine
A boar. And then returning to thy home,
See that thou offer hallowed hecatombes
To all the ever-living ones who dwell
In the broad heaven, to each in order due.   165
So at the last thy death shall come to thee
Far from the sea, and gently take thee off
In a serene old age that ends among
A happy people. I have told thee true.'
He spake, and thus I answered him: 'The gods,   170
Tiresias, have decreed as thou hast said.
But tell, and tell me truly—I behold
The soul of my dead mother; there she sits
In silence by the blood, and will not deign
To look upon her son nor speak to him.   175
Instruct me, mighty prophet, by what means
To make my mother know me for her son.'
I spake, and instantly the seer replied:
'Easily that is told; I give it thee
To bear in mind. Whoever of the dead   180
Thou sufferest to approach and drink the blood

Will speak the truth; those whom thou dost forbid
To taste the blood will silently withdraw.'
The soul of King Tiresias, saying this,
Passed to the abode of Hades; he had given   185
The oracle I asked. I waited still
Until my mother, drawing near again,
Drank the dark blood; she knew me suddenly,
And said in piteous tones these winged words:
'How didst thou come, my child, a living man,   190
Into this place of darkness? Difficult
It is for those who breathe the breath of life
To visit these abodes, through which are rolled
Great rivers, fearful floods—the first of these
Oceanus, whose waters none can cross   195
On foot, or save on board a trusty bark.
Hast thou come hither on thy way from Troy,
A weary wanderer with thy ship and friends?
And hast thou not been yet at Ithaca,
Nor in thine island palace seen thy wife?'   200
She spake, I answered: "Tis necessity,
Dear mother, that has brought me to the abode
Of Hades, to consult the Theban seer,
Tiresias. Not to the Achaean coast
Have I returned, nor reached our country, yet   205
Continually I wander; everywhere
I meet misfortune—even from the time
When, in the noble Agamemnon's train,
I came to Ilium, famed for steeds, and made
War on its dwellers. Tell me now, I pray,   210
And truly, how it was that fate on thee
Brought the long sleep of death? by slow disease?
Or, stealing on thee, did the archer-queen,

Artemis, slay thee with her silent shafts?
And tell me of my father, and the son   215
Left in my palace. Rests the sway I bore
On them, or has another taken it,
Since men believe I shall return no more?
And tell me of my wedded wife, her thoughts
And purposes, and whether she remains   220
Yet with my son. Is she the guardian still
Of my estates, or has the noblest chief
Of those Achaeans led her thence a bride?'
I spake; my reverend mother answered thus:
'Most certain is it that she sadly dwells   225
Still in thy palace. Weary days and nights
And tears are hers. No man has taken yet
Thy place as ruler, but Telemachus
Still has the charge of thy domain, and gives
The liberal feasts which it befits a prince   230
To give, for all invite him. In the fields
Thy father dwells, and never in the town
Is seen; nor beds nor cloaks has he, nor mats
Of rich device, but, all the winter through,
He sleeps where sleep the laborers, on the hearth,   235
Amid the dust, and wears a wretched garb;
And when the summer comes, or autumn days
Ripen the fruit, his bed is on the ground,
And made of leaves, that everywhere are shed
In the rich vineyards. There he lies and grieves,   240
And, cherishing his sorrow, mourns thy fate,
And keenly feels the miseries of age.
And thus I underwent my fate and died;
For not the goddess of the unerring bow
Stealing upon me smote me in thy halls   245

With silent arrows, nor did slow disease
Come o'er me, such as, wasting cruelly
The members, takes at last the life away;
But constant longing for thee, anxious thoughts
Of thee, and memory of thy gentleness,   250
Odysseus, made an end of my sweet life.'
She spake; I longed to take into my arms
The soul of my dead mother. Thrice I tried,
Moved by a strong desire, and thrice the form
Passed through them like a shadow or a dream.   255
And then did the great sorrow in my heart
Grow sharper, and in winged words I said:
'Beloved mother, why wilt thou not keep
Thy place, that I may clasp thee, so that here,
In Hades' realm and in each other's arms,   260
We each might in the other soothe the sense
Of misery? Hath mighty Proserpine
Sent but an empty shade to meet me here,
That I might only grieve and sigh the more?'
I spake, and then my reverend mother said: 255
'Believe not that Zeus's daughter Proserpine
Deceives thee. 'Tis the lot of all our race
When they are dead. No more the sinews bind
The bones and flesh, when once from the white bones
The life departs. Then like a dream the soul   260
Flies off, and flits about from place to place.
But haste thou to the light again, and mark
What I have said, that thou in after days
Mayst tell it to thy wife on thy return.'
Thus we conferred. Meantime the women came   275
Around me, moved by mighty Proserpine;
In throngs they gathered to the dark red blood.

Then, as I pondered how to question each,
This seemed the wisest—from my sturdy thigh
I plucked the trenchant sword, and suffered not   280
All that were there to taste the blood at once;
So one by one they came, and each in turn
Declared her lineage. Thus I questioned all.
"Then saw I high-born Tyro first, who claimed
To be the daughter of that blameless man   285
Salmoneus, and who called herself the wife
Of Cretheus, son of Aeolus. She loved
Enipeus, hallowed river, fairest stream
Of all that flow on earth, and often walked
Beside its pleasant waters. He whose arms   290
Surround the islands, Poseidon, once put on
The river's form, and at its gulfy mouth
Met her; the purple waters stood upright
Around them like a wall, and formed an arch,
And hid the god and woman. There he loosed   295
The virgin zone of Tyro, shedding sleep
Upon her. Afterward he took her hand
And said: 'Rejoice, O maiden, in our love,
For with the year's return shalt thou bring forth
Illustrious sons; the embraces of the gods   300
Are not unfruitful. Rear them carefully.
And now return to thy abode, and watch
Thy words, and keep thy secret. Thou must know
That I am Poseidon, he who shakes the earth.'
He spake, and plunged into the billowy deep.   305
And she became a mother, and brought forth
Pelias and Neleus, valiant ministers
Of mighty Zeus. On the broad lands
Of Iaolchos Pelias dwelt, and reared

Vast flocks of sheep, while Neleus made his home   310
In Pylos midst the sands. The queenly dame,
His mother, meanwhile brought forth other sons
To Cretheus—Aeson first, and Pheres next,
And Amythaon, great in horsemanship.

And after her I saw Antiope,   315
The daughter of Asopus—her who made
A boast that she had slumbered in the arms
Of Zeus. Two sons she bore—Amphion one,
The other Zethus—and they founded Thebes
With its seven gates, and girt it round with towers;   320
For, valiant as they were, they could not dwell
Safely in that great town unfenced by towers.
And after her I saw Amphitryon's wife,
Alcmena, her who brought forth Hercules,
The dauntless hero of the lion-heart—   325
For she had given herself into the arms
Of mighty Zeus. I also saw
Megara there, a daughter of the house
Of haughty Creion. Her Amphitryon's son,
Untamable in strength, had made his wife.   330
"The mother, too, of Oedipus I saw,
Beautiful Epicaste, who in life
Had done unwittingly a heinous deed—
Had married her own son, who, having slain
Her father first, espoused her; but the gods   335
Published abroad the rumor of the crime.
He in the pleasant town of Thebes bore sway
O'er the Cadmeians; yet in misery
He lived, for so the offended gods ordained.
And she went down to Hades and the gates   340
That stand forever barred; for, wild with grief,

She slung a cord upon a lofty beam
And perished by it, leaving him to bear
Woes without measure, such as on a son
The furies of a mother might inflict.   345
"And there I saw the dame supremely fair,
Chloris, whom Neleus with large marriage-gifts
Wooed, and brought home a bride; the youngest she
Among the daughters of Iasus' son,
Amphion, ruler o'er Orchomenus,   350
The Minyeian town, and o'er the realm
Of Pylos. Three illustrious sons she bore
To Neleus—Nestor, Chromius, and a chief
Of lofty bearing, Periclymenus.
She brought forth Pero also, marvelous   355
In beauty, wooed by all the region round;
But Neleus would bestow the maid on none
Save him who should drive off from Phylace
The beeves, broad-fronted and with crooked horns,
Of valiant Iphicles—a difficult task.   360
One man alone, a blameless prophet, dared
Attempt it; but he found himself withstood
By fate, and rigid fetters, and a force
Of rustic herdsmen. Months and days went by,
And the full year, led by the hours, came round.   365
The valiant Iphicles, who from the seer
Had heard the oracles explained, took off
The shackles, and the will of Zeus was done.
"Then saw I Leda, wife of Tyndarus,
Who bore to Tyndarus two noble sons,   370
Castor the horseman, Pollux skilled to wield
The cestus. Both of them have still a place
Upon the fruitful earth; for Zeus

Gave them such honor that they live by turns
Each one a day, and then are with the dead   375
Each one by turns; they rank among the gods.
The wife of Aloeus next appeared.
Iphidameia, who, as she declared,
Had won the love of Poseidon. She brought forth
Two short-lived sons—one like a god in form,   380
Named Otus; and the other, far renowned,
Named Ephialtes. These the bounteous earth
Nourished to be the tallest of mankind,
And goodliest, save Orion. When the twain
Had seen but nine years of their life, they stood   385
In breadth of frame nine cubits, and in height
Nine fathoms. They against the living gods
Threatened to wage, upon the Olympian height,
Fierce and tumultuous battle, and to fling
Ossa upon Olympus, and to pile   390
Pelion, with all its growth of leafy woods,
On Ossa, that the heavens might thus be scaled.
And they, if they had reached their prime of youth,
Had made their menace good. The son of Zeus
And amber-haired Latona took their lives   395
Ere yet beneath their temples sprang the down
And covered with its sprouting tufts the chin.
"Phaedra I saw, and Procris, and the child
Of the wise Minos, Ariadne, famed
For beauty, whom the hero Theseus once   400
From Crete to hallowed Athens' fertile coast
Led, but possessed her not. Artemis gave
Ear to the tale which Bacchus brought to her,
And in the isle of Dia slew the maid.
And Maera I beheld, and Clymene,   405

And Eriphyle, hateful in her guilt,
Who sold her husband for a price in gold.
But vainly might I think to name them all—
The wives and daughters of heroic men
Whom I beheld—for first the ambrosial night   410
Would wear away. And now for me the hour
Of sleep is come, at my good ship among
My friends, or haply here. Meantime the care
For my return is with the gods and you."
He spake, and all were silent: all within   415
The shadows of those palace-halls were held
Motionless by the charm of what he said.
And thus the white-armed Queen Arete spake:
"Phaeacians, how appears this man to you
In form, in stature, and well-judging mind?   420
My guest he is, but each among you shares
The honor of the occasion. Now, I pray,
Dismiss him not in haste, nor sparingly
Bestow your gifts on one in so much need;
For in your dwellings is much wealth, bestowed   425
Upon you by the bounty of the gods."
Then also Echeneus, aged chief,
The oldest man of the Phaeacians, spake:
"My friends, the word of our sagacious queen
Errs not, nor is ill-timed, and yours it is   430
To hearken and obey: but all depends
Upon Alcinous—both the word and deed."
And then in turn Alcinous spake: "That word
Shall be fulfilled, if I am ruler here
O'er the Phaeacians, skilled in seamanship.   435
But let the stranger, though he long for home,
Bear to remain till morning, that his store

Of gifts may be complete. To send him home
Shall be the charge of all, but mostly mine,
Since mine it is to hold the sovereign power."   440
And then the wise Odysseus said: "King
Alcinous, eminent o'er all thy race!
Shouldst thou command me to remain with thee
Even for a twelvemonth, and at length provide
For my return, and give me princely gifts,   445
Even that would please me; for with fuller hands,
The happier were my lot on my return
To my own land. I should be honored then,
And meet a kinder welcome there from all
Who see me in my Ithaca once more."   450
And then again in turn Alcinous spake:
"Odysseus, when we look on thee, we feel
No fear that thou art false, or one of those,
The many, whom the dark earth nourishes,
Wandering at large, and forging lies, that we   455
May not suspect them. Thou hast grace of speech
And noble thoughts, and fitly hast thou told,
Even as a minstrel might, the history
Of all thy Argive brethren and thy own.
Now say, and frankly, didst thou also see   460
Any of those heroic men who went
With thee to Troy, and in that region met
Their fate? A night immeasurably long
Is yet before us. Let us have thy tale
Of wonders. I could listen till the break   465
Of hallowed morning, if thou canst endure
So long to speak of hardships thou hast borne."
He spake, and wise Odysseus answered thus:
"O King Alcinous, eminent beyond

All others of thy people. For discourse   470
There is a time; there is a time for sleep.
If more thou yet wouldst hear, I will not spare
To give the story of the greater woes
Of my companions, who were afterward
Cut off from life; and though they had escaped   475
The cruel Trojan war, on their return
They perished by a woman's fraud and guilt.
When chaste Proserpina had made the ghosts
Of women scatter right and left, there came
The soul of Agamemnon, Atreus' son.   480
He came attended by a throng of those
Who in the palace of Aegisthus met
A fate like his and died. When he had drunk
The dark red blood, he knew me at a look,
And wailed aloud, and, bursting into tears,   485
Stretched out his hands to touch me; but no power
Was there of grasp or pressure, such as once
Dwelt in those active limbs. I could not help
But weep at sight of him, for from my heart
I pitied him, and spake these winged words: 490
'Most glorious son of Atreus, king of men!
How, Agamemnon, has the fate that brings
To man the everlasting sleep of death
O'ertaken thee? Did Poseidon, calling up
The winds in all their fury, make thy fleet   495
A wreck, or did thine enemies on land
Smite thee, as thou wert driving off their beeves
And their fair flocks, or fighting to defend
Some city, and the helpless women there?'
I spake, and Agamemnon thus replied: 500
'Son of Laertes, nobly born and wise,

'Twas not that Poseidon calling up the winds
In all their fury wrecked me in my fleet,
Nor hostile warriors smote me on the land.
But that Aegisthus, bent upon my death,   505
Plotted against me with my guilty wife,
And bade me to his house and slew me there?
Even at the banquet, as a hind might slay
A bullock at the stall. With me they slew
My comrades, as a herd of white-toothed swine   510
Are slaughtered for some man of large estates,
Who makes a wedding or a solemn feast.
Thou hast seen many perish by the sword
In the hard battle, one by one, and yet
Thou wouldst have pitied us, hadst thou beheld   515
The slain beside the wine-jar, and beneath
The loaded tables, while the pavement swam
With blood. I heard Cassandra's piteous cry,
The cry of Priam's daughter, stricken down
By treacherous Clytemnestra at my side.   520
And there I lay, and, dying, raised my hands
To grasp my sword. The shameless woman went
Her way, nor stayed to close my eyes, nor press
My mouth into its place, although my soul
Was on its way to Hades. There is naught   525
That lives more horrible, more lost to shame,
Than is the woman who has brought her mind
To compass deeds like these—the wretch who plans
So foul a crime—the murder of the man
Whom she a virgin wedded. I had looked   539
For a warm welcome from my children here,
And all my household in my ancient home.
This woman, deep in wickedness, hath brought

Disgrace upon herself and all her sex,

Even those who give their thoughts to doing good.'   535

He spake, and I replied: 'O, how the God

Who wields the thunder, Zeus, must hate

The house of Atreus for the women's sake!

At first we fell by myriads in the cause

Of Helen; Clytemnestra now hath planned   540

This guile against thee while thou wert afar.'

I spake, and instantly his answer came:

'Therefore be not compliant to thy wife,

Nor let her hear from thee whatever lies

Within thy knowledge. Tell her but a part,   545

And keep the rest concealed. Yet is thy life,

Odysseus, in no danger from thy spouse:

For wise and well instructed in the rules

Of virtuous conduct is Penelope,

The daughter of Icarius. When we went   550

To war, we left her a young bride; a babe

Was at her breast, a boy, who now must sit

Among grown men; and fortunate is he,

For certainly his father will behold

The youth on his return, and he embrace   520

His father, as is meet. But as for me,

My consort suffered not my eyes to feed

Upon the sight of my own son; for first

She slew me. This, then, I admonish thee—

Heed thou my words. Bring not thy ship to land   560

Openly in thy country, but by stealth,

Since now no longer can we put our trust

In woman. Meantime, tell me of my son,

And faithfully, if thou hast heard of him

As living, whether in Orchomehus,   565

Or sandy Pylos, or in the broad realm
Of Menelaus, Sparta; for not yet
Has my Orestes passed from earth and life.'
He spake, and I replied: 'Why ask of me
That question, O Atrides? I know not   570
Whether thy son be living or be dead,
And this is not a time for idle words.'
Thus in sad talk we stood, and freely flowed
Our tears. Meanwhile the ghosts of Peleus' son
Achilles, and Patroclus, excellent   575
Antilochus, and Ajax, all drew near—
Ajax for form and stature eminent
O'er all the Greeks save Peleus' faultless son.
Then did the soul of fleet Aeacides
Know me, and thus in winged words he said: 580
'Odysseus! what hath moved thee to attempt
This greatest of thy labors? How is it
That thou hast found the courage to descend
To Hades, where the dead, the bodiless forms
Of those whose work is done on earth, abide?'   585
He spake; I answered: 'Greatest of the Greeks!
Achilles, son of Peleus! 'Twas to hear
The counsel of Tiresias that I came,
If haply he might tell me by what means
To reach my rugged Ithaca again;   590
For yet have I not trod my native coast,
Nor even have drawn nigh to Greece I meet
Misfortunes everywhere. But as for thee,
Achilles, no man lived before thy time,
Nor will hereafter live, more fortunate   595
Than thou—for while alive we honored thee
As if thou wert a god, and now again

In these abodes thou rulest o'er the dead;
Therefore, Achilles, shouldst thou not be sad.'
I spake; Achilles quickly answered me: 600
'Noble Odysseus, speak not thus of death,
As if thou couldst console me. I would be
A laborer on earth, and serve for hire
Some man of mean estate, who makes scant cheer,
Rather than reign o'er all who have gone down   605
To death. Speak rather of my noble son,
Whether or not he yet has joined the wars
To fight among the foremost of the host.
And tell me also if thou aught hast heard
Of blameless Peleus—whether he be yet   610
Honored among his many Myrmidons,
Or do they hold him now in small esteem
In Hellas and in Phthia, since old age
Unnerves his hands and feet, and I no more
Am there, beneath the sun, to give him aid,   615
Strong as I was on the wide plain of Troy,
When warring for the Achaean cause I smote
That valiant people. Could I come again,
But for a moment, with my former strength,
Into my father's palace, I would make   620
That strength and these unconquerable hands
A terror to the men who do him wrong,
And rob him of the honor due a king.'
He spake; I answered: 'Nothing have I heard
Of blameless Peleus, but I will relate   625
The truth concerning Neoptolemus,
Thy son, as thou requirest. Him I took
From Scyros in a gallant bark to join
The well-armed Greeks. Know, then, that when we sat

In council, planning to conduct the war   630
Against the city of Troy, he always rose
The first to speak, nor were his words unwise.
The godlike Nestor and myself alone
Rivaled him in debate. And when we fought
About the city walls, he loitered not   635
Among the others in the numerous host,
But hastened on before them, giving place
To no man there in valor. Many men
He slew in desperate combat, whom to name
Were past my power, so many were they all   640
Whom in the cause of Greece he struck to earth.
Yet one I name, Eurypylus, the son
Of Telephus, who perished by his sword
With many of his band, Citeians, led
To war because of liberal gifts bestowed   645
Upon their chieftain's wife; the noblest he
Of men, in form, whom I have ever seen,
Save Memnon. When into the wooden steed,
Framed by Epeius, we the chiefs of Greece
Ascended, and to me was given the charge   650
Of all things there, to open and to shut
The close-built fraud, while others of high rank
Among the Greeks were wiping off their tears,
And their limbs shook, I never saw thy son
Turn pale in his fine face, or brush away   655
A tear, but he besought me earnestly
That he might leave our hiding-place, and grasped
His falchion's hilt, and lifted up his spear
Heavy with brass, for in his mind lie smote
The Trojan crowd already. When at last   660
We had o'erthrown and sacked the lofty town

Of Priam, he embarked upon a ship,
With all his share of spoil—a large reward—-
Unhurt, not touched in combat hand to hand,
Nor wounded from afar, as oftentimes   665
Must be the fortune of a fight, for Ares
Is wont to rage without regard to men.'
I spake. The soul of swift Aeacides
Over the meadows thick with asphodel
Departed with long strides, well pleased to hear   670
From me the story of his son's renown.
The other ghosts of those who lay in death
Stood sorrowing by, and each one told his griefs;
But that of Ajax, son of Telamon,
Kept far aloof, displeased that I had won   675
The victory contending at the fleet
Which should possess the arms of Peleus' son.
His goddess-mother laid them as a prize
Before us, and the captive sons of Troy
And Pallas were the umpires to award   680
The victory. And now how much I wish
I had not conquered in a strife like that,
Since for that cause the dark earth hath received
The hero Ajax, who in nobleness
Of form and greatness of exploits excelled   685
All other Greeks, except the blameless son
Of Peleus. Then I spake in soothing words:
'O Ajax, son of blameless Telamon!
Wilt thou not even in death forget the wrath
Caused by the strife for those accursed arms?   690
The gods have made them fatal to the Greeks,
For thou, the bulwark of our host, didst fall,
And we lamented thee as bitterly

When thou wert dead as we had mourned the son
Of Peleus. Nor was any man to blame;   695
'Twas Zeus who held in vehement hate
The army of the warlike Greeks, and laid
This doom upon thee. Now, O king, draw near,
And hear our voice and words, and check, I pray,
The anger rising in thy generous breast.'   700
I spake; he answered not, but moved away
To Erebus, among the other souls
Of the departed. Yet would I have had
Speech of him, angry as he was, or else
Have spoken to him further, but my wish   705
Was strong to see yet others of the dead.
Then I beheld the illustrious son of Zeus,
Minos, a golden scepter in his hand,
Sitting to judge the dead, who round the king
Pleaded their causes. There they stood or sat   710
In Hades' halls—a pile with ample gates.
And next I saw the huge Orion drive,
Across the meadows green with asphodel,
The savage beast whom he had slain; he bore
The brazen mace, which no man's power could break.   715
And Tityus there I saw—the mighty earth
His mother—overspreading, as he lay,
Nine acres, with two vultures at his side,
That, plucking at his liver, plunged their beaks
Into the flesh; nor did his hands avail   720
To drive them off, for he had offered force
To Zeus's proud wife Latona, as she went
To Pytho, through the pleasant Panopeus.
And next I looked on Tantalus, a prey
To grievous torments, standing in a lake   725

That reached his chin. Though painfully athirst,
He could not drink; as often as he bowed
His aged head to take into his lips
The water, it was drawn away, and sank
Into the earth, and the dark soil appeared   730
Around his feet; a god had dried it up.
And lofty trees drooped o'er him, hung with fruit—
Pears and pomegranates, apples fair to sight,
And luscious figs, and olives green of hue.
And when that ancient man put forth his hands   735
To pluck them from their stems, the wind arose
And whirled them far among the shadowy clouds.
There I beheld the shade of Sisyphus
Amid his sufferings. With both hands he rolled
A huge stone up a hill. To force it up,   740
He leaned against the mass with hands and feet;
But, ere it crossed the summit of the hill
A power was felt that sent it rolling back,
And downward plunged the unmanageable rock
Before him to the plain. Again he toiled   745
To heave it upward, while the sweat in streams
Ran down his limbs, and dust begrimed his brow.
Then I beheld the mighty Hercules—
The hero's image—for he sits himself
Among the deathless gods, well pleased to share   750
Their feasts, and Hebe of the dainty feet—
A daughter of the mighty Zeus
And golden-sandaled Hera—is his wife.
Around his image flitted to and fro
The ghosts with noise, like fear-bewildered birds.   755
His look was dark as night. He held in hand
A naked bow, a shaft upon the string,

And fiercely gazed, like one about to send
The arrow forth. Upon his breast he wore
The formidable baldric, on whose band   760
Of gold were sculptured marvels—forms of bears,
Wild boars, grim lions, battles, skirmishings,
And death by wounds, and slaughter. He who wrought
That band had never done the like before,
Nor could thereafter. As I met his eye,   765
The hero knew me, and, beholding me
With pity, said to me in winged words:
'Son of Laertes, nobly born and wise,
And yet unhappy; surely thou dost bear
A cruel fate, like that which I endured   770
While yet I saw the brightness of the sun.
The offspring of Cronus-son Zeus
Am I, and yet was I compelled to serve
One of a meaner race than I, who set
Difficult tasks. He sent me hither once   775
To bring away the guardian hound; he deemed
No harder task might be. I brought him hence;
I led him up from Hades, with such aid
As Hermes and the blue-eyed Pallas gave.'
Thus having spoken, he withdrew again   780
Into the abode of Hades. I remained
And kept my place, in hope there yet might come
Heroes who perished in the early time,
And haply I might look on some of those—
The ancients, whom I greatly longed to see—   785
On Theseus and Pirithous, glorious men,
The children of the gods. But now there flocked
Already round me, with a mighty noise,
The innumerable nations of the dead;

And I grew pale with fear, lest from the halls   790
Of Hades the stem Proserpine should send
The frightful visage of the monster-maid,
The Gorgon. Hastening to my ship, I bade
The crew embark, and cast the hawsers loose.
Quickly they went on board, and took their seats   795
Upon the benches. Through Oceanus
The current bore my galley, aided first
By oars and then by favorable gales."

BOOK XII

Now when our bark had left Oceanus   1
And entered the great deep, we reached the isle
Aeaea, where the Morning, child of Dawn,
Abides, and holds her dances, and the Sun
Goes up from earth. We landed there and drew   5
Our galley up the beach; we disembarked
And laid us down to sleep beside the sea,
And waited for the holy Morn to rise.
Then when the rosy-fingered Morn appeared,
The child of Dawn, I sent my comrades forth   10
To bring from Circe's halls Elpenor's corse.
And where a headland stretched into the deep
We hewed down trees, and held the funeral rites
With many tears; and having there consumed
The body and the arms with fire, we built   15
A tomb, and reared a column to the dead,
And on its summit fixed a tapering oar.
All this was duly done; yet was the news
Of our return from Hades not concealed
From Circe. She attired herself in haste   20
And came; her maids came with her, bringing bread

And store of meats and generous wine; and thus
Spake the wise goddess, standing in the midst:
'Ah, daring ones! who, yet alive, have gone
Down to the abode of Hades; twice to die   25
Is yours, while others die but once. Yet now
Take food, drink wine, and hold a feast today,
And with the dawn of morning ye shall sail;
And I will show the way, and teach you all
Its dangers, so that ye may not lament   30
False counsels followed, either on the land
Or on the water, to your grievous harm.'
She spake; and our confiding minds were swayed
Easily by her counsels. All that day
Till set of sun we sat and banqueted   35
Upon the abundant meats and generous wines;
And when the Sun went down, and darkness came,
The crew beside the fastenings of our bark
Lay down to sleep, while Circe took my hand,
Led me apart, and made me sit, and took   40
Her seat before me, and inquired of all
That I had seen. I told her faithfully,
And then the mighty goddess Circe said:
Thus far is well; now heedfully attend
To what I say, and may some deity   45
Help thee remember it! Thou first wilt come
To where the Sirens haunt. They throw a spell
O'er all who pass that way. If unawares
One finds himself so nigh that he can hear
Their voices, round him nevermore shall wife   50
And lisping children gather, welcoming
His safe return with joy. The Sirens sit
In a green field, and charm with mellow notes

The comer, while beside them lie in heaps
The bones of men decaying underneath   55
The shriveled skins. Take heed and pass them by.
First fill with wax well kneaded in the palm
The ears of thy companions, that no sound
May enter. Hear the music, if thou wilt,
But let thy people bind thee, hand and foot,   60
To the good ship, upright against the mast,
And round it wind the cord, that thou mayst hear
The ravishing notes. But shouldst thou then entreat
Thy men, commanding them to set thee free,
Let them be charged to bind thee yet more fast   65
With added bands. And when they shall have passed
The Sirens by, I will not judge for thee
Which way to take; consider for thyself;
I tell thee of two ways. There is a pile
Of beetling rocks, where roars the mighty surge   70
Of dark-eyed Amphitrite; these are called
The Wanderers by the blessed gods. No birds
Can pass them safe, not even the timid doves,
Which bear ambrosia to our father Zeus,
But ever doth the slippery rock take off   75
Some one, whose loss the God at once supplies,
To keep their number full. To these no bark
Guided by man has ever come, and left
The spot unwrecked; the billows of the deep
And storms of fire in air have scattered wide   80
Timbers of ships and bodies of drowned men.
One only of the barks that plough the deep
Has passed them safely—Argo, known to all
By fame, when coming from Aeaeta home—
And her the billows would have dashed against   85

The enormous rocks, if Hera, for the sake
Of Jason, had not come to guide it through.
Two are the rocks; one lifts to the broad heaven
Its pointed summit, where a dark gray cloud
Broods, and withdraws not; never is the sky   90
Clear o'er that peak, not even in summer days
Or autumn; nor can man ascend its steeps,
Or venture down—so smooth the sides, as if
Man's art had polished them. There in the midst
Upon the western side toward Erebus   95
There yawns a shadowy cavern; thither thou,
Noble Odysseus, steer thy bark, yet keep
So far aloof that, standing on the deck,
A youth might send an arrow from a bow
Just to the cavern's mouth. There Scylla dwells,   100
And fills the air with fearful yells; her voice
The cry of whelps just littered, but herself
A frightful prodigy—a sight which none
Would care to look on, though he were a god.
Twelve feet are hers, all shapeless; six long necks,   105
A hideous head on each, and triple rows
Of teeth, close set and many, threatening death.
And half her form is in the cavern's womb,
And forth from that dark gulf her heads are thrust,
To look abroad upon the rocks for prey—no   110
Dolphin, or dogfish, or the mightier whale,
Such as the murmuring Amphitrite breeds
In multitudes. No mariner can boast
That he has passed by Scylla with a crew
Unharmed; she snatches from the deck, and bears   115
Away in each grim mouth, a living man.
Another rock, Odysseus, thou wilt see,

Of lower height, so near her that a spear,
Cast by the hand, might reach it. On it grows
A huge wild fig-tree with luxuriant leaves.   120
Below, Charybdis, of immortal birth,
Draws the dark water down; for thrice a day
She gives it forth, and thrice with fearful whirl
She draws it in. O, be it not thy lot
To come while the dark water rushes down!   125
Even Poseidon could not then deliver thee.
Then turn thy course with speed toward Scylla's rock,
And pass that way; 'Twere better far that six
Should perish from the ship than all be lost.'
She spake, and I replied: 'O goddess, deign   130
To tell me truly, cannot I at once
Escape Charybdis and defend my friends
Against the rage of Scylla when she strikes?'
I spake; the mighty goddess answered me:
'Rash man! dost thou still think of warlike deeds,   135
And feats of strength? And wilt thou not give way
Even to the deathless gods? That pest is not
Of mortal mold; she cannot die, she is
A thing to tremble and to shudder at,
And fierce, and never to be overcome.   140
There is no room for courage; flight is best.
And if thou shouldst delay beside the rock
To take up arms, I fear lest once again
She fall on thee with all her heads, and seize
As many men. Pass by the monster's haunt   145
With all the speed that thou canst make, and call
Upon Crataeis, who brought Scylla forth
To be the plague of men, and who will calm
Her rage, that she assault thee not again.

Then in thy voyage shalt thou reach the isle   150
Trinacria, where, in pastures of the Sun,
His many beeves and fading sheep are fed—
Seven herds of oxen, and as many flocks
Of sheep, and fifty in each flock and herd.
They never multiply; they never die.   155
Two shepherdesses tend them, goddesses,
Nymphs with redundant locks—Lampelia one,
The other Phaethusa. These the nymph
Naeera to the overgoing Sun
Brought forth, and when their queenly mother's care   160
Had reared them, she appointed them to dwell
In far Trinacria, there to keep the flocks
And oxen of their father. If thy thoughts
Be fixed on thy return, so that thou leave
These flocks and herds unharmed, ye all will come   165
To Ithaca, though after many toils.
But if thou rashly harm them, I foretell
Destruction to thy ship and all its crew;
And if thyself escape, thou wilt return
Late and in sorrow, all thy comrades lost.'   170
She spake; the Morning on her golden throne
Looked forth; the glorious goddess went her way
Into the isle, I to my ship, and bade
The men embark and cast the hawsers loose.
And straight they went on board, and duly manned   175
The benches, smiting as they sat with oars,
The hoary waters. Circe, amber-haired,
The mighty goddess of the musical voice,
Sent a fair wind behind our dark-prowed ship
That gaily bore us company, and filled   180
The sails. When we had fairly ordered all

On board our galley, we sat down, and left
The favoring wind and helm to bear us on,
And thus in sadness I bespake the crew:
'My friends! it were not well that one or two   185
Alone should know the oracles I heard
From Circe, great among the goddesses;
And now will I disclose them, that ye all,
Whether we are to die or to escape
The doom of death, may be forewarned. And first   190
Against the wicked Sirens and their song
And flowery bank she warns us. I alone
May hear their voice, but ye must bind me first
With bands too strong to break, that I may stand
Upright against the mast; and let the cords   195
Be fastened round it. If I then entreat
And bid you loose me, make the bands more strong.'
Thus to my crew I spake, and told them all
That they should know, while our good ship drew near
The island of the Sirens, prosperous gales   200
Wafting it gently onward. Then the breeze
Sank to a breathless calm; some deity
Had hushed the winds to slumber. Straightway rose
The men and furled the sails and laid them down
Within the ship, and sat and made the sea   205
White with the beating of their polished blades,
Made of the fir-tree. Then I took a mass
Of wax and cut it into many parts,
And kneaded each with a strong hand. It grew
Warm with the pressure, and the beams of him   210
Who journeys round the earth, the monarch Sun.
With this I filled the ears of all my men
From first to last. They bound me, in their turn,

Upright against the mast-tree, hand and foot,

And tied the cords around it. Then again   215

They sat and threshed with oars the hoary deep.

And when, in running rapidly, we came

So near the Sirens as to hear a voice

From where they sat, our galley flew not by

Unseen by them, and sweetly thus they sang: 220

'O world-renowned Odysseus! thou who art

The glory of the Achaeans, turn thy bark

Landward, that thou mayst listen to our lay

No man has passed us in his galley yet,

Ere he has heard our warbled melodies.   225

He goes delighted hence a wiser man;

For all that in the spacious realm of Troy

The Greeks and Trojans by the will of Heaven

Endured we know, and all that comes to pass

In all the nations of the fruitful earth.'   230

'Twas thus they sang, and sweet the strain. I longed

To listen, and with nods I gave the sign

To set me free; they only plied their oars

The faster. Then up sprang Eurylochus

And Perimedes, and with added cords   235

Bound me, and drew the others still more tight.

And when we now had passed the spot, and heard

No more the melody the Sirens sang,

My comrades hastened from their ears to take

The wax, and loosed the cords and set me free.   240

As soon as we had left the isle, I saw

Mist and a mountain billow, and I heard

The thunder of the waters. From the hands

Of my affrighted comrades flew the oars,

The deep was all in uproar; but the ship   245

Stopped there, for all the rowers ceased their task.
I went through all the ship exhorting them
With cheerful words, man after man, and said:
'Reflect, my friends, that we are not untried
In evil fortunes, nor in sadder plight   250
Are we than when within his spacious cave
The brutal Cyclops held us prisoners;
Yet through my valor we escaped, and through
My counsels and devices, and I think
That ye will live to bear this day's events   253
In memory like those. Now let us act.
Do all as I advise; go to your seats
Upon the benches, smiting with your oars
These mighty waves, and haply Zeus will grant
That we escape the death which threatens us.   260
Thee, helmsman, I adjure—and heed my words,
Since to thy hands alone is given in charge
Our gallant vessel's rudder—steer thou hence
From mist and tumbling waves, and well observe
The rock, lest where it juts into the sea   265
Thou heed it not, and bring us all to wreck.'
I spake, and quickly all obeyed my words.
Yet said I naught of Scylla—whom we now
Could not avoid—lest all the crew in fear
Should cease to row, and crowd into the hold.   270
And then did I forget the stern command
Which Circe gave me, not to arm myself
For combat. In my shining arms I cased
My limbs, and took in hand two ponderous spears,
And went on deck, and stood upon the prow—   275
For there it seemed to me that Scylla first
Would show herself—that monster of the rocks—

To seize my comrades. Yet I saw her not,
Though weary grew my eyes with looking long
And eagerly upon those dusky cliffs.   280
Sadly we sailed into the strait, where stood
On one hand Scylla, and the dreaded rock
Charybdis on the other, drawing down
Into her horrid gulf the briny flood;
And as she threw it forth again, it tossed   285
And murmured as upon a glowing fire
The water in a cauldron, while the spray,
Thrown upward, fell on both the summit-rocks;
And when once more she swallowed the salt sea,
It whirled within the abyss, while far below   290
The bottom of blue sand was seen. My men
Grew pale with fear; we looked into the gulf
And thought our end was nigh. Then Scylla snatched
Six of my comrades from our hollow bark,
The best in valor and in strength of arm.   295
I looked to my good ship; I looked to them,
And saw their hands and feet still swung in air
Above me, while for the last time on earth
They called my name in agony of heart.
As when an angler on a jutting rock   300
Sits with his taper rod, and casts his bait
To snare the smaller fish, he sends the horn
Of a wild bull that guards his line afar
Into the water, and jerks out a fish,
And throws it gasping shoreward; so were they   305
Uplifted gasping to the rocks, and there
Scylla devoured them at her cavern's mouth,
Stretching their hands to me with piercing cries
Of anguish. 'twas in truth the saddest sight,

Whatever I have suffered and where'er   310
Have roamed the waters, that mine eyes have seen.
Escaping thus the rocks, the dreaded haunt
Of Scylla and Charybdis, we approached
The pleasant island of the Sun, where grazed
The oxen with broad foreheads, beautiful,   315
And flocks of sheep, the fatlings of the god
Who makes the round of heaven. While yet at sea
I heard from my black ship the low of herds
In stables, and the bleatings of the flocks,
And straightway came into my thought the words   320
Of the blind seer Tiresias, him of Thebes,
And of Aeaean Circe, who had oft
Warned me to shun the island of the god
Whose light is sweet to all. And then I said
To my companions with a sorrowing heart: 325
'My comrades, sufferers as ye are, give ear.
I shall disclose the oracles which late
Tiresias and Aeaean Circe gave.
The goddess earnestly admonished me
Not to approach the island of the Sun,   330
Whose light is sweet to all, for there she said
Some great misfortune lay in wait for us.
Now let us speed the ship and pass the isle.'
I spake; their hearts were broken as they heard,
And bitterly Eurylochus replied: 335
'Austere art thou, Odysseus; thou art strong
Exceedingly; no labor tires thy limbs;
They must be made of iron, since thy will
Denies thy comrades, overcome with toil
And sleeplessness, to tread the land again,   340
And in that isle amid the waters make

A generous banquet. Thou wouldst have us sail
Into the swiftly coming night, and stray
Far from the island, through the misty sea.
By night spring up the mighty winds that make
A wreck of ships, and how can one escape
Destruction, should a sudden hurricane
Rise from the south or the hard-blowing west,
Such as, in spite of all the sovereign gods,
Will cause a ship to founder in the deep?
Let us obey the dark-browed Night, and take
Our evening meal, remaining close beside
Our gallant bark, and go on board again
When morning breaks, and enter the wide sea.'
So spake Eurylochus; the rest approved.
And then I knew that some divinity
Was meditating evil to our band,
And I bespake him thus in winged words:
'Eurylochus, ye force me to your will,
Since I am only one. Now all of you
Bind yourselves to me firmly, by an oath,
That if ye haply here shall meet a herd
Of beeves or flock of sheep, ye will not dare
To slay a single ox or sheep, but feed
Contented on the stores that Circe gave.'
I spake, and readily my comrades swore
As I required; and when that solemn oath
Was taken, to the land we brought and moored
Our galley in a winding creek, beside
A fountain of sweet water. From the deck
Stepped my companions and made ready there
Their evening cheer. They ate and drank till thirst
And hunger were appeased, and then they thought

345

350

355

360

365

370

Of those whom Scylla from our galley's deck
Snatched and devoured; they thought and wept till sleep   375
Stole softly over them amid their tears.
Now came the third part of the night; the stars
Were sinking when the Cloud-compeller Zeus
Sent forth a violent wind with eddying gusts,
And covered both the earth and sky with clouds,   330
And darkness fell from heaven. When Morning came,
The rosy-fingered daughter of the Dawn,
We drew the ship into a spacious grot.
There were the seats of nymphs, and there we saw
The smooth fair places where they danced. I called
A council of my men, and said to them: 3 86
'My friends, in our good ship are food and drink;
Abstain we from these beeves, lest we be made
To suffer; for these herds and these fair flocks
Are sacred to a dreaded god, the Sun—   390
The all-beholding and all-hearing Sun.'
I spake, and all were swayed by what I said
Full easily. A month entire the gales
Blew from the south, and after that no wind
Save east and south. While yet we had our bread   395
And ruddy wine, my comrades spared the beeves,
Moved by the love of life. But when the stores
On board our galley were consumed, they roamed
The island in their need, and sought for prey,
And snared with barbed hooks the fish and birds—   400
Whatever came to hand—till they were gaunt
With famine. Meantime I withdrew alone
Into the isle, to supplicate the gods,
If haply one of them might yet reveal
The way of my return. As thus I strayed   405

Into the land, apart from all the rest,
I found a sheltered nook where no wind came,
And prayed with washed hands to all the gods
Who dwell in heaven. At length they bathed my lids
In a soft sleep. Meantime, Eurylochus   410
With fatal counsels thus harangued my men:
'Hear, my companions, sufferers as ye are,
The words that I shall speak. All ways of death
Are hateful to the wretched race of men;
But this of hunger, thus to meet our fate,   415
Is the most fearful. Let us drive apart
The best of all the oxen of the Sun,
And sacrifice them to the immortal ones
Who dwell in the broad heaven. And if we come
To Ithaca, our country, we will there   420
Build to the Sun, whose path is o'er our heads,
A sumptuous temple, and endow its shrine
With many gifts and rare. But if it be
His will, approved by all the other gods,
To sink our bark in anger, for the sake   425
Of these his high-horned oxen, I should choose
Sooner to gasp my life away amid
The billows of the deep, than pine to death
By famine in this melancholy isle.'
So spake Eurylochus; the crew approved.   430
Then from the neighboring herd they drove the best
Of all the beeves; for near the dark-prowed ship
The fair broad-fronted herd with crooked horns
Were feeding. Round the victims stood my crew,
And, offering their petitions to the gods,   435
Held tender oak-leaves in their hands, just plucked
From a tall tree, for in our good ship's hold

Was no white barley now. When they had prayed,
And slain and dressed the beeves, they hewed away
The thighs and covered them with double folds   440
Of caul, and laid raw slices over these.
Wine had they not poured in sacrifice
Upon the burning flesh; they poured instead
Water, and roasted all the entrails thus.
Now when the thighs were thoroughly consume   445
And entrails tasted, all the rest was carved
Into small portions, and transfixed with spits.
Just then the gentle slumber left my lids.
I hurried to the shore and my good ship,
And, drawing near, perceived the savory steam   450
From the burnt-offering. Sorrowfully then
I called upon the ever-living gods:
'O Father Zeus, and all ye blessed gods,
Who live forever, 'twas a cruel sleep
In which ye lulled me to my grievous harm;   455
My comrades here have done a fearful wrong.'
Lampetia, of the trailing robes, in haste
Flew to the Sun, who journeys round the earth,
To tell him that my crew had slain his beeves,
And thus in anger he bespake the gods: 460
'O Father Zeus, and all ye blessed gods
Who never die, avenge the wrong I bear
Upon the comrades of Laertes' son,
Odysseus, who have foully slain my beeves,
In which I took delight whene'er I rose   465
Into the starry heaven, and when again
I sank from heaven to earth. If for the wrong
They make not large amends, I shall go down
To Hades, there to shine among the dead.'

The cloud-compelling Zeus replied: 470
'Still shine, O Sun! among the deathless gods
And mortal men, upon the nourishing earth.
Soon will I cleave, with a white thunderbolt,
Their galley in the midst of the black sea.'
This from Calypso of the radiant hair 475
I heard thereafter; she herself, she said,
Had heard it from the herald Hermes.
When to the ship I came, beside the sea,
I sternly chid them all, man after man,
Yet could we think of no redress; the beeves 480
Were dead; and now with prodigies the gods
Amazed my comrades—the skins moved and crawled,
The flesh both raw and roasted on the spits
Lowed with the voice of oxen. Six whole days
My comrades feasted, taking from the herd 435
The Sun's best oxen. When Cronus's Zeus
Brought the seventh day, the tempest ceased; the wind
Fell, and we straightway went on board. We set
The mast upright, and, spreading the white sails,
We ventured on the great wide sea again. 490
When we had left the isle, and now appeared
No other land, but only sea and sky,
The son of Cronus caused a lurid cloud
To gather o'er the galley, and to cast
Its darkness on the deep. Not long our ship 495
Ran onward, ere the furious west-wind rose
And blew a hurricane. A strong blast snapped
Both ropes that held the mast; the mast fell back;
The tackle dropped entangled to the hold;
The mast, in falling on the galley's stern, 500
Dashed on the pilot's head and crushed the bones,

And from the deck he plunged like one who dives
Into the deep; his gallant spirit left
The limbs at once. Zeus thundered from on high,
And sent a thunderbolt into the ship,   505
That, quaking with the fearful blow, and filled
With stifling sulfur, shook my comrades off
Into the deep. They floated round the ship
Like seamews; Zeus had cut them off
From their return. I moved from place to place,
Still in the ship, until the tempest's force   510
Parted the sides and keel. Before the waves
The naked keel was swept. The mast had snapped
Just at the base, but round it was a thong
Made of a bullock's hide; with this I bound,   515
The mast and keel together, took my seat
Upon them, and the wild winds bore me on.
The west-wind ceased to rage; but in its stead
The south-wind blew, and brought me bitter grief.
I feared lest I must measure back my way   520
To grim Charybdis. All night long I rode
The waves, and with the rising sun drew near
The rock of Scylla and the terrible
Charybdis as her gulf was drawing down
The waves of the salt sea. There as I came   525
I raised myself on high till I could grasp
The lofty fig-tree, and I clung to it
As clings a bat—for I could neither find
A place to plant my feet, nor could I climb,
So distant were the roots, so far apart   530
The long huge branches overshadowing
Charybdis. Yet I firmly kept my hold
Till she should throw the keel and mast again

Up from the gulf. They, as I waited long,
Came up again, though late—as late as one   535
Who long has sat adjudging strifes between
Young suitors pleading in the market-place
Rises and goes to take his evening meal;
So late the timbers of my bark returned,
Thrown from Charybdis. Then I dropped amid   540
The dashing waves, and came with hands and feet
On those long timbers in the midst, that they
Might bear my weight. I sat on them and rowed
With both my hands. The father of the gods
And mortals suffered not that I should look   545
On Scylla's rock again, else had I not
Escaped a cruel death. For nine long days
I floated on the waters; on the tenth
The gods at nightfall bore me to an isle—
Ogygia, where Calypso, amber-haired,   550
A mighty goddess, skilled in song, abides,
Who kindly welcomed me, and cherished me.
Why should I speak of this? Here in these halls
I gave the history yesterday to thee
And to thy gracious consort, and I hate   555
To tell again a tale once fully told."

BOOK XIII

He spake, and all within those shadowy halls   1
Were silent; all were held in mute delight.
Since thou hast come, Odysseus, as a guest,
To this high pile and to these brazen rooms,
So long a sufferer, thou must not depart   5
Upon thy homeward way a wanderer still.
And this let me enjoin on each of you.
Who in this palace drink at our repasts
The choice red wine, and listen to the bard:
Already in a polished chest are laid   10
Changes of raiment, works of art in gold,
And other gifts, which the Phaeacian chiefs
Have destined for our guest; now let us each
Bestow an ample tripod and a vase, is
And we in an assembly of the realm   15
Will see the cost repaid, since otherwise
Great would the burden be that each must bear."
So spake Alcinous; they approved, and sought
Alcinous then took up the word and said:
Their homes to sleep, but when the child of Dawn,   20
The rosy-fingered Morn, appeared, they came,

All bringing to the ship their gifts of brass
In honor of the guest. The mighty prince
Alcinous, going through the ship, bestowed
The whole beneath the benches, that no one   25
Of those who leaned to pull the oar might thence
Meet harm or hindrance. Then they all went back
To the king's palace, and prepared a feast.
The mighty prince Alcinous offered up
For them an ox to cloud-compelling Zeus,   30
The son of Cronus, ruler over all.
They burned the thighs, and held high festival,
And all was mirth. Divine Demodocus
The bard, whom all men reverenced, sang to them.
Meantime Odysseus often turned to look   35
At the bright Sun, and longed to see him set,
So eager was the hero to set sail
Upon his homeward way. As when a swain
Awaits his evening meal, for whom all day
Two dark-brown steers have dragged the solid plough   40
Through fallow grounds, and welcome is the hour
Of sunset, calling him to his repast,
And wearily he walks with failing knees,
So welcome to Odysseus did the light
Of day go down. Then did he hold discourse   45
With the Phaeacians, lovers of the sea,
And chiefly with Alcinous, speaking thus:
"O monarch most illustrious of thy race,
Alcinous, now when ye have duly poured
Wine to the gods, be pleased to send me hence   50
In peace, and fare ye well! All that my heart
Could wish have ye provided bounteously,
An escort and rich gifts; and may the gods

Bestow their blessing with them! May I meet
My blameless wife again, and find my friends   55
Prosperous! And ye whom I shall leave behind,
Long may ye make the wives of your young years
And children happy! May the gods vouchsafe
To crown with every virtue you and them,
And may no evil light upon your isle!"   60
He spake; the assembly all approved his words,
And bade send forth the stranger on his way,
Who spake so nobly. Then the mighty prince
Alcinous turned, and to the herald said:
"Now mix the wine, Pontonous, in a jar,   65
And bear a part to all beneath our roof,
That we with prayers to Father Zeus
May send the stranger to his native land."
He spake; Pontonous mingled for the guests
The generous wine, and went with it to each,   70
Who poured it on the ground, from where they sat,
To all the dwellers of the ample heaven;
And then the great Odysseus, rising up,
Placed the round goblet in Arete's hands,
And thus bespake the queen with winged words: 75
"Farewell, O queen, through the long years, till age
And death, which are the lot of all, shall come.
Now I depart, but mayst thou, here among
Thy people, and the children of thy love,
And King Alcinous, lead a happy life!"   80
So spake the high-born chieftain, and withdrew,
And crossed the threshold. King Alcinous sent
A herald with him to direct his way
To the fleet ship and border of the deep.
Arete also sent her servant-maids—   85

One bearing a fresh cloak and tunic, one
A coffer nobly wrought, and yet a third
Bread and red wine; and when they reached the ship
Beside the sea, the diligent crew received
Their burdens, and bestowed within the hold   90
The food and drink, but spread upon the deck
And at the stern a mat and linen sheet,
That there Odysseus undisturbed might sleep.
He went on board and silently lay down,
While all the rowers in due order took   95
Their seats upon the benches. Loosing first
The hawser from the perforated rock,
They bent them to their task, and flung the brine
Up from the oar, while on the chieftain's lids
Lighted a sweet and deep and quiet sleep,   100
Most like to death. As, smitten by the lash,
Four harnessed stallions spring on high and dart
Across the plain together; so the prow
Rose leaping forward, while behind it rolled
A huge dark billow of the roaring sea.   105
Safely and steadily the galley ran,
Nor could a falcon, swiftest of the birds,
Have kept beside it, with such speed it flew,
Bearing a hero who was like the gods
In wisdom, and whose sufferings in the wars   110
And voyages among the furious waves
Were great and many, though he slumbered now
In peace, forgetful of misfortunes past.
Now when that brightest star, the harbinger
Of Morning, daughter of the Dawn, arose,   115
The bark had passed the sea, and reached the isle.
A port there is in Ithaca, the haunt

Of Phorcys, Ancient of the Sea. Steep shores
Stretch inward toward each other, and roll back
The mighty surges which the hoarse winds hurl   120
Against them from the ocean, while within
Ships ride without their hawsers when they once
Have passed the haven's mouth. An olive-tree
With spreading branches at the farther end
Of that fair haven stands, and overbrows   125
A pleasant shady grotto of the nymphs
Called Naiads. Cups and jars of stone are ranged
Within, and bees lay up their honey there.
There from their spindles wrought of stone the nymphs
Weave their sea-purple robes, which all behold   130
With wonder; there are ever-flowing springs.
Two are the entrances: one toward the north
By which men enter; but a holier one
Looks toward the south, nor ever mortal foot
May enter there. By that way pass the gods.   135
They touched the land, for well they knew the spot.
The galley, urged so strongly by the arms
Of those who plied the oar, ran up the beach
Quite half her length. And then the crew came forth
From the good ship, and first they lifted out   140
Odysseus with the linen and rich folds
Of tapestry, and laid him on the sands
In a deep slumber. Then they also took
The presents from the hold, which, as he left
Their isle, the princes of Phaeacia gave   145
By counsel of wise Pallas. These they piled
Close to the olive-tree, without the way,
That none, in passing, ere Odysseus woke,
Might do their owner wrong. Then homeward sailed

The crew; but Poseidon, who could not forget 150
The threats which he had uttered long before
Against the godlike chief Odysseus, thus
Sought to explore the will of Zeus:
"O Father Zeus! I shall no more be held
In honor with the gods, since mortal men, 155
The people of Phaeacia, though their race
Is of my lineage, do not honor me.
I meant Odysseus should not reach his home
Save with much suffering, though I never thought
To hinder his return, for thou hadst given 160
Thy promise and thy nod that it should be.
Yet these Phaeacians, in a gallant bark,
Have borne him o'er the deep, and while he slept,
Have laid him down in Ithaca, and given
Large gifts, abundant store of brass and gold, 165
And woven work, more than he could have brought
From captured Ilium, if he had returned
Safely, with all his portion of the spoil."
Then cloud-compelling Zeus replied:
"Earth-shaker, ruler of a mighty realm! 170
What hast thou said? The gods deny thee not
Due honor; perilous it were for them
To show contempt for one who stands in age
And might above them all. But if among
The sons of men be one who puts such trust 175
In his own strength as not to honor thee,
Do as seems good to thee, and as thou wilt."
Promptly the god who shakes the shores replied;
"What thou dost bid me I would do at once,
But that I fear and would avoid thy wrath. 180
I would destroy that fair Phaeacian bark

In its return across the misty sea
From bearing home Odysseus, that no more
May the Phaeacians lend an escort thus
To wandering men, and I would also cause   185
A lofty mount to rise and hide their town."
Then spake again the Cloud-compeller Zeus:
"Thus were it best, my brother: when the crowd
Of citizens already see the ship
Approaching, then transform it to a rock   190
In semblance of a galley, that they all
May gaze in wonder; thus wilt thou have caused
A lofty mount to stand before their town."
This when the shaker of the shores had heard,
He flew to Scheria, the Phaeacian isle,   195
And stood, until that galley, having crossed
The sea, came swiftly scudding. He drew near
And smote it with his open palm, and made
The ship a rock, fast rooted in the bed
Of the deep sea, and then he went his way.   200
Then winged words were spoken in that throng
Of the Phaeacians, wielders of long oars,
And far renowned in feats of seamanship.
And, looking on each other, thus they said:
"Ha! what has stayed our good ship on the sea?   205
This moment we beheld her hastening home."
'Twas thus they talked, unweeting of the cause.
But then Alcinous to the assembly said:
'Yes! now I call to mind the ancient words
Of prophecy—my father's—who was wont   210
To say that Poseidon sorely is displeased
That we should give to every man who comes
Safe escort to his home. In coming times—

Such was my father's prophecy—the god
Would yet destroy a well-appointed bark   215
Of the Phaeacians on the misty deep
Returning from an escort, and would cause
A lofty mount to stand before our town.
So prophesied the aged man; his words
Are here fulfilled. Now do as I appoint,   220
And let us all obey. Henceforth refrain
From bearing to their homes the strangers thrown
Upon our coast; and let us sacrifice
To Poseidon twelve choice bullocks of the herd,
That he may pity us, nor hide our town   225
With a huge mountain from the sight of men."
He spake, and they were awed and straightway brought
The bullocks for the sacrifice. So prayed
To sovereign Poseidon the Phaeacian chiefs
And princes, standing round the altar-fires.   230
Now woke the great Odysseus from his sleep
In his own land, and yet he knew it not.
Long had he been away, and Pallas now,
The goddess-child of Zeus, had cast a mist
Around him, that he might not yet be known   235
To others, and that she might tell him first
What he should learn; nor even might his wife,
Nor friends, nor people, know of his return,
Ere he avenged upon the suitor crew
His wrongs, and therefore all things wore to him   240
Another look—the footways stretching far,
The bights where ships were moored, the towering rocks,
And spreading trees. He rose and stood upright,
And gazed upon his native coast and wept,
And smote his thigh, and said in bitter grief: 245

"Ah me! what region am I in, among
What- people? lawless, cruel, and unjust?
Or are they hospitable men, who fear
The gods? And where shall I bestow these goods,
And whither go myself? Would that they all   250
Were still with the Phaeacians, and that I
Had found some other great and mighty king
Kindly to welcome me, and send me back
To my own land. I know not where to place
These treasures, and I must not leave them here,   255
Lest others come and seize them as a spoil
Nay, these Phaeacian chiefs and counselors
Were not, in all things, either wise or just.
They gave their word to land me on the coast
Of pleasant Ithaca, and have not kept   260
Their promise. O, may Zeus avenge this wrong!
He who protects the suppliant, who beholds
All men with equal eye, and punishes
The guilty. Now will I review my stores
And number them again, that I may see   265
If those who left me here have taken aught."
Thus having said, he numbered all his gifts—
Beautiful tripods, cauldrons, works of gold,
And gorgeous woven raiment; none of these
Were wanting. Then he pined to see again   270
His native isle, and slowly paced the beach
Of the loud sea, lamenting bitterly.
There Pallas came to meet him in the shape
Of a young shepherd, delicately formed,
As are the sons of kings. A mantle lay   275
Upon her shoulder in rich folds; her feet
Shone in their sandals: in her hand she bore

A javelin. As Odysseus saw, his heart
Was glad within him, and he hastened on,
And thus accosted her with winged words: 280
"Fair youth, who art the first whom I have met
Upon this shore, I bid thee hail, and hope
Thou meetest me with no unkind intent.
Protect what thou beholdest here and me;
I make my suit to thee as to a god,   285
And come to thy dear knees. And tell, I pray,
That I may know the truth, what land is this?
What people? who the dwellers? may it be
A pleasant isle, or is it but the shore
Of fruitful mainland shelving to the sea?"   290
And then the goddess, blue-eyed Pallas, said:
"Of simple mind art thou, unless perchance
Thou comest from afar, if thou dost ask
What country this may be. It is not quite
A nameless region; many know it well   295
Of those who dwell beneath the rising sun,
And those, behind, in Evening's dusky realm.
Rugged it is, and suited ill to steeds,
Yet barren it is not, though level grounds
Are none within its borders. It is rich   300
In corn and wine, for seasonable rains
And dews refresh its soil. Large flocks of goats
And herds of beeves are pastured here; all kinds
Of trees are in its forests, and its springs
Are never dry. The fame of Ithaca,   305
Stranger, has travelled to the Trojan coast,
Though that, I hear, lies far away from Greece."
She spake; Odysseus, the great sufferer,
Rejoiced to be in his own land, whose name

Pallas, the child of aegis-bearing Zeus,   310
Had just now uttered. Then with winged words
He spake, but not the truth; his artful speech
Put that aside, forever in his breast
The power of shrewd invention was awake:
"In the broad fields of Crete, that lie far off   315
Beyond the sea, I heard of Ithaca,
To which I now am come with these my goods.
I left as many for my sons and fled,
For I had slain Orsilochus, the fleet
Of foot, the dear son of Idomeneus,   320
Who overcame by swiftness in the race
The foremost runners in the realm of Crete.
He sought to rob me wholly of my share
Of Trojan spoil, for which I had endured
Hardships in war with heroes, and at sea   325
Among the angry waves. The cause was this:
I would not in the siege of Troy submit
To serve his father, but, apart from him,
I led a troop, companions of my own.
The youth returning from the fields I met,   330
And smote him with the spear—for near the way
I lay in ambush with a single friend.
A night exceeding dark was in the sky;
No human eye beheld, nor did he know
Who took his life. When I had slain him thus   335
With the sharp spear I hastened to a ship
Of the Phoenicians, and besought their aid,
And gave them large reward, and bade them steer
To Pylos, bearing me, and leave me there,
Or where the Epeians hold the hallowed coast   340
Of Elis. But the force of adverse winds

Drove them unwilling thence; they meant no fraud.
We wandered hither, just at night we came;
And rowing hard, the seamen brought their ship
Within the port. No word was said of food,   345
Though great our need. All disembarked in haste
And lay upon the shore. Deep was the sleep
That stole upon my weary limbs. The men
Took from the hold my goods, and, bearing them
To where I slumbered on the sand, set sail   350
For populous Sidonia, leaving me
Here quite alone with sorrow in my heart."
He spake; the blue-eyed goddess, Pallas, smiled,
And touched the chief caressingly. She seemed
A beautiful and stately woman now,   355
Such as are skilled in works of rare device,
And thus she said to him in winged words:
"Full shrewd were he, a master of deceit,
Who should surpass thee in the ways of craft,
Even though he were a god—thou unabashed   360
And prompt with shifts, and measureless in wiles!
Thou canst not even in thine own land refrain
From artful figments and misleading words,
As thou hast practiced from thy birth. But now
Speak we of other matters, for we both   365
Are skilled in stratagem. Thou art the first
Of living men in counsel and in speech,
And I am famed for foresight and for craft
Among the immortals. Dost thou not yet know
Pallas Athene, child of Zeus, whose aid   370
Is present to defend thee in all time
Of peril, and but lately gained for thee
The favor of the whole Phaeacian race?

And hither am I come to frame for thee
Wise counsels, and to hide away the stores   375
Given by the opulent Phaeacian chiefs
At thy departure. I shall also tell
What thou must yet endure beneath the roof
Of thine own palace, by the will of fate.
Yet bear it bravely, since thou must, nor speak   380
To any man or woman of thyself
And of thy wandering hither, but submit
To many things that grieve thee, silently,
And bear indignities from violent men."
Odysseus, the sagacious, thus rejoined: 385
"O goddess, it is hard for mortal man
To know thee when he meets thee, though his sight
Be of the sharpest, for thou puttest on
At pleasure any form. Yet this I know,
That thou wert kind to me when we, the sons   390
Of Greece, were warring in the realm of Troy.
But when we had o'erthrown the lofty town
Of Priam, and embarked, and when some god
Had scattered the Achaeans, after that,
Daughter of Zeus, I never saw thee more,   395
Never perceived thee entering my bark
And guarding me from danger—but I roamed
Ever from place to place, my heart weighed down
By sorrow, till the gods delivered me,
And till thy counsels in the opulent realm   400
Of the Phaeacians brought my courage back,
And thou thyself didst guide me to the town.
And now in thy great father's name I pray—
For yet I cannot think that I am come
To pleasant Ithaca, but have been thrown   405

Upon some other coast, and fear that thou
Art jesting with me, and hast spoken thus
But to deceive me—tell me, is it true
That I am in my own beloved land?"
And then the goddess, blue-eyed Pallas, said: 410
"Such ever are thy thoughts, and therefore I
Must not forsake thee in thy need. I know
How prompt thy speech, how quick thy thought, how shrewd
Thy judgment. If another man had come
From such long wanderings, he had flown at once   415
Delighted to his children and his wife
In his own home. But thou desirest not
To ask or hear of them till thou hast put
Thy consort to the trial of her truth—
Her who now sits within thy halls and waits   420
In vain for thee, and in perpetual grief
And weeping wears her nights and days away.
I never doubted—well, in truth, I knew
That thou, with all thy comrades lost, wouldst reach
Thy country, but I dreaded to withstand   425
My father's brother Poseidon, who was wroth,
And fiercely wroth, for that thou hadst deprived
His well-beloved son of sight. But now
Attend, and I will show thee Ithaca
By certain tokens; mark them and believe.   430
The port of Phorcys, Ancient of the Deep,
Is here; and there the spreading olive-tree,
Just at the haven's head; and, close beside,
The cool dark grotto, sacred to the nymphs
Called Naiads—a wide-vaulted cave where once   435
Thou earnest oft with chosen hecatombs,
An offering to the nymphs—and here thou seest

The mountain Neritus with all his woods."
So spake the goddess, and dispersed the mist,
And all the scene appeared. Odysseus saw   440
Well pleased, rejoicing in his own dear land,
And, stooping, kissed the bountiful earth, and raised
His hands, and thus addressed the nymphs in prayer:
"Nymphs, Naiads, born to Zeus, I did not hope
To be with you again. With cheerful prayers   445
I now salute you. We shall bring you soon
Our offerings, as of yore, if graciously
Zeus's daughter, huntress-queen, shall grant me yet
To live, and bless my well-beloved son."
And then the goddess, blue-eyed Pallas, said: 450
"Be of good cheer, and let no anxious thought
Disturb thy mind. Let us bestir ourselves
To hide away, the treasures thou hast brought
Within this hallowed grot in some recess
Where they may lie in safety; afterward   455
Will we take counsel what should next be done."
The goddess said these words, and took her way
Into the shadowy cavern, spying out
Its hiding-places; while Odysseus brought
The treasures thither in his arms—the gold,   460
The enduring brass, the raiment nobly wrought—
Which the Phaeacians gave him. These they laid
Together in due order; Pallas then,
The daughter of the aegis-bearer Zeus,
Closed up the opening with a massive rock.   465
Then, sitting by the sacred olive-tree,
They plotted to destroy the haughty crew
Of suitors, and the blue-eyed Pallas said:
"O nobly born, and versed in many wiles,

Son of Laertes! now the hour is come   470
To think how thou shalt lay avenging hands
Upon the shameless crew who, in thy house,
For three years past have made themselves its lords,
And wooed thy noble wife and brought her gifts,
While, pining still for thy return, she gave   475
Hopes to each suitor, and by messages
Made promises to all, though cherishing
A different purpose in her secret heart."
Odysseus, the sagacious, answered her:
"Ah me, I should have perished utterly,   480
By such an evil fate as overtook
Atrides Agamemnon, in the halls
Of my own palace, but for thee, whose words,
O goddess, have revealed what I should know.
Now counsel me how I may be avenged.   485
Be ever by my side, and strengthen me
With courage, as thou didst when we o'erthrew
The towery crest of Ilium. Would thou wert
Still my ally, as then! I would engage,
O blue-eyed Pallas, with three hundred foes,   490
If thou, dread goddess, wouldst but counsel me."
And then the blue-eyed Pallas spake again:
"I will be present with thee. When we once
Begin the work, thou shalt not leave my sight;
And many a haughty suitor with his blood   495
And brains shall stain thy spacious palace floor.
Now will I change thine aspect, so that none
Shall know thee. I will wither thy fair skin,
And it shall hang on crooked limbs; thy locks
Of auburn I will cause to fall away,   500
And round thee fling a cloak which all shall see

With loathing. I will make thy lustrous eyes
Dull to the sight, and thus shalt thou appear
A squalid wretch to all the suitor train,
And to thy wife, and to the son whom thou   505
Didst leave within thy palace. Then at first
Repair thou to the herdsman, him who keeps
Thy swine; for he is loyal, and he loves
Thy son and the discreet Penelope.
There wilt thou find him as he tends his swine,   510
That find their pasturage beside the rock
Of Corax, and by Arethusa's founts
On nourishing acorns they are fed, and drink
The dark clear water, whence the flesh of swine
Is fattened. There remain, and carefully   515
Inquire of all that thou wouldst know, while I,
Taking my way to Sparta, the abode
Of lovely women, call Telemachus,
Thy son, Odysseus, who hath visited
King Menelaus in his broad domain,   520
To learn if haply thou art living yet."
Odysseus, the sagacious, answered her:
"Why didst not thou, to whom all things are known,
Tell him concerning me? Must he too roam
And suffer on the barren deep, and leave   525
To others his estates, to be their spoil?"
And then the blue-eyed goddess spake again:
"Let not that thought distress thee. It was I
Who sent him thither, that he might deserve
The praise of men. No evil meets him there;   530
But in the halls of Atreus' son he sits,
Safe mid the abounding luxuries. 'Tis true
That even now the suitors lie in wait,

In their black ship, to slay him ere he reach
His native land; but that will hardly be   535
Before the earth shall cover many a one
Of the proud suitors who consume thy wealth."
So Pallas spake, and touched him with her wand,
And caused the blooming skin to shrivel up
On his slow limbs, and the fair hair to fall,   540
And with an old man's wrinkles covered all
His frame, and dimmed his lately glorious eyes.
Another garb she gave—a squalid vest;
A ragged, dirty cloak, all stained with smoke;
And over all the huge hide of a stag,   545
From which the hair was worn. A staff, beside,
She gave, and shabby scrip with many a rent,
Tied with a twisted thong. This said and done,
They parted; and the goddess flew to seek
Telemachus in Sparta's sacred town.   550

BOOK XIV

Then from the haven up the rugged path   1
Odysseus went among the woody heights.
He sought the spot where Pallas bade him meet
The noble swineherd, who of all that served
The great Odysseus chiefly had in charge   5
To bring the day's supplies. He found him there
Seated beneath the portico, before
His airy lodge, that might be seen from far,
Well built and spacious, standing by itself.
Eumaeus, while his lord was far away,   10
Had built it, though not bidden by the queen,
Nor old Laertes, with the stones he drew
From quarries thither. Round it he had set
A hedge of thorns, encircling these with sakes
Close set and many, cloven from the heart   15
Of oak. Within that circuit he had made
Twelve sties, beside each other, for the swine
To lie in. Fifty wallowed in each sty,
All females; there they littered. But he males
Were fewer, and were kept without and these   20
The suitor train made fewer everyday,

Feeding upon them, for Eumaeus sent
Always the best of all his fading herd.
These numbered twice nine score. Beside them slept
Four mastiffs, which the master swineherd fed,   25
Savage as wolves. Eumaeus to his feet
Was fitting sandals, which he carved and shaped
From a stained ox-hide, while the other hinds
Were gone on different errands—three to drive
The herds of swine—a fourth was sent to take   30
A fatling to the city, that the crew
Of arrogant suitors, having offered him
In sacrifice, might feast upon his flesh.
The loud-mouthed dogs that saw Odysseus come
Ran toward him, fiercely baying. He sat down   35
At once, through caution, letting fall his staff
Upon the ground, and would have suffered there
Unseemly harm, within his own domain,
But then the swineherd, following with quick steps,
Rushed through the vestibule, and dropped the hide.   40
He chid the dogs and, pelting them with stones,
Drove them asunder, and addressed the king:
"O aged man, the mastiffs of the lodge
Had almost torn thee, and thou wouldst have cast
Bitter reproach upon me. Other griefs   45
And miseries the gods have made my lot.
Here sorrowfully sitting I lament
A godlike master, and for others tend
His fading swine; while, haply hungering
For bread, he wanders among alien men so   50
In other kingdoms, if indeed he lives
And looks upon the sun. But follow me,
And come into the house, that there, refreshed

With food and wine, old man, thou mayst declare
Whence thou dost come and what thou hast endured."   55
So the good swineherd spake, and led the way
Into the lodge, and bade his guest sit down,
And laid thick rushes for his seat, and spread
On these a wild goat's shaggy hide to make
A soft and ample couch. Rejoiced to meet   60
So kind a welcome, thus Odysseus spake:
"May Zeus and all the deathless gods
Bestow on thee, my host, in recompense
Of this kind welcome, all thy heart's desire!"
And then, Eumaeus, thou didst answer thus: 65
"My guest, it were not right to treat with scorn
A stranger, though he were of humbler sort
Than thou, for strangers and the poor are sent
By Zeus; our gifts are small, though gladly given,
As it must ever be with those who serve   70
Young masters, whom they fear. The gods themselves
Prevent, no doubt, the safe return of him
Who loved me much, and would ere this have given
What a kind lord is wont to give his hind—
A house, a croft, the wife whom he has wooed,   75
Rewarding faithful services which God
Hath prospered, as he here hath prospered mine.
Thus would my master, had he here grown old,
Have recompensed my toils; but he is dead.
O that the house of Helen, for whose sake   80
So many fell, had perished utterly!
For he went forth at Agamemnon's call,
Honoring the summons, and on Ilium's coast,
Famed for its coursers, fought the sons of Troy."
He spake, and girt his tunic round his loins,   85

And hastened to the sties in which the herds
Of swine were lying. Thence he took out two
And slaughtered them, and singed them, sliced the flesh,
And fixed it upon spits, and, when the whole
Was roasted, brought and placed it reeking hot,   90
Still on the spits and sprinkled with white meal,
Before Odysseus. Then he mingled wine
Of delicate flavors in a wooden bowl,
And opposite Odysseus sat him down,
And thus with kindly words bespake his guest: 95
"Feast, stranger, on these porkers. We who serve
May feed on them; it is the suitor train
That banquet on the fatted swine—the men
Who neither fear heaven's anger nor are moved
By pity. The great gods are never pleased   100
With violent deeds; they honor equity
And justice. Even those who land as foes
And spoilers upon foreign shores, and bear
Away much plunder by the will of Zeus,
Returning homeward with their laden barks,   105
Feel, brooding heavily upon their minds,
The fear of vengeance. But these suitors know—
For haply they have heard some god declare—
That he, the king, is dead; they neither make
Their suit with decency, nor will withdraw   110
To their own homes, but at their ease devour
His substance with large waste, and never spare.
Of all the days and nights which Zeus
Gives to mankind is none when they require
A single victim only, or but two,   115
For sacrifice, and lavishly they drain
His wine-jars. Once large revenues were his.

No hero on the dark-soiled continent
Nor in the isle of Ithaca possessed
Such wealth as he, nor even twenty men   120
Together. Hear me while I give the amount.
Twelve herds of kine that on the mainland graze
Are his, as many flocks of sheep, of swine
As many droves; as many flocks of goats
Are tended there by strangers, and by hinds,   125
His servants. Here moreover, in the fields
Beyond us, graze eleven numerous flocks
Of goats, attended by his trusty men,
Each one of whom brings daily home a goat,
The finest of the fatlings. I meantime   130
Am keeper of these swine, and from the drove
I choose and to the palace send the best."
So spake the swineherd, while Odysseus ate
The flesh with eager appetite, and drank
The wine in silence, meditating woe   135
To all the suitors. When the meal was o'er,
And he was strengthened by the food, his host
Filled up with wine the cup from which he drank,
And gave it to Odysseus, who, well pleased,
Received it, and with winged words replied: 140
"What rich and mighty chief was he, my friend,
Of whom thou speakest, and who purchased thee?
Thou sayest that he died to swell the fame
Of Agamemnon. Tell his name, for I
Perchance know somewhat of him. Zeus   145
And the great gods know whether I have seen
The man, and have some tidings for thy ear;
For I have wandered over many lands."
And then again the noble swineherd spake:

"O aged man, no wanderer who should bring 150
News of Odysseus e'er would win his wife
And son to heed the tale. For roving men,
In need of hospitality, are prone
To falsehood, and will never speak the truth.
The vagabond who comes to Ithaca 155
Goes straightway to my mistress with his lies.
Kindly she welcomes him, and cherishes
And questions him, while tears abundantly
Fall from her lids—such tears as women shed
Whose lords have perished in a distant land. 160
Thou too, old man, perchance, couldst readily
Frame a like fable, if someone would give
A change of raiment for thy news—a cloak
And tunic. But the dogs and fowls of air
Have doubtless fed upon the frame from which 165
The life has passed, and torn from off his bones
The skin, or fishes of the deep have preyed
Upon it, and his bones upon the shore
Lie whelmed in sand. So is he lost to us,
And sorrow is the lot of all his friends, 170
Mine most of all; for nowhere shall I find
So kind a master, though I were to come
Into my father's and my mother's house,
Where I was born and reared. Nor do I pine
So much to look on them with my own eyes, 175
And in my place of birth, as I lament
Odysseus lost. Though he be far away,
Yet must I ever speak, O stranger guest,
His name with reverence, for exceedingly
He loved me and most kindly cared for me; 180
And though he is to be with us no more,

I hold him as an elder brother still."
Odysseus, the great sufferer, thus replied:
"Since then, my friend, thou dost not say nor think
That he will come again, nor wilt believe   185
My words, I now repeat, but with an oath,
Odysseus will return. Let this reward
Be given for my good news: the very hour
When he once more is in his house, bestow
On me a comely change of raiment—cloak   190
And tunic—nor will I accept the gift,
Though great my need, until he comes again.
For as the gates of hell do I detest
The man who, tempted by his poverty,
Deceives with lying words. Now Zeus   195
Bear witness, and this hospitable board
And hearth of good Odysseus where I sit,
That all which I foretell will come to pass.
This very year Odysseus will return.
He, when this month goes out, and as the next   200
Is entering, will be here in his domain,
To be avenged on those, whoe'er they be,
That dare insult his wife and noble son."
And then, Eumaeus, thou didst answer thus:
"Old man, I shall not give thee that reward,   205
For never will Odysseus come again
To his own palace. Drink thy wine in peace,
And let us give our thoughts to other things.
Remind me not of this again; my heart
Grows heavy in my bosom when I hear   210
My honored master named. But leave the oath
Unsworn, and may Odysseus come, as we
Earnestly wish—I and Penelope,

And old Laertes, and the godlike youth
Telemachus. And then, again, I bear   215
Perpetual sorrow for Telemachus,
My master's son, to whom the gods had given
A generous growth like that of some young plant,
And who, I hoped, would prove no less in worth
Than his own father, and of eminent gifts   220
In form and mind. Some god, perchance some man.
Hath caused that mind to lose its equal poise,
And he is gone to Pylos the divine
For tidings of his father. Meanwhile here
The arrogant suitors plan to lie in wait   225
For him as he returns, that utterly
The stock of great Arcesius from our isle
May perish, and its name be heard no more.
Speak we no more of him, be it his fate
To fall or flee; but O, may Cronus's son   230
Protect him with his arm! And now, old man,
Relate, I pray, thy fortunes; tell me true,
That I may know who thou mayst be, and whence
Thou earnest, where thy city lies, and who
Thy parents were, what galley landed thee   235
Upon our coast, and how the mariners
Brought thee to Ithaca, and of what race
They claim to be; for I may well suppose
Thou hast not come to Ithaca on foot."
Odysseus, the sagacious, answered him: 240
"I will tell all and truly. Yet if here
Were store of food, and wine for many days,
And we might feast at ease within thy lodge
While other labored, I should hardly end
In a whole year the history of the woes   245

Which I have borne, and of the many toils
Which it hath pleased the gods to lay on me.
"It is my boast that I am of the race
Who dwell in spacious Crete, a rich man's son,
Within whose palace many other sons   250
Were born and reared, the offspring of his wife;
But me a purchased mother whom he made
His concubine brought forth to him. And yet
Castor Hylacides, from whom I sprang,
Held me in equal favor with the rest;   255
And he himself was honored like a god
Among the Cretan people, for his wealth
And for his prosperous life and gallant sons.
But fate and death o'ertook and bore him down
To Hades' realm, and his magnanimous sons   260
Divided his large riches, casting lots.
Small was the portion they assigned to me;
They gave a dwelling, but my valor won
A bride, the daughter of a wealthy house—
Tor I was not an idler, nor in war   265
A coward; but all that is with the past,
And thou, who seest the stubble now, mayst guess
What was the harvest, ere calamities
Had come so thick upon me. Once did Ares
And Pallas lend me courage, and the power   270
To break through ranks of armed men. Whene'er
I formed an ambush of the bravest chiefs,
And planned destruction to the enemy,
My noble spirit never set the fear
Of death before me; I was ever first   275
To spring upon the foes, and with my spear
To smite them as they turned their steps to flee.

Such was I once in war; to till the fields
I never liked, nor yet the household cares
By which illustrious sons are reared. I loved 280
Ships well appointed, combats, polished spears
And arrows. Things that others hold in dread
Were my delight; some god inclined to them
My mind—so true it is that different men
Rejoice in different labors. Ere the sons 285
Of Greece embarked for Troy, I served in war
Nine times as leader against foreign foes,
With troops and galleys under me, and then
I prospered; from the mass of spoil I chose
The things that pleased me, and obtained by lot 290
Still other treasures. Thus my household grew
In riches, and I was revered and great
Among the Cretans. When all-seeing Zeus
Decreed the unhappy voyage to the coast
Of Troy, they made the great Idomeneus 295
And me commanders of the fleet. No power
Had we—the public clamor was so fierce—
To put the charge aside. Nine years we warred—
We sons of Greece—and in the tenth laid waste
The city of Priam, and embarked for home. 300
Our fleets were scattered by the gods. For me
Did all-disposing Zeus ordain
A wretched lot. But one short month I dwelt
Happy among my children, with the wife
Wedded to me in youth, and my large wealth. 305
And then I planned a voyage to the coast
Of Egypt, with a gallant fleet, and men
Of godlike valor. I equipped nine ships,
And quickly came the people to embark.

Six days on shore my comrades banqueted,   310
And many a victim for the sacrifice
And for the feast I gave; the seventh we sailed
From Crete's broad isle before a favoring wind
That blew from the clear north, and easily
We floated on as down a stream. No ship   315
Was harmed upon its way; in health and ease
We sat, the wind and helmsmen guiding us,
And came upon the fifth day to the land
Of Egypt, watered by its noble streams.
I bade my comrades keep beside our ships   320
Upon the strand, and watch them well. I placed
Sentries upon the heights. Yet confident
In their own strength, and rashly giving way
To greed, my comrades ravaged the fair fields
Of the Egyptians, slew them, and bore off   325
Their wives and little ones. The rumor reached
The city soon; the people heard the alarm
And came together. With the early morn
All the great plain was thronged with horse and foot,
And gleamed with brass; while Zeus, the Thunderer, sent   330
A deadly fear into our ranks, where none
Dared face the foe. On every side was death.
The Egyptians hewed down many with the sword,
And some they led away alive to toil
For them in slavery. To my mind there came   335
A thought, inspired by Zeus; yet I could wish
That I had met my fate, and perished there
In Egypt, such have been my sorrows since.
I took the well-wrought helmet from my head,
And from my shoulders dropped the shield, and flung   340
The javelin from my hand, and went to meet

The monarch in his chariot, clasped his knees
And kissed them. He was moved to pity me,
And spared me. In his car he seated me,
And bore me weeping home. Though many rushed   345
At me with ashen spears, to thrust me through—
For furious was their anger—he forbade.
He feared the wrath of Zeus, the stranger's friend
And foe of wrong. Seven years I dwelt among
The Egyptians, and I gathered in their land   350
Large wealth, for all were liberal of their gifts.
But with the eighth revolving year there came
A shrewd Phoenician, deep in guile, whose craft
Had wrought much wrong to many. With smooth words
This man persuaded me to go with him   355
Into Phoenicia, where his dwelling lay
And his possessions. With him I abode
For one whole year; and when its months and days
Were ended, and another year began,
He put me in a ship to cross the sea   360
To Lybia. He had framed a treacherous plot,
By making half the vessel's cargo mine,
To lure me thither, and to sell me there
For a large price. I went on board constrained,
But with misgivings. Under a clear sky,   365
With favoring breezes from the north, we ran
O'er the mid sea, beyond the isle of Crete.
When we had left the isle, and saw no land
But only sky and sea, Cronus-son bade
A black cloud gather o'er our roomy ship.   370
The sea grew dark below. On high the God
Thundered again and yet again, and sent
A bolt into our ship, which, as it felt

The lightning, reeled and shuddered, and was filled
With sulfur-smoke. The seamen from the deck   375
Fell headlong, and were tossed upon the waves
Like seamews round our galley, which the God
Forbade them to regain. But Zeus
Gave to my hands, bewildered as I was,
Our dark-prowed galley's mast, unbroken yet,   380
That by its aid I might escape. I wound
My arms around it, and the raging winds
Swept me along. Nine days they bore me on,
And on the tenth dark night a mighty surge
Drifted me, as it rolled, upon the coast   385
Of the Thesprotians. There the hero-king
Of the Thesprotians freely sheltered me
And fed me; for his well-beloved son
Had found me overcome with cold and toil,
And took me by the hand and raised me up,   390
And led me to his father's house, and gave
Seemly attire, a tunic and a cloak.
"There heard I of Odysseus. Pheidon told
How he received him as a guest and friend,
When on his homeward voyage. Then he showed   395
The wealth Odysseus gathered, brass and gold,
And steel divinely wrought. That store might serve
To feed, until ten generations pass,
Another household. But the chief himself.
So Pheidon said, was at Dodona then;   400
For he had gone to hear from the tall oak
Of Zeus the counsel of the God,
Whether to land in opulent Ithaca,
After long years of absence, openly
Or in disguise."The monarch took an oath   405

In his own palace, pouring to the gods
Their wine, that even then the ship was launched,
And the crew ready to attend him home.
But me he first dismissed. There was a ship
Of the Thesprotians just about to make   410
A voyage to Dulichium, rich in fields
Of wheat. He bade them take me faithfully
To King Acastus; but another thought
Found favor with the crew, a wicked scheme
To plunge me deeper in calamity.   415
And when our ship had sailed away from land,
They hastened to prepare me for a life
Of slavery. They took my garments off,
Mantle and cloak, and clothed me in a vest
And cloak, the very rags which thou dost see.   420
The evening brought them to the pleasant fields
Of Ithaca. They bound me in the ship
With a strong cord, and disembarked, and took
A hasty meal upon the ocean-side;
Easily did the gods unbind my limbs.   425
I wrapped a tattered cloth about my head,
And, slipping from the polished rudder, brought
My bosom to the sea, and spread my hands,
And swam away. I soon had left the crew
At distance; then I turned and climbed the shore,   430
Where it was dark with forest, and lay close
Within its shelter, while they wandered round
And grumbled, but they ventured not to pass
Into the island farther on their search.
They turned, and went on board their roomy bark.   435
Thus mightily the gods delivered me,
And they have brought me to a wise man's lodge,

And now I see it is my lot to live."
Then thou, Eumaeus, thus didst make reply:
"Unhappy stranger, thou hast deeply moved   440
My heart in telling all that thou hast borne,
And all thy wanderings. Yet are some things wrong.
Thou hast not spoken of Odysseus well.
Why should a man like thee invent such tales,
So purposeless? Of one thing I am sure   445
Concerning his return—the gods all hate
My master, since they neither caused his death
In the great war of Troy, nor, when the war
Was over, suffered him to die at home,
And in the arms of those who loved him most;   450
For then would all the Greeks have reared to him
A monument, and mighty would have been
The heritage of glory for his son;
But now ingloriously the harpy brood
Have torn him. I, apart among my swine,   455
Go never to the town, unless, perchance,
The sage Penelope requires me there,
When someone comes with tidings from abroad.
Then those who sorrow for their absent lord,
And those who waste his substance, both inquire   460
News of the king. For me, it suits me not
Ever to ask for tidings, since the day
When an Aetolian with a flattering tale
Deceived me. He had slain a man, and came
Wandering in many lands to my abode,   465
And kindly I received him. He had seen,
He said, my master with Idomeneus,
Among the Cretans, putting in repair
His galleys, shattered by a furious storm,

And in the summertime he would be here,   470
Or in the autumn, bringing ample wealth,
And his brave comrades with him. Seek not then,
O aged sufferer, whom some deity
Has guided hither, to amuse my grief
With fictions that may bring back pleasant thoughts,   475
Since not for them I minister to thee
And love thee, but through reverence for Zeus—
The stranger's friend—-and pity for thyself."
Odysseus, the sagacious, spake again:
"Within thy bosom thou dost bear a heart   430
Of slow belief, since not the oath I take
Persuades or even 'moves thee. Make we now
A covenant, and let the gods who dwell
Upon Olympus be our witnesses,
That when thy master comes to this abode   435
Thou wilt bestow a tunic and a cloak,
And wilt dispatch me clothed in seemly garb
Hence to Dulichium, whither I would go.
But if he come not as I have foretold,
Then charge thy servants that they cast me down   440
From a tall rock, that never beggar more
May think to cozen thee with lying tales."
The noble swineherd answered him and said:
"Great would my honor be, and I should gain
Great praise for worth among the sons of men,   495
If, having welcomed thee into my lodge
And spread the board for thee, I took thy life;
Then boldly might I pray to Cronus's son.
But see, the supper hour is come, and soon
Will my companions be within, and they   500
Will make a liberal banquet ready here."

Thus did the twain confer. Now came the swine,
And those who tended them. They penned the herd
In their enclosure, and a din of cries
Rose as they entered. Then the swineherd called   505
To his companions: "Bring the best of all,
And we will make an offering for the sake
Of one who comes from far and is my guest.
And we will also feast, for we have toiled
Long time in tendance of this white-toothed herd,   510
And others waste, unpunished, what we rear."
So spake he, and began to cleave the wood
With the sharp steel; the others chose and brought
A fatted brawn, and placed him on the hearth.
Nor was the swineherd careless of the rites   515
Due to the gods—such was his piety.
From off the white-toothed victim first he sheared
The bristles of the forehead, casting them
Into the flames, and prayed to all the gods
For wise Odysseus and his safe return.   520
Next, with a fragment of the oaken trunk
Which he had just then cleft, he smote the boar,
And the life left it. Then they cut its throat,
And, having singed it, quickly hewed the parts
Asunder, while the swineherd took and laid,   525
On the rich fat, raw portions from the limbs
For sacrifice, and other parts he cast,
Sprinkled with flour of meal, into the flames;
The rest they duly sliced and fixed on spits,
And roasted carefully, and drew it back,   530
And heaped it on the board. And now arose
The swineherd to divide the whole, for well
He knew the duty of a host. He made

Seven parts; and one he offered to the Nymphs,
To Hermes, son of Maia, one, and both   535
With prayer; the rest he set before the guests,
But, honoring Odysseus, gave to him
The white-toothed victim's ample chine. The king,
The wise Odysseus, was well pleased, and said:
"Eumaeus, be thou ever dear to Zeus   540
As to myself, since with thy benefits
Thou freely honorest such a one as I."
And thou, Eumaeus, madest answer thus:
"Eat, venerable stranger, and enjoy
What is before us. At his pleasure God   545
Gives or withholds; his power is over all."
He spake, and burned to the eternal gods
The firstlings, and poured out the dark red wine,
And to Odysseus, spoiler of walled towns,
Who sat beside the table, gave the cup.   550
Meantime to each Mesaulius brought the bread—
A servant whom Eumaeus, while his lord
Was far away, had taken for himself,
Without the order of Penelope
Or old Laertes; from the Taphian tribe   555
With his own goods he bought him. Now the guests
Put forth their hands and shared the ready feast;
And when their thirst and hunger were appeased
Mesaulius took the bread away, and all,
Satiate with food and wine, lay down to rest.   560
Then came the darkness on, without a moon;
And Zeus the whole night long sent down
The rain, and strong the showery west-wind blew.
And now to try the swineherd, if with all
His kindly ministrations to his guest   565

lie yet would spare to him his cloak, or bid
Another do the like, Odysseus spake:
"Eumaeus, hearken thou, and all the rest,
Thy comrades, while I utter boastful words.
Wine makes me foolish, it can even cause   570
The wise to sing and laugh a silly laugh
And dance, and often to the lips it brings
Words that were better left unsaid. But since
I have begun to prattle, I will not
Keep back my thought. I would I were as young   575
And in the same full strength as when I formed
Part of an ambush near the walls of Troy.
The leaders were Odysseus, and the son
Of Atreus, Menelaus, with myself
The third, for they desired it. When we reached   580
The city and the lofty walls we lay
Couched in a marshy spot among the reeds
And thick-grown shrubs, with all our armor on.
'Twas an inclement night, and the north-wind
Blew bitter chill, the cold snow fell and lay   585
White like hoar-frost; ice gathered on our shields.
The rest had cloaks and tunics, and they slept
At ease, their shoulders covered with their shields.
I only, when I joined the squadron, left
My cloak unwisely, for I had not thought   590
Of such fierce cold. I went but with my shield
And my embroidered girdle. When the night
Was in its later watches, and the stars
Were turning toward their set, I thus bespake
Odysseus near me, thrusting in his side   595
My elbow, and he listened readily:
"Son of Laertes, nobly born and wise!

Odysseus, I shall not be long among
The living; for I perish with the cold.
I have no cloak; some god misled my thought,   600
So that I brought one garment and no more,
And now I see there is no help for me.'
I spake, and instantly his mind conceived
This stratagem—such was his readiness
In council and in battle—and he said   605
To me in a low voice: 'Be silent now,
And let no others of the Achaeans hear!'
And leaning on his elbow thus he spake:
'Hear me, my friends: a dream has come from heaven
Into my sleep. Far from our ships we lie;   610
And now let someone haste to bear from us
This word to Agamemnon, Atreus' son,
The shepherd of the people, that he send
More warriors to this ambush from the fleet'
He spake, and Thoas instantly arose—   615
Andraemon's son—and threw his purple cloak
Aside, and hastened toward the fleet. I took
Gladly the garment he had left, and lay
Till Morning in her golden chariot came.
And now I would that I were young again,   620
And in the vigor of my prime, for then
Some one among the swineherds in the stalls
Would find, I think, a cloak for me, through love
And reverence of such a man; but now
They hold me in slight favor, dressed in rags."   625
And thus, Eumaeus, thou didst make reply:
"O aged man! we see no cause of blame
In thy recital, and of all thy words
Not one is unbecoming or inapt.

Thou shalt not lack for garments, nor aught else   630
That any suppliant in his poverty
Might hope for at our hands tonight. With morn
Gird thou thy tatters on again; for here
We have not many cloaks, nor many a change
Of raiment—only one for each of us.   635
But when the son of our Odysseus comes
Again, he will provide thee with a cloak
And tunic, and will send thee where thou wilt."
He spake and rose, and made his guest a bed
Close to the hearth, and threw on it the skins   640
Of sheep and goats, and there Odysseus lay,
O'er whom the swineherd spread a thick large cloak,
Which he had often worn for a defense
When a wild winter storm was in the air.
Thus slept Odysseus with the young men near.   645
A couch within, and distant from his charge,
Pleased not the swineherd, who first armed himself,
And then went forth. Odysseus gladly saw
That while he was in distant lands his goods
Were watched so faithfully. Eumaeus hung   650
About his sturdy shoulders a sharp sword,
And wrapped a thick cloak round him, tempest-proof,
And took the hide of a huge pampered goat,
And a well-pointed javelin for defense
Both against dogs and men. So went he forth   655
To take his rest where lay the white-toothed swine,
Herded and slumbering underneath a rock,
Whose hollow fenced them from the keen north-wind.

BOOK XV

Then Pallas, hastening to the mighty realm   1
Of Lacedaemon, sought the illustrious son
Of great Odysseus, to remind the youth
Of home, and bid him think of his return.
She found Telemachus and Nestor's son   5
Upon their couches in the portico
Of Menelaus, the renowned. Deep sleep
Held Nestor's son; but to Telemachus
The welcome slumber came not, for his thoughts
Uneasily through all the quiet night   10
Dwelt on his father. Now beside his bed
The blue-eyed Pallas took her stand and spake:
"Telemachus, it is no longer well
That thou shouldst wander from thy home, and leave
All thy possessions, and those arrogant men   15
That crowd thy halls. Beware, lest they devour
Thy substance utterly, dividing all
Among them, and this journey be for naught.
Make suit to Menelaus, great in war,
Quickly to send thee home, that thou mayst join   20
Thy blameless mother in thy halls; for now

289

Her father and her brothers counsel her
To wed Eurymachus, whose gifts exceed
Those of the other suitors, and besides
He offers a yet richer bridal dower.　　　　　　　　25
It were not hard without thy leave to take
Wealth from a palace. What a wife will do
Thou knowest. 'tis her pleasure to increase
The riches of the man whom she has wed.
Care of her former children has she none,　　　　30
Nor memory of the husband whom she took
While yet a maid, and who is in his grave;
Of these she never speaks. Return thou, then,
And give thy goods in charge to one among
The handmaids of thy household who shall seem　　35
The fittest for the trust, until the gods
Bring thee a noble wife. Another word
Have I for thee, and bear thou it in mind:
The chief among the suitors in the strait
Between the rugged Samos and the isle　　　　40
Of Ithaca are lurking, in the hope
To slay thee on thy voyage home; but this
I think they cannot do before the earth
Hold many of the suitor-crew who make
Thy wealth a spoil. Steer thou thy gallant bark　　45
Far from the isles; sail only in the night.
Some god, whoever it may be that keeps
Watch over thee, will send a prosperous gale.
When to the nearest shore of Ithaca
Thou comest in thy ship, let it go on, so　　　50
With all thy comrades, to the town, while thou
Repairest to the keeper of thy swine,
Whose heart is faithful to thee. There remain

With him that night, and send him to the town
With tidings to the sage Penelope   55
That thou art come from Pylos and art safe."
So having said, the goddess took her way
Up to the Olympian height. Telemachus
Touched with his heel and wakened Nestor's son
From a soft slumber, and bespake him thus: 60
"Rise, Nestor's son, Peisistratus, and bring
The firm paced steeds and yoke them to the car,
And we will now set forth upon our way."
And Nestor's son, Peisistratus, replied:
"Telemachus, whatever be our haste,   65
It were not well in darkness to begin
Our journey, and the morn will soon be here.
Remain till Menelaus, Atreus' son,
The hero mighty with the spear, shall come,
And bring his gifts, and place them in our car,   70
And send us on our way with kindly words.
Well does a guest remember all his days
The generous host who shows himself his friend."
He spake, and quickly on her car of gold
Appeared the Morn. Then Menelaus came,   75
The great in battle, from his couch beside
The fair-haired Helen. When Telemachus
Knew of the king's approach, the hero threw
In haste his tunic o'er his noble form,
And over his broad shoulders flung a cloak   80
Of ample folds. Then, going forth, the son
Of great Odysseus met the king and said:
"Atrides Menelaus, loved of Zeus
And sovereign of the people, send me hence,
I pray, to the dear country of my birth,   85

For earnestly I long to be at home."
And Menelaus, great in war, replied:
"Telemachus, I will not keep thee long,
Since thou so much desirest to return.
I am displeased with him who as a host   90
Is lavish of his love, for he will hate
Beyond due measure; best it is to take
The middle way. It is alike a wrong
To thrust the unwilling stranger out of doors,
And to detain him when he longs to go.   95
While he is with us we should cherish him,
And, when he wishes, help him to depart
Remain until I bring thee worthy gifts
And place them in thy chariot, that thine eyes
May look on them; and I will give command   100
That in the palace here the women spread
A liberal feast from stores that lie within.
But if, in turning from thy course, thou choose
To pass through Hellas and the midland tract
Of Argos, I will yoke my steeds and go   105
With thee, and show the cities thronged with men;
Nor will they send us empty-handed thence,
But bring us gifts which we may bear away—
Tripod, perchance, or cauldron wrought of brass,
Perchance a pair of mules or golden cup."   110
Then spake discreet Telemachus in turn:
"Atrides Menelaus, loved of Zeus
And sovereign of the people, rather far
Would I return to my own home; for there
Is no man left in charge of what is mine,"   115
And I must go, lest, while I vainly seek
My father, I may perish, or may lose

Some valued treasure from my palace rooms."
The valiant Menelaus heard, and bade
His wife and maidens spread without delay   120
A ready banquet from the stores within.
Then Eteoneus from his morning sleep,
Son of Boetheus, came, for very near
His dwelling was. The sovereign bade him light
A fire and roast the flesh, and he obeyed.   125
And then into the fragrant treasure-room
Descended Menelaus, not alone;
Helen and Megapenthes went with him.
And when they came to where the treasures lay,
Atrides took a double goblet up,   130
And bade his son, young Megapenthes, bear
A silver beaker thence, while Helen stood
Beside the coffers where the embroidered robes
Wrought by her hands were laid. The glorious dame
Took one and brought it forth, most beautiful   135
In needlework, and amplest of them all.
The garment glittered like a star, and lay
Below the other robes. Then, passing through
The palace halls, they found Telemachus,
And thus the fair-haired Menelaus spake: 140
"Telemachus, may Zeus the Thunderer,
Husband of Hera, grant thee to return
According to thy wish! I give thee here
Of all the treasures which my house contains
The fairest and most precious. I present   145
A goblet all of silver, save the lips,
And they are bound with gold; it is the work
Of Hephaestus. Phaedimus the hero, king
Of the Sidonians, gave it me when once

His palace sheltered me. He gave it me   150
At parting, and I now would have it thine."
Atrides spake, and gave into his hands
The double goblet. Megapenthes next
Before him set the shining beaker wrought
Of silver. Rosy Helen, holding up   155
The robe, drew near, and spake to him and said:
"I also bring to thee, dear son, a gift,
The work of Helen's hands, which thou shalt keep,
In memory of her, until the day
Of thy desired espousals, when thy bride   160
Shall wear it. Let it in the meantime lie
Within thy halls, in thy dear mother's care;
And mayst thou soon and happily arrive
At thy fair palace and thy native coast."
So spake she, placing in his hands the robe.   165
He took it, and was glad. Peisistratus
Was moved with wonder as he saw, and laid
The presents in the car. The fair-haired king
Then led them to the hall, and seated them
On thrones and couches, where a maiden brought   170
Water in a fair golden ewer, and o'er
A silver basin poured it for their hands,
And near them set a table smoothly wrought
The matron of the palace brought them bread
And many a delicate dish to please the taste   175
From stores within the house. Then to the board
Boetheus' son drew near and carved the meats,
And gave to each a portion, while the son
Of glorious Menelaus poured the wine.
The guests put forth their hands and shared the food   180
That lay prepared before them. When the calls

Of thirst and hunger ceased, Telemachus
And Nestor's famous son brought forth and yoked
The steeds, and climbed into the sumptuous car,
And drove from out the echoing portico.   185
Atrides Menelaus, amber-haired,
Went forth with them, and, holding in his hand
A golden cup of generous wine, poured out
An offering for their voyage to the gods.
Before the steeds he took his stand, and first   190
Drank from the cup, and then bespake the guests:
"Now fare ye well, young men, and when ye come
To Nestor, shepherd of the people, give
Greetings from me; for he was kind to me
As if he were a father, when the sons   195
Of Greece were warring in the realm of Troy."
Then spake in turn discreet Telemachus:
"Assuredly I shall relate to him,
As soon as I am with him, all that thou,
foster-child of Zeus, hast bid me say;   200
And would to heaven I might as surely tell
Odysseus in his palace, when again
I come to Ithaca, how welcome thou
Hast made me here, and how I came away
With treasures rich and many from thy court."   205
As thus he spake, an eagle to the right
Appeared, that, flying, bore a large white goose,
Clutched from the tame flock in the palace court;
And men and women ran the way he flew,
And shouted after him. Before the steeds   210
Of the young men, and still on the right hand,
The bird went sweeping on. They saw well pleased,
And every heart was gladdened. To the rest

Peisistratus, the son of Nestor, said:

"Now tell me, Menelaus, loved of Zeus,   215

Prince of the people! does the god who sends

This portent mean the sign for us or thee?"

He spake; and Menelaus, dear to Ares,

Paused, thinking how to answer him aright,

When thus the long-robed Helen interposed: 220

"Listen to me, and I will prophesy

As the gods prompt me, and as I believe

The event will be. Just as this eagle came

From the wild hills, his birthplace and his haunt,

And seized and bore away the water-fowl   225

Reared near our halls, so will Odysseus come,

After much hardship and long wanderings,

To his own home, to be avenged: perchance

Already is at home, and meditates

An evil end to all the suitor crew."   230

Then spake discreet Telemachus in turn:

"May Hera's husband, Zeus the Thunderer,

So order the event, and I will there

Make vows to thee as to a deity."

He spake and touched the coursers with the lash;   235

And through the city rapidly they went

And toward the plain, and all day long they shook

The yoke upon their necks. The sun went down;

The roads all lay in darkness as they came

To Pherae, and the house of Diocles,   240

Whose father was Orsilochus, and he

The offspring of Alpheius. There that night

They slept; their host was liberal of his cheer.

But when appeared the daughter of the Dawn,

The rosy-fingered Morn, they yoked the steeds   245

And climbed the sumptuous car, and drove afield
From underneath the echoing portico.
The son of Nestor plied the lash; the steeds
Flew not unwillingly, and quickly reached
The lofty citadel of Pylos. There   250
Telemachus bespake his comrade thus:
"Wilt thou consent to do what I shall ask,
O son of Nestor? 'tis our boast that we
Are friends because our fathers were; besides,
We are of equal age, and journeying thus   255
Has made our friendship firmer. Take me not,
O foster-child of Zeus, beyond the spot
Where lies my galley, lest against my will
The aged Nestor should detain me here
Through kindness, when I needs must hasten home."   260
He spake, and then the son of Nestor mused
How what his friend desired might best be done.
And this seemed wisest after careful thought:
He turned the chariot to the ship and shore,
And taking out the garments and the gold—   265
Beautiful gifts which Menelaus gave—
He put them in the galley's stern, and thus
Bespake Telemachus with winged words:
"Embark in haste, and summon all thy crew
On board before I reach my home and tell   270
The aged king. I know how vehement
His temper is; he will not let thee go,
But hastening hither to enforce thy stay,
At Pylos, will not, I am sure, go back
Without thee; his displeasure will be great."   275
He spake, and toward the Pylian city turned
His steeds with flowing manes, and quickly reached

His home. Meantime Telemachus held forth
To his companions, thus exhorting them:
"My friends, make ready all things in our ship   280
And mount the deck, for we must now set sail."
He spake, they hearkened and obeyed, and leaped
On board and manned the benches. While he thus
Was hastening his departure, offering prayer
And pouring wine to Pallas at the stern,   285
A stranger came, a seer, a fugitive
From Argos, where his hand had slain a man.
Melampus was his ancestor, who dwelt
Some time in Pylos, mother of fair flocks—
Rich, and inhabiting a sumptuous house   290
Among the Pylians. Afterward he joined
Another people, fleeing from his home
And from the mighty Neleus, haughtiest
Of living men, who, seizing his large wealth,
Held it a year by force. Melampus lay   295
Meantime within the house of Phylacus
Fast bound, and suffering greatly, both because
Of Neleus' daughter, and of his own mind
Distempered by the unapproachable
Erinnys. Yet did he escape from death,   300
And drove the lowing herds to Phylace
And Pylos, and avenged his cruel wrong
On Neleus, carrying off his child to be
A consort for his brother. Then he came
Into the realm of Argos, famed for steeds;   305
For there it was decreed that he should dwell,
And rule o'er many of the Argive race.
And there he took a wife and built a house—
A lofty pile; and there to him were born

Antiphates and Mantius, valiant men.   310
Antiphates was father of a son,
The brave Oicleus, and to him was born
Amphioraus, one of those whose voice
Rouses the nations. aegis-bearing Zeus
And Phoebus loved him with exceeding love;   315
Yet reached he not the threshold of old age,
But, through the treachery of his bribed wife,
Perished too soon at Thebes. To him were born
Two sons, Alcmaeon and Amphilochus.
Clytus and Polyphides were the sons   320
Of Mantius; but Aurora, she who fills
A golden chariot, bore away to heaven
Clytus for his great beauty, there to dwell
Among the immortals, while Apollo gave
To Polyphides of the noble mind   325
To be a prophet, first of living men,
Since now Amphiaraus was no more.
His father had displeased him, and he went
To Hyperesia, where he dwelt, and there
Revealed to all what yet should come to pass.   330
It was his son who now approached; his name
Was Theoclymenus; he saw the prince
Telemachus, who stood beside the swift
Black ship, and, pouring a libation, prayed;
And thus he said to him in winged words: 335
"My friend, whom here beside this bark I find
Making a pious offering, I entreat
Both by that offering and the deity,
And by thy life, and by the lives of these
Who follow thee, declare to me the truth,   340
And keep back naught of all that I inquire—

Who art thou, from what race of men, and where
Thy city lies, and who thy parents are."
Then spake in turn discreet Telemachus:
Stranger, to every point I answer thee.   345
I am by race a son of Ithaca,
My father was Odysseus when alive,
But he has died a miserable death;
Long years has he been absent, and I came
With my companions here, and this black ship,   350
To gather tidings of my father's fate."
Then said the godlike Theoclymenus:
"I too, like thee, am far away from home;
For I have slain a man of my own tribe,
And he had many brothers, many friends,   355
In Argos famed for steeds. Great is the power
Of those Achaeans, and I flee from them
And the black doom of death, to be henceforth
A wanderer among men. O, shelter me
On board thy galley! I, a fugitive,   360
Implore thy mercy, lest they overtake
And slay me; they are surely on my track."
And thus discreet Telemachus replied:
"If thou desire to come on board my ship,
I shall not hinder thee. Come with us then,   365
And take a friendly share in what we have."
So saying he received his brazen spear,
And laid it on the good ship's deck, and went
Himself on board, and, taking at the stern
His place, he seated Theoclymenus   370
Beside him. Then the mariners cast loose
The hawsers, and Telemachus gave forth
The order to prepare for sea. They heard

And eagerly obeyed; they raised the mast,
A pine-tree stem—and, bringing it to stand   375
In its deep socket, bound it there with cords,
And hoisted by their strongly twisted thongs
The ship's white sails. The blue-eyed Pallas sent
A favorable and fresh-blowing wind,
That swept the sky to drive more speedily   380
The galley through the salt-sea waves. They came
To Cruni, and to Chalcis pleasantly
Watered by rivers. Now the sun went down;
Night closed around their way, but onward still
A favorable wind from Zeus   385
Toward Pherae bore them, and the hallowed coast
Of Elis, where the Epeian race bear sway,
And then among the isles whose rocky peaks
Rise from the waters. Here Telemachus
Mused thoughtfully on what his fate might be—   390
To perish by the ambush or escape.
Meantime Odysseus and the swineherd sat
At meat within the lodge; the other men
Were at the board, and when the calls of thirst
And hunger ceased, Odysseus spake to try   395
The swineherd, whether he were bent to show
Yet further kindness, and entreat his stay,
Or whether he would send him to the town.
"Eumaeus, hearken thou, and all the rest.
Tomorrow is my wish to go to town,   400
That I may beg, and be no charge to thee
And thy companions. Give me thy advice,
And send a trusty guide to show the way.
There will I roam the streets, for so I must,
And haply someone there will give a cup   405

Of wine and cake of meal. And when I find
The house of great Odysseus, I will tell
The sage Penelope the news I bring.
Nay, I would even go among the crew
Of arrogant suitors, who perhaps might give   410
A meal, for there is plenty at their feasts,
And I would do whatever they require.
For let me tell thee, and do thou give heed,
There lives no man who can contend with me
In menial tasks—to keep alive a fire   415
With fuel, cleave dry wood, and carve and roast
The meat and pour the wine—whate'er is done
By poor men waiting on the better sort."
And thou, Eumaeus, keeper of the swine,
Didst answer in displeasure: "Woe is me!   420
How could thy bosom harbor such a thought?
O stranger! thou must surely be resolved
To perish if thy purpose be to go
Among the suitor crew, whose insolence
And riot reach the iron vault of heaven.   425
Not such attendants minister to them
As thou art, but fair youths arrayed in cloaks
And tunics, with sleek heads and smooth of face.
These wait at polished tables heavily
Loaded with bread and flesh and wine. Stay thou   430
Content among us, sure that no one here
Is wearied by thy presence, neither I
Nor any of my fellows. When he comes,
The dear son of Odysseus will provide
For thee the garments thou dost need—a cloak   435
And tunic—and will send thee where thou wilt."
Odysseus, the great sufferer, answered thus:

"I pray that thou mayst be as dear to Zeus,
The great All-Father, as thou art to me,
Since through thy kindness I enjoy a pause   440
Amid my weary wanderings. There is naught
Worse than a wandering life. Unseemly cares
A hungry stomach brings to homeless men;
Hardship and grief are theirs. But since thou wilt
That I remain and wait for thy young lord,   445
Speak to me of the mother of thy chief
Odysseus, and his father, whom he left
Just on the threshold of old age, if yet
They live, and still may look upon the sun;
Or have they died, and passed to Hades' realm?"   450
And then in turn the master swineherd spake:
"Rightly and truly will I answer thee,
Stranger! still Laertes lives, but prays
Continually to Zeus that he may die
In his own house; for sorely he laments   455
His son long absent, and his excellent wife,
Bride of his youth, whose death has brought on him
Sharp sorrow, and old age before its time.
By a sad death she died—through wasting grief
For her lost, glorious son. May no one here,   460
No friend of mine, nor one who has bestowed
A kindness on me, die by such a death!
While yet she lived, great as her sorrow was,
I loved to speak with her and hear her words
For she had reared me with her youngest-born—   465
Her daughter, long-robed Ctimena. With her
Was I brought up, and scarcely less than her
Was held in honor. When at length we came
Into the pleasant years of youth, they sent

The princess hence to Samos, and received   470
Large presents; but to me her mother gave
Garments of price, a tunic and a cloak,
And sandals for my feet, and sent me forth
Into the fields, and loved me more and more.
All this is over now, yet must I say   475
My calling has been prospered by the gods.
From this I have the means to eat and drink,
And wherewithal to feast a worthy guest;
But from the queen I never have a word
Or deed of kindness, since that evil came   480
Upon her house—that crew of lawless men.
Greatly the servants would rejoice to speak
Before their mistress, and inquire her will,
And eat and drink, and carry to their homes
Some gift, for gifts delight a servant's heart."   485
Again Odysseus, the sagacious, spake:
"Swineherd Eumaeus, thou, while yet a child,
Wert doubtless strangely tossed about the world,
Far from thy kindred and thy native land.
Now tell me, was the spacious town wherein   490
Thy father and thy mother dwelt laid waste?
Or wert thou left among the flocks and herds
Untended, and borne off by hostile men,
Who came in ships and sold thee to the lord
Of these possessions for a worthy price?"   495
And then the master swineherd spake again:
"Since thou dost ask me, stranger, hear my words
In silence; sit at ease and drink thy wine.
These nights are very long; there's time enough
For sleep, and time to entertain ourselves   500
With talk. It is not fitting to lie down

Ere the due hour arrive, and too much sleep
Is hurtful. Whosoever here shall feel
The strong desire, let him withdraw and sleep,
And rise with early morn and break his fast   505
And tend my master's swine. Let us remain
Within, and drink and feast, and pass the time
Gaily, relating what we have endured,
Each one of us; for in the after time
One who has suffered much and wandered far   510
May take a pleasure even in his griefs.
"But let me tell what thou hast asked of me:
Beyond Ortygia lies an island named
Syria; thou must have heard of it. The sun
Above it turns his course. It is not large,   515
But fruitful, fit for pasturage, and rich
In flocks, abounding both in wine and wheat.
There never famine comes, nor foul disease
Fastens on wretched mortals; but when men
Grow old, Apollo of the silver bow   520
Comes with Diana, aims his silent shafts,
And slays them. There two cities stand, and share
The isle between them. There my father reigned,
The godlike Ctesias, son of Ormenus,
And both the cities owned him as their king.   525
"There came a crew of that seafaring race,
The people of Phoenicia, to our isle.
Shrewd fellows they, and brought in their black ship
Large store of trinkets. In my father's house
Was a Phoenician woman, large and fair,   530
And skillful in embroidery. As she came
A laundress to their ship, those cunning men
Seduced her. One of them obtained her love—

For oft doth love mislead weak womankind,
Even of the more discreet. Her paramour   535
Asked who she was, and whence. She pointed out
The lofty pile in which my father dwelt.
'At Sidon, rich in brass, I had my birth—
A daughter of the opulent Arybas;
And once, as I was coming from the fields,   540
The Taphian pirates seized and bore me off,
And brought me to this isle and sold me here,
At that man's house; much gold he paid for me.'
Then said her paramour: 'Wilt thou not then
Return with us, that thou mayst see again   545
Father and mother, and their fair abode?
For yet they live, and rumor says are rich.'
To this the woman answered: 'I consent
If first ye take an oath—ye mariners—
And pledge your faith to bear me safely home.'   550
She spake, and they complied, and when the oath
Was duly taken, thus the woman said:
'Now hold your peace; let none of all the crew
Speak to me more, in meeting on the road
Or at the fountain, lest someone should tell   555
The old man at the house, and he suspect
Some fraud and bind me fast, and plot your death.
Lock up your words within your breast; make haste
To buy supplies, and when the ship is full
Of all things needful, let a messenger   560
Come to me at the palace with all speed;
And I will bring with me whatever gold
My hands may find, and something else to pay
My passage. I am nurse to the young heir
Of the good man who dwells in yonder halls—   565

A shrewd boy for his years, who oft goes out
With me—and I will lead him to the ship,
And he will bring, in any foreign land
To which ye carry him, a liberal price.'
The woman spake, and to our fair abode   570
Departed. The Phoenician crew remained
Until the twelvemonth's end, and filled their ship
With many things, and, when its roomy hull
Was fully laden, sent a messenger
To tell the woman. He, a cunning man,   575
Came to my father's house, and brought with him
A golden necklace set with amber beads.
The palace maidens and the gracious queen,
My mother, took it in their hands, and gazed
Upon it, and debated of its price.   580
Meantime the bearer gave the sign, and soon
Departed to the ship. The woman took
My hand and led me forth. Within the hall
She found upon the tables ready placed
The goblets for my father's guests, his peers;   585
But they were absent, and in council yet
Amid a great assembly. She concealed
Three goblets in her bosom, and bore off
The theft. I followed thoughtlessly. The sun
Went down, and darkness brooded o'er the ways.   590
Briskly we walked, and reached the famous port
And the fast-sailing ship. They took us both
On board, and sailed. Along its ocean path
The vessel ran, and Zeus bestowed
A favorable wind. Six days we sailed,   595
Both night and day; but when Cronus-son Zeus
Brought the seventh day, Diana, archer-queen,

Struck down the woman, and with sudden noise
Headlong she plunged into the hold, as dives
A sea-gull. But the seamen cast her forth   600
To fishes and to sea-calves. I was left
Alone and sorrowful. The winds and waves
Carried our galley on to Ithaca;
And there Laertes purchased me, and thus
I first beheld the land in which I dwell."   605
And then again the great Odysseus spake:
"Eumaeus, the sad story of thy wrongs
And sufferings moves me deeply; yet hath Zeus
Among thy evil fortunes given this good.
That, after all thy sufferings, thou art lodged   610
With a good master, who abundantly
Provides thee meat and drink; thou leadest here
A pleasant life, while I am come to thee
From wandering long and over many lands."
So talked they with each other. No long time   615
They passed in sleep, for soon the Morning came,
Throned on her car of gold. Beside the shore
The comrades of Telemachus cast loose
The sails, took down the mast, and with their oars
Brought in the vessel to its place. They threw   620
The anchors out and bound the hawsers fast,
And went upon the sea-beach, where they dressed
Their morning meal, and mingled purple wine.
Then, when the calls of thirst and hunger ceased,
Discreet Telemachus bespake the crew: 625
"Take the black ship to town. I visit first
The fields, and see my herdsmen, and at eve
Will come to town. Tomorrow I will give
The parting feast, rich meats and generous wine."

Then said the godlike Theoclymenus: 630
"Whither, my son, am I to go? What house
Of all the chiefs of rugged Ithaca
Shall I seek shelter in? with thee, perhaps,
In thine own palace where thy mother dwells."
And thus discreet Telemachus replied: 635
"I would have asked thee at another time
To make our house thy home, for there would be
No lack of kindly welcome. 'Twere not well
To ask thee now, for I shall not be there,
Nor will my mother see thee—since not oft   640
Doth she appear before the suitor-train,
But in an upper room, apart from them,
Weaves at her loom a web. Another man
I name, Eurymachus, the illustrious son
Of the sage Polybus, to be thy host.   645
The noblest of the suitors he, and seeks
Most earnestly to wed the queen, and take
The rank Odysseus held. Olympian Zeus,
Who dwells in either, knows the fatal day
That may o'ertake the suitors ere she wed."   650
As thus he spake, a falcon on the right
Flew by, Apollo's messenger. A dove
Was in his talons, which he tore, and poured
The feathers down between Telemachus
And where the galley lay. When this was seen   655
By Theoclymenus, he called the youth
Apart, alone, and took his hand and said:
"The bird that passed us, O Telemachus,
Upon the right, flew not without a god
To guide him. When I saw it; well I knew   660
The omen. Not in Ithaca exists

A house, of a more kingly destiny
Than thine, and ever will its power prevail."
And thus discreet Telemachus replied:
"O stranger, may thy saying come to pass: 665
Then shalt thou quickly know me for thy friend,
And be rewarded with such liberal gifts
That all who meet thee shall rejoice with thee."
Then turning to Piraeus he bespake
That faithful follower thus: "Piraeus, son   670
Of Clytius, thou who ever wert the first
To move, at my command, of all the men
Who went with me to Pylos, take, I pray,
This stranger to thy house, and there provide
For him, and honor him until I come."   675
Piraeus, mighty with the spear, replied:
"Telemachus, however long thy stay,
This man shall be my guest, nor ever lack
Beneath my roof for hospitable care."
He spake, and climbed the deck, and bade his men   680
Enter the ship and cast the fastenings loose.
Quickly they came together, went on board
And manned the benches, while Telemachus
Bound the fair sandals to his feet, and took
His massive spear with its sharp blade of brass   685
That lay upon the deck. The men unbound
The hawsers, shoved the galley forth, and sailed
Townward, as they were bidden by the son
Of great Odysseus. Meantime the quick feet
Of the young chieftain bore him on until   690
He reached the lodge where his great herds of swine
Were fed, and, careful of his master's wealth,
Beside his charge the worthy swineherd slept.

BOOK XVI

Meantime Odysseus and that noble hind   1
The swineherd, in the lodge, at early dawn
Lighted a fire, prepared a meal, and sent
The herdsmen forth to drive the swine afield.
The dogs, so apt to bark, came fawning round,   5
And barked not as Telemachus drew near.
Odysseus heard the sound of coming feet,
And marked the crouching dogs, and suddenly
Bespake Eumaeus thus with winged words:
"Eumaeus, without doubt some friend of thine,   10
Or someone known familiarly, is near.
There is no barking of the dogs; they fawn
Around him, and I hear the sound of feet."
Scarce had he spoken, when within the porch
Stood his dear son. The swineherd starting up,   15
Surprised, let fall the vessels from his hands
In which he mingled the rich wines, and flew
To meet his master; kissed him on the brow;
Kissed both his shining eyes and both his hands,
With many tears. As when a father takes   20
Into his arms a son whom tenderly

He loves, returning from a distant land
In the tenth year—his only son, the child
Of his old age, for whom he long has borne
Hardship and grief—so to Telemachus   25
The swineherd clung, and kissed him o'er and o'er,
As one escaped from death, and, shedding still
Warm tears, bespake him thus with winged words:
"Thou comest, O Telemachus! the light
Is not more sweet to me. I never thought   30
To see thee more when thou hadst once embarked
For Pylos. Now come in, beloved child,
And let my heart rejoice that once again
I have thee here, so newly come from far.
For 'tis not often that thou visitest   35
Herdsmen and fields, but dwellest in the town—
Such is thy will—beholding day by day
The wasteful pillage of the suitor-train."
And thus discreet Telemachus replied:
"So be it, father; for thy sake I came   40
To see thee with these eyes, and hear thee speak
And tell me if my mother dwells within
The palace yet; or has some wooer led
The queen away, his bride, and does the couch
Of great Odysseus lie untapestried, as   45
With ugly cobwebs gathering over it?"
And then the master swineherd spake in turn:
"Most true it is that with a constant mind
The queen inhabits yet thy palace halls,
And wastes in tears her wretched nights and days."   50
So speaking he received his brazen lance,
And over the stone threshold passed the prince
Into the lodge. Odysseus yielded up

His seat to him; Telemachus forbade.
"Nay, stranger, sit; it shall be ours to find   55
Elsewhere a seat in this our lodge, and he
Who should provide it is already here."
He spake; Odysseus turned, and took again
His place; the swineherd made a pile of twigs
And covered it with skins, on which sat down so   60
The dear son of Odysseus. Next he brought
Dishes of roasted meats which yet remained,
Part of the banquet of the day before,
And heaped the canisters with bread, and mixed
The rich wines in a wooden bowl. He sat   65
Right opposite Odysseus. All put forth
Their hands and shared the meats upon the board;
And when the calls of thirst and hunger ceased,
Thus to the swineherd said Telemachus:
"Whence, father, is this stranger, and how brought   70
By seamen to the coast of Ithaca?
And who are they that brought him?—for I deem
He came not over to our isle on foot."
And thus, Eumaeus, thou didst make reply:
"True answer will I make to all. He claims   75
To be a son of the broad isle of Crete,
And says that in his wanderings he has passed
Through many cities of the world, for so
Some god ordained; and now, escaped by flight
From a Thesprotian galley, he has sought so   80
A refuge in my lodge. Into thy hands
I give him; deal thou with him as thou wilt.
He is thy suppliant, and makes suit to thee."
Then spake discreet Telemachus again:
"Eumaeus, thou hast uttered words that pierce   85

My heart with pain; for how can I receive
A stranger at my house? I am a youth
Who never yet has trusted in his arm
To beat the offerer of an insult back.
And in my mother's mind the choice is yet   90
Uncertain whether to remain with me
The mistress of my household, keeping still
Her constant reverence for her husband's bed,
And still obedient to the people's voice,
Or whether she shall follow as a bride   95
Him of the Achaean suitors in my halls
Who is accounted worthiest, and who brings
The richest gifts. Now, as to this thy guest,
Since he has sought thy lodge, I give to him
A cloak and tunic, seemly of their kind,   100
A two-edged sword, and sandals for his feet.
And I will send him to whatever coast
He may desire to go. Yet, if thou wilt,
Lodge him beneath thy roof, and I will send
Raiment and food, that he may be no charge   105
To thee or thy companions. To my house
Among the suitor-train I cannot bear
That he should go. Those men are insolent
Beyond all measure; they would scoff at him,
And greatly should I grieve. The boldest man   110
Against so many might contend in vain,
And greater is their power by far than mine."
Then spake Odysseus, the great sufferer:
"O friend—since I have liberty to speak—
My very heart is wounded when I hear   115
What wrongs the suitors practice in thy halls
Against a youth like thee. But give me leave

To ask if thou submittest willingly,
Or do thy people, hearkening to some god,
Hate thee with open hatred? Dost thou blame   120
Thy brothers?—for in brothers men confide
Even in a desperate conflict. Would that I
Were young again, and with the will I have,
Or that I could become Odysseus' son,
Or were that chief himself returned at last   125
From all his wanderings—and there yet is hope
Of his return—then might another strike
My head off if I would not instantly
Enter the house of Laertiades
And make myself a mischief to them all.   130
But should they overcome me, thus alone
Contending with such numbers, I would choose
Rather in mine own palace to be slain
Than every day behold such shameful deeds—
Insulted guests, maid-servants foully dragged   135
Through those fair palace chambers, wine-cask drained,
And gluttons feasting idly, wastefully,
And others toiling for them without end."
Then spake again discreet Telemachus:
"Stranger, thou shalt be answered faithfully.   140
Know, then, the people are by no means wroth
With me, nor have I brothers to accuse,
Though in a desperate conflict men rely
Upon a brother's aid. Cronus-son Zeus
Confines our lineage to a single head.   145
The king Arcesius had an only son,
Laertes, and to him was only born
Odysseus; and Odysseus left me here,
The only scion of his house, and he

Had little joy of me. Our halls are filled   150
With enemies, the chief men of the isles—
Dulichium, Samos, and Zacynthus dark
With forests, and the rugged Ithaca—
So many woo my mother and consume
Our substance. She rejects not utterly   155
Their hateful suit, nor yet will give consent
And end it. They go on to waste my wealth,
And soon will end me also; but the event
Rests with the gods. And go thou now with speed,
Eumaeus, father, to Penelope,   160
And say that I am safe, and just returned
From Pylos. I remain within the lodge.
And then come back as soon as thou hast told
The queen alone. Let none of all the Greeks
Hear aught; for they are plotting harm to me."   165
Then thus, Eumaeus, thou didst make reply:
"Enough, I see it all, thy words are said
To one who understands them. But, I pray,
Direct me whether in my way to take
A message to Laertes, the distressed.   170
While sorrowing for Odysseus he o'ersaw
The labors of the field, and ate and drank,
As he had appetite, with those who wrought.
But since thy voyage to the Pylian coast
They say he never takes his daily meals   175
As he was wont, nor oversees the work,
But sits and mourns and sighs and pines away,
Until his limbs are shriveled to the bone."
Then spake discreet Telemachus again:
"'Tis sad, but we must leave him to his grief   180
A little while. Could everything be made

To happen as we mortals wish, I then
Would first desire my father's safe return.
But thou, when thou hast given thy message, haste
Hither again, nor wander through the fields   185
To him; but let my mother send at once
The matron of her household, privately,
To bear the tidings to the aged man."
He spake to speed the swineherd, who took up
His sandals, bound them on, and bent his way   190
Townward. Not unperceived by Pallas went
Eumaeus from the lodge. She came in shape
A woman beautiful and stately, skilled
In household arts, the noblest. Near the gate
She stood, right opposite. Odysseus saw;   195
Telemachus beheld her not; the gods
Not always manifest themselves to all.
Odysseus and the mastiffs saw the dogs
Barked not, but, whimpering, fled from her and sought
The stalls within. She beckoned with her brows;   200
Odysseus knew her meaning and came forth,
And passed the great wall of the court, and there
Stood near to Pallas, who bespake him thus:
"Son of Laertes, nobly born and wise,
Speak with thy son; conceal from him the truth   205
No longer, that, prepared to make an end
Of that vile suitor-crew, ye may go up
Into the royal town. Nor long will I
Be absent; I am ready for the assault."
Thus spake the goddess. Putting forth a wand   210
Of gold, she touched the chief. Beneath that touch
His breast was covered with a new-blanched robe
And tunic. To his frame it gave new strength;

His swarthy color came again, his cheeks
Grew full, and the beard darkened on his chin.   215
This done, she disappeared. Odysseus came
Into the lodge again; his son beheld
Amazed and overawed, and turned his eyes
Away, as if in presence of a god,
And thus bespake the chief with winged words: 220
"O stranger, thou art other than thou wert;
Thy garb is not the same, nor are thy looks;
Thou surely art some deity of those
Whose habitation is the ample heaven.
Be gracious to us, let us bring to thee   225
Such sacrifices as thou wilt accept
And gifts of graven gold; be merciful."
Odysseus, the great sufferer, thus replied:
"I am no god; how am I like the gods?
I am thy father, he for whom thy sighs   230
Are breathed, and sorrows borne, and wrongs endured."
He spake and kissed his son, and from his lids
Tears fell to earth, that long had been restrained.
And then Telemachus, who could not think
The stranger was his father, answered thus: 235
"Nay, thou art not my father, thou art not
Odysseus; rather hath some deity
Sought to deceive me, that my grief may be
The sharper; for no mortal man would do
What has been done, unless some god should come   240
To aid him, and to make him young or old
At pleasure; for thou wert a moment since
An aged man, and sordidly arrayed,
And now art like the gods of the wide heaven."
Odysseus, the sagacious, answered thus: 245

"It is not well, Telemachus, to greet
With boundless wonder and astonishment
Thy father in this lodge. Be sure of this,
That no Odysseus other than myself
Will ever enter here. I, who am he,   250
Have suffered greatly and have wandered far,
And in the twentieth year am come again
To mine own land. Thou hast beheld today
A wonder wrought by Pallas, huntress-queen,
Who makes me what she will, such power is hers—   255
Sometimes to seem a beggar, and in turn
A young man in a comely garb. The gods
Whose home is in the heavens can easily
Exalt a mortal man, or bring him low."
He spake and sat him down. Telemachus   260
Around his glorious father threw his arms,
And shed a shower of tears. Both felt at heart
A passionate desire to weep; they wept
Aloud—and louder were their cries than those
Of eagles, or the sharp-clawed vulture tribe,   265
Whose young the hinds have stolen, yet unfledged.
Still flowed their tears abundantly; the sun
Would have gone down and left them weeping still,
Had not Telemachus at length inquired:
"Dear father, tell me in what galley came   270
The mariners who brought thee. Of what race
Claim they to be? For certainly, I think,
Thou cam'st not hither travelling on foot."
Odysseus, the great sufferer, thus replied:
"My son, thou shalt be answered faithfully.   275
Men of a race renowned for seamanship,
Phaeacians, brought me hither. They convey

Abroad the strangers coming to their isle,
And, bearing me in one of their swift barks
Across the sea, they landed me asleep   280
In Ithaca. Rich were the gifts they gave—
Much brass and gold, and garments from the loom
These, so the gods have counseled, lie concealed
Among the hollow rocks, and I am come,
Obeying Pallas, to consult with thee   285
How to destroy our enemies. Give now
The number of the suitors: let me know
How many there may be, and who they are,
That with a careful judgment I may weigh
The question whether we shall fall on them—   290
We two alone—or must we seek allies."
Then spake discreet Telemachus again:
"O father, I have heard of thy great fame
My whole life long—how mighty is thy arm,
How wise thy counsels. Thou hast said great things,   295
And I am thunderstruck. It cannot be
That two alone should stand before a crowd
Of valiant men. They are not merely ten—
These suitors—nor twice ten, but many more;
Hear, then, their number. From Dulichium come   300
Fifty and two, the flower of all its youth,
With whom are six attendants. Samos sends
Twice twelve, and twenty more Achaean chiefs
Come from Zacynthus. Twelve from Ithaca;
The noblest of the isle are these—with whom   305
Medon the herald comes—a bard, whose song
Is heavenly—and two servants skilled to spread
The banquet. Should we in the palace halls
Assault all these, I fear lest the revenge

For all thy wrongs would end most bitterly   310
And grievously for thee. Now, if thy thought
Be turned to some ally, bethink thee who
Will combat for us with a willing heart."
Again Odysseus, the great sufferer, spake:
"Then will I tell thee; listen, and give heed.   315
Think whether Pallas and her father, Zeus,
Suffice not for us. Need we more allies? "
And then discreet Telemachus rejoined:
"Assuredly the twain whom thou hast named
Are mighty as allies; for though they sit   320
On high among the clouds, they yet bear rule
Both o'er mankind and o'er the living gods."
Once more Odysseus, the great sufferer, spake
"Not long will they avoid the fierce affray
When in my halls the strength of war is tried   325
Between me and the suitor crew. Now go
With early morning to thy home, and there
Mingle among the suitors. As for me,
The swineherd afterward shall lead me hence
To town, a wretched beggar seemingly,   330
And very old. If there they scoff at me
In mine own palace, let thy faithful heart
Endure it, though I suffer; though they seize
My feet, and by them drag me to the door,
Or strike at me with weapon-blades, look on   335
And bear it; yet reprove with gentle words
Their folly. They will never heed reproof;
The day of their destruction is at hand.
And this I tell thee further, and be sure
To keep my words in memory. As soon   340
As Pallas, goddess of wise counsel, gives

The warning, I shall nod to thee, and thou,
When thou perceivest it, remove at once
All weapons from my halls to a recess
High in an upper chamber. With soft words   345
Quiet the suitors when they ask thee why.
Say, 'I would take them where there comes no smoke,
Since now they seem no longer like to those
Left by Odysseus when he sailed for Troy,
But soiled and tarnished by the breath of fire.   350
This graver reason, also, Cronus's son
Hath forced upon my mind—that ye by chance,
When full of wine and quarrelling, may wound
Each other, and disgrace the feast, and bring
Shame on your wooing; for the sight of steel   355
Draws men to bloodshed.' Say but this, and leave
Two swords for us, two spears, two oxhide shields,
Against the day of combat. Pallas then,
And Zeus the All-disposer, will unman
Their hearts. Moreover, let me say to thee—   360
And keep my words in memory—if thou be
My son, and of my blood, let no man hear
That now Odysseus is within the isle;
Let not Laertes hear of it, nor him
Who keeps the swine, nor any of the train   365
Of servants, nor Penelope herself,
While thou and I alone search out and prove
The women of the household, and no less
The serving-men, to know who honors us,
And bears us reverence in his heart, and who   370
Contemns us, and dishonors even thee."
Then answered his illustrious son and said:
"Father, thou yet wilt know my heart, and find

That of a careless and too easy mood
I am not; but a search like this, I think,   375
Would profit neither of us, and I pray
That thou wilt well consider it. Long time
Wouldst thou go wandering from place to place,
O'er thy estates, to prove the loyalty
Of every one, while in thy halls at ease   380
The suitors wastefully consume thy wealth.
Yet would I counsel that the women's faith
Be proved, that the disloyal may be marked
And the innocent go free. As for the men,
I would not now inquire from farm to farm;   385
That may be done hereafter, if indeed
Thou hast a sign from aegis-bearing Zeus."
So talked they with each other. The good ship
Which brought Telemachus and all his friends
From Pylos kept meantime upon its way   390
To Ithaca. There, entering the deep port,
The seamen hauled the black ship up the beach;
And then the ready servants took away
The arms, and to the house of Clytius bore
The costly gifts. A herald from the ship   395
Went forward to the palace of the king
With tidings to the sage Penelope
That now her son was come and in the fields,
And that the ship at his command had reached
The city, lest the royal dame might feel   400
Fear for his safety, and give way to tears.
The herald and the noble swineherd met,
Each bearing the same message to the queen.
Entering the palace of the godlike king,
And standing midst the maids, the herald said: 405

"O lady, thy beloved son is come."
But close beside the queen the swineherd stood,
And told her everything which her dear son
Had bid him say; and, having thus fulfilled
His errand, left the palace and its court.   410
Then were the suitors vexed and sorrowful,
And going from the palace, and without
The great wall that enclosed the court, sat down
Before the gates, and there Eurymachus,
The son of Polybus, harangued the throng: 415
"Behold, my friends, Telemachus has done
A marvelous thing; this voyage, which we thought
He could not make, is made. Now let us launch
A ship, the best that we can find, and man
With fishermen the benches, sending it   420
To find our friends, and hasten their return."
Scarce had he spoken when Amphinomus,
In turning where he stood, beheld a bark
Enter the port's deep waters, with a crew
That furled the sails and held the oars in hand.   425
He laughed, well pleased, and to the suitors said:
"There needs no message to be sent, for they
Are here already. Haply hath some god
Given them the knowledge, or perchance they saw,
But could not overtake, the prince's ship."   430
He spake; they rose and hastened to the strand,
And quickly drew the galley up the beach.
The ready servants bore the arms away;
Then met they all in council, suffering none
Save of the suitor-train to meet with them—   435
None, either young or old. Eupeithes' son,
Antinous, standing forth, bespake them thus:

"How strangely do the gods protect this man
From evil. All day long spy after spy
Has sat and watched upon the airy heights,   440
And when the sun was set we never slept
On land, but ever in our gallant ship
Sailed, waiting for the holy morn, and lay
In constant ambush for Telemachus,
To seize and to destroy him. Yet behold,   445
Some deity has brought him home. And now
Frame we a plan to cut off utterly
Telemachus, and leave him no escape;
For certainly I think that while he lives
The end we aim at cannot be attained.   450
Shrewd is the youth in counsel and device,
And we no longer have, as once we had,
The people's favor. Let us quickly act,
Ere he can call a council of the Greeks.
That he will do without delay, and there   455
Will rise in wrath to tell them how we planned
His death by violence, and failed; and they
Who hear assuredly will not approve
The plotted mischief. They may drive us forth
With outrage from our country to a land   460
Of strangers. Let us be the first to strike,
And slay him in the fields or on the way,
And, taking his possessions to ourselves,
Share equally his wealth. Then may we give
This palace to his mother, and the man   465
Whom she shall wed, whoever he may be.
Or if this plan mislike you, and ye choose
That he should live, and keep the fair estate
That was his father's, let us not go on

Thronging the palace to consume his wealth   470
In revelry, but each with liberal gifts
Woo her from his own dwelling; and let him
Who gives most generously, and whom fate
Most favors, take the lady as his bride."
He spake, and all were mute. Amphinomus   475
The illustrious son of royal Nisus, rose.
The grandson of Aretias, it was he
Who led the suitors from Dulichium's fields,
Grassy and rich in corn. Penelope
Liked best his words, for generous was his thought   480
And with a generous purpose thus he spake:
"Nay, friends, not mine is the advice to slay
Telemachus. It is a fearful thing
To take a royal life. Then let us first
Inquire the pleasure of the gods. For if   485
The oracles of mighty Zeus
Approve it, I would do the deed myself,
Or bid another do it; but if they
Consent not, 'tis my counsel to forbear."
He spake, and all approved. At once they rose,   490
And, entering the palace, sat them down
On shining thrones. Meantime Penelope
Had formed the purpose to appear before
The arrogant suitors, for the news was brought
Into her chamber of the plot to slay   495
Her son; the herald Medon overheard,
And told her all. So to the hall she went
With her attendant maids. The glorious dame
Drew near the suitor-train, and took her stand
Beside a column of the stately pile,   500
And with a delicate veil before her cheeks

Began to speak, and chid Antinous thus:
"Antinous, mischief-plotter, insolent!
The rumor is that thou excellest all
Of thy own age among the Ithacans   505
In understanding and in speech. Yet such
Thou never wert. Ferocious as thou art,
Why seek the death of my Telemachus,
And treat with scorn the suppliants of whose prayer
Zeus is the witness? An unholy thing   510
It is when men against their fellow-men
Plot mischief. Dost thou then forget that once
Thy father came to us a fugitive,
In terror of the people, who were wroth
Because he joined the Taphian pirate-race,   515
And plundered the Thesprotians, our allies.
The people would have slain him, and have torn
His heart out, and have pillaged his large wealth;
Odysseus checked their rage, and held them back,
Fierce as they were. Now thou dost waste his goods   520
Most shamefully, and woo his wife, and slay
His son, and multiply my woes. Cease now,
I charge thee, and persuade the rest to cease."
Eurymachus, the son of Polybus,
Replied: "O daughter of Icarius, sage   525
Penelope, take heart; let no such thought
Possess thy mind. There is no man on earth,
Nor will there be, who shall lay violent hands
Upon Telemachus, thy son, while I
Am living, and yet keep the gift of sight.   530
I say, and will perform it—his black blood
Shall flow and bathe my spear. Odysseus oft,
Spoiler of realms, would take me on his knee,

And put the roasted meats into my hands,
And give me ruddy wine. I therefore hold   535
Telemachus of all mankind most dear,
And I will bid him have no fear of death
From any of the suitors. If it come,
Sent by the gods, he cannot then escape."
So spake he to appease her, while he planned,   540
The murder of her son. The queen went up
To the fair upper chambers, and there wept
Odysseus, her dear spouse, till o'er her lids
The blue-eyed Pallas poured the balm of sleep.
At evening to Odysseus and his son   545
The noble swineherd went, while busily
They made the supper ready, having slain
A porker one year old. Then instantly
Stood Pallas by Odysseus, and put forth
Her wand and touched him, making him again   550
Old, and clad sordidly in beggar's weeds,
Lest that the swineherd, knowing at a look
His master, might not keep the knowledge locked
In his own breast, but, hastening forth, betray
The secret to the chaste Penelope.   555
Then to the swineherd said Telemachus:
"Noble Eumaeus, welcome; what reports
Are in the town? Have those large-minded men,
The suitors, left their ambush and returned,
Or are they waiting yet for me to pass?"   560
And thus, Eumaeus, thou didst make reply:
"Of that, indeed, I never thought to ask,
In going through the town. My only care
Was to return, as soon as I had given
My message, with such speed as I could make,   565

I met a messenger, a herald sent
By thy companions, who was first to tell
Thy mother of thy safe return. Yet this
I know, for I beheld it with my eyes.
When outside of the city, where the hill   570
Of Hermes stands, I saw a gallant bark
Entering the port, and carrying many men.
Heavy it was with shields and two-edged spears;
'Twas they, I thought, and yet I cannot tell."
He spake; Telemachus the valiant looked   575
Upon his father with a smile unmarked
By good Eumaeus. When their task was done,
And the board spread, they feasted. No one lacked
His portion of the common meal. Their thirst
And hunger satisfied, they laid them down   530
To rest, and so received the gift of sleep.

BOOK XVII

Now when the rosy-fingered Morn looked forth,—   1
The daughter of the Dawn—Telemachus,
The dear son of the great Odysseus, bound
The shapely sandals underneath his feet,
And took the massive spear that fitted well   5
His grasp, and, as he stood in act to go
Up to the town, bespake the swineherd thus:
"Father, I hasten to the town, that there
My mother may behold me; for I think
She will not cease to grieve, and fear, and weep,   10
Till her eyes rest on me. I leave with thee
The charge of leading our unfortunate guest
Into the city, there to beg his bread.
Whoever will may give him food and drink.
All men I cannot feed, and I have cares   15
Enough already. If he chafe at this,
The worse for him. I like to speak my mind."
And thus Odysseus, the sagacious, spake:
"Nor do I wish, my friend, to loiter here.
Better it is for one like me to beg   20
In town than in the country. In the town,

Whoever chooses will bestow his dole;
But here, if I remain about the stalls,
I am no longer of an age to do
All that a master may require. Go thou;   25
This man, at thy command, will lead me hence,
As soon as I have warmed me at the fire,
And the air grows milder. This keen morning-cold
May end me, and the way, ye say, is long."
He ended; from the lodge Telemachus   30
Passed quickly, meditating to destroy
The suitors. Coming to his stately home,
He leaned his spear against a column's shaft,
And, crossing the stone threshold, entered in.
First Eurycleia, who had been his nurse,   35
Beheld him, as she spread the beautiful thrones
With skins, and ran to him with weeping eyes;
And round him other handmaids of the house
Of resolute Odysseus thronged. They gave
Fond welcome, kissing him upon the brow   40
And shoulders. Issuing from her chamber next
The chaste Penelope, like Dian's self
In beauty, or like golden Aphrodite, came,
And, weeping, threw her arms about her son,
And kissed him on his forehead and on both   45
His glorious eyes, and said, amidst her tears:
"Light of my eyes! O my Telemachus!
Art thou, then, come? I never thought again
To see thee, when I heard thou hadst embarked
For Pylos—secretly, and knowing me   50
Unwilling—in the hope to gather there
Some tidings of thy father. Tell me now
All that has happened, all that thou hast seen."

And thus discreet Telemachus replied:

"Nay, mother, waken not my griefs again,   55

Nor move my heart to rage. I have just now

Escaped a cruel death. But go and bathe,

And put fresh garments on, and when thou com'st

Into thy chamber with thy maidens, make

A vow to all the gods that thou wilt burn   60

A sacrifice of chosen hecatombs

When Zeus shall have avenged our wrongs.

Now must I hasten to the market-place

In quest of one who came with me a guest

From Pylos. Him, with all my faithful crew,   65

I sent before me to this port, and bade

Piraeus lead him to his own abode,

There to be lodged and honored till I came."

He spake, nor flew his words unheeded by.

The princess bathed, and put fresh garments on,   70

And vowed to all the gods a sacrifice

Of chosen hecatombs when Zeus

Should punish the wrongdoers. While she prayed,

Telemachus went forth, his spear in hand.

Two fleet dogs followed him. Athena shed   75

A godlike beauty o'er his form and face,

And all the people wondered as he came.

The suitors thronged around him with smooth words,

Yet plotting mischief in their hearts. He turned

From their assembly hastily, and took   80

His place where Mentor sat with Antiphus,

And Halitherses—all his father's friends

And his from the beginning. While they asked

Of all that he had seen, Piraeus came,

The famous spearman, bringing through the town   85

The stranger with him to the market-place.
Nor long Telemachus delayed, but came
To meet his guest, and then Piraeus said:
"Telemachus, dispatch to where I dwell
Thy serving-women I would send to thee,   90
At once, the gifts which Menelaus gave."
And then discreet Telemachus replied:
"We know not yet, Piraeus, what may be
The event; and if the suitors privily
Should slay me in the palace, and divide   95
The inheritance among them, I prefer
That thou, instead of them, shouldst have the gifts;
But should they meet the fate which I have planned,
And be cut off, then shalt thou gladly bring
The treasures, which I gladly will receive."   100
So spake the prince, and to the palace led
The unhappy man, his guest. When now they reached
The stately pile, they both laid down their cloaks
Upon the benches, and betook themselves
To the well-polished baths. The attendant maids   105
There ministered and smoothed their limbs with oil,
And each received a tunic at their hands,
And fleecy mantle. Then they left the baths
And took their seats. A damsel came, and poured
Water from a fair ewer wrought of gold   110
Into a silver basin for their hands,
And spread a polished table near their seats;
And there the matron of the household placed
Bread, and the many dishes which her stores
Supplied. The queen was seated opposite,   115
Beside a column of the pile, and twirled
A slender spindle, while the son and guest

Put forth their hands and shared the meal prepared.
And when the calls of hunger and of thirst
Had ceased, thus spake the sage Penelope: 120
"Telemachus, when I again go up
Into my chamber, I shall lay me down
Upon the couch which, since Odysseus sailed
For Troy with Atreus' sons, has been to me
A couch of mourning, sprinkled with my tears.   125
And now thou hast not chosen to reveal,
Ere yet the haughty suitors throng again
Into these halls, what in thy voyage thou
Hast haply heard concerning his return."
And thus discreet Telemachus replied: 130
"Then, mother, will I truly tell thee all.
We went to Pylos, and saw Nestor there,
The shepherd of the people. Kindly he
Received me in his stately home, as one
Might welcome back a wandering son returned   135
From foreign lands. Such welcome I received
Both from the king and his illustrious sons.
But he had heard, he said, from living man,
No tidings of the much-enduring chief
Odysseus, whether he were yet alive   140
Or dead. He therefore sent me with his steeds
And chariot to the court of Atreus' son,
The warlike Menelaus. There I saw
The Argive Helen, for whose sake the Greeks
And Trojans, by the appointment of the gods,   145
Suffered so much. The valiant king inquired
What wish of mine had brought me to the town
Of hallowed Lacedaemon. I replied,
And truly told him all, and everything

In order. Then he answered me, and said: 150
'So then! these men, unwarlike as they are,
Aspire to occupy a brave man's bed,
As when a hart hath left two suckling fawns,
Just born, asleep in a strong lion's lair.
And roams for pasturage the mountain slopes   155
And grassy lawns, the lion suddenly
Comes back, and makes a cruel end of both,
So will Odysseus bring a sudden doom
Upon the suitors. Would to Father Zeus,
And Pallas, and Apollo, that the chief,   160
Returning mighty, as he was when once
In well-built Lesbos, at a wrestling-match,
He rose to strive with Philomelides,
And threw him heavily, and all the Greeks
Rejoiced—would he might come as then he was!
Short-lived would then the suitors be, and taste   166
A bitter marriage-feast. But now, to come
To what thou hast inquired, I will not seek
To turn from it, and talk of other things,
Nor will deceive. Of all that I was told   170
By the Ancient of the Deep, whose words are true,
I will not hide a single word from thee.
He saw thy father in an isle, he said,
A prey to wasting sorrows, and detained,
Unwilling, in the palace of the nymph   175
Calypso. To the country of his birth
He cannot come; no ships are there with oars
And crew to bear him o'er the great wide sea.'
Thus Menelaus, mighty with the spear,
The son of Atreus, said. And having now   180
Fulfilled my errand, I returned. The gods

Gave favoring winds, and sent me swiftly home."
He ended, and the queen was deeply moved.
Then Theoclymenus, the godlike, said:
"O gracious consort of Laertes' son,   185
King Menelaus knew not all. Hear now
What I shall say—for I will prophesy,
And truly, nor will keep back aught from thee.
Let Zeus, the mightiest of the gods,
And this thy hospitable board, and this   190
The hearth of great Odysseus, where I find
A refuge, be my witnesses, that now
Odysseus is in his own land again,
And sits or walks observant of the deeds
Of wrong, and planning vengeance, yet to fall   195
On all the suitors; such the augury:
Which I beheld when in the gallant bark
I sat and told it to Telemachus."
And thus the sage Penelope replied:
"O stranger! may thy saying be fulfilled!   200
Then shalt thou have such thanks and such rewards
That all who greet thee shall rejoice with thee."
So talked they with each other. In the space
Before the palace of Odysseus stood
The suitors, pleased with hurling quoits and spears   205
On the smooth pavement, where their insolence
So oft was seen. But when the supper-hour
Was near, and from the fields the cattle came,
Driven by the herdsmen, Medon—he whom most
They liked of all the heralds, and who sat   210
Among them at the feast—bespake them thus:
"Youths! since ye now have had your pastime here?
Come in, and help prepare the evening meal;

At the due hour a banquet is not ill."
He spake; the suitors hearkened and obeyed,   215
And rose, and came into the halls, and laid
Their cloaks upon the benches and the thrones,
And slaughtered well-fed sheep and fatling goats,
And made a victim of a pampered brawn,
And a stalled ox, preparing for the feast.   220
Meantime Odysseus and that noble hind
The swineherd hastened to begin their walk
To town, and thus the master swineherd spake:
"Since, stranger, 'tis thy wish to pass today
Into the city, as my master bade—   225
Though I by far prefer that thou remain
A guardian of the stalls, yet much I fear
My master, and am sure that he would chide,
And harsh the upbraidings of a master are—
Let us depart; the day is now far spent,   230
And chill will be the air of eventide."
Odysseus, the sagacious, answered thus:
"Enough; I know; thy words are heard by one
Who understands them. Let us then depart.
Lead thou the way; and if thou hast a staff,   235
Cut from the wood to lean on, give it me,
Since, as thou say'st, we have a slippery road."
He spake, and o'er his shoulders flung a scrip,
Old, cracked, and hanging by a twisted thong.
Eumaeus gave the staff he asked, and both   240
Went forth; the dogs and herdsmen stayed to guard
The lodge. The swineherd led his master on
Townward, a squalid beggar to the sight,
And aged, leaning on a staff, and wrapped
In sordid rags. There by the rugged way,   245

As they drew near the town, they passed a fount
Wrought by the hand of man, and pouring forth
Its pleasant streams, from which the citizens
Drew water. Ithacus and Neritus
Founded it with Polyctor, and a grove   250
Of alders feeding on the moistened earth
Grew round it on all sides. The ice-cold rill
Gushed from a lofty rock, upon whose brow
An altar stood, at which the passers-by
Worshiped, and laid their offerings for the Nymphs.   255
There did Melanthius, son of Dolius, meet
The twain, as he was driving to the town
The finest goats of all the flocks, to make
A banquet for the suitors; with him went
Two shepherds, following the flock. As soon   260
As he beheld Eumaeus and his guest,
He railed at them with rude and violent words,
That made the anger of Odysseus rise.
"See that vile fellow lead the vile about!
Thus ever doth some god join like with like.   265
Thou worthless swineherd! whither wouldst thou take
This hungry, haunting beggar-man, this pest
Of feasts, who at the posts of many a door
Against them rubs his shoulders, asking crusts,
Tripods or cauldrons never. Shouldst thou leave   270
The wretch to me, to watch my stalls, and sweep
The folds, and bring fresh branches to the kids,
He might by drinking whey get stouter thighs.
But he has learned no good, and will refuse
To work; he better likes to stroll about   275
With that insatiable stomach, asking alms
To fill it. Let me tell thee what is sure

To happen to him, should he ever come
Into the palace of the glorious chief
Odysseus. Many a footstool will be flung   280
Around him by the hands of those who sit
As guests, and they will tear the fellow's sides."
He spake, and in his folly thrust his heel
Against the hero's thigh. The blow moved not
Odysseus from his path, nor swerved he aught,   285
But meditated whether with a blow
Of his good staff to take the fellow's life,
Or lift him in the air and dash his head
Against the ground. Yet he endured the affront
And checked his wrath. The swineherd spake, and chid   290
The offender, and thus prayed with lifted hands:
"Nymphs of the fountain, born to Zeus!
If e'er in sacrifice Odysseus burned
To you the thighs of lambs and goats, o'erlaid
With fat, be pleased to grant the prayer I make,   295
That, guided by some deity, the chief
May yet return. Then thy rude boasts would cease
Melanthius, which thou utterest in thy way
From place to place while wandering through the town.
Unfaithful shepherds make a perishing flock."   300
Melanthius, keeper of the goats, rejoined:
"'Tis wonderful how flippant is the cur,
And shrewd! But I shall carry him on board
A good black ship, far off from Ithaca,
And there will sell him for a goodly price.   305
Would that Apollo of the silver bow
Might in the palace slay Telemachus
This very hour, or that the suitors might,
As certainly as that the day which brings

Odysseus to his home will never dawn!"   310
He spake, and left them there. They followed on
Slowly. Melanthius hastened, and was soon
At the king's palace gate, and, entering, took
A seat right opposite Eurymachus,
Whose favorite he was. The attendants there   315
Brought meats, the matron of the household bread,
And both were set before them. Meantime stopped
Odysseus with the noble swineherd near
The palace, for around them in the air
Came the sweet murmurs of a lyre. Just then   320
Phemius, the minstrel, had begun his song,
Odysseus took the swineherd's hand, and said:
"Eumaeus, this must be the noble pile
In which Odysseus dwelt, for easily
'Tis known among the others that are near.   325
Rooms over rooms are here; around its court
Are walls and battlements, and folding-doors
Shut fast the entrance; no man may condemn
Its strength. And I perceive that many guests
Banquet within; the smoke of fat goes up,   330
And the sweet lyre is heard; the gods have given
Its music to accompany the feast."
And then, Eumaeus, thou didst make reply:
"Thou speakest rightly, and in other things
Thou art not slow of thought. Now let us think   335
What we shall do. First enter, if thou wilt,
The sumptuous rooms, while I remain without;
Or, if it please thee, I will enter first,
While thou remainest; yet delay not long,
Lest someone, seeing thee, should deal a blow,   340
Or drive thee hence. I pray thee, think of this."

Odysseus, the great sufferer, answered thus:
"Enough; I know; thy words are heard by one
Who understands them. Go before me, then,
And leave me here. I am not quite unused   345
To blows and stripes, and patient is my mood,
For greatly have I suffered, both at sea
And in the wars; and I submit to bear
This also. But the stomach's eagerness
Is desperate, and is not to be withstood,   350
And many are the mischiefs which it brings
Upon the race of men; it fits out fleets
That cross the barren deep arrayed for war,
And carry death and woe to hostile realms."
So talked the twain. A dog was lying near,   355
And lifted up his head and pricked his ears.
'Twas Argus, which the much-enduring man
Odysseus long before had reared, but left
Untried, when for the hallowed town of Troy
He sailed. The young men oft had led him forth   350
In eager chase of wild goats, stags, and hares;
But now, his master far away, he lay
Neglected, just before the stable doors,
Amid the droppings of the mules and beeves,
Heaped high till carried to the spacious fields   365
Of which Odysseus was the lord. There lay
Argus, devoured with vermin. As he saw
Odysseus drawing near, he wagged his tail
And dropped his ears, but found that he could come
No nearer to his master. Seeing this,   370
Odysseus wiped away a tear unmarked
By the good swineherd, whom he questioned thus:
"Eumaeus, this I marvel at—this dog,

That lies upon the dunghill, beautiful
In form, but whether in the chase as fleet   375
As he is fairly shaped I cannot tell.
Worthless, perchance, as house-dogs often are,
Whose masters keep them for the sake of show."
And thus, Eumaeus, thou didst make reply:
"The dog belongs to one who died afar.   380
Had he the power of limb which once he had
For feats of hunting when Odysseus sailed
For Troy and left him, thou wouldst be amazed
Both at his swiftness and his strength. No beast
In the thick forest depths which once he saw,   385
Or even tracked by footprints, could escape.
And now he is a sufferer, since his lord
Has perished far from his own land. No more
The careless women heed the creature's wants;
For, when the master is no longer near,   390
The servants cease from their appointed tasks,
And on the day that one becomes a slave
The Thunderer, Zeus, takes half his worth away."
He spake, and, entering that fair dwelling-place,
Passed through to where the illustrious suitors sat,   395
While over Argus the black night of death
Came suddenly as soon as he had seen
Odysseus, absent now for twenty years.
Telemachus, the godlike, was the first
To mark the swineherd coming through the hall,   400
And, nodding, called to him. The swineherd looked
About him, and beheld a seat on which
The carver of the feast was wont to sit,
Distributing the meats. He bore it thence
And placed it opposite Telemachus,   405

And at his table. Then he sat him down,
And thither came the herald, bringing him
A portion of the feast, and gave him bread
From the full canister. Soon after him
Odysseus entered, seemingly an old   410
And wretched beggar, propped upon a staff,
And wrapped in sordid weeds. He sat him down
On the ashen threshold, just within the doors,
And leaned against a shaft of cypress-wood,
Which some artificer had skillfully   415
Wrought by a line, and smoothed. Telemachus
Called to the swineherd, bade him come, and took
A loaf that lay in the fair canister,
And all the flesh which his two hands could grasp.
"Bear this to yonder stranger; bid him go   420
And ask a dole from every suitor here.
No beggar should be bashful in his need."
He spake, the hind obeyed, and, drawing near
Odysseus, said to him in winged words:
"These from Telemachus, who bids thee ask   425
A dole from every suitor, for he says
No beggar should be bashful in his need."
Odysseus, the sagacious, answered thus:
"May Zeus, the sovereign, make Telemachus
A happy man among the sons of men,   430
And grant him all his heart desires in life!"
He spake, and took the gift in both his hands,
And laid it down upon his tattered scrip
Close to his feet. Then, while the poet sang,
He ate, and, just as he had supped, the bard   435
Closed his divine recital. Then ensued
Great clamor in the hall, but Pallas came

And moved Odysseus to arise, and ask
From every suitor there a dole of bread,
That he might know the better from the worse,   440
Though none were to be spared. From right to left
He took his way, and asked of every man,
With outstretched hand, as if he had been long
A beggar. And they pitied him, and gave,
And looked at him with wonder, and inquired   445
One of another who he was, and whence.
Then spake Melanthius, keeper of the goats:
"Give ear, ye suitors of the illustrious queen.
As to this stranger, I have seen him once.
The swineherd brought him; but I know him not,   450
And of what race he is I cannot tell."
He spake; Antinous chid the swineherd thus:
"Why hast thou brought him, too well known thyself?
Have we not vagabonds enough? enough
Of sturdy beggars, pests of every feast.   455
Or is it a light matter that they throng
Hither to waste the substance of thy lord,
And therefore thou art with this fellow here?"
And thus, Eumaeus, thou didst make reply:
"Antinous, high as is thy station, thou   460
Hast spoken ill. What man goes ever forth
To bid a stranger to his house, unless
The stranger be of those whose office is
To serve the people, be he seer, or leech,
Or architect, or poet heaven-inspired,   465
Whose song is gladly heard? All these are called
To feasts wherever men are found; but none
Call in the poor, to live upon their means.
Antinous, thou, of all the suitor-train,

Dost ever with the greatest harshness treat   470
The servants of Odysseus, chiefly me.
I heed it not while sage Penelope
Dwells in the palace with her godlike son."
Then interposed discreet Telemachus:
"Nay, have no strife of words with him, I pray.   475
Antinous takes delight in bitter words,
And rails, and stirs up railing in the rest."
And then he turned, and thus with winged words
Bespake Antinous: "Truly thou dost care
For me as might a father for a son,   480
Bidding me drive a stranger from my door
With violent words—which God forbid. Take now
Somewhat and give to him. I grudge it not,
Nay, I advise it. Fear not to offend
My mother, or displease a single one   485
Of all the household of the godlike chief,
Odysseus. But thou hast not thought of this.
It suits thee best to feast and never give."
Antinous thus rejoined: "O utterer
Of big and braggart words! Telemachus,   490
If all the other suitors would bestow
As much as I will, he would not be seen
Within these halls for three months yet to come."
So speaking, he brought forward to the sight,
From underneath the board, a stool, on which   495
Rested his dainty feet. The others all
Gave somewhat to Odysseus, till his scrip
Was filled with meat and bread. Then as he went
Back to the threshold, there to feast on what
The Greeks had given him in his rounds, he stopped   500
Beside Antinous, and bespake him thus:

"Give somewhat also, friend. Thou dost not seem
One of the humbler rank among the Greeks,
But of the highest. Kingly is thy look;
It therefore will become thee to bestow   505
More freely than the rest, and I will sound
Thy praise through all the earth. Mine too was once
A happy lot, for I inhabited
A palace filled with goods, and often gave
To wanderers, whosoever they might be   510
That sought me out, and in whatever need.
And I had many servants, and large store
Of everything by which men live at ease
And are accounted rich. Cronus-son Zeus—
Such was his pleasure—brought me low; for, moved   515
By him, I joined me to a wandering band
Of pirates, and to my perdition sailed
Upon a distant voyage to the coast
Of Egypt. In the river of that land
I stationed my good ships, and bade my men   520
Remain with them and watch them well. I placed
Sentries upon the heights. Yet confident
In their own strength, and rashly giving way
To greed, my comrades ravaged the fair fields
Of the Egyptians, slew them, and bore off   525
Their wives and little ones. The rumor reached
The city soon; the people heard the alarm
And came together. With the dawn of day
All the great plain was thronged with horse and foot,
And gleamed with brass, while Zeus, the Thunderer, sent   530
A deadly fear into our ranks, where none
Dared face the foe. On every side was death.
The Egyptians hewed down many with the sword,

And some they led away alive to toil
For them in slavery. Me my captors gave 535
Into a stranger's hands, upon his way
To Cyprus, where he reigned, a mighty king,
Demetor, son of Jasus. Thence at last
I came through many hardships to this isle."
Antinous lifted up his voice, and said: 540
"What god hath sent this nuisance to disturb
The banquet? Take thyself to the mid-hall,
Far from thy table, else expect to see
An Egypt and a Cyprus of a sort
That thou wilt little like. Thou art a bold 545
And shameless beggar. Thou dost take thy round
And ask from each, and foolishly they give,
And spare not nor consider; well supplied
Is each, and freely gives what is not his."
Then sage Odysseus said as he withdrew: 550
"'Tis strange; thy mind agrees not with thy form.
Thou wouldst not give a suppliant even salt
In thine own house—thou who, while sitting here,
Fed at another's table, canst not bear
To give me bread from thy well-loaded board." 555
He spake. Alcinous grew more angry still,
And frowned and answered him with winged words:
"A Dealer in saucy words! I hardly think
That thou wilt leave this palace unchastised."
He spake, and raised the footstool in his hand, 560
And smote Odysseus on the lower part
Of the right shoulder. Like a rock he stood,
Unmoved beneath the blow Antinous gave,
But shook his head in silence as he thought
Of vengeance. Then, returning, he sat down 565

Upon the threshold, where he laid his scrip
Well filled, and thus bespake the suitor-train:
"Hear me, ye suitors of the illustrious queen.
Grief or resentment no man feels for blows
Received by him while fighting for his own—   570
His beeves or white-woolled sheep. But this man here,
Antinous, dealt that blow on me because
I have an empty stomach; hunger brings
Great mischiefs upon men. If there be gods
Or furies who avenge the poor, may death   575
O'ertake Antinous ere his marriage-day!"
He ended. Then again Eupeithes' son,
Antinous, spake: "Eat, stranger, quietly;
Sit still, or get thee hence; our young men else
Who hear thy words will seize thee by the feet   580
Or hands, and drag thee forth and flay thee there."
He spake, and greatly were the rest incensed,
And one of those proud youths took up the word:
"Antinous, it was ill of thee to smite
That hapless wanderer. Madman! what if he   585
Came down from heaven and were a god! The gods
Put on the form of strangers from afar,
And walk our towns in many different shapes,
To mark the good and evil deeds of men."
Thus spake the suitors, but he heeded not   590
Their words. Telemachus, who saw the blow,
Felt his heart swell with anger and with grief,
Yet from his eyelids fell no tear; he shook
His head in silence, pondering to repay
The wrong. Meantime the sage Penelope   595
Heard of the stranger smitten in her halls,
And thus bespake the maidens of her train:

"Would that Apollo, mighty with the bow,
Might smite thee also!" Then Eurynome,
The matron of the household, said in turn: 600
"O, were our prayers but heard, not one of these
Should look upon the golden morn again!"
Then spake again the sage Penelope:
"Mother, they all are hateful; everyone
Plots mischief, but Antinous most of all;   605
And he is like black death, to be abhorred.
A friendless stranger passes through these halls,
Compelled by need, and asks an alms of each,
And all the others give, and fill his scrip;
Antinous flings a footstool, and the blow   610
Bruises the shoulder of the suppliant man."
So talked they with each other where they sat
In the queen's chamber, 'mid the attendant train
Of women, while meantime Odysseus took
The evening meal. The queen then bade to call   615
The noble swineherd, and bespake him thus:
"My worthy friend Eumaeus, go and bring
The stranger hither. I would speak with him,
And ask if anywhere he saw or heard
Aught of Odysseus; for he seems like one   620
Whose wanderings have been in many lands."
And thus, Eumaeus, thou didst make reply:
"Would that these Greeks, O queen, would hold their peace,
Then might this stranger in thy hearing speak
Words full of consolation. For three nights   625
I had him with me, for three days I made
My lodge his home—for at the very first
He came to me, escaping from his ship—
Nor when he left me had he told of all

That he had suffered. As a hearer looks   630
Upon a minstrel whom the gods have taught
To sing the poems that delight all hearts,
And, listening, longs to listen without end;
So, as the stranger sat beneath my roof,
He held me charmed. He was the ancestral friend,
He said, of thy Odysseus, and his home   635
Was Crete, where dwells the stock of Minos yet.
From Crete he came, and much had suffered since,
Driven on from place to place. And he had heard
Some tidings of Odysseus yet alive—   640
So he affirmed—in a rich region near
The realm of the Thesprotians, and prepared
To bring much riches to his native isle."
Then spake the sage Penelope again:
"Go, call him hither, that he may relate   645
His story in my presence. Let these men,
As it may please them, sitting at our gates
Or in our halls, amuse themselves, for light
Are they of heart. Unwasted in their homes
Lie their possessions, and their bread and wine   650
Are only for their servants, while themselves
Frequent our palace, day by day, and slay
Our beeves and sheep and fatling goats, and feast,
And drink abundantly the dark red wine,
And all with lavish waste. No man is here,   655
Such as Odysseus was, to drive away
This pest from our abode. Should he return
To his own land, he and his son would take
Swift vengeance on the men who do him wrong."
She ended. Suddenly Telemachus   660
Sneezed loudly, so that all the palace rang;

And, laughing as she heard, Penelope
Bespake Eumaeus thus with winged words:
"Go, call the stranger. Dost thou not perceive
My son has sneezed as to confirm my words.   665
Not unfulfilled will now remain the doom
That waits the suitors; none will now escape
Death and the Fates. This further let me say,
And thou remember it; if what he tells
Be true, I will bestow on him a change   670
Of fair attire, a tunic and a cloak."
She spake, the swineherd went, and, drawing near
Odysseus, said to him in winged words:
"Stranger and father, sage Penelope,
The mother of the prince, hath sent for thee.   675
Though sorrowing, she is minded to inquire
What of her husband thou canst haply say;
And should she find that all thy words are true,
She will bestow a tunic and a cloak,
Garments which much thou needest. For thy food,
What will appease thy hunger thou wilt find   680
Among the people; ask, and each will give."
Odysseus, much-enduring man, replied:
"Eumaeus, faithfully will I declare
All that I know to sage Penelope,   685
The daughter of Icarius. Well I knew
Her husband, and with like calamities
We both have suffered. But I greatly dread
This reckless suitor-crew, whose riotous acts
And violence reach to the iron heavens.   690
Even now, when that man dealt me, as I passed,
A painful blow, though I had done no harm,
None interposed, not even Telemachus,

In my defense. Now, therefore, ask, I pray,
Penelope that she will deign to wait   695
Till sunset in her rooms, though strong her wish
To hear my history. Of her husband then,
And his return, she may inquire, while I
Sit by the blazing hearth; for scant have been
My garments, as thou knowest, since the clay   700
When first I came, a suppliant, to thy door."
He spake; the swineherd went, and as he crossed
The threshold of Penelope she said:
"Thou bringst him not, Eumaeus? What may be
The wanderer's scruple? Fear of some one here?   705
Or in a palace is he filled with awe?
To be a bashful beggar is most hard."
And thus, Eumaeus, thou didst answer her:
"Rightly he speaks, and just as one would think
Who shuns the encounter of disorderly men.   710
He prays that thou wilt wait till set of sun;
And better were it for thyself, O queen,
To speak with him and hear his words alone."
Then spake discreet Penelope again:
"Whoe'er may be the stranger, not unwise   715
He seems; for nowhere among men are done
Such deeds of wrong and outrage as by these."
She spake, and the good swineherd, having told
The lady all, went forth among the crowd
Of suitors, drawing near Telemachus,   720
And bowed his head beside him that none else
Might hear, and said to him in winged words:
"I go, my friend, to tend the swine and guard
What there thou hast, thy sustenance and mine.
The charge of what is here belongs to thee.   725

Be thy first care to save thyself, and watch
To see that mischief overtake thee not—
For many are the Achaeans plotting it,
Whom Zeus destroy ere we become their prey!"
Then spake discreet Telemachus in turn: 730
"So be it, father, and, when thou hast supped,
Depart, but with the morning come, and bring
Choice victims for the sacrifice. The care
Of all things here is with the gods and me."
He spake; the swineherd sat him down again 735
Upon his polished seat, and satisfied
His appetite and thirst with food and wine.
Then he departed to his herd, and left
The palace and the court before it thronged
With revelers, who gave the hour to song, 740
And joined the dance; for evening now was come.

BOOK XVIII

There came a common beggar, wont to ask   1
Alms through the town of Ithaca, well-known
For greediness of stomach, gluttonous
And a wine-bibber, but of little strength
And courage, though he seemed of powerful mold.   5
Arnaeus was the name which at his birth
Flis mother gave him, but the young men called
The fellow Irus, for it was his wont
To go on errands, as a messenger,
When he was ordered. Coming now, he thought   10
To drive Odysseus out of his own house,
And railed at him, and said in winged words:
"Hence with thee! Leave the porch, old man,
Lest thou be taken by the foot and dragged
Away from it. Dost thou not see how all   15
Around us nod, to bid me drag thee out?
I am ashamed to do it. Rise and go,
Else haply we may have a strife of blows."
Odysseus, the sagacious, frowned and said:
"Wretch! there is nothing that I do or say   20
To harm thee aught. I do not envy thee

What others give thee, though the dole be large;
And ample is this threshold for us both.
Nor shouldst thou envy others, for thou seemst
A straggler like myself. The gods bestow   25
Wealth where they list. But do not challenge me
To blows, lest, aged as I am, thou rouse
My anger, and I make thy breast and lips
Hideous with blood. Tomorrow then will be
A quiet day for me, since thou, I trust,   30
In all the time to come, wilt never more
Enter the palace of Laertes' son."
The beggar Irus angrily rejoined:
"Ye gods! this glutton prattles volubly,
Like an old woman at the chimney-side.   35
Yet could I do him mischief, smiting him
On both his sides, and dashing from his cheeks
The teeth to earth, as men are wont to deal
With swine that eat the wheat. Now gird thyself,
Let these men see us fighting. How canst thou   40
Think to contend with one so young as I?"
Thus fiercely did they wrangle as they stood
Beside the polished threshold and before
The lofty gates. The stout Antinous heard,
And, laughing heartily, bespake the rest: 45
"Here, friends, is what we never yet have had.
Behold the pleasant pastime which the gods
Provide for us. These men—the stranger here,
And Irus—quarrel, and will come to blows.
Let us stand by and bring the combat on."   50
He spake. All rose with laughter and came round
The ragged beggars, while Eupeithes' son,
Antinous, in these words harangued the rest:

"Ye noble suitors, hear me. At the fire
Already lie the paunches of two goats,   55
Preparing for our evening meal, and both
Are filled with fat and blood. Whoever shows
Himself the better man in this affray,
And conquers, he shall take the one of these
He chooses, and shall ever afterward   60
Feast at our table, and no man but he
Shall ever come among us asking alms."
He ended. All approved his words, and thus
Odysseus, craftily dissembling, said:
"O friends, it is not well that one so old   65
As I, and broken by calamity,
Should fight a younger man; but hunger bids,
And I may be o'ercome by blows. But now
Swear all a solemn oath, that none of you,
To favor Irus, wickedly will raise   70
His mighty hand to smite me, and so aid
My adversary to my overthrow."
He spake; the suitor-train, assenting, took
The oath, and when they all were duly sworn,
The high-born prince Telemachus began: 75
"O stranger, if thy manly heart be moved
To drive him hence, fear no one else of all
The Achaeans. Whosoever strikes at thee
Has many to contend with. I am here
The host. Antinous and Eurymachus,   80
Wise men and kings, agree with me in this."
He spake, and all approved. Odysseus drew
And girt his tatters round his waist and showed
His large and shapely thighs. Unclothed appeared
His full broad shoulders, and his manly breast   85

And sinewy arms. Athena stood by him,
And with a mighty breadth of limb endued
The shepherd of the people. Earnestly
The suitors gazed, and wondered at the sight,
And each one, turning to his neighbor, said: 90
"Irus, poor Irus, on himself has drawn
An evil fate, for what a sinewy thigh
His adversary shows beneath his rags!"
So talked they, while the heart of Irus sank
Within him; yet the attendants girding him   95
Forcibly drew him forward, sore afraid,
The muscles quivering over every limb.
And then Antinous spake, and chid him thus:
"Now, boaster, thou deservest not to live,
Nay, nor to have been bora, if thou dost fear   100
And quake at meeting one so old as he,
So broken with the hardships he has borne.
And now I tell thee what will yet be done,
Should he approve himself the better man,
And conquer. I will have thee sent on board   105
A galley to Epirus, and its king,
The foe of all men living, Echetus,
And he will pare away thy nose and ears
With the sharp steel, and, wrenching out the parts
Of shame, will cast them to be torn by dogs."   110
He spake, and Irus shook through all his frame
With greater terror, yet they dragged him on
Into the midst. Both champions lifted up
Their arms. The godlike, much-enduring man,
Odysseus, pondered whether so to strike   115
His adversary that the breath of life
Might leave him as he fell, or only smite

To stretch him on the earth. As thus he mused,
The lighter blow seemed wisest, lest the Greeks
Should know who dealt it. When the hands of both   120
Were thus uplifted, Irus gave a blow
On his right shoulder, while Odysseus smote
Irus beneath the ear, and broke the bone
Within, and brought the red blood from his mouth.
He fell amid the dust, and shrieked and gnashed   125
His teeth, and beat with jerking feet the ground.
The suitor-train threw up their hands and laughed
Till breathless, while Odysseus seized his feet
And drew him o'er the threshold to the court
And the porch doors, and there, beside the wall,   130
Set him to lean against it, gave a staff
Into his hands, and said in winged words:
"Sit there, and scare away the dogs and swine,
But think not, wretched creature, to bear rule
Over the stranger and the beggar tribe,   135
Or worse than this may happen to thee yet."
He spake, and o'er his shoulders threw the scrip
That yawned with chinks, and by a twisted thong
Was fastened; then he turned to take his seat
Upon the threshold, while the suitor-train   140
Went back into the palace with gay shouts
Of laughter, and bespake him blandly thus:
"Stranger, may Jove and all the other gods
Grant thee what thou desirest, and whate'er
Is pleasant to thee! Thou hast put an end   145
To this importunate beggar's rounds among
The people. We shall send him off at once
Into Epirus, and to Echetus,
Its king, the foe of every living man."

So talked the suitors, and the omen made   150
Odysseus glad. Meantime Antinous placed
The mighty paunch before the victor, filled
With blood and fat, and from the canister
Amphinomus brought forth two loaves, and raised
A golden cup and drank to him, and said: 155
"Hail, guest and father! happy be thy days
Henceforth, though dark with many sorrows now!"
Odysseus, the sagacious, answered thus:
"Amphinomus, thou seemest most discreet,
And such thy father is, of whom I hear   160
A worshipful report, the good and rich
Dulichian Nisus. Thou, as I am told,
Art son to him, and thou art seemingly
A man of pertinent speech. I therefore say
To thee, and bid thee hear and mark me well,   165
No being whom earth nourishes to breathe
Her air and move upon her face is more
The sport of circumstance than man. For while
The gods give health, and he is strong of limb,
He thinks no evil in the coming days   170
Will overtake him. When the blessed gods
Visit him with afflictions, these he bears
Impatiently and with a fretful mind.
Such is the mood of man, while yet he dwells
On earth; it changes as the All-Father gives   175
The sunshine or withholds it. I was once
Deemed fortunate among my fellow-men,
And many things that were unjust I did;
For in my strength and in my father's power,
And valor of my brothers, I had put   180
My trust. Let no man, therefore, dare to be

Unjust in aught, but tranquilly enjoy
Whatever good the gods vouchsafe to give.
Yet are these suitors guilty of foul wrong,
Wasting the substance and dishonoring   185
The wife of one who will not, as I deem,
Remain long distant from his friends and home,
But is already near. O, may some god
Remove thee from this danger to thy home!
Nor mayst thou meet him when he shall return   190
To his own land. For when he comes once more
Beneath this roof, and finds the suitors here,
Not without bloodshed will their parting be."
He spake, and, pouring out a part, he drank
The wine, and gave the goblet to the prince,   195
Who crossed the hall, and sorrowfully shook
His head, for now already did his heart
Forebode the coming evil. Not by this
Did he escape his death. Athena laid
A snare for him, that he might fall beneath,   200
The strong arm of Telemachus. He went
And took the seat from which he lately rose.
Then blue-eyed Pallas moved Penelope,
Sage daughter of Icarius, to appear
Before the suitors, that their base intent   205
Might be more fully seen, and she might win
More honor from her husband and her son.
Wherefore she forced a laugh, and thus began:
"Eurynome, I would at length appear,
Though not till now, before the suitor-train,   210
Detested as they are. I there would speak
A word of timely warning to my son,
And give him counsel not to trust himself

Too much among the suitors, who are fair
In speech, but mean him foully in their hearts."   215
Eurynome, the household matron, said:
"Assuredly, my child, thou speakest well.
Go now, and warn thy son, and keep back naught.
First bathe, and, ere thou go, anoint thy cheeks,
Nor show them stained with tears. It is not well   220
To sorrow without end. For now thy son
Is grown, and thou beholdest him at length
What thou didst pray the gods, when he was born,
That he might yet become, a bearded man."
And then the sage Penelope rejoined: 225
"Though anxious for my sake, persuade me not,
Eurynome, to bathe, nor to anoint
My cheeks with oil. The gods inhabiting
Olympus took away their comeliness
When in his roomy ships my husband sailed;   230
But bid Antinoe come, and call with her
Hippodameia, that they both may stand
Beside me in the hall. I will not go
Alone among the men, for very shame."
She spake, the aged dame went forth to bear   235
The message, and to bring the women back.
While blue-eyed Pallas had yet other cares,
She brought a balmy sleep, and shed it o'er
The daughter of Icarius, as she lay
Reclined upon her couch, her limbs relaxed   240
In rest. The glorious goddess gave a dower
Of heavenly graces, that the Achaean chiefs
Might look on her amazed. She lighted up
Her fair face with a beauty all divine,
Such as the queenly Cytherea wears   245

When in the mazes of the dance she joins
The Graces. Then she made her to the sight
Of loftier stature and of statelier size,
And fairer than the ivory newly carved.
This having done, the gracious power withdrew,   250
While from the palace came the white-armed maids,
And prattled as they came. The balmy sleep
Forsook their mistress at the sound. She passed
Her hands across her cheeks, and thus she spake:
"'Twas a sweet sleep that, in my wretchedness,   255
Wrapped me just now. Would that, this very hour,
The chaste Diana by so soft a death
Might end me, that my days might be no more
Consumed in sorrow for a husband lost,
Of peerless worth, the noblest of the Greeks."   260
She spake, and from the royal bower went down,
Yet not alone; two maidens went with her.
And when that most august of womankind
Drew near the suitors, at the door she stopped
Of that magnificent hall, and o'er her cheeks   265
Let fall the lustrous veil, while on each side
A modest maiden stood. The suitors all
Felt their knees tremble, and were sick with love,
And all desired her. Then the queen bespake
Telemachus, her well-beloved son: 270
"Telemachus, thy judgment is not firm,
Nor dost thou think aright. While yet a boy
Thy thought was wiser. Now that thou art grown,
And on the verge of manhood, so that one
Who comes from far and sees thy noble part   275
And stature well may say thou art the son
Of a most fortunate father, yet to think

And judge discreetly thou art not as then,
For what a deed is this which has been done
Even here! Thou hast allowed a stranger guest   280
To be assaulted rudely. How is this?
If one who sits a guest beneath our roof
Be outraged thus, be sure it brings to thee
Great shame and rank dishonor among men."
To this discreet Telemachus replied: 285
"Mother, I cannot take it ill that thou
Shouldst be offended. But of many things
I have a clear discernment, and can weigh
The good and bad. I was till now a child,
Yet even now I cannot always see   290
The wiser course. These men bewilder me,
As, sitting side by side, they lay their plots
Against me, and I have no helper here.
When Irus and the stranger fought, the strife
Had no such issue as the suitors wished.   295
The stranger conquered. Would to Father Jove,
To Pallas and Apollo, that the crew
Of suitors here might sit with nodding heads
Struck down upon the spot, within these halls
Or in the courts, and all with powerless limbs,   300
As Irus sits beside the gate and nods,
Like one o'ercome with wine, nor can he stand
Upon his feet, nor go to where he dwells,
If home he has, so feeble are his limbs."
So talked the twain awhile; then interposed   305
Eurymachus, and thus bespake the queen:
"Sage daughter of Icarius! if all those
Who in Iasian Argos have their homes
Should once behold thee, a still larger crowd

Of suitors would tomorrow come and feast   310
Within thy halls, so much dost thou excel
In mind and form and face all womankind."
To this the sage Penelope replied:
"Eurymachus, the immortals took away
Such grace of form and face as once was mine,   315
What time the sons of Argos sailed for Troy,
And with them went Odysseus, my espoused.
Should he return, and take again in charge
My household, greater would my glory be,
And prized more highly. I am wretched now,   320
Such woes the gods have heaped upon my head.
He, when he left his native island, grasped
My right hand at the wrist, and said to me:
"Think not, dear wife, that all the well-armed Greeks
Will come back safe from Troy. The Trojan men,   325
They say, are brave in war, expert to cast
The spear and wing the arrow, skilled to rein
The rapid steeds by which the bloody strife
Of battle-fields is hurried to its close;
And therefore whether God will bring me back,   330
Or I shall fall in Troy, I cannot know.
Take charge of all things here. I leave with thee
My father and my mother in these halls.
Be kind to them as now, nay, more than now,
Since I shall not be here. When thou shalt see   335
My son a bearded man, take to thyself
A husband, whom thou wilt, and leave thy house.'
Such were his words, and they have been fulfilled.
The night will come in which I must endure
This hateful marriage, wretched that I am,   340
To whom the will of Jupiter forbids

All consolation, and this bitter thought
Weighs evermore upon my heart and soul.
The custom was not thus in other times;
When suitors wooed a noble wife, the child   345
Of some rich house, contending for her smile,
They came with beeves and fading sheep to feast
The damsel's friends, and gave munificent gifts,
But wasted not the wealth that was not theirs."
She spake, Odysseus was rejoiced to see   350
That thus she sought to draw from each a gift,
With fair and artful words. Yet were his thoughts
Intent on other plans. Eupeithes' son,
Antinous, thus made answer to the queen:
"Sage daughter of Icarius, only deign   355
To take the gifts which any of the Greeks
Will bring—nor is it gracious to reject
A present—yet be sure we go not hence,
To our estates nor elsewhere, till thou make
A bridegroom of the best Achaean here."   360
So spake Antinous. All approved his words,
And each sent forth a herald for his gift.
The herald of Antinous brought to him
A robe of many colors, beautiful
And ample, with twelve golden clasps, which each   365
Had its well-fitted eye. Eurymachus
Received a golden necklace, richly wrought,
And set with amber beads, that glowed as if
With sunshine. To Eurydamas there came
A pair of earrings, each a triple gem,   370
Daintily fashioned and of exquisite grace.
Two servants bore them. From Pisander's house—
Son of the Prince Polyctor—there was brought

A collar of rare beauty. Thus did each
Bestow a different yet becoming gift   375
And then that most august of women went
Back to the upper chambers with her maids,
Who bore the sumptuous presents, while below
The suitors turned them to the dance and song,
Amused till evening came. Its darkness stole   380
Over their pastime. Then they brought and placed
Three hearths to light the palace, heaping them
With wood, well dried and hard and newly cleft.
With this they mingled flaming brands. The maids
Of the great sufferer, Odysseus, fed   385
The fire by turns. To them the hero spake:
"Ye maidens of a sovereign absent long,
Withdraw to where your high-born mistress sits;
There turn the spindle, seeking to amuse
Her lonely hours; there comb with your own hands   390
The fleece, and I will see that these have light.
Even though they linger till the Morn is here
In her bright car, they cannot overcome
My patience. I am practiced to endure."
So spake he, and the maidens, as they heard,   395
Cast at each other meaning looks, and laughed,
And one Melantho, of the rosy cheeks,
Railed at him impudently. She was born
To Dolius, but Penelope had reared
The damsel as a daughter of her own,   400
And given her, for her pleasure, many things;
Yet for the sorrows of Penelope
Melantho little cared. Eurymachus
Had made the girl his paramour. She spake,
And chid Odysseus with unmannerly words: 405

"Outlandish wretch! thou must be one whose brain
Is turned, since thou wilt neither go to sleep
Within a smithy, nor in any place
Of public shelter, but wilt stay and prate
Among this company with no restraint   410
Or reverence. Either wine has stolen away
Thy senses, or thy natural mood, perchance,
Prompts thee to chatter idly. Art thou proud
Of conquering Irus, that poor vagabond?
Beware lest some one of robuster arms   415
Than Irus seize and thrust thee out of doors
With a bruised head and face begrimed with blood."
The sage Odysseus frowned on her and said:
"Impudent one, Telemachus shall hear
From me the saucy words which thou hast said,   420
And he will come and hew thee limb from limb."
He spake; the damsels, frightened at his words,
Fled through the hall, and shook in every limb
With terror, lest his threat should be fulfilled.
He meantime stood beside the kindled hearths   425
And fed the flames, and, looking on the crowd
Of suitors, brooded in his secret heart
O'er plans that would not fail to be fulfilled.
But Pallas suffered not the suitors yet
To cease from railing speeches, all the more   430
To wound the spirit of Laertes' son.
Eurymachus, the son of Polybus,
Began to scoff at him, and thus he spake
To wake the ready laughter of the rest:
"Hear me, ye suitors of the illustrious queen.   435
I speak the thought that comes into my mind.
Led by some god, no doubt, this man has come

Into the palace; for the light we have
Of torches seems to issue from the crown
Of his bald pate, a head without a hair."   440
So said Eurymachus, and then bespake
Odysseus, the destroyer of walled towns:
"Stranger, if I accept thee, wilt thou serve
Upon the distant parts of my estate?
There shalt thou have fair wages, and shalt bring   445
The stones in heaps together, and shalt plant
Tall trees, and I will feed thee through the year,
And give thee clothes, and sandals for thy feet.
But thou art used, no doubt, to idle ways,
And never dost thou work with walling hands,   450
But dost prefer to roam the town and beg,
Purveying for thy gluttonous appetite."
Odysseus, the sagacious, answered thus:
"Eurymachus, if we were matched in work
Against each other in the time of spring   455
When days are long, and both were mowing grass,
And I had a curved scythe in hand and thou
Another, that we might keep up the strife
Till nightfall, fasting, 'mid the abundant grass;
Or if there were a yoke of steers to drive,   460
The sturdiest of their kind, sleek, large, well fed,
Of equal age, and equal strength to bear
The labor, and both strong, and if the field
Were of four acres, with a soil through which
The plough could cleave its way—then shouldst thou see   465
How evenly my furrow would be turned.
Or should the son of Cronus send today
"War from abroad, and I had but a shield,
Two spears, and, fitted to my brows, a helm

Of brass, thou wouldst behold me. pressing on   470
Among the foremost warriors, and would see
No cause to rail at my keen appetite.
But arrogantly thou dost bear thyself,
And pitilessly; thou in thine own eyes
Art great and mighty, since thou dost consort   475
With few, and those are not the best of men.
Yet should Odysseus come to his own land,
These gates that seem so wide would suddenly
Become too narrow for thee in thy flight."
He spake. Eurymachus grew yet more wroth,   480
And frowned on him, and said in winged words:
"Wretch! I shall do thee mischief. Thou art bold,
And babblest unabashed among us all.
The wine, perhaps, is in thy foolish head,
Or thou art always thus, and ever prone   485
To prattle impudently. Art thou proud
Of conquering Irus, that poor vagabond?"
Thus having said, he brandished in the air
A footstool; but Odysseus, to escape
The anger of Eurymachus, sat down   490
Before the knees of the Dulichiain prince,
Amphinomus. The footstool flew, and struck
On the right arm the cupbearer. Down fell
The beaker ringing; he who bore it lay
Stretched in the dust. Then in those shadowy halls   495
The suitors rose in tumult. One of them
Looked at another by his side, and said:
"Would that this vagabond had met his death
Ere he came hither. This confusion, then,
Had never been. 'Tis for a beggar's sake   500
We wrangle, and the feast will henceforth give

No pleasure; we shall go from bad to worse."
Then rose in majesty Telemachus,
And said: "Ye are not in your senses sure,
Unhappy men, who cannot eat and drink   505
In peace. Some deity, no doubt, has moved
Your minds to frenzy. Now, when each of you
Has feasted well, let each withdraw to sleep,
Just when he will. I drive no man away."
He spake; the suitors heard, and bit their lips,   510
And wondered at Telemachus, who spake
So resolutely. Then Amphinomus,
The son of Nisus Aretiades,
Stood forth, harangued the suitor-crowd, and said:
"O friends! let no one here with carping words   515
Seek to deny what is so justly said,
Nor yet molest the stranger, nor do harm
To any of the servants in the halls
Of the great chief Odysseus. Now let him
Who brings the guests their wine begin and fill   520
The cups, that, pouring to the gods their part,
We may withdraw to sleep. The stranger here
Leave me within the palace, and in charge
Of him to whom he came, Telemachus."
He ended. All were pleased, and Mutlus then,   525
Hero and herald from Dulichium's coast,
And follower of the prince Amphinomus,
Mingled a jar of wine, and went to each,
Dispensing it. They to the blessed gods
Poured first a part, and then they drank themselves   530
The generous juice. And when the wine was poured,
And they had drunk what each desired, they went
Homeward to slumber, each in his abode.

BOOK XIX

Now was the godlike chief Odysseus left   1
In his own palace, planning, with the aid
Of Pallas, to destroy the suitor-train,
And thus bespake his son with winged words:
"Now is the time, Telemachus, to take   5
The weapons that are here, and store them up
In the inner rooms. Then, if the suitors ask
The reason, answer them with specious words:
Say, 'I have put them where there comes no smoke.
Since even now they do not seem the arms   10
Left by Odysseus when he sailed for Troy,
So tarnished are they by the breath of fire;
And yet another reason sways my mind,
The prompting of some god, that ye, when flushed
With wine and in the heat of a dispute,   15
May smite and wound each other, and disgrace
The banquet and your wooing; for the sight
Of steel doth draw men onto violence.'"
He ended, and Telemachus obeyed
His father's words, and calling forth his nurse, 20
The aged Eurycleia, said to her:

"Go, nurse, and see the women all shut up
In their own place, while in our inner room
I lay away my father's beautiful arms,
Neglected long, and sullied by the smoke,   25
While he was absent. I was then a child,
But now would keep them from the breath of fire."
And thus the nurse, Dame Eurycleia, said:
"Would that at length, my child, thou didst exert
Thy proper wisdom here, and take in charge   30
Thy house and thy possessions. But who goes
With thee to bear a torch, since none of these,
Thy handmaids, are allowed to light thy way?"
And thus discreet Telemachus replied:
"This stranger. No man may be idle here   35
Who eats my bread, though from a distant land."
He spake, nor flew his words in vain. The nurse
Closed all the portals of that noble pile.
Odysseus and his glorious son in haste
Bore off the helmets, and the bossy shields,   40
And the sharp spears, while Pallas held to them
A golden lamp, that shed a fair clear light.
Then to his father spake Telemachus:
"Father! my eyes behold a marvel. All
The palace walls, each beautiful recess,   45
The fir-tree beams, the aspiring columns, shine,
Before my eyes, as with a blaze of fire.
Some god is surely here, some one of those
Who make their dwelling in the high broad heaven.'
Odysseus, the sagacious, answered thus: 50
"Keep silence; give thy thought no speech, nor ask
Concerning aught. Such is the wont of those
Who dwell upon Olympus. Now withdraw

To rest upon thy couch, while I remain,
For I would move thy mother and her maids   55
To ask of what concerns me. She, I deem,
Full sadly will inquire of many things."
He spake; Telemachus departed thence,
By torchlight, to his chamber, there to rest
Where he was wont to lie when gentle sleep   60
Came over him. There lay he down to wait
The hallowed morning, while Odysseus, left
Within the palace, meditated still
Death to the suitors with Athena's aid.
The sage Penelope now left her bower;   65
Like Artemis or golden Aphrodite came
The queen. Beside the hearth they placed for her
The throne where she was wont to sit, inlaid
With ivory and silver, which of yore
The artisan Icmalius wrought. They laid   70
Close to the throne a footstool, over which
Was spread an ample fleece. On this sat down
The sage Penelope. Her white-armed train
Of handmaids came with her; they cleared away
The abundant feast, and bore the tables off,   75
And cups from which those insolent men had drunk;
They laid upon the ground the lighted brands,
And heaped fresh fuel round them, both for light
And warmth. And now Melantho once again
Bespake Odysseus with unmannerly words: so   80
"Stranger, wilt thou forever be a pest,
Ranging the house at night to play the spy
Upon the women? Leave the hall, thou wretch!
And gorge thyself without, else wilt thou go
Suddenly, driven by blows and flaming brands."   85

The sage Odysseus frowned on her, and said:
"Pert creature! why so fiercely rail at me?
Is it that I am squalid and ill-clad,
And forced by want to beg from hand to hand?
Such is the fate of poor and wandering men.   90
I too was opulent once, inhabiting
A plenteous home among my fellow-men,
And often gave the wanderer alms, whoe'er
He might be and in whatsoever need;
And I had many servants, and large store   95
Of things by which men lead a life of ease
And are called rich. But Zeus, the son
Of Cronus, put an end to this, for so
It pleased the god. Now, therefore, woman, think
That thou mayst lose the beauty which is now   100
Thy pride among the serving-women here;
Thy mistress may be wroth, and make thy life
A hard one or Odysseus may come back—
And there is hope of that. Or if it be
That he has perished, and returns no more,   105
There still remains his son Telemachus,
Who by Apollo's grace is now a man,
And no one of the women in these halls
May think to misbehave, and yet escape
His eye, for he no longer is a boy."   110
He spake; Penelope, the prudent, heard,
And, calling to her maid, rebuked her thus:
"O bold and shameless! I have taken note
Of thy behavior; thou hast done a wrong
For which thy head should answer. Well thou know'st,   115
For thou hast heard me say, that I would ask
The stranger in these halls if aught he knows

Of my Odysseus, for whose sake I grieve."
Then to the matron of the household turned
The queen, and thus bespake Eurynome: 120
"Bring now a seat, Eurynome, and spread
A fleece upon it, where the stranger guest
May sit at ease, and hear what I shall say,
And answer me, for I have much to ask."
She spake; the ancient handmaid brought with speed   125
A polished seat, and o'er it spread a fleece.
Odysseus, much-enduring chief, sat down,
And thus the sage Penelope began:
"First will I ask thee who thou art, and whence,
Where is thy birthplace, and thy parents who?"   130
Odysseus, the sagacious, answered thus:
"O lady, none in all the boundless earth
Can speak of thee with blame. Thy fame has reached
To the great heavens. It is like the renown
Of some most excellent king, of godlike sway   135
O'er many men and mighty, who upholds
Justice in all his realm. The dark-soiled earth
Brings wheat and barley forth; the trees are bowed
With fruit; the meadows swarm with noble herds,
The sea with fish, and under his wise reign   140
The people prosper. Therefore ask, I pray,
Of other things, while I am underneath
Thy palace-roof, but of my race and home
Inquire not, lest thou waken in my mind
Unhappy memories. I am a man   145
Of sorrow, and it would become me ill
To sit lamenting in another's house
And shedding tears. Besides, a grief indulged
Doth grow in violence. Thy maids would blame,

And thou perhaps, and ye would call my tears   150
The maudlin tears of one o'ercome with wine."
Then spake the sage Penelope again:
"Stranger, such grace of feature and of form
As once I had the immortals took away,
What time the Argive warriors sailed for Troy,   155
And my Odysseus with them. Could he now
Return to rule my household as of yore,
The wider and the brighter were my fame.
But now I lead a wretched life, so great
And many are the evils which some god   160
Heaps on me. For the chieftains who bear sway-
Over the isles—Dulichium, and the fields
Of Samos, and Zacynthus dark with woods,
And those who rule in sunny Ithaca—
Woo me against my will, and waste away   165
My substance. Therefore have I small regard
For strangers and for suppliants, and the tribe
Of heralds, servants of the public weal,
But, pining for Odysseus, wear away
My life. The suitors urge the marriage rite,   170
And I with art delay it. Once some god
Prompted me to begin an ample web,
Wide and of subtle texture, in my rooms.
And then I said: 'Youths, who are pressing me
To marriage, since Odysseus is no more,   175
Urge me no further till I shall complete—
That so the threads may not be spun in vain—
This shroud for old Laertes, when grim fate
And death's long sleep at last shall overtake
The hero; else among the multitude is   180
Of Grecian women I shall bear the blame,

If one whose ample wealth so well was known
Should lie in death without a funeral robe.'
I spake, and easily their minds were swayed
By what I said, and I began to weave   185
The ample web, but raveled it again
By torchlight every evening. For three years
I foiled them thus; but when the fourth year came,
And brought its train of hours and changing moons,
And many days had passed, they came on me,   190
And through my maidens' fault, a careless crew,
They caught me at my fraud, and chid me sore.
So, though unwilling, I was forced to end
My task, and cannot longer now escape
The marriage, nor is any refuge left.   195
My parents both exhort me earnestly
To choose a husband, and my son with grief
Beholds the suitors wasting his estate,
And he already is a man and well
Can rule his household; Zeus bestows   200
Such honor on him. Now, I pray, declare
Thy lineage, for thou surely art not sprung
From the old fabulous oak, nor from a rock."
Odysseus, the sagacious, answered her:
"O royal consort of Laertes' son!   205
Wilt thou still ask my lineage? I will then
Disclose it, but thou wakest in my heart
New sorrows. So it ever is with one
Who long, like me, is far away from home,
Wandering in many realms, and suffering much;   210
But since thou dost require it, thou shalt hear.
Crete is a region lying in the midst
Of the black deep, a fair and fruitful land,

Girt by the waters. Many are the men,
Nay, numberless, who make it their abode,   215
And ninety are its cities. Different tongues
Are spoken by the dwellers of the isle.
In part they are Achaeans, and in part
Are Cretans of the soil, a gallant stock;
There dwell Cydonians, Dorians of three tribes,   320
And proud Pelasgians. Their great capital
Is Cnossus, where the monarch Minos dwelt,
He who at every nine years' end conferred
With Zeus almighty; and to him was born
Deucalion, my brave father, who begat   325
Me and Idomeneus, the King of Crete.
To Ilium in his beaked galleys sailed
Idomeneus with Atreus' sons. My name—
A name well known—is Aethon. 'Twas at Crete
I saw Odysseus, who received from me   230
The welcome due a guest. A violent wind
Had driven him from Maleia and the course
That led to Ilium, and had carried him
To Crete, and lodged him in the dangerous port
Amnisus, close to Ilithyia's cave,   235
Where scarce his fleet escaped the hurricane.
Thence came he to the city, and inquired
For King Idomeneus, who was, he said,
His dear and honored guest; but he had sailed
Ten days before, perhaps eleven, for Troy,   240
In his beaked galleys. To the palace there
I led Odysseus, and with liberal cheer
Welcomed the chief, for plentifully stored
The royal dwelling was. I also gave
Meal from the public magazines to him   245

And those who followed him, and dark red wine
Brought from the country round, and beeves to slay
In sacrifice, that so their hearts might feel
No lack of aught. Twelve days the noble Greeks
Remained with us. A violent north-wind,   250
Which scarcely suffered them to stand upright
On shore, withstood them. Some unfriendly power
Had bid it blow; but on the thirteenth day
Its fury ceased, and the fleet put to sea."
Thus went he on, inventing tales that seemed   255
Like truth. She listened, melting into tears
That flowed as when on mountain height the snow,
Shed by the west-wind, feels the east-wind's breath,
And flows in water, and the hurrying streams
Are filled; so did Penelope's fair cheeks   260
Seem to dissolve in tears—tears shed for him
Who sat beside her even then. He saw
His weeping wife, and pitied her at heart;
Yet were his eyes like iron or like horn,
And moved not in their lids; for artfully   265
He kept his tears from falling. When the queen
Had ceased to weep, she answered him and said:
"Now, stranger, let me prove thee, if in truth
Thou didst receive, as thou hast just declared,
In thine abode, my husband and his train   270
Of noble friends. Describe the garb he wore;
How looked he, and the friends he brought with him?"
Odysseus, the sagacious, answered her:
"O lady, hard it is to answer thee,
So long have I been far away from home.   275
'Tis now the twentieth year since he was there
And left the isle, but, as my memory bids,

So will I speak. A fleecy purple cloak
Odysseus wore, a double web; the clasp
Was golden, with two fastenings, and in front   280
It showed a work of rare design—a hound
That held in his fore-paws a spotted fawn,
Struggling before his open mouth. Although
The figures were of gold, we all admired
The hound intent to break his victim's neck,   285
The fawn that, writhing, plied her nimble feet
To free herself. Around the hero's chest
And waist I saw a lustrous tunic worn,
Soft, like the thin film of the onion dried,
And bright as sunshine; many ladies looked   290
With wonder on it. Yet consider this;
I know not whether thus attired he left
His home, or whether, in the voyage thence,
Some comrade gave the garments, or perhaps
Some friendly host, for he was very dear   295
To many; among the Greeks were few like him.
I gave him, from myself, a brazen sword,
And a fair purple cloak, a double web,
Besides a tunic reaching to his feet,
And with due honors sent him on his way   300
In his good ship. There came and went with him
A herald somewhat older than himself;
Let me portray him—hunchbacked, swarthy skinned,
And curly haired, Eurybates his name.
Odysseus honored him above the rest   305
Of his companions, for they thought alike."
He ceased; the queen was moved to deeper grief,
For she remembered all the tokens well
Of which he spake; and when that passionate gust

Of weeping ceased, she spake again and said: 310
"Stranger, till now thy presence in these halls
Has only moved my pity; thou henceforth
Art dear and honored. It was I who gave
The garments thou hast told me of; these hands
Folded them in my chamber. I put on   315
The glittering clasp to be his ornament,
And now I never shall behold him more
Returning to his own dear land and home;
So cruel was the fate that took him hence
To Ilium, in his roomy ship, a town   320
Of evil omen never to be named."
Odysseus, the sagacious, answered thus:
"O gracious consort of Laertes' son!
Let not thy grief for him whom thou hast lost
Wither thy beauty longer, and consume   325
Thy heart. And yet I blame thee not at all;
For any wife in losing him to whom
She gave herself while yet a maid, and bore
Children, will mourn him, though he be in worth
Below Odysseus, who, as fame declares,   330
Is like the gods. But cease to grieve, and hear
What I shall say, and I shall speak the truth,
Nor will I hide from thee that I have heard,
But lately from Odysseus, yet alive,
And journeying homeward, in the opulent realm   335
Of the Thesprotians, whence he brings with him
Much and rare treasure, gathered there among
The people. His beloved friends he lost,
And his good ship; the black deep swallowed them
In coming from Trinacria, for his crew   340
Had slaughtered there the oxen of the Sun.

The Sun and Zeus were angry; therefore all
His comrades perished in the billowy sea;
But him upon his galley's keel the wind
Drove to the coast where the Phaeacians dwell,   345
The kinsmen of the gods. They welcomed him,
And honored him as if he were a god,
And gave him many things, and would have sent
The hero safely to his native isle;
And here Odysseus would have been long since,   350
But that he deemed it wise to travel far,
And gather wealth—for well Odysseus knew,
Beyond all other men, the arts of gain,
And none in these could think to rival him;
So Pheidon, king of the Thesprotians said,   355
Who also, in his palace, swore to me—
As to the gods of heaven he poured the wine —
That even then a galley was drawn down
Into the water, and already manned
With rowers, who should take Odysseus home.   360
But me he first dismissed, for at the time
A bark of the Thesprotians left the port,
Bound for Dulichium's cornfields. Ere I went
He showed the treasures of Odysseus stored
In the king's palace—treasures that might serve   365
To feed the household of another chief
To the tenth generation. He who owned
That wealth was at Dodona, so the king
Declared, inquiring, at the lofty oak
Of Zeus, the counsel of the god   370
How to return to his dear native land,
So long a wanderer—whether openly
Or else by stealth. So he is safe, and soon

Will he be nearer to us; for not long
Can he remain away from all his friends
And fatherland. To this I plight my oath; 375
Let Zeus, the greatest and the best of gods,
Be witness, and this hearth of the good prince
Odysseus, where I sit, that every word
Which I have said to thee will be fulfilled. 380
Within the year Odysseus will return,
As this month passes and the next comes in."
Then spake the sage Penelope again:
"Would that it might be thus, O stranger guest,
As thou hast said; then shouldst thou have such thanks." 385
And bounty at my hands that every one
Who meets thee should rejoice with thee. And yet
The thought abides with me, and so indeed
It must be, that Odysseus will no more
Return, nor wilt thou find an escort hence; 390
For now no master like Odysseus rules—
And what a man was he!—within these walls,
To welcome or dismiss the honored guest.
But now, ye maidens, let the stranger bathe,
And spread his couch with blankets, fleecy cloaks, 395
And showy tapestries, that he may lie
Warm till the Morning, in her golden car,
Draw near; then with the early morn again
Bathe and anoint him, that he may sit down
Beside Telemachus prepared to take 400
His morning meal. Ill shall he fare who dares
Molest the stranger; he shall have no place
Or office here, however he may rage.
And how, O stranger, wouldst thou learn that I
In mind and thoughtful wisdom am above 405

All other women, if I let thee sit
Squalid and meanly clad at banquets here?
Short is the life of man, and whoso bears
A cruel heart, devising cruel things,
On him men call down evil from the gods   410
While living, and pursue him, when he dies
With scoffs. But whoso is of generous heart
And harbors generous aims, his guests proclaim
His praises far and wide to all mankind,
And numberless are they who call him good."   415

Odysseus, the sagacious, answered thus:
"O gracious consort of Laertes' son!
Such cloaks and splendid coverings please me not,
Since in my long-oared bark I left behind
The snowy peaks of Crete. I still will lie,   420
As I am wont through many a sleepless night,
On a mean couch to wait the holy Morn
Upon her car of gold. I do not like
This washing of the feet. No maiden here
That ministers to thee may touch my foot;   425
But if among them be some aged dame
And faithful, who has suffered in her life
As I have suffered, she may touch my feet."

And thus the sage Penelope rejoined:
"Dear guest—for never to these halls has come   430
A stranger so discreet or better liked
By me, so wisely thou dost speak, and well,
I have an aged prudent dame, whose care
Reared my unfortunate husband. She received
The nursling when his mother brought him forth,   435
And she, though small her strength, will wash thy feet.
Rise, prudent Eurycleia, thou shalt wash

The feet of one whose years must be the same
As thy own master's; such is doubtless now
Odysseus, with such wrinkled feet and hands. 440
For quickly doth misfortune make men old."
She spake; the aged handmaid hid her face
With both her hands, and, shedding bitter tears,
Thus sorrowfully to the queen replied:
"My heart is sad for thee, my son; and yet 445
I can do nothing. Can it be that Zeus
Hates thee beyond all other? Though thyself
So reverent to the gods? No man on earth
Has burned so many thighs of fatling beasts
And chosen hecatombs as thou to Zeus 450
The Thunderer, with prayer that thou mayst reach
A calm old age, and rear thy glorious son
To manhood; yet the god hath cut thee off
From thy return forever. Even now
Perchance the women of some princely house 455
Which he has entered in some distant land
Scoff at him as these wretched creatures scoff
At thee, O stranger, who, to shun their taunts
And insults, wilt not suffer them to wash
Thy feet. The sage Penelope commands, 460
And I am not unwilling. I will wash
Thy feet, both for her sake and for thy own;
For deeply am I moved at sight of thee.
Hear what I say: of strangers in distress
Come many hither, yet have I beheld 465
No one who bears, in shape and voice and feet,
Such likeness to our absent lord as thou."
Odysseus, the sagacious, thus replied:
"O aged woman, so has it been said

By all who have beheld both him and me.   470
They all declare that we are very like
Each other; thou in this hast spoken well."
He spake; she took a shining vase designed
For washing feet, and poured cold water
In large abundance, and warm water next.   475
Odysseus, who had sat before the hearth.
Moved to a darker spot, for in his mind
The thought arose that she might find a scar
Upon his limbs in handling them, and thus
His secret would be known. She came and bathed   480
His feet, and found the scar. 'Twas where a boar
With his white tooth had gashed the limb, as once
He journeyed to Parnassus, where he paid
A visit to Autolycus and his sons,
His mother's noble father, who excelled   485
All men in craft and oaths, such was the gift
Conferred on him by Hermes; for to him
Autolycus made grateful offerings,
The thighs of lambs and kids, and evermore
The god was with him. Once Autolycus   490
Came to the opulent realm of Ithaca,
And found his daughter with a son new born;
There Eurycleia placed upon his knees
The infant, just as he had supped, and said:
"Give this dear babe, Autolycus, a name—   495
Thy daughter's son, vouchsafed to many prayers."
And thus Autolycus in answer spake:
"Daughter and son-in-law, be his the name
That I shall give. In coming to his isle
I bear the hate of many—both of men   500
And women—scattered o'er the nourishing earth;

Name him Odysseus therefore, and when, grown
To man's estate, he visits the proud halls
Reared at Parnassus, where his mother dwelt
And my possessions lie, I will bestow   505
A share on him, and send him home rejoiced."
And therefore went Odysseus to receive
The promised princely gifts. Autolycus
And all his sons received him with kind words.
And friendly grasp of hands. Amphithea there—   510
His mother's mother—took him in her arms,
And kissed his brow and both his beautiful eyes.
Then to his noble sons Autolycus
Called to prepare a feast, and they obeyed.
They brought and slew a steer of five years old,   515
And flayed and dressed it, hewed the joints apart,
And sliced the flesh, and fixed it upon spits,
Roasted it carefully, and gave to each
His part. So all the day till set of sun
They feasted, to the full content of all.   520
And when the sun had set, and earth grew dark,
They laid them down, and took the gift of sleep.
But when the rosy-fingered Morn appeared,
Born of the Dawn, forth issued the young men,
The children of Autolycus, with hounds,   525
To hunt, attended by their noble guest,
Odysseus. Up the steeps of that high, mount
Parnassus, clothed with woods, they climbed, and soon
Were on its airy heights. The sun, new risen
From the deep ocean's gently flowing stream,   530
Now smote the fields. The hunters reached a dell;
The hounds before them tracked the game; behind
Followed the children of Autolycus.

The generous youth Odysseus, brandishing
A spear of mighty length, came pressing on   535
Close to the hounds. There lay a huge wild boar
Within a thicket, where moist-blowing winds
Came not, nor in his brightness could the sun
Pierce with his beams the covert, nor the rain
Pelt through, so closely grew the shrubs. The ground   540
Was heaped with sheddings of the withered leaves.
Around him came the noise of dogs and men
Approaching swiftly. From his lair he sprang
And faced them, with the bristles on his neck
Upright, and flashing eyes. Odysseus rushed   545
Before the others, with the ponderous spear
Raised high in his strong hand intent to smite.
The boar was first to strike; he dealt a blow
Sidelong, and gashed his foe above the knee,
And tore the flesh, but left untouched the bone.   550
Odysseus, striking with his burnished spear
The boar's right shoulder, drove the weapon through.
He fell with piercing cries amid the dust,
And the life left him. Then, around their guest
The kindly children of Autolycus   555
Came and bound up with care the wound, and stanched
With spells the dark blood of the blameless youth,
And hastened with him to their father's home.
And when Autolycus and they his sons
Had seen him wholly healed, they loaded him   560
With presents, and, rejoicing for his sake,
Sent him rejoicing back to Ithaca.
His father and his gracious mother there
Rejoiced in turn, and asked him of the scar,
And how it came, and he related all—   565

How by the white tusk of a savage boar
The wound was given on the Parnassian heights,
As he was hunting with her father's sons.
The aged woman, as she took the foot
Into her hands, perceived by touch the scar,   570
And, letting fall the limb, it struck the vase.
Loud rang the brass, the vase was overturned,
And poured the water forth. At once a rush
Of gladness and of grief came o'er her heart.
Tears filled her eyes, and her clear voice was choked.   575
She touched Odysseus on the chin, and said:
"Dear child! thou art Odysseus, of a truth.
I knew thee not till I had touched the scar."
So speaking, toward Penelope she turned
Her eyes, about to tell her that her lord   580
Was in the palace; but the queen saw not,
And all that passed was unperceived by her,
For Pallas turned her thoughts another way.
Meantime, Odysseus on the nurse's throat
Laid his right hand, and with the other drew   535
The aged woman nearer him, and said:
"Nurse, wouldst thou ruin me, who drew long since
Milk from thy bosom, and who now return,
After much suffering borne for twenty years,
To mine own land? Now then, since thou hast learned   599
The truth—by prompting of some god, no doubt—
Keep silence, lest some others in the house
Should learn it also. Else—I tell thee this,
And will perform my word—if God permit
That I o'ercome the arrogant suitor-crew,   595
Nurse as thou art, I spare not even thee,
When in these halls the other maidens die."

Then thus the prudent Eurycleia said:

"What words, my son, have passed thy lips? for well

Thou knowest my firm mind; it never yields.   600

Like solid rock or steel I keep my trust.

This let me tell thee, and, I pray thee, keep

My words in mind. If, by the aid of God,

Thou overcome the arrogant suitor-crew,

Then will I name the handmaids that disgrace   605

Thy household, and point out the innocent."

Odysseus, the sagacious, thus rejoined:

"Why name them, nurse? It needs not. I myself

Shall watch them, and shall know them all. Hold thou

Thy peace, and leave the issue with the gods."   610

He spake; the aged woman left the place

To bring a second bath, for on the floor

The first was spilled. When she had bathed his feet

And made them smooth with oil, Odysseus drew

Close to the hearth his seat again, to take   615

The warmth, and with his tatters hid the scar.

And thus the sage Penelope began:

"Stranger, but little longer will I yet

Inquire; the hour of grateful rest is near

For those who, though unhappy, can receive   620

The balm of slumber. Yet for me some god

Appoints immeasurable grief. All day

In sorrows and in sighs, my solace is

To oversee my maidens at their tasks

Here in the palace; but when evening comes,   625

And all betake themselves to rest, I lie

Upon my couch, and sorrows thick and sharp

Awake new misery in my heart. As when,

In the fresh spring, the swarthy Nightingale,

Daughter of Pandarus, among thick leaves   630
Sings sweetly to the woods, and, changing oft
The strain, pours forth her voice of many notes,
Lamenting the beloved Itylus,
Her son by royal Zethos, whom she smote
Unwittingly, and slew; with such quick change   635
My mind is tossed from thought to thought. I muse
Whether to keep my place beside my son,
And hold what here is mine, my dower, my maids
And high-roofed halls, as one who still reveres
Her husband's bed, and heeds the public voice,   640
Or follow one of the Achaean chiefs,
The noblest of the wooers, and the one
Who offers marriage presents without stint.
My son's green years, while he was yet a boy,
Unripe in mind, allowed me not to wed,   645
And leave his father's home; but he is grown,
And on the verge of manhood. He desires
That I should leave the palace, for his wrath
Is great against the men who waste his wealth.
Hear, and interpret now a dream of mine: 650
Within these courts are twenty geese that eat
Corn from the water, and I look on them
Pleased and amused. From off a mountain came
A hook-beaked eagle, broke their necks, and left
Their bodies strewn about the palace dead,   655
And soared again into the air of heaven.
I wept and moaned, although it was a dream;
And round me came the fair-haired Grecian maids
Lamenting wildly that the bird of prey
Had slain my geese. Then came the eagle back,   660
And took his perch upon the jutting roof,

And thus bespake me in a human voice:
"'O daughter of Icarius, the renowned!
Let not thy heart be troubled; this is not
A dream, but a true vision, and will be   665
Fulfilled. The geese denote the suitor-train,
And I, who was an eagle once, am come,
Thy husband, now to end them utterly.'
He spake; my slumbers left me, and I looked,
And saw the geese that in the palace still   670
Were at their trough, and feeding as before."
And thus Odysseus, the sagacious, said:
"Lady, the dream that visited thy sleep
Cannot be wrested to another sense.
Odysseus has himself revealed to thee   675
The way of its fulfillment. Death is near
The suitors, and not one escapes his doom."
Then spake the sage Penelope again:
"Of dreams, O stranger, some are meaningless
And idle, and can never be fulfilled.   680
Two portals are there for their shadowy shapes,
Of ivory one, and one of horn. The dreams
That come through the carved ivory deceive
With promises that never are made good;
But those which pass the doors of polished horn,   685
And are beheld of men, are ever true.
And yet I cannot hope that my strange dream
Came through them, though my son and I would both
Rejoice if it were so. This let me say,
And heed me well. Tomorrow brings to us   690
The hateful morn which takes me from my home,
The palace of Odysseus. I shall now
Propose a contest. In the palace court

Odysseus in a row set up twelve stakes,
Like props that hold a galley up; each stake   695
Had its own ring; he stood afar, and sent
An arrow through them all. I shall propose
This contest to the suitors. He who bends
The bow with easy mastery, and sends
Through the twelve rings an arrow, I will take   700
To follow from the palace where I passed
My youthful married life—a beautiful home,
And stored with wealth; a home which I shall long
Remember, even in my nightly dreams."
Odysseus, the sagacious, answered thus: 705
"O gracious consort of Laertes' son!
Let not this contest be delayed; the man
Of ready wiles, Odysseus, will be here
Ere, tampering with the hero's polished bow,
The suitors shall prevail to stretch the cord,   710
And send an arrow through the rings of steel."
And thus the sage Penelope rejoined:
"Stranger, if, sitting in the palace here,
Thou still wouldst entertain me as thou dost,
Sleep would not fall upon my lids; and yet   715
Sleepless the race of mortals cannot be,
So have the gods ordained, who measure out
His lot to man upon the nourishing earth.
I to the upper rooms withdraw, to take
My place upon the couch which has become   720
To me a place of sorrow and of tears
Since my Odysseus went away to Troy,
That fatal town which should be named no more.
And I will lay me down; but thou remain
Within these walls, and make the floor thy bed,   725

Or let these maidens spread a couch for thee."
Penelope, thus having spoken, went
Up to her royal bower, but not alone;
Her maids went with her. When they were within,
She wept for her dear husband, till at length   730
The blue-eyed Pallas graciously distilled
Upon her closing lids the balm of sleep.

BOOK XX

The noble chief, Odysseus, in the porch   1
Lay down to rest. An undressed bullock's hide
Was under him, and over that the skins
Of sheep, which for the daily sacrifice
The Achaeans slew. Eurynome had spread   5
A cloak above him. There he lay awake,
And meditated how he yet should smite
The suitors down. Meantime, with cries of mirth
And laughter, came the women forth to seek
The suitors' arms. Odysseus, inly moved   10
With anger, pondered whether he should rise
And put them all to death, or give their shame
A respite for another night, the last.
His heart raged in his bosom. As a hound
Growls, walking round her whelps, when she beholds 15
A stranger, and is eager for the attack,
So growled his heart within him, and so fierce
Was his impatience with that shameless crew.
He smote his breast, and thus he chid his heart:
"Endure it, heart! thou didst bear worse than this. 20
When the grim Cyclops of resistless strength

Devoured thy brave companions, thou couldst still
Endure, till thou by stratagem didst leave
The cave in which it seemed that thou must die."
Thus he rebuked his heart, and, growing calm,   25
His heart submitted; but the hero tossed
From side to side. As when one turns and turns
The stomach of a bullock filled with fat
And blood before a fiercely blazing fire
And wishes it were done, so did the chief   30
Shift oft from side to side, while pondering how
To lay a strong hand on the multitude
Of shameless suitors—he but one, and they
So many. Meantime Pallas, sliding down
From heaven, in form a woman, came, and there   35
Beside his bed stood over him, and spake:
"Why, most unhappy of the sons of men,
Art thou still sleepless? This is thine abode,
And here thou hast thy consort and a son
Whom any man might covet for his own."   40
Odysseus, the sagacious, answered thus:
"Truly, O goddess, all that thou hast said
Is rightly spoken. This perplexes me—
How to lay hands upon these shameless men,
When I am only one, and they a throng   45
That fill the palace. Yet another thought,
And mightier still—if, by thy aid and Zeus's,
I slay the suitors, how shall I myself
Be safe thereafter? Think, I pray, of this."
And thus in turn the blue-eyed Pallas said: 50
"O faint of spirit! in a humbler friend
Than I am, in a friend of mortal birth
And less far-seeing, one might put his trust;

But I am born a goddess, and protect
Thy life in every danger. Let me say,   55
And plainly say, if fifty armed bands
Of men should gather round us, eager all
To take thy life, thou mightest drive away,
Unharmed by them, their herds and pampered flocks.
But give thyself to sleep. To wake and watch   60
All night is most unwholesome. Thou shalt find
A happy issue from thy troubles yet."
She spake, and, shedding slumber on his lids,
Upward the glorious goddess took her way
Back to Olympus, when she saw that sleep   65
Had seized him, making him forget all care
And slackening every limb. His faithful wife
Was still awake, and sat upright and wept
On her soft couch, and after many tears
The glorious lady prayed to Dian thus: 70
"Goddess august! Artemis, child of Zeus!
I would that thou wouldst send into my heart
A shaft to take my life, or that a storm
Would seize and hurl me through the paths of air,
And cast me into ocean's restless streams,   75
As once a storm, descending, swept away
The daughters born to Pandarus. The gods
Had slain their parents, and they dwelt alone
As orphans in their palace, nourished there
By blessed Aphrodite with the curds of milk,   80
And honey, and sweet wine, while Hera gave
Beauty and wit beyond all womankind,
And chaste Artemis dignity of form,
And Pallas every art that graces life.
Then, as the blessed Aphrodite went to ask   85

For them, of Zeus the Thunderer, on the heights
Of his Olympian mount, the crowning gift
Of happy marriage—for to Zeus is known
Whatever comes to pass, and what shall be
The fortune, good or ill, of mortal men—   90
The Harpies came meantime, bore off the maids,
And gave them to the hateful sisterhood
Of Furies as their servants. So may those
Who dwell upon Olympus make an end
Of me, or fair-haired Dian strike me down,   95
That, with the image of Odysseus still
Before my mind, I may not seek to please
One of less worth. This evil might be borne
By one who weeps all day, and feels at heart
A settled sorrow, yet can sleep at night.   100
For sleep, when once it weighs the eyelids down,
Makes men unmindful both of good and ill,
And all things else. But me some deity
Visits with fearful dreams. There lay by me,
This very night, one like him, as he was   105
When with his armed men he sailed for Troy;
And I was glad, for certainly I deemed
It was a real presence, and no dream."
She spake. Just then, upon her car of gold,
Appeared the Morn. The great Odysseus heard   110
That voice of lamentation; anxiously
He mused; it seemed to him as if the queen
Stood over him and knew him. Gathering up
In haste the cloak and skins on which he slept,
He laid them in the palace on a seat, us   115
But bore the bull's hide forth in open air,
And lifted up his hands and prayed to Zeus:

"O Father Zeus, and all the gods! if ye
Have led me graciously, o'er land and deep,
Across the earth, and, after suffering much,   120
To mine own isle, let one of those who watch
Within the palace speak some ominous word,
And grant a sign from thee without these walls."
So prayed he. All-providing Zeus
Hearkened, and thundered from the clouds around   125
The bright Olympian peaks. Odysseus heard
With gladness. From a room within the house,
In which the mills of the king's household stood,
A woman, laboring at the quern, gave forth
An omen also. There were twelve who toiled   130
In making flour of barley and of wheat—
The strength of man. The rest were all asleep;
Their tasks were done; one only, of less strength
Than any other there, kept toiling on.
She paused a moment, stopped the whirling stone,   135
And spake these words—a portent for the king:
"O Father Zeus, the king of gods and men!
Thou hast just thundered from the starry heaven,
And yet there is no cloud. To some one here
It is a portent. O perform for me,   140
All helpless as I am, this one request!
Let now the suitors in this palace take
Their last and final pleasant feast today—
These men who make my limbs, with constant toil,
In grinding corn for them, to lose their strength,   145
Once let them banquet here, and then no more."
She spake; the omen of the woman's words
And Zeus's loud thunder pleased Odysseus well;
And now he deemed he should avenge himself

Upon the guilty ones. The other maids   150
Of that fair palace of Odysseus woke
And came together, and upon the hearth
Kindled a steady fire. Telemachus
Rose from his bed in presence like a god,
Put on his garments, hung his trenchant sword   155
Upon his shoulder, tied to his fair feet
The shapely sandals, took his massive spear
Tipped with sharp brass, and, stopping as he reached
The threshold, spake to Eurycleia thus:
"Dear nurse, have ye with honor fed and lodged   160
Our guest, or have ye suffered him to find
A lodging where he might, without your care?
Discerning as she is, my mother pays
High honor to the worse among her guests,
And sends the nobler man unhonored hence."   165
And thus the prudent Eurycleia said:
"My child, blame not thy mother; she deserves
No blame. The stranger sat and drank his wine,
All that he would, and said, when pressed to eat,
That he desired no more. And when he thought   170
Of sleep, she bade her maidens spread his couch;
But he refused a bed and rugs, like one
Inured to misery, and beneath the porch
Slept on an undressed bull's hide and the skins
Of sheep, and over him we cast a cloak."   175
She spake; Telemachus, his spear in hand,
Went forth, his fleet dogs following him. He sought
The council where the well-greaved Greeks were met.
Meantime the noble Eurycleia, child
Of Ops, Pisenor's son, bespake the maids: 180
"Come, some of you, at once, and sweep the floor,

And sprinkle it, and on the shapely thrones
Spread coverings of purple tapestry;
Let others wipe the tables with a sponge,
And cleanse the beakers and the double cups,   185
While others go for water to the fount,
And bring it quickly, for not long today
The suitors will be absent from these halls.
They will come early to the general feast."
She spake; the handmaids hearkened and obeyed,   190
And twenty went to the dark well to draw
The water, while the others busily
Bestirred themselves about the house. Then came
The servants of the chiefs, and set themselves
Neatly to cleave the wood. Then also came   195
The women from the well. The swineherd last
Came with three swine, the fattest of the herd.
In that fair court he let them feed, and sought
Odysseus, greeting him with courteous words:
"Hast thou, O stranger, found among these Greeks   200
More reverence? Art thou still their mark of scorn?"
Odysseus, the sagacious, answered thus:
"O that the gods, Eumaeus, would avenge
The insolence of those who meditate
Violent deeds, and make another's house   205
Their plotting-place, and feel no touch of shame!"
So talked they with each other. Now appeared
Melanthius, keeper of the goats. He brought
Goats for the suitors' banquet; they were choice
Beyond all others. With him also came   210
Two goatherds. In the echoing portico
He bound his goats. He saw Odysseus there,
And thus accosted him with railing words:

"Stranger, art thou still here, the palace pest,
And begging still, and wilt thou ne'er depart?   215
We shall not end this quarrel, I perceive,
Till thou hast tried the flavor of my fist.
It is not decent to be begging here
Continually; the Greeks have other feasts."
He spake; Odysseus answered not, but shook   220
His head in silence, planning fearful things.
Philoetius now, a master-herdsman, came,
And for the banquet of the suitors led
A heifer that had never yeaned, and goats
The fatlings of the flock; they came across   225
The ferry, brought by those whose office is
To bear whoever comes from shore to shore.
He bound his animals in the sounding porch,
And went and, standing by the swineherd, said:
"Who, swineherd, is the stranger newly come   230
To this our palace? of what parents born,
And of what race, and where his native land?
Unhappy seemingly, yet like a king
In person. Sorrowful must be the lot
Of men who wander to and fro on earth,   235
When even to kings the gods appoint distress."
He spake, and, greeting with his offered hand
Odysseus, said in winged words aloud:
"Stranger and father, hail! and mayst thou yet
Be happy in the years to come at least,   240
Though held in thrall by many sorrows now.
Yet thou, All-father Zeus! art most austere
Of all the gods, not sparing even those
Who have their birth from thee, but bringing them
To grief and pain. The sweat is on my brow   245

When I behold this stranger, and my eyes
Are filled with tears when to my mind comes back
The image of Odysseus, who must now,
I think, be wandering, clothed in rags like thee,
Among the abodes of men, if yet indeed   250
He lives and sees the sweet light of the sun.
But if that he be dead, and in the abode
Of Hades, woe is me for his dear sake!
The blameless chief, who when I was a boy
Gave to me, in the Cephalenian fields,   255
The charge of all his beeves; and they are now
Innumerable; the broad-fronted race
Of cattle never would have multiplied
So largely under other care than mine.
Now other masters bid me bring my beeves   260
For their own feasts. They little heed his son,
The palace-heir; as little do they dread
The vengeance of the gods; they long to share
Among them the possessions of the king,
So many years unheard from. But this thought   265
Comes to my mind again, and yet again:
Wrong were it, while the son is yet alive,
To drive the cattle to a foreign land,
Where alien men inhabit; yet 'tis worse
To stay and tend another's beeves, and bear   270
This spoil. And long ago would I have fled
To some large-minded monarch, since this waste
Is not to be endured, but that I think
Still of my suffering lord, and hope that yet
He may return and drive the suitors hence."   275
Odysseus, the sagacious, answering, said:
"Herdsman, since thou dost seem not ill inclined,

Nor yet unwise, and I perceive in thee
A well-discerning mind, I therefore say,
And pledge my solemn oath—Zeus, first of gods,   280
Be witness, and this hospitable board
And hearth of good Odysseus, which has here
Received me—while thou art within these halls
Odysseus will assuredly return,
And, if thou choose to look, thine eyes shall see   285
The suitors slain, who play the master here."
And thus the master of the herds rejoined:
"Stranger, may Zeus make good thy words!
Then shalt thou see what strength is in my arm."
Eumaeus also prayed to all the gods,   290
That now the wise Odysseus might return.
So talked they with each other, while apart
The suitors doomed Telemachus to death,
And plotted how to take his life. Just then
A bird—an eagle—on the left flew by,   295
High up; his talons held a timid dove.
And then Amphinomus bespake the rest:
"O friends, this plan to slay Telemachus
Must fail. And now repair we to the feast."
So spake Amphinomus, and to his words   300
They all gave heed, and hastened to the halls
Of the divine Odysseus, where they laid
Their cloaks upon the benches and the thrones,
And slaughtering the choice sheep, and fading goats,
And porkers, and a heifer from the herd,   305
Roasted the entrails, and distributed
A share to each. Next mingled they the wine
In the large bowls. The swineherd brought a cup
To everyone. Philoetius, chief among

The servants, gave from shapely canisters 310
The bread to each. Melanthius poured the wine.
Then putting forth their hands, they all partook
The ready banquet. With a wise design,
Telemachus near the stone threshold placed
Odysseus, on a shabby seat, beside 315
A little table, but within the walls
Of that strong-pillared pile! He gave him there
Part of the entrails, and poured out for him
The wine into a cup of gold, and said:
"Sit here, and drink thy wine among the rest, 320
And from the insults and assaults of these
It shall be mine to guard thee. For this house
Is not the common property of all;
Odysseus first acquired it, and for me—
And you, ye suitors, keep your tongues from taunts 325
And hands from force, lest there be wrath and strife."
He spake; the suitors, as they heard him, bit
Their pressed lips, wondering at Telemachus,
Who uttered such bold words. Antinous then,
Eupeithes' son, bespake his fellows thus: 330
"Harsh as they are, let us, O Greeks, endure
These speeches of Telemachus. He makes
High threats, but had Cronus-son Zeus allowed,
We should, ere this, and in these very halls,
Have quieted our loud-tongued orator." 335
So spake the suitor, but Telemachus
Heeded him not. Then through the city came
The heralds with a hallowed hecatomb,
Due to the gods. The long-haired people thronged
The shady grove of Phoebus, archer-god. 340
Now when the flesh was roasted and was drawn

From off the spits, and each was given his share,
They held high festival. The men who served
The banquet gave Odysseus, where he sat,
A portion equal to their own, for so   345
His own dear son Telemachus enjoined.
Yet did not Pallas cause the haughty crew
Of suitors to refrain from stinging taunts,
That so the spirit of Laertes' son
Might be more deeply wounded. One there was   350
Among the suitors, a low-thoughted wretch;
Ctesippus was his name, and his abode
Was Samos. Trusting in his father's wealth,
He wooed the wife of the long-absent king
Odysseus. To his insolent mates he said: 355
"Hear me, ye noble suitors, while I speak.
This stranger has received an equal share,
As is becoming; for it were not just
Nor seemly to pass by, in such a feast,
The guests, whoe'er they may be, that resort   360
To this fair mansion of Telemachus.
I also will bestow on him a gift
Of hospitality, and he in turn
May give it to the keeper of the bath,
Or any other of the menial train   365
That serve the household of Odysseus here."
So speaking, with his strong right hand he flung
A bullock's foot, which from a canister
Hard by he plucked. Odysseus gently bowed
His head, and shunned the blow, and grimly smiled.   370
The missile struck the solid wall, and then
Telemachus rebuked the suitor thus:
"Ctesippus, well hast thou escaped with life,

Not having hit the stranger, who himself
Shrank from the blow; else had I pinned thee through   375
With my sharp spear. Instead of wedding feast,
Thy father would have celebrated here
Thy funeral rites. Let no man in these halls
Bear himself insolently in my sight
Hereafter, for my reason now is ripe   380
To know the right from wrong. I was of late
A child, and now it is enough to bear
That ye should slay our sheep, and drink our wine,
And eat our bread—for what can one man do
Against so many? Cease this petty war   335
Of wrong and hatred; but if ye desire
To take my life, 'tis well; 'twere better so.
And rather would I die by violence
Than live to see these most unmanly deeds—
Guests driven away, and women-servants hauled   390
Through these fair rooms by brutal wassailers."
He ended, and the assembly all sat mute
Till Agelaus spake, Damastor's son:
"O friends! let no man here with carping words
Gainsay what is so rightly said, nor yet   393
Insult the stranger more, nor one of those
Who serve the household of the godlike chief
Odysseus in his palace. I would say
This word in kindness to Telemachus
And to his mother; may it please them both!   400
While yet the hope was cherished in your hearts
That wise Odysseus would return, no blame
Could fasten on the queen that she remained
Unwedded, and resisted those who came
To woo her in the palace. Better so,   405

Had he come home again. Yet now, is clear,
He comes no more. Go then, Telemachus,
And, sitting by thy mother, bid her wed
The noblest of her wooers, and the one
Who brings the richest gifts; and thou possess   410
Thy father's wealth in peace, and eat and drink
At will, while she shall find another home."
And thus discreet Telemachus replied:
"Nay, Agelaus, for I swear by Zeus,
And by my father's sufferings, who has died,   415
Or yet is wandering, far from Ithaca,
That I do nothing to delay the choice
And marriage of my mother. I consent
That she become the wife of whom she list,
And him who offers most. But I should feel   420
Great shame to thrust her forth against her will,
And with unfilial speeches; God forbid!"
He ended here, and Pallas, as he spake,
To inextinguishable laughter moved
The suitors. There they sat with wandering minds;   425
They swallowed morsels foul with blood; their eyes
Were filled with tears; their hearts foreboded woe.
Then spake the godlike Theoclymenus:
"Unhappy men! what may this evil be
That overtakes you? Every brow and face   430
And each one's lower limbs are wrapped in night,
And moans arise, and tears are on your cheeks.
The walls and all the graceful cornices
Between the pillars are bedropped with blood,
The portico is full, these halls are full   435
Of shadows, hastening down to Erebus
Amid the gloom. The sun is blotted out

From heaven, and fearful darkness covers all."
He spake, and loud they laughed. Eurymachus,
The son of Polybus, in answer said: 440
"The stranger prattles idly; he is come
From some far land. Conduct him through the door,
Young men, and send him to the market-place,
Since all things here are darkened to his eyes."
Then spake the godlike Theoclymenus: 445
"Eurymachus, from thee I ask no guide,
For I have eyes and ears, and two good feet,
And in my breast a mind as sound as they,
And by the aid of these I mean to make
My way without; for clearly I perceive   450
A coming evil, which no suitor here
Will yet escape—no one who, in these halls
Of the great chief, Odysseus, treats with scorn
His fellow-man, and broods o'er guilty plans."
He spake, and, hastening from that noble pile,   455
Came to Piraeus, in whose house he found
A welcome. All the suitors, as he went,
Looked at each other, and, the more to vex
Telemachus, kept laughing at his guests.
And thus an insolent youth among them said: 460
"No man had ever a worse set of guests
Than thou, Telemachus. For what a wretch
That wandering beggar is, who always wants
His bread and wine, and is unfit for work,
And has no strength; in truth, a useless load   465
Upon the earth he treads. The other guest
Rises to play the prophet. If thou take
My counsel, which I give thee for thy good,
Let them at once be put on board a bark

Of many oars, and we will send them hence   470
To the Sicilians; they will bring a price."
So talked the suitors, but he heeded not
Their words, and, looking toward his father, held
His peace, expecting when he would lay hands
Upon that insolent crew. Penelope,   475
Sage daughter of Icarius, took her place
Right opposite upon a sumptuous seat,
And heard the words of every man who spake
Within the hall. They held that midday feast
With laughter—a luxurious feast it was,   480
And mirthful; many victims had been slain
To furnish forth the tables; but no feast
Could be more bitter than the later one,
To which the goddess and that valiant man
Would bid the guilty crew of plotters soon.   485

BOOK XXI

Pallas, the goddess of the azure eyes,   1
Woke in the mind of sage Penelope,
The daughter of Icarius, this design—
To put into the suitors' hands the bow
And gray steel rings, and to propose a game   5
That in the palace was to usher in
The slaughter. So she climbed the lofty stair,
Up from the hall, and took in her plump hand
The fair carved key; its wards were wrought of brass,
And ivory was the handle. Soon she reached   10
The furthest room with her attendant maids.
There lay the treasures of Odysseus—brass
And gold, and steel divinely wrought. There lay
His bow unstrung; there lay his quiver charged
With arrows; many were the deadly shafts   15
It held, a stranger's gift, who met him once
In Lacedaemon, Iphitus by name,
The son of Eurytus, and like the gods
In presence. In Messene met the twain,
And in the mansion of Orsilochus,   20
The warlike. Thither had Odysseus come
To claim a debt from all the region round;

For rovers from Messene to their ships
Had driven and carried off from Ithaca
Three hundred sheep and those who tended them.   25
For this Odysseus, though a stripling yet,
Came that long voyage, on an embassy,
Sent by his father and the other chiefs.
And Iphitus had come in search of steeds
Which he had lost—twelve mares, and under them   30
Twelve hardy mules, their foals. That errand brought
The doom of death upon him. For he came,
In journeying, to the abode of Hercules,
The mighty hero-son of Zeus,
Famed for his labors, who, in his own house,   35
Slew Iphitus, the stranger. Cruel wretch!
Who reverenced not the vengeance of the gods,
Nor what was due to his own board, at which
He placed his guest, and slew him afterward,
And in his stables kept the goodly mares.   40
'Twas when this guest was seeking for his steeds
He met Odysseus, and bestowed on him
The bow, which mighty Eurytus once bore,
And dying in his lofty palace left
The weapon to his son. Odysseus gave   45
In turn a trenchant sword and massive lance,
A pledge of kindly hospitality,
Begun, but not continued till they sat
Each at the other's table; for the son
Of Zeus first took the life of him who gave so   50
The bow, the godlike son of Eurytus.
That bow Odysseus, when he went to war
In his black galleys, never took with him,
But left it in his palace, to be kept

In memory of a beloved friend,   55
And only bore it in his own domain.
Now when the glorious lady reached the room,
And stood upon the threshold, wrought of oak
And polished by the workman's cunning hand,
Who stretched the line upon it, and set up   60
Its posts, and hung its shining doors, she loosed
With a quick touch the thong that held the ring,
Put in the key, and with a careful aim
Struck back the sounding bolts. As when a bull
Roars in the field, such sound the beautiful doors, 65
Struck with the key, gave forth, and instantly
They opened to her. Up the lofty floor
She stepped, where stood the coffer that contained
The perfumed garments. Reaching forth her hand,
The queen took down the bow, that hung within   70
Its shining case, and sat her down, and laid
The case upon her knees, and, drawing forth
The monarch's bow, she wept aloud. As soon
As that new gush of tears had ceased to fall,
Back to the hall she went, and that proud throng   75
Of suitors, bearing in her hand the bow
Unstrung, and quiver, where the arrows lay
Many and deadly. Her attendant maids
Brought also down a coffer, where were laid
Much brass and steel, provided by the king   80
For games like these. The glorious lady then,
In presence of the suitors, stood beside
The columns that upheld the stately roof.
She held a lustrous veil before her cheeks,
And, while on either side of her a maid   85
Stood modestly, bespake the suitors thus:

"Hear, noble suitors! ye who throng these halls,
And eat and drink from day to day, while long
My husband has been gone; your sole excuse
For all this lawlessness the claim ye make   90
That I become a bride. Come then, for now
A contest is proposed. I bring to you
The mighty bow that great Odysseus bore.
Whoe'er among you he may be whose hand
Shall bend this bow, and send through these twelve rings   95
An arrow, him I follow hence, and leave
This beautiful abode of my young years,
With all its plenty—though its memory,
I think, will haunt me even in my dreams."
She spake, and bade the master of the swine,   100
The good Eumaeus, place the bow and rings
Of hoary steel before the suitor-train.
In tears he bore the bow and laid it down.
The herdsman also wept to see again
His master's bow. Antinous called to both   105
With a loud voice, and chid them angrily:
"Ye silly rustics, who can never see
Beyond the hour, why trouble with your tears
The lady who had grief enough besides
For her lost husband? Sit and share the feast   110
In silence, or go forth and leave the bow;
A difficult contest it will be for us,
Nor, as I think, will this fair bow be bent
With ease, since surely there is no man here
Such as Odysseus was. I saw him once,   115
While but a child, and still remember him."
He spake, yet in his secret heart believed
That he should bend the bow, and send a shaft

Through all the rings. And yet he was the first
To taste the steel—an arrow from the hand   120
Of the great chief Odysseus—whom he wronged
In his own palace, and to equal wrong
Encouraged others. Then Telemachus
Rose in his sacred might, and thus began:
"Alas! it must be that Cronus-son Zeus   125
Has made me lose my wits. Wise as she is,
My mother promises to leave her home
And follow someone else, and yet I laugh,
And am delighted in my foolish heart.
Come then, since such a contest is proposed,   130
Ye suitors! and for such a woman too.
The like is not in all the lands of Greece,
Argos, Mycenae, or the hallowed shore
Of Pylos, or in Ithaca itself,
Or the dark mainland coast. Ye know it well;   135
Why should I praise my mother? Come then, all;
Let there be no excuses for delay,
Nor longer leave the bow untried, that we
May see the event. I too am moved to try;
And if I bend the bow, and send a shaft   140
Through all the rings, my gracious mother then
Will not, to my great grief, renounce her home,
And, following another, leave me here,
Although my prowess even now might win
The glorious prizes that my father won."   145
He spake and, rising, from his shoulders took
The purple cloak, and laid the trenchant sword
Aside; and first he placed the rings of steel
In order, opening for them in the ground
A long trench by a line, and stamping close   150

The earth around them. All admired the skill
With which he ranged them, never having seen
The game before. And then he took his place
Upon the threshold, and essayed the bow;
And thrice he made the attempt, and thrice gave o'er,   155
Yet hoping still to draw the cord, and send
An arrow through the rings. He would have drawn
The bow at the fourth trial, but a nod
Given by his father caused him to forbear,
Though eager for the attempt. And then again   160
The princely youth bespake the suitors thus:
"Well, this is strange! I may hereafter prove
A craven and a weakling, or perchance
Am yet too young, and cannot trust my arm
To do me right against the man who first   165
Assaults me. Come then, ye whose strength excels
My own, and try the bow, and end the strife."
He spake, and setting down the bow to lean
Against the firm smooth panels of the wall,
And the swift shaft against the bow's fair curve,   170
He took again his seat upon the throne
From which he rose. And then Eupeithes' son,
Antinous, to the crowd of suitors said:
"Rise one by one, my friends, from right to left.
Begin where he begins who pours the wine."   175
So spake Antinous, and the rest approved.
Then rose Leiodes, son of Oenops, first.
He was their seer, and always had his seat
Beside the ample bowl. From deeds of wrong
He shrank with hatred, and was sore incensed   180
Against the suitors all. He took the bow
And shaft, and, going to the threshold, stood

And tried the bow, yet bent it not; it galled
His hands, for they were soft, and all unused
To such a task; and thus at length he spake: 185
"O friends, I bend it not; another hand
Must try. This bow, upon this very spot,
Will take from many a prince the breath of life.
And better were it thus to die, by far,
Than, living, fail of that intent for which   190
We haunt this place, and still from day to day
Assemble. There is many a one whose wish
And hope are strong to wed Penelope,
The consort of Odysseus; but so soon
As he shall see and try the hero's bow   195
Let him with marriage presents seek to gain
Some other bride among the long-robed dames,
Achaia's daughters. Let him leave the queen
To wed the suitor who shall bring to her
The richest gifts, and him whom fate appoints."   200
He spake, and setting down the bow to lean
Against the firm smooth panels of the wall,
And the swift shaft against the bow's fair curve,
He took again his seat upon the throne
From which he rose. Antinous then took up   205
The word and answered, and reproached him thus:
"What words are these, Leiodes, that have passed
Thy lips? harsh words and fearful—that this bow
Shall take from many princes here the breath
Of life, and all because thou hast no power   210
To bend it? Thy good mother bore thee not
To draw the bow and send the arrow forth,
But others of the noble suitor-train
Are here, by whom this bow shall yet be bent."

Then to Melanthius, keeper of the goats,   215
Antinous gave this bidding. "Light a fire
With speed, Melanthius, in the palace here,
And place a seat before it. Lay a fleece
Upon the seat, and bring us from within
An ample roll of fat, that we young men   220
By warming and anointing may make soft
The bow, and draw the cord, and end the strife."
He spake; Melanthius kindled instantly
A glowing fire, and near it placed a seat,
And on the seat a fleece, and from within   225
Brought forth an ample roll of fat, with which
The young men, having warmed it, smeared the bow
And tried, but bent it not, too weak by far
For such a feat. Antinous kept aloof,
He and the godlike youth Eurymachus,   230
Two princes who in might excelled the rest.
The herdsman of Odysseus meantime left
The palace, and with him the swineherd went,
And after them Odysseus. When they all
Were now without the gate and palace court,   235
Odysseus spake to them, and blandly said:
"Herdsman and swineherd, shall I say to you
Somewhat, or shall I keep it back? My heart
Moves me to say it. Should Odysseus come,
Led by some god, and suddenly, what aid   240
Would he receive from you? Would ye take part
With him, or with the suitors? Frankly speak;
And tell me what your hearts would bid you do."
Then answered thus the keeper of the herds:
"O Father Zeus! wouldst thou but grant my wish,   245
And let some god conduct him hither, then

Shall it be seen what might is in these hands!"
So also did Eumaeus offer prayer
To all the deities, that speedily
The wise Odysseus might return; and when   250
The chief perceived in all its truth the thought
And purpose of their hearts, he spake and said:
"Know, then, that I myself am he, at home
Again, returning in the twentieth year,
And after many sufferings, to the land   255
That saw my birth. I know that I am come
Welcome to you alone of all my train
Of servants, since I hear no others pray
For my return. Hear, then, what I engage
Shall be hereafter. If some god o'ercome   260
For me these arrogant suitors, I will give
To each of you a wife and lands, and build
For each a house near mine, and ye shall be
The friends and brothers of Telemachus
Thenceforth. And now, that ye may surely know   265
And trust me, I will show a token here—
A scar which once the white tooth of a boar
Made, when long since, on the Parnassian mount,
I hunted with Autolycus's sons."
Thus having said, he drew from the broad scar   270
The covering rags; they looked and knew it well,
And wept, and round Odysseus threw their arms,
And kissed in that embrace the hero's head
And shoulders, while Odysseus also kissed
Their heads and hands. The sun would have gone down   275
Upon their weeping, but for him. He said:
"Cease now from tears, lest some one from the hall
Should see us, and report of us within.

Now let us enter, not in company—
I first, and ye thereafter, one by one,   280
And let the sign be this: the others all—
The haughty suitors—will refuse to me
The bow and quiver. When thou bearest it,
My noble friend Eumaeus, through the halls,
Bring it and place it in my hands, and charge   285
The women to make fast the solid doors;
And then if any one of them should hear
A groan or other noise of men within,
Let her not issue forth, but silently
Pursue her task. Meantime be it thy care,   290
My good Philoetius, with a key to lock
The portals of the court and fix the chain."
Thus having said, into that noble pile
He passed again, and took the seat from which
He lately rose, and afterward, in turn,   295
Entered the servants of the godlike chief.
Eurymachus was busy with the bow,
Turning and warming it before the blaze
On both its sides. He could not bend it thus.
There came a deep sigh from his boastful heart,   300
And greatly was he vexed, and sadly said:
"Alas! great cause of grief indeed is here
For me and all. 'tis not that I lament
So much the losing of the bride, although
That also vexes me—there yet remain   305
Many fair ladies of the Achaean stock,
Both in the sea-girt lands of Ithaca
And other regions—yet if we be found
To fall in strength of arm so far below
The great Odysseus that we cannot bend   310

His bow, our sons will hear of it with shame."
Eupeithes' son, Antinous, answered thus:
"Not so, Eurymachus, as thou thyself
Shouldst know. This day is held a solemn feast
Of Phoebus by the people. Who would draw   315
The bow today? Nay, lay it by in peace,
And suffer all the rings to stand as now;
For no man, as I think, will dare to come
Into the palace of Laertes' son
And take them hence. Let him who bears the cup   320
Begin to serve the wine, that, having poured
Part to the gods, we may lay down the bow,
And with the morning let Melanthius come—
The goatherd—bringing with him from the flock
The choicest goats, that we may burn the thighs,   325
An offering to the god of archery,
Apollo, Then will we again essay
The bow, and bring the contest to an end."
So spake Antinous, and they all approved.
Then heralds came, and on the suitors' hands   330
Poured water; youths filled up the cups with wine,
Beginning at the right, and gave to each
His share; and when they all had poured a part,
And each had drunk, the shrewd Odysseus thus
With artful speech bespake the suitor-train: 335
"Hearken, ye suitors of the illustrious queen,
To what my heart is prompting me to say;
But chiefly to Eurymachus I make
My suit, and to Antinous, who so well
Hath counseled to lay by the bow and trust   340
The gods. Tomorrow Phoebus will bestow
The needed strength on whomsoe'er he will;

But let me take that polished bow, and try
Among you, whether still the power that dwelt
In these once pliant limbs abides in them,   345
Or whether happily it has passed from me
Amid my wanderings and a life of want."
He spake, and all were vehemently moved
With anger, for they feared that he would bend
The bow, and thus Antinous, railing, spake: 350
"Thou worthless vagabond, without a spark
Of reason, art thou not content to sit
And banquet with the proudest, where no part
Of all the feast escapes thee, hearing all
That we are saying, which no other man,   355
Stranger and beggar, is allowed to hear!
This good wine makes thee foolish, as wine oft
Makes those who swallow it too greedily,
And drink not with due stint. It maddened once
Eurytion, the famed Centaur, in the halls   360
Of the large-souled Pirithous. He had come
Among the Lapithae, and when inflamed
With wine to madness, in those very halls
Did lawless deeds. The heroes were incensed.
They rushed upon him, dragged him through the porch   365
And out of doors, and there cut off his nose
And ears, and he departed, frenzied still,
Land bearing in bewilderment of mind
His punishment, whence war arose between
Centaurs and men; yet surely he had brought   370
The evil on himself, when overcome
With wine. Such fearful mischief I foretell
Will light on thee, if thou shouldst bend this bow,
Nor canst thou hope for favor here among

The people. We will send thee speedily,   375
In a black galley, to King Echetus,
The enemy of humankind, from whom
Thou shalt find no escape. Drink, then, in peace
Thy wine, and seek no strife with younger men."
Then spake the sage Penelope again: 330
"Truly, Antinous, it becomes thee not,
Nor is it just, to vex the stranger guests
Who seek the palace of Telemachus.
Dost thou, then, think that, should this stranger bend,
Proud as he is of his great strength of arm,   385
The mighty bow that once Odysseus bore,
He leads me hence a bride? No hope of that
Is in his heart, and let no one of you
Who banquet here allow a thought like that
To vex him; 'tis a thing that cannot be."   390
Then to the queen, Eurymachus, the son
Of Polybus, replied: "We do not fear,
Sage daughter of Icarius, that this man
Will lead thee hence a bride; it cannot be.
We fear the speech of men and women both.   395
The very meanest of the Achaean race
Will say: 'Degenerate men are these, who seek
To wed the consort of a glorious chief,
Not one of whom can draw the bow he bore;
And now there comes a wandering beggar-man,   400
Who draws the bow with ease, and sends a shaft
Through all the rings of steel.' Thus will they speak,
And this will be to us a cause of shame!"
And then the sage Penelope rejoined:
"Eurymachus, it cannot be that those   405
Should earn the general praise who make the wealth

Of a most worthy man their spoil, and bring
Dishonor on his house. The stranger's frame
Is powerful and well knit; he claims to be
Of noble parentage. Now let him take   410
The bow, and we will see the event; but this
I promise, and will make my promise good,
If he should bend it—if Apollo give
To him that glory—he shall have from me
A tunic and a cloak, fair garments both,   415
And a keen javelin, his defense against
Both dogs and men, a two-edged sword besides,
And sandals for his feet, and I engage
To send him whither he desires to go."
Then spake discreet Telemachus again: 420
"Mother, in all Achaia there is none
Who has more power than I can claim, to grant
Or to deny the bow to whom I will.
No one of those who rule the rugged coast
Of Ithaca, or isles where Elis breeds   425
Her mares, may interpose to thwart my will,
If on the stranger I bestow the bow
To be his own, and bid him take it hence.
Withdraw, O queen, into thy bower; direct
Thy household tasks, the distaff and the web,   430
And bid thy maidens speed the work. The bow
Belongs to men, and most to me; for here,
Within these walls, the authority is mine."
The queen, astonished, heard him and withdrew,
But kept her son's wise sayings in her heart.   435
And then ascending to her bower, among
Her maids, she wept her well-beloved lord,
Odysseus, till the blue-eyed Pallas came,

And poured upon her lids the balm of sleep.
Meantime the worthy swineherd bore the bow   440
In hand, and all along the palace-halls
The suitor-crew were chiding him aloud,
And thus an insolent youth among them spake:
"Thou awkward swineherd, whither goest thou
With the curved bow? Thy own fleet dogs which thou   445
Hast reared shall soon devour thee, far from men
And midst thy herds of swine, if we find grace
With Phoebus and the other deathless gods."
Such were their words; the swineherd where he stood
Set down the bow in fear, for many a voice   450
Called to him in the hall. On the other side
Shouted Telemachus with threatening words:
"Nay, father, carry on the bow, nor think
To stop at every man's command; lest I,
Though younger than thyself, cast stones at thee,   455
And chase thee to the fields, for I in strength
Excel thee. Would that I excelled as far
In strength of arm the suitors in these halls,
Then would I roughly through the palace-gates
Drive many who are plotting mischief now."   460
He spake, and all with hearty laughter heard
His words, and for their sake allowed their wrath
Against the prince to cool. The swineherd went
Forward, along the hall, and, drawing near
The wise Odysseus, gave into his hands   465
The bow; and then he called the nurse aside,
Dame Eurycleia, and bespake her thus:
"Sage Eurycleia, from Telemachus
I charge thee to make fast the solid doors,
And then, if any of the maids should hear   470

A groan or other noise of men within,
Let her not issue forth, but silently
Pursue the task in hand, and keep her place."
He spake, nor were his words in vain. The dame
Made fast the doors of that magnificent hall,   475
While silently Philoetius hastened forth
And locked the portals of the high-walled court.
A cable of the bark of Byblos lay
Beneath the portico—it once had served
A galley—and with this the herdsman tied   480
The portals, and, returning, took the seat
Whence he had risen, but ever kept his eye
Fixed on his lord. Odysseus, meantime, held
The bow, and, turning it, intently eyed
Side after side, and tried each part in turn,   485
For fear that worms, while he was far away,
Had pierced the horn. At this, a youth among
The suitors, turning to his neighbor, said:
"Lo an inspector and a judge of bows!
Perhaps he has a bow like that at home,   490
Or else would make one like it. How he shifts
The thing with busy hands from side to side—
The vagabond, well trained in knavish tricks!"
Then also said another insolent youth:
"May he in all things be as fortunate   495
As now, when he shall try to bend that bow!"
"Such was their talk; but when the wary chief
Had poised and shrewdly scanned the mighty bow,
Then, as a singer, skilled to play the harp,
Stretches with ease on its new fastenings   500
A string, the twisted entrails of a sheep,
Made fast at either end, so easily

Odysseus bent that mighty bow. He took
And drew the cord with his right hand; it twanged
With a clear sound as when a swallow screams.   505
The suitors were dismayed, and all grew pale.
Zeus in loud thunder gave a sign from heaven.
The much-enduring chief, Odysseus, heard
With joy the friendly omen, which the son
Of crafty Cronus sent him. He took up   510
A winged arrow, that before him lay
Upon a table, drawn; the others still
Were in the quiver's womb; the Greeks were yet
To feel them. This he set with care against
The middle of the bow, and toward him drew   515
The cord and arrow-notch, just where he sat,
And, aiming opposite, let fly the shaft.
He missed no ring of all; from first to last
The brass-tipped arrow threaded every one.
Then to Telemachus Odysseus said: 520
"Telemachus, the stranger sitting here
Hath not disgraced thee. I have neither missed
The rings, nor found it hard to bend the bow;
Nor has my manly strength decayed, as these
Who seek to bring me to contempt pretend;   525
And now the hour is come when we prepare
A supper for the Achaeans, while the day
Yet lasts, and after supper the delights
Of song and harp, which nobly grace a feast."
He spake, and nodded to Telemachus,   530
His well-beloved son, who girded on
His trenchant sword, and took in hand his spear,
And, armed with glittering brass for battle, came
And took his station by his father's seat.

BOOK XXII

Then did Odysseus cast his rags aside,   1
And, leaping to the threshold, took his stand
On its broad space, with bow and quiver filled
With arrows. At his feet the hero poured
The winged shafts, and to the suitors called: 5
"That difficult strife is ended. Now I take
Another mark, which no man yet has hit.
Now shall I see if I attain my aim,
And, by the aid of Phoebus, win renown."
He spake; and, turning, at Antinous aimed   10
The bitter shaft—Antinous, who just then
Had grasped a beautiful two-eared cup of gold,
About to drink the wine. He little thought
Of wounds and death; for who, when banqueting
Among his fellows, could suspect that one   15
Alone against so many men would dare,
However bold, to plan his death, and bring
On him the doom of fate? Odysseus struck
The suitor with the arrow at the throat.
The point came through the tender neck behind,   20
Sideways he sank to earth; his hand let fall

The cup; the dark blood in a thick warm stream
Gushed from the nostrils of the smitten man.
He spurned the table with his feet, and spilled
The viands; bread and roasted meats were flung   25
To lie polluted on the floor. Then rose
The suitors in a tumult, when they saw
The fallen man; from all their seats they rose
Throughout the hall, and to the massive walls
Looked eagerly; there hung no buckler there,   30
No sturdy lance for them to wield. They called
Thus to Odysseus with indignant words:
"Stranger! in evil hour hast thou presumed
To aim at men; and thou shalt henceforth bear
Part in no other contest. Even now   35
Is thy destruction close to thee. Thy hand
Hath slain the noblest youth in Ithaca.
The vultures shall devour thy flesh for this."
So each one said; they deemed he had not slain
The suitor wittingly; nor did they see,   40
Blind that they were, the doom which in that hour
Was closing round them all. Then with a frown
The wise Odysseus looked on them, and said:
"Dogs! ye had thought I never would come back
From Ilium's coast, and therefore ye devoured   45
My substance here, and offered violence
To my maid-servants, and pursued my wife
As lovers, while I lived. Ye dreaded not
The gods who dwell in the great heaven, nor feared
Vengeance hereafter from the hands of men;   50
And now destruction overhangs you all."
He spake, and all were pale with fear, and each
Looked round for some escape from death. Alone

Eurymachus found voice, and answered thus:
"If thou indeed be he, the Ithacan   55
Odysseus, now returned to thine old home,
Well hast thou spoken of the many wrongs
Done to thee by the Achaeans in thy house
And in thy fields. But there the man lies slain
Who was the cause of all. Antinous first   60
Began this course of wrong. Nor were his thoughts
So much of marriage as another aim—
Which Cronus's son denied him—to bear rule
Himself o'er those who till the pleasant fields
Of Ithaca, first having slain thy son   65
In ambush. But he now has met his fate.
Spare, then, thy people. We will afterward
Make due amends in public for the waste
Here in thy palace of the food and wine.
For each of us shall bring thee twenty beeves,   70
And brass and gold, until thy heart shall be
Content. Till then we cannot blame thy wrath."
Sternly the wise Odysseus frowned, and said:
"Eurymachus, if thou shouldst offer me
All that thou hast, thy father's wealth entire,   75
And add yet other gifts, not even then
Would I refrain from bloodshed, ere my hand
Avenged my wrongs upon the suitor-crew.
Choose then to fight or flee, whoever hopes
Escape from death and fate; yet none of you   85
Will now, I think, avoid that bitter doom.'
He spake. At once their knees and head grew faint,
And thus Eurymachus bespake the rest:
"This man, O friends, to his untamable arm
Will give no rest, but with that bow in hand,   90

And quiver, will send forth from where he stands
His shafts, till he has slain us all. Prepare
For combat then, and draw your swords, and hold
The tables up against his deadly shafts,
And rush together at him as one man,   90
And drive him from the threshold through the door.
Then, hurrying through the city, let us sound
The alarm, and soon he will have shot his last."
He spake, and, drawing his keen two-edged sword
Of brass, sprang toward him with a dreadful cry,   95
Just as the great Odysseus, sending forth
An arrow, smote the suitor on the breast,
Beside the nipple. The swift weapon stood
Fixed in his liver; to the ground he flung
The sword, and, reeling giddily around   100
The table, fell; he brought with him to earth
The viands and the double cup, and smote
The pavement with his forehead heavily,
And in great agony. With both his feet
He struck and shook his throne, and darkness came   105
Over his eyes. Then rushed Amphinomus
Against the glorious chief, and drew his sword
To thrust him from the door. Telemachus
O'ertook him, and between his shoulders drove
A brazen lance. Right through his breast it went,   110
And he fell headlong, with his forehead dashed
Against the floor. Telemachus drew back,
And left his long spear in Amphinomus,
Lest, while he drew it forth, someone among
The Achaeans might attack him with the sword,   115
And thrust him through or hew him down. In haste
He reached his father's side, and quickly said:

"Now, father, will I bring to thee a shield,
Two javelins, and a helmet wrought of brass,
Well fitted to the temples. I will case   120
Myself in armor, and will also give
Arms to the swineherd. and to him who tends
The beeves; for men in armor combat best"
And wise Odysseus answered: "Bring them then,
And quickly, while I yet have arrows here   125
For my defense, lest, when I am alone,
They drive me from my station at the door."
He spake. Obedient to his father's word,
Telemachus was soon within the room
In which the glorious arms were laid. He took   130
Four bucklers thence, eight spears, and helmets four
Of brass, each darkened with its horsehair crest,
And bore them forth, and quickly stood again
Beside his father. But he first encased
His limbs in brass; his followers also put   135
Their shining armor on, and took their place
Beside the wise Odysseus, eminent
In shrewd devices. He, while arrows yet
Were ready to his hand, with every aim
Brought down a suitor; side by side they fell.   140
But when the shafts were spent, the archer-king
Leaned his good bow beside the shining wall,
Against a pillar of the massive pile,
And round his shoulders slung a fourfold shield,
And crowned his martial forehead with a helm   145
Wrought fairly, with a heavy horsehair crest
That nodded gallantly above, and took
In hand the two stout lances tipped with brass.
In the strong wall there was a postern door,

And, near the outer threshold of the pile,   150
A passage from it to a narrow lane,
Closed with well-fitting doors. Odysseus bade
The noble swineherd take his station there,
And guard it well, as now the only way
Of entrance. Agelaus called aloud   155
To all his fellows, and bespake them thus:
"Friends! will no one among you all go up
To yonder postern door, and make our plight
Known to the people? Then the alarm would spread,
And this man haply will have shot his last."   160
Melanthius, keeper of the goats, replied:
"Nay, noble Agelaus; 'tis too near
The palace gate; the entrance of the lane
Is narrow, and a single man, if brave,
Against us all might hold it. I will bring   165
Arms from the chamber to equip you all;
For there within, and nowhere else, I deem,
Odysseus and his son laid up their arms."
Thus having said, the keeper of the goats,
Melanthius, climbed the palace stairs, and gained   170
The chamber of Odysseus. Taking thence
Twelve shields, as many spears, as many helms
Of brass, with each its heavy horsehair plume,
He came, and gave them to the suitors' hands.
Then sank the hero's heart, and his knees shook   175
As he beheld the suitors putting on
Their armor, and uplifting their long spears.
The mighty task appalled him, and he thus
Bespake Telemachus with winged words:
"Telemachus, some woman here, or else   180
Melanthius, makes the battle hard for us."

And thus discreet Telemachus replied:
"Father, I erred in this. I was the cause,
And no one else; I left the solid door
Ajar; the spy was shrewder far than I.   185
Now, good Eumaeus, shut the chamber door,
And see if any of the palace-maids
Have brought these arms, or if I rightly fix
The guilt upon Melanthius, Dolius' son."
So talked they with each other, while again   190
Melanthius, stealing toward the chamber, thought
To bring yet other shining weapons thence.
The noble swineherd marked him as he went,
And quickly drawing near Odysseus said:
"Son of Laertes! nobly born and wise!   195
The knave whom we suspect is on his way
Up to thy chamber. Tell me now, I pray,
And plainly, shall I make an end of him,
If I may prove the stronger man, or bring
The wretch into thy presence, to endure   200
The vengeance due to all the iniquities
Plotted by him against thee in these halls?"
Odysseus, the sagacious, answered thus:
"Telemachus and I will keep at bay
The suitors in this place, however fierce   205
Their onset, while ye two bind fast his hands
And feet behind his back, and bringing him
Into the chamber, with the door made fast
Behind you, tie him with a double cord,
And draw him up a lofty pillar close   210
To the timbers of the roof, that, swinging there,
He may live long and suffer grievous pain."
He spake; they hearkened and obeyed, and went

Up to the chamber unperceived by him
Who stood within and searched a nook for arms.   215
On each side of the entrance, by its posts,
They waited for Melanthius. Soon appeared
The goatherd at the threshold of the room,
Bearing a beautiful helmet in one hand,
And in the other a broad ancient shield,   220
Defaced by age and mold. Laertes once,
The hero, bore it when a youth, but now
Long time it lay unused, with gaping seams.
They sprang and seized the goatherd, dragging him
Back to the chamber by the hair; and there   225
They cast him, in an agony of fear,
Upon the floor, and bound his hands and feet
With a stout cord behind his back, as bade
The great Odysseus, much-enduring son
Of old Laertes. Round him then they looped   230
A double cord, and swung him up beside
A lofty pillar, till they brought him near
The timbers of the roof. And then didst thou,
Eumaeus, say to him in jeering words:
"Melanthius, there mayst thou keep watch all night   235
On a soft bed, a fitting place for thee;
And when the Mother of the Dawn shall come
Upon her golden seat from ocean's streams,
Thou wilt not fail to see her. Thou mayst then
Drive thy goats hither for the suitors' feast."   240
They left him in that painful plight, and put
Their armor on, and closed the shining door,
And went, and by Odysseus, versed in wiles,
Stood breathing valor. Four were they who stood
Upon that threshold, while their foes within   245

Were many and brave. Then Pallas, child of Zeus,
Drew near, like Mentor both in shape and voice.
Odysseus saw her, and rejoiced and said:
"Come, Mentor, to the aid of one who loves
And has befriended thee, thy peer in age."   250
Thus said Odysseus, but believed he spake
To Pallas, scatterer of hosts. Fierce shouts
Came from the suitors in the hall, and first,
Thus Agelaus railed, Damastor's son:
"Mentor, let not Odysseus wheedle thee   255
To join him, and make war on us, for this
Our purpose is, and it will be fulfilled:
When by our hands the father and the son
Are slain, thou also shalt be put to death
For this attempt, and thy own head shall be   260
The forfeit. When we shall have taken thus
Thy life with our good weapons, we will seize
On all thou hast, on all thy wealth within
Thy dwelling or without, and, mingling it
With the possessions of Odysseus, leave   265
Within thy palaces no son of thine
Or daughter living, and no virtuous wife
Of thine, abiding here in Ithaca."
He spake, and woke new anger in the heart
Of Pallas, and she chid Odysseus thus: 270
"Odysseus, thou art not, in might of arm
And courage, what thou wert when waging war
Nine years without a pause against the men
Of Troy for Helen's sake, the child of Zeus,
And many didst thou slay in deadly strife,   275
And Priam's city, with its spacious streets,
Was taken through thy counsels. How is it

That, coming to thy own possessions here
And thy own palace, thou dost sadly find
Thy ancient valor fail thee in the strife   280
Against the suitors? Now draw near, my friend,
And stand by me, and see what I shall do,
And own that Mentor, son of Alcimus,
Amid a press of foes requites thy love."
She spake, but gave not to Odysseus yet   285
The certain victory; for she meant to put
To further proof the courage and the might
Both of Odysseus and his emulous son.
To the broad palace roof she rose, and sat
In shape a swallow. Agelaus now,   290
Damastor's son, cheered on with gallant words
His friends; so also did Amphimedon,
Eurynomus, and Demoptolemus,
Polyctor's son, Peisander, and with these
Sagacious Polybus. These six excelled   295
In valor all the suitors who survived,
And they were fighting for their lives. The bow
And the fleet shafts had smitten down their peers.
Thus to his fellows Agelaus spake:
"O friends, this man will now be forced to stay   300
His fatal hand. See, Mentor leaves his side,
After much empty boasting, and those four
Are at the entrance gate alone. Now aim
At him with your long spears—not all at once,
Let six first hurl their weapons, and may Zeus   305
Grant that we strike "Odysseus down, and win
Great glory! For the others at his side
We care but little, if their leader fall."
He spake; they hearkened. Eagerly they cast

Their lances. Pallas made their aim to err.   310
One struck a pillar of the massive pile;
One struck the paneled door; one ashen shaft,
Heavy with metal, rang against the wall.
And when they had escaped that flight of spears,
Hurled from the crowd, the much-enduring man,   315
Odysseus, thus to his companions said:
"Now is the time, my friends, to send our spears
Into the suitor-crowd, who, not content
With wrongs already done us, seek our lives."
He spake, and, aiming opposite, they cast   320
Their spears. The weapon which Odysseus flung
Slew Demoptolemus; his son struck down
Euryades; the herdsman smote to death
Peisander, and the swineherd Elatus.
These at one moment fell, and bit the dust   325
Of the broad floor. Back flew the suitor-crowd
To a recess; and after them the four
Rushed on, and plucked their weapons from the dead.
Again the suitors threw their spears; again
Did Pallas cause their aim to err. One struck   330
A pillar of the massive pile, and one
The paneled door; another ashen shaft,
Heavy with metal, rang against the wall.
Yet did the weapon of Amphimedon
Strike lightly on the wrist Telemachus.   335
The brass just tore the skin. Ctesippus grazed
The shoulder of Eumaeus with his spear,
Above the shield; the spear flew over it
And fell to earth. Then they who stood beside
The sage Odysseus, versed in wiles, once more   340
Flung their keen spears. The spoiler of walled towns,

Odysseus, slew Eurydamas; his son
Struck down Amphimedon; the swineherd took
The life of Polybus; the herdsman smote
Ctesippus, driving through his breast the spear,
And called to him, and gloried o'er his fall: 345
"O son of Polytherses, prompt to rail!
Beware of uttering, in thy foolish pride,
Big words hereafter; leave it to the gods,
Mightier are they than we. See, I repay   350
The hospitable gift of a steer's foot,
Which once the great Odysseus from thy hand
Received, as he was passing through this hall."
Thus spake the keeper of the horned herd.
Meantime, Odysseus slew Damastor's son   355
With his long spear, in combat hand to hand.
Telemachus next smote Evenor's son,
Leiocritus. He sent the brazen spear
Into his bowels; through his body passed
The weapon, and he fell upon his face.   360
His forehead struck the floor. Then Pallas held
On high her fatal aegis. From the roof
She showed it, and their hearts grew wild with fear.
They fled along the hall as flees a herd
Of kine, when the swift gadfly suddenly   365
Has come among them, and has scattered them
In springtime, when the days are growing long.
Meantime, like falcons with curved claws and beaks,
That, coming from the mountain summits, pounce
Upon the smaller birds, and make them fly   370
Close to the fields among the snares they dread,
And seize and slay, nor can the birds resist
Or fly, and at the multitude of prey

The fowlers' hearts are glad; so did the four
Smite right and left the suitors hurrying through   375
The palace-hall, and fearful moans arose
As heads were smitten by the sword, and all
The pavement swam with blood. Leiodes then
Sprang forward to Odysseus, clasped his knees,
And supplicated him with winged words: 380
"I come, Odysseus, to thy knees. Respect
And spare me. Never have I said or done,
Among the women of thy household, aught
That could be blamed, and I essayed to check
The wrongs of other suitors. Little heed   385
They gave my counsels, nor withheld their hands
From evil deeds, and therefore have they drawn
Upon themselves an evil fate. But I,
Who have done nothing—I their soothsayer—
Must I too die? Then is there no reward   390
Among the sons of men for worthy deeds."
Odysseus, the sagacious, frowned and said:
"If then, in truth, thou wert as thou dost boast,
A soothsayer among these men, thy prayer
Within these palace-walls must oft have been   395
That far from me might be the blessed day
Of my return, and that my wife might take
With thee her lot, and bring forth sons to thee,
And therefore shalt thou not escape from death."
He spake, and seizing with his powerful hand   400
A falchion lying near, which from the grasp
Of Agelaus fell when he was slain,
Just at the middle of the neck he smote
Leiodes, while the words were on his lips,
And the head fell, and lay amid the dust.   405

Phemius, the son of Terpius, skilled in song,
Alone escaped the bitter doom of death.
He by constraint had sung among the train
Of suitors, and was standing now beside
The postern door, and held his sweet-toned lyre,   410
And pondered whether he should leave the hall,
And sit before the altar of the great
Herceian Zeus, where, with Laertes, once
Odysseus oft had burned the thighs of beeves,
Or whether he should fling himself before   415
Odysseus, as a suppliant, at his knees.
This to his thought seemed wisest—to approach
Laertes' son, and clasp his knees. He placed
His sweet harp on the floor, between the cup
And silver-studded seat, and went and clasped   420
The hero's knees, and said in winged words:
"I come, Odysseus, to thy knees. Respect
And spare me. It will be a grief to thee,
Hereafter, shouldst thou slay a bard, who sings
For gods and men alike. I taught myself   425
This art; some god has breathed into my mind
Songs of all kinds, and I could sing to thee
As to a god. O, seek not then to take
My life! Thy own dear son Telemachus
Will bear me witness that not willingly   430
Nor for the sake of lucre did I come
To sing before the suitors at their feasts
And in thy palace, but was forced to come
By numbers and by mightier men than I."
He ceased; Telemachus, the mighty, heard   435
And thus bespake his father at his side:
"Refrain; smite not the guiltless with the sword;

And be the herald, Medon, also spared,
Who in our palace had the care of me
Through all my childhood; if he be not slain   440
Already by Philoetius, or by him
Who tends the swine, or if he have not met
Thyself, when thou wert ranging through the hall."
He spake, and the sagacious Medon heard,
As crouching underneath a throne he lay,   445
Wrapped in the skin just taken from a steer,
To hide from the black doom of death. He came
From where he lay, and quickly flung aside
The skin, and, springing forward, clasped the knees
Of the young prince, and said in winged words: 450
"Dear youth, behold me here; be merciful;
Speak to thy father, that he put not forth
His sword to slay me, eager as he is
For vengeance, and incensed against the men
Who haunt these halls to make his wealth a spoil,   455
And in their folly hold thyself in scorn."
He spake; the sage Odysseus smiled and said:
"Be of good cheer, since this my son protects
And rescues thee. Now mayst thou well perceive,
And say to other men, how much more safe   460
Is doing good than evil. Go thou forth
Out of this slaughter to the open court,
Thou and the illustrious bard, and sit ye there,
While here within I do what yet I must."
He spake; they moved away and left the hall,   465
And by the altar of almighty Zeus
Sat looking round them, still in fear of death.
Meantime, Odysseus passed with searching look
O'er all the place, to find if yet remained

A single one of all the suitor-crew 470
Alive, and skulking from his bitter doom.
He saw that all had fallen in blood and dust,
Many as fishes on the shelving beach
Drawn from the hoary deep by those who tend
The nets with myriad meshes. Poured abroad 475
Upon the sand, while panting to return
To the salt sea they lie, till the hot sun
Takes their life from them; so the suitors lay
Heaped on each other. Then Odysseus took
The word, and thus bespake Telemachus: 480
"Go now, Telemachus, and hither call
The nurse, Dame Eurycleia. I would say
Somewhat to her that comes into my thought."
So spake the chief. Telemachus obeyed
The word, and smote the door, and called the nurse: 435
"Come hither, ancient dame, who hast in charge
To oversee the women in their tasks;
My father calls thee, and would speak with thee."
He spake; nor flew the word in vain; she flung
Apart the portals of those stately rooms, 490
And came in haste. Before her went the prince.
Among the corpses of the slain they found
Odysseus, stained with blood, and grimed with dust.
As when a lion, who has just devoured
A bullock of the pasture, moves away, 495
A terror to the sight, with breast and cheeks
All bathed in blood; so did Odysseus seem,
His feet and hands steeped in the blood of men.
She, when she saw the corpses and the pools
Of blood, and knew the mighty task complete, 500
Was moved to shout for joy. Odysseus checked

Her eager zeal, and said in winged words:
"Rejoice in spirit, dame, but calm thyself,
And shout not. To exult aloud o'er those
Who lie in death is an unholy thing.   505
The pleasure of the gods, and their own guilt,
Brought death on these; for no respect had they
To any of their fellow-men—the good
Or evil—whosoever he might be
That came to them, and thus on their own heads   510
They drew this fearful fate. Now name to me
The women of the palace; let me know
Who is disloyal, and who innocent."
Then thus the well-beloved nurse replied:
"My son, I will declare the truth. There dwell   515
Here in thy palace fifty serving-maids,
Whom we have taught to work, to comb the fleece
And serve the household. Twelve of these have walked
The way of shame. To me they give no heed,
Nor to Penelope herself. Thy son   520
Has just now grown to manhood, and the queen
Has never suffered him to rule the maids;
But let me now, ascending to her room—
The royal bower—apprise thy wife, to whom
Some deity has sent the gift of sleep."   525
Odysseus, the sagacious, answered thus:
"Wake her not yet, but go and summon all
The women who have wrought these shameful deeds."
He spake; the matron through the palace went
To seek the women, and to bid them come.   530
Meanwhile, Odysseus called Telemachus,
The herdsman and the swineherd to his side,
And thus commanded them with winged words:

"Begin to carry forth the dead, and call
The women to your aid; and next make clean,   535
With water and with thirsty sponges, all
The sumptuous thrones and tables. When ye thus
Have put the hall in order, lead away
The serving-maids, and in the space between
The kitchen vault and solid outer wall   540
Smite them with your long swords till they give up
The ghost, and lose the memory evermore
Of secret meetings with the suitor-train."
He spake; the women came, lamenting loud
With many tears, and carried forth the dead,   545
Leaning upon each other as they went,
And placed them underneath the portico
Of the walled court. Odysseus gave command,
Hastening their task, as all unwillingly
They bore the corpses forth. With water next,   550
And thirsty sponges in their hands, they cleansed
The sumptuous thrones and tables. Then the prince,
Telemachus, with shovels cleared the floor,
The herdsman and the swineherd aiding him,
And made the women bear the rubbish forth.   555
And now when all within was once again
In seemly order, they led forth the maids
From that fair pile into the space between
The kitchen vault and solid outer wall,
A narrow space from which was no escape,   560
And thus discreet Telemachus began:
"I will not take away these creatures' lives
By a pure death—these who so long have heaped
Reproaches on my mother's head and mine,
And played the wanton with the suitor-crew."   565

He spake, and made the hawser of a ship
Fast to a lofty shaft; the other end
He wound about the kitchen vault. So high
He stretched it that the feet of none who hung
On it might touch the ground. As when a flock   570
Of broad-winged thrushes or wild pigeons strike
A net within a thicket, as they seek
Their perch, and find unwelcome durance there,
So hung the women, with their heads a-row,
And cords about their necks, that they might die   575
A miserable death. A little while,
And but a little, quivered their loose feet
In air. They led Melanthius from the hall
And through the porch, cut off his nose and ears,
Wrenched out the parts of shame, a bloody meal   580
For dogs, and in their anger from the trunk
Lopped hands and feet. Then having duly washed
Their feet and hands, they came into the hall,
And to Odysseus; they had done their work.
And then to the dear nurse Odysseus said: 585
"Bring sulfur, dame, the cure of noxious air,
And fire, that I may purge the hall with smoke;
And go, and bid Penelope come down,
With her attendant women, and command
That all the handmaids of the household come."   590
And thus in turn Dame Eurycleia spake:
"Well hast thou said, my son, but suffer me
To bring thee clothes, a tunic and a cloak,
Nor with those rags on thy broad shoulders stand
In thine own palace; it becomes thee not."   595
Odysseus, the sagacious, answered thus:
"First let a fire be kindled in this hall."

He spake, and Eurycleia, the dear nurse,
Obeyed, and brought the sulfur and the fire.
Odysseus steeped in smoke the royal pile.   600
Both hall and court. The matron, passing through
The stately palace of Odysseus, climbed
The stair to find and summon all the maids.
And forth they issued, bearing in their hands
Torches, and, crowding round Odysseus, gave   605
Glad greeting, seized his hands, embraced him, kissed
His hands and brow and shoulders. The desire
To weep for joy o'ercame the chief; his eyes
O'erflowed with tears; he sobbed; he knew them all.

BOOK XIII

Up to the royal bower the matron went   1
With an exulting heart, to tell the queen
That her beloved husband was within.
With knees that faltered not, and quick light step
She went; and, standing by her mistress, said: 5
"Awake, Penelope, dear child, and see
With thine own eyes what thou hast pined for long.
Odysseus has returned; thy lord is here,
Though late, and he has slain the arrogant crew
Of suitors, who disgraced his house, and made   10
His wealth a spoil, and dared insult his son."
And thus discreet Penelope replied:
"The gods, dear nurse, have made thee mad; for they
Have power to change the wisest men to fools,
And make the foolish wise, and they have warped is   15
Thy mind once sound. How canst thou mock me thus,
Amidst my sorrows, with such idle tales?
Why wake me from the pleasant sleep that closed
My lids so softly? Never have I slept
So sweetly since Odysseus went from me   20
To that bad city, which no tongue should name.

Go, then; return into the lower rooms.
Had any of my women save thyself
Brought such a message to disturb my sleep,
I would have sent her back into the hall
With angry words; thy years are thy excuse."
But Eurycleia, the dear nurse, rejoined:
"Nay, my dear child, I mock thee not. Most true
It is that thy Odysseus has returned,
And here he is at home, as I have said.
The stranger whom they scoffed at in the hall
Is he; and long Telemachus has known
That he was here, but wisely kept from all
His father's secret, till he should avenge
Upon those violent men their guilty deeds."
She ended, and her mistress, overjoyed,
Sprang from her couch, embraced the aged dame,
And wept, and said to her in winged words:
"Tell me, dear nurse, and truly, if indeed
Odysseus have returned as thou hast said.
How smote he those proud suitors?—he alone,
And they so many, gathered in the hall."
And thus the well-beloved nurse replied:
"I saw it not, nor knew of it. I heard
Only the moanings of the slain, while we
The maids, affrighted, sat in a recess
Of that well-vaulted chamber; the firm doors
Closed us all in, until at length thy son,
Sent by his father, called me forth. I found
Odysseus standing midst the dead that lay
Heaped on each other, everywhere along
The solid pavement. Thou wouldst have rejoiced
To see him like a lion with the stains

25

30

35

40

45

50

Of slaughter on him. Now the suitors lie
Before the portals of the palace-court,   55
And he has kindled a great fire, and steeps
In smoke the noble hall. He bade me come
To call thee. Follow me, that ye may give
Your hearts to gladness—for ye have endured
Great sorrows both, and your long-cherished hope   60
Is now fulfilled. He hath returned alive
To his dear home, and finds thee and his son
Yet in his palace, and hath terribly
Avenged himself upon the guilty men
Who under his own roof have done him wrong."   65
Then spake the sage Penelope again:
"Beloved nurse, exult not overmuch,
Nor rashly boast. Well is it known to thee,
Were he to come beneath this roof again,
How welcome he would be to all, but most   70
To me and to the son to whom we gave
His being. Yet thy tidings are not true.
Some one of the immortals must have slain
The arrogant suitors, angry to behold
Their foul injustice and their many crimes;   75
For no respect had they to mortal man,
Good he might be, or bad, whome'er they met;
And therefore have they made an evil end.
But my Odysseus must have perished far
From Ithaca, cut off from his return."   80
Then Eurycleia, the dear nurse, rejoined:
"What words are these, my child, that pass thy lips?
Sayst thou, then, that thy husband, who now stands
Upon thy hearthstone, never will return?
O slow of faith! but thou wert ever thus.   85

Come, then, I give a certain proof. I saw
Myself, when he was at the bath, the scar
Left on him by the white tusk of a boar,
And would have told thee, but he laid his hands
Upon my mouth, and would not suffer me   90
To bear the tidings, such his forecast was.
Now follow me.; I give my life in pledge.
If I deceive thee, slay me ruthlessly."
Then spake discreet Penelope again:
"Dear nurse, though thou in many things art wise,   95
Think not to scan the counsels of the gods,
Who live forever. Yet will we descend,
And meet my son, and look upon the slain,
And see the avenger by whose hand they fell."
She spake, and from the royal bower went down,   100
Uncertain whether she should stand aloof
And question there her lord, or haste to him
And clasp his hands in hers and kiss his brow.
But having passed the threshold of hewn stone,
Entering she took her seat right opposite   105
Odysseus, in the full glow of the fire,
Against the other wall. Odysseus sat
Beside a lofty column with his eyes
Cast down, and waiting for his high-born wife
To speak when she had seen him. Long she sat   110
In silence, for amazement overpowered
Her senses. Sometimes, looking in his eyes,
She saw her husband there, and then again,
Clad in those sordid weeds, she knew him not.
Then spake Telemachus, and chid her thus: 115
"Mother, unfeeling mother! hard of heart
Art thou; how else couldst thou remain aloof?

How keep from taking, at my father's side,
Thy place, to talk with him, and question him?
No other wife could bring herself to bear   120
Such distance from a husband, just returned
After long hardships, in the twentieth year
Of absence, to his native land and her.
Mother! thy heart is harder than a stone."
And thus the sage Penelope replied: 125
"Dear child, my faculties are overpowered
With wonder, and I cannot question him,
Nor even speak to him, nor fix my looks
Upon his face. But if it be indeed
Odysseus, and he have returned, we soon   130
Shall know each other; there are tokens known
To both of us, to none but him and me."
She ended, and the much-enduring chief
Odysseus, smiling at her words, bespake
Telemachus at once, in winged words: 135
"Suffer thy mother, O Telemachus,
To prove me; she will know me better soon.
My looks are sordid, and my limbs are wrapped
In tattered raiment, therefore does she think
Meanly of me, and cannot willingly   140
Believe that I am he. But let us now
Consider what most wisely may be done.
He who hath slain, among a tribe of men,
A single one with few to avenge his death,
Flees from his kindred and his native land;   145
But we have slain the champions of the realm,
The flower of all the youth of Ithaca.
Therefore, I pray thee, think what shall be done."
And then discreet Telemachus replied:

"Look thou to that, dear father; for they say   150
That thou of all mankind wert wont to give
The wisest counsels. None of mortal birth
In this was deemed thy peer. We follow thee
With cheerful hearts; nor will our courage fail,
I think, in aught that lies within our power."   155
Odysseus, the sagacious, answered thus:
"Then will I tell thee what I deem most wise.
First take the bath, and then array yourselves
In tunics, bid the palace-maidens choose
Fresh garments; let the godlike bard, who bears   160
The clear-toned harp, be leader, and strike up
A melody to prompt the festive dance,
That all may say who hear it from without—
Whether the passers by or dwellers near—
'It is a wedding.' Else throughout the land   165
The rumor of the slaughter we have wrought
Among the suitors may have spread before
We reach our wooded farm, and there consult
Beneath the guidance of Olympian Zeus."
He spake; they hearkened and obeyed. They took   170
The bath, and then they put their garments on.
The maids arrayed themselves; the godlike bard
Took the curved harp, and woke in all the love
Of melody, and of the graceful dance.
The spacious pile resounded to the steps   175
Of men and shapely women in their mirth,
And one who stood without was heard to say:
"Someone, no doubt, has made the long-wooed queen
His bride at last; a worthless woman she,
Who could not, for the husband of her youth,   180
Keep his fair palace till he came again."

Such words were said, but they who uttered them
Knew little what had passed. Eurynome,
The matron of the palace, meantime took
Magnanimous Odysseus to the bath   185
In his own dwelling, smoothed his limbs with oil,
And threw a gorgeous mantle over him
And tunic. Pallas on the hero's head
Shed grace and majesty; she made him seem
Taller and statelier, made his locks flow down   190
In curls like blossoms of the hyacinth,
As when a workman skilled in many arts,
And taught by Pallas and Athena, twines
A golden border round the silver mass,
A glorious work; so did the goddess shed   195
Grace o'er his face and form. So from the bath
He stepped, like one of the immortals, took
The seat from which he rose, right opposite
Penelope, and thus addressed the queen:
"Lady, the dwellers of the Olympian heights   200
Have given thee an impenetrable heart
Beyond all other women. Sure I am
No other wife could bring herself to bear
Such distance from a husband just returned
After long hardships, in the twentieth year   205
Of absence, to his native land and her.
Come, nurse, prepare a bed, where by myself
I may lie down; an iron heart is hers."
To this the sage Penelope replied:
"Nay, sir, 'tis not through pride or disregard,   210
Or through excess of wonder, that I act
Thus toward thee. Well do I remember thee
As thou wert in the day when thy good ship

Bore thee from Ithaca. Bestir thyself,
Dame Eurycleia, and make up with care   215
A bed without the chamber, which he framed
With his own hands; bear out the massive bed,
And lay upon it seemly coverings,
Fleeces and mantles for his nightly rest."
She spake to try her husband; but, displeased,   220
Odysseus answered thus his virtuous queen:
"O woman, thou hast said unwelcome words.
Who hath displaced my bed? That task were hard
For long-experienced hands, unless some god
Had come to shift its place. No living man,   225
Even in his prime of years, could easily
Have moved it, for in that elaborate work
There was a mystery; it was I myself
Who shaped it, no one else. Within my court
There grew an olive-tree with full-leaved boughs,   230
A tall and flourishing tree; its massive stem
Was like a column. Round it I built up
A chamber with cemented stones until
The walls were finished; then I framed a roof
Above it, and put on the well-glued doors   235
Close fitting. Next I lopped the full-leaved boughs,
And, cutting off the trunk above the root,
Smoothed well the stump with tools, and made of it
A post to bear the couch. I bored the wood
With wimbles, placed on it the frame, and carved   240
The work till it was done, inlaying it
With silver, gold, and ivory. I stretched
Upon it thongs of oxhide brightly dyed
In purple. Now, O wife, I cannot know
Whether my bed remains as then it was,   245

Or whether someone from the root has hewn
The olive trunk, and moved it from its place."
He spake, and her knees faltered and her heart
Was melted as she heard her lord recount
The tokens all so truly; and she wept,   250
And rose, and ran to him, and flung her arms
About his neck, and kissed his brow, and said:
"Odysseus, look not on me angrily,
Thou who in other things art wise above
All other men. The gods have made our lot   255
A hard one, jealous lest we should have passed
Our youth together happily, and thus
Have reached old age. I pray, be not incensed,
Nor take it ill that I embraced thee not
As soon as I beheld thee, for my heart   260
Has ever trembled lest someone who comes
Into this isle should cozen me with words;
And they who practice fraud are numberless.
The Argive Helen, child of Zeus,
Would ne'er have listened to a stranger's suit   265
And loved him, had she known that in the years
To come the warlike Greeks would bring her back
To her own land. It was a deity
Who prompted her to that foul wrong. Her thought
Was never of the great calamity   270
Which followed, and which brought such woe on us.
But now, since thou, by tokens clear and true,
Hast spoken of our bed, which human eye
Has never seen save mine and thine, and those
Of one handmaiden only, Actoris—   275
Her whom my father gave me when I came
To this thy palace, and who kept the door

Of our close chamber—thou hast won my mind
To full belief, though hard it was to win."
She spake, and he was moved to tears; he wept   280
As in his arms he held his dearly loved
And faithful wife. As welcome as the land
To those who swim the deep, of whose stout bark
Poseidon has made a wreck amidst the waves,
Tossed by the billow and the blast, and few   285
Are those who from the hoary ocean reach
The shore, their limbs all crested with the brine,
These gladly climb the sea-beach, and are safe—
So welcome was her husband to her eyes.
Nor would her fair white arms release his neck,   290
And there would rosy-fingered Mom have found
Both weeping, but the blue-eyed Pallas planned
That thus it should not be; she stayed the night
When near its close, and held the golden Morn
Long in the ocean deeps, nor suffered her   295
To yoke her steeds that bring the light to men—
Lampas and Phaethon, swift steeds that bear
The Morning on her way. Odysseus then,
The man of forecast, thus bespake his queen:
"Not yet, O wife, have we attained the close   300
Of all our labors. One remains which yet
I must achieve, toilsome, and measureless
In difficulty; for so prophesied
The spirit of Tiresias, on the day
When to the abode of Hades I went down   305
To ask the seer concerning the return
Of my companions, and my own. But now
Seek we our couch, dear wife, that, softly laid,
We may refresh ourselves with welcome sleep."

Then spake in turn the sage Penelope: 310
"Whenever thou desirest it thy couch
Shall be made ready, since the gods vouchsafe
To bring thee back into thy pleasant home
And to thy native land. But now that thou
Hast spoken of it, and some deity   315
Is prompting thee, declare what this new task
May be. Hereafter I shall hear of it,
No doubt, nor were it worse to know it now."
Odysseus, the sagacious, answered thus:
"Dear wife, why wilt thou ask? why press me thus?   320
Yet will I tell thee truly, nor will keep
Aught from thee, though thou wilt not gladly hear,
Nor I relate. Tiresias bade me pass
Through city after city, till I found
A people who know not the sea, nor eat   325
Their food with salt, who never yet beheld
The red-prowed galley, nor the shapely oars,
Which are the wings of ships. And this plain sign
He gave, nor will I keep it back from thee,
That when another traveler whom I meet   330
Shall say it is a winnowing-fan I bear
On my stout shoulder, there he bade me plant
The oar upright in earth, and offer up
To monarch Poseidon there a ram, a bull,
And sturdy boar, and then, returning home,   335
Burn hallowed hecatombs to all the gods
Who dwell in the broad heaven, each one in turn.
At last will death come over me, afar
From ocean, such a death as peacefully
Shall take me off in a serene old age,   340
Amid a people prosperous and content.

All this, the prophet said, will come to pass."
And then the sage Penelope rejoined:
"If thus the immortals make thy later age
The happier, there is hope that thou wilt find   345
Escape from evil in the years to come."
So talked they with each other. Meantime went
Eurynome, attended by the nurse,
And in the light of blazing torches dressed
With soft fresh drapery a bed; and when   350
Their busy hands had made it full and high,
The aged dame withdrew to take her rest
In her own chamber, while Eurynome,
Who kept the royal bower, upheld a torch
And thither led the pair, and, when they both   355
Were in the chamber, went her way. They took
Their place delighted in the ancient bed.
The prince, the herdsman, and the swineherd ceased
Meantime to tread the dance, and bade the maids
Cease also, and within the palace-rooms   360
Dark with night's shadow, sought their place of rest.
Then came the time of pleasant mutual talk,
In which that noblest among women spake
Of wrongs endured beneath her roof from those
Who came to woo her—an insatiate crew—   365
Who made of beeves and fatlings of the flock
Large slaughter, and drained many a wine-cask dry.
Then nobly born Odysseus told what woes
His valor brought on other men; what toils
And suffering he had borne; he told her all,   370
And she, delighted, heard him, nor did sleep
Light on her eyelids till his tale was done.
And first he told her how he overcame

The people of Ciconia; how he passed
Thence to the rich fields of the race who feed   375
Upon the lotus; what the Cyclops did,
And how upon the Cyclops he avenged
The death of his brave comrades, whom the wretch
Had piteously slaughtered and devoured.
And how he came to Aeolus, and found   380
A friendly welcome, and was sent by him
Upon his voyage; yet 'twas not his fate
To reach his native land; a tempest caught
His fleet, and far across the fishy deep
Bore him away, lamenting bitterly.   385
And how he landed at Telepylus,
Among the Laestrigonians, who destroyed
His ships and warlike comrades, he alone
In his black ship escaping. Then he told
Of Circe, her deceit and many arts,   390
And how he went to Hades' dismal realm
In his good galley, to consult the soul
Of him of Thebes, Tiresias, and beheld
All his lost comrades and his mother—her
Who brought him forth, and trained him when a child.   395
And how he heard the Sirens afterward,
And how he came upon the wandering rocks,
The terrible Charybdis, and the crags
Of Scylla—which no man had ever passed
In safety; how his comrades slew for food   400
The oxen of the Sun; how Zeus,
The Thunderer, with a bolt of fire from heaven
Smote his swift bark; and how his gallant crew
All perished, he alone escaped with life.
And how he reached Ogygia's isle, he told,   405

And met the nymph Calypso, who desired
That he would be her husband, and long time
Detained and fed him in her vaulted grot,
And promised that he ne'er should die, nor know
Decay of age, through all the days to come;   410
Yet moved she not the purpose of his heart.
And how he next through many hardships came
To the Phaeacians, and they welcomed him
And honored him as if he were a god,
And to his native country in a bark   415
Sent him with ample gifts of brass and gold
And raiment. As he uttered this last word,
Sleep softly overcame him; all his limbs
Lay loose in rest, and all his cares were calmed.
The blue-eyed Pallas had yet new designs;   420
And when she deemed Odysseus was refreshed
With rest and sleep, in that accustomed bed,
She called the Morning, daughter of the Dawn,
To rise from ocean in her car of gold,
And shed her light on men. Odysseus rose   425
From his soft couch, and thus enjoined his spouse:
"O wife! enough of misery have we borne
Already—thou in weeping for my long
Unhappy absence—I for years withheld
By Zeus and all the other gods   430
From my return to this dear land, although
I pined for home. Now since upon this couch
We take the place so earnestly desired,
Take thou the charge of all that I possess
Here in the palace. For the herds and flocks   435
Which those high-handed suitors have devoured,
I shall seize many others as a spoil;

The rest the Greeks will bring me, till my stalls
Are filled again. I hasten to my farm
Embowered in trees, to greet the aged man   440
My excellent father, who continually
Grieves for me. Prudent as thou art, I give
This charge; a rumor, with the rising sun,
Will quickly go abroad that I have slain
The suitors in the palace. Now withdraw,   445
Thou and thy maidens, to the upper room,
And sit and look not forth, nor ask of aught."
So spake the chief, and on his shoulders braced
His glorious armor. Then he called his son,
The herdsman, and the swineherd, bidding them   450
To take in hand their weapons. They obeyed,
And, having armed themselves in brass, they threw
The portals open. As they all went forth,
Odysseus led the way. The early light
Was on the earth, but Pallas, shrouding them   455
In darkness, led them quickly through the town.

BOOK XXIV

Cyllenian Hermes summoned forth the souls   1
Of the slain suitors. In his hand he bore
The beautiful golden wand, with which at will
He shuts the eyes of men, or opens them
From sleep. With this he guided on their way   5
The ghostly rout; they followed, uttering
A shrilly wail. As when a flock of bats,
Deep in a dismal cavern, fly about
And squeak, if one have fallen from the place
Where, clinging to each other and the rock,   10
They rested, so that crowd of ghosts went forth
With shrill and plaintive cries. Before them moved
Beneficent Hermes through those dreary ways,
And past the ocean stream they went, and past
Leucadia's rock, the portals of the Sun,   15
And people of the land of dreams, until
They reached the fields of asphodel, where dwell
The souls, the bodiless forms of those who die.
And there they found the soul of Peleus' son,
His friend Patroclus, and the blameless chief   20
Antilochus, and Ajax, who excelled

463

In stature and in form all other Greeks
Save the great son of Peleus. These were grouped
Around Achilles. Then approached the ghost
Of Agamemnon, Atreus' son; he seemed   25
In sorrow, and around him others stood,
Who in the palace of Aegisthus met
Their fate and died. The son of Peleus took
The word, and spake to Agamemnon thus:
"Atrides, we had thought that Zeus, who wields   30
The thunder, favored thee, through all thy years,
Beyond all other men—thou didst bear rule
Over so many and such valiant men
Upon the plain of Troy, where we of Greece
Endured such sufferings. Yet all too soon   35
The cruel doom of death, which no man born
Of woman can escape, has fallen on thee.
O, if amid the honors of thy sway
That doom had overtaken thee, while yet
In Troy's far realm, then would the assembled Greeks   40
Have built a tomb to thee! Thou wouldst have left
A heritage of glory to thy son;
Now hast thou died a most unhappy death."
And then the soul of Agamemnon said:
"Fortunate son of Peleus, godlike chief   45
Achilles, who didst die upon the field
Of Ilium, far from Argos, while there fell
Around thee many of the bravest sons
Of Troy and Greece, who fought for thee, and thou
Wert lying in thy mighty bulk, amid   50
Whirlwinds of dust, forgetful evermore
Of horsemanship. All that day long we fought,
Nor stayed our hands till Zeus, to part us, sent

A hurricane. When we had borne thee thence
And brought thee to the fleet, upon a bier   55
We laid thee, pouring o'er thy shapely limbs
Warm water, and anointing them with oil.
Round thee the Achaeans stood in tears, hot tears,
And cut their hair away. From ocean's depth
Thy mother, when she heard the tidings, rose   60
With her immortal sea-nymphs. Mournfully
Came o'er the waves the sound of their lament.
Trembled the Greeks with fear, and, rushing forth,
Would have sought refuge in their roomy ships,
If Nestor, wise in ancient lore, and known   65
For counsels ever safe, had not restrained
Their haste, and thus declared his prudent thought:
"'Stay, Argives, youths of Greece; think not of flight!
It is his mother; from the sea she comes
To her dead son, and brings her deathless nymphs.'   70
"He spake; his words withheld the valiant Greeks
From flight. And now around thee came and stood
The daughters of the Ancient of the Deep,
Lamenting bitterly. Upon thy corse
They put ambrosial robes. The Muses nine   75
Bewailed thee with sweet voices, answering
Each other. Then wouldst thou have seen no one
Of all the Argive host with eyes unwet,
The Muses' song so moved them. Seventeen days
And nights we mourned thee—both the immortal ones so   80
And mortals. On the eighteenth day we gave
Thy body to the fire, and at the pile
Slew many fatling ewes, and many an ox
With crooked horns. In raiment of the gods
The fire consumed thee 'midst anointing oils   85

And honey. Many heroes of our host
In armor and in chariots, or on foot,
Contended round thy funeral pyre in games,
And mighty was the din. And when at length
The fires of Hephaestus had consumed thy flesh,   90
We gathered up at morning thy white bones,
Achilles, pouring over them pure wine
And fragrant oils. Thy mother brought a vase
Of gold, which Bacchus gave, she said, the work
Of Hephaestus the renowned, and in it now,   95
Illustrious son of Peleus, thy white bones
Are lying, and with thine are mingled those
Of dead Patroclus Menoetiades.
Apart we placed the ashes of thy friend
Antilochus, whom thou didst honor most   100
After the slain Patroclus. O'er all these
The sacred army of the warlike Greeks
Built up a tomb magnificently vast
Upon a cape of the broad Hellespont,
There to be seen, far off upon the deep,   105
By those who now are born, or shall be born
In future years. Thy mother, having first
Prayed to the gods, appointed noble games,
Within the circus, for the Achaean chiefs.
Full often have I seen the funeral rites   110
Of heroes, when the youth, their chieftain dead,
Were girded for the games, and strove to win
The prizes; but I most of all admired
Those which the silver-footed Thetis gave
To mark thy burial, who wert loved by all us   115
The immortals. So thou hast not lost by death
Thy fame, Achilles, and among the tribes

Of men thy glory will be ever great;
But what hath it availed me to have brought
The war on Ilium to an end, since Zeus   120
Doomed me to be destroyed on my return,
Slain by Aegisthus and my guilty wife?"
So talked they with each other. Now approached
The herald Argus-queller, bringing down
The souls of suitors by Odysseus slain.   125
Both chiefs moved toward them, wondering at the sight.
The soul of Agamemnon, Atreus' son,
Knew well-renowned Amphimedon, whose birth
Was from Melanthius, and by whom he once
Was welcomed to his house in Ithaca;   130
And him the son of Atreus first bespake:
"Amphimedon, what sad mischance has brought
You all, who seem like chosen men, and all
Of equal age, into these drear abodes
Beneath the earth? 'twere hard indeed to find,   135
In a whole city, nobler forms of men.
Has Poseidon wrecked you in your ships at sea
With fierce winds and huge waves, or armed men
Smitten you on the land, while carrying off
Their beeves and sheep, or fighting to defend.   140
Your wives and city? Tell me, for I claim
To have been once your guest. Rememberest thou
I lodged in thy own palace when I came
With godlike Menelaus, and besought
Odysseus to unite his gallant fleet   145
To ours, and sail for Troy. A whole month long
Were we in crossing the wide sea, and hard
We found the task to gain as our ally
Odysseus, the destroyer of walled towns."

The soul of dead Amphimedon replied: 150
"Atrides Agamemnon, far renowned,
And king of men, I well remember all
Of which thou speakest; I will now relate,
And truly, how we met our evil end.
We wooed the wife of the long-absent chief   155
Odysseus; she rejected not, nor yet
Granted our suit, detested as it was,
But, meditating our destruction, planned
This shrewd device. She laid upon the loom
Within her rooms a web of delicate threads,   160
Ample in length and breadth, and thus she said
To all of us: 'Young princes, who are come
To woo me—since Odysseus is no more,
My noble husband—urge me not, I pray,
To marriage, till I finish in the loom—   165
That so my threads may not be spun in vain—
A funeral vesture for the hero-chief
Laertes, when his fatal hour shall come,
With death's long sleep; else some Achaean dame
Might blame me, should I leave without a shroud   170
Him who in life possessed such ample wealth.'
Such were her words, and easily they won
Upon our generous minds. So went she on
Weaving that ample web, and every night
Unraveled it by torchlight. Three full years   175
She practiced thus, and by the fraud deceived
The Grecian youths; but when the hours had brought
The fourth year round, a woman who knew all
Revealed the mystery, and we ourselves
Saw her unraveling the ample web.   180
Thenceforth constrained, and with unwilling hands,

She finished it. And when at length she showed
The vesture she had woven, the broad web
That she had bleached to brightness like the sun's
Or like the moon's, some hostile deity   185
Brought back Odysseus to a distant nook
Of his own fields, and to his swineherd's lodge.
And thither also came in his black ship
His son, returning from the sandy coast
Of Pylos. Thence the twain, when they had planned   190
To slay the suitors, came within the walls
Of the great city; first Telemachus,
And after him Odysseus, with his guide
The swineherd. He was clad in sordid weeds,
And seemed a wretched beggar, very old,   195
Propped on a staff. In that disguise of rags
None knew him, as he suddenly appeared,
Not even the oldest of us all. Harsh words
And blows we gave him. He endured them all
Awhile with patience, smitten and reviled   200
In his own palace. Moved at length by Zeus,
He and his son Telemachus bore off
The shining weapons from the hall, to lie
In a far chamber, and barred all the doors.
Then, prompted by her husband's craft, the queen   205
Proposed a game of archery, with bow
And rings of hoary steel, to all of us
Ill-fated suitors. This drew on our death.
Not one of us could bend that sturdy bow,
None had the strength. But as it passed from us   210
Into Odysseus' hands, we loudly chid
The bearer, and forbade him, but in vain.
Telemachus alone with stern command

Bade him deliver it. When in his hands

The much-enduring chief, Odysseus, took   215

The bow, he drew the string with ease, and sent

A shaft through all the rings. He sprang and stood

Upon the threshold; at his feet he poured

The winged arrows, cast a terrible glance

Around him, and laid King Antinous dead,   220

Then sent the fatal shafts at those who stood

Before him; side by side they fell and died.

Some god, we saw, was with them, as they rushed

Upon us mightily, and chased us through

The palace, slaying us on every side;   225

And fearful were the groans of dying men,

As skulls were cloven, and the pavement swam

With blood. Such, Agamemnon, was the fate

By which we perished. Now our bodies lie

Neglected at the palace; for not yet   230

Our kindred, dwelling in our homes, have heard

The tidings, nor have come to cleanse our wounds

From the dark blood, and lay us on the bier

With tears—such honors as are due the dead."

In turn the soul of Agamemnon spake: 235

"Son of Laertes, fortunate and wise,

Odysseus! thou by feats of eminent might

And valor dost possess thy wife again.

And nobly minded is thy blameless queen,

The daughter of Icarius, faithfully   240

Remembering him to whom she gave her troth

While yet a virgin. Never shall the fame

Of his great valor perish, and the gods

Themselves shall frame, for those who dwell on earth,

Sweet strains in praise of sage Penelope.   245

Not such was she who treacherously slew
The husband of her youth—she of the house
Of Tyndarus. Her name among mankind
Shall be the hateful burden of a song;
And great is the dishonor it has brought   250
On women, even the faithful and the good."
So talked they with each other, standing there
In Hades' realm beneath the vaulted earth.
Meantime Odysseus, hastening from the town,
Came to the fair fields of Laertes, tilled   255
With care. Laertes, after years of toil,
Acquired them. There his dwelling stood; a shed
Encircled it, where ate and sat and slept
The servants of the household, who fulfilled
His slightest wish. An old Sicilian dame   260
Was there, who waited, in that distant spot,
On her old master with assiduous care.
And then Odysseus to his followers said:
"Go into that fair dwelling, and with speed
Slay for our feast the fattest of the swine.   265
I go to prove my father; I would learn
Whether he knows me when he sees my face,
Or haply knows me not, so long away."
He spake, and laid his weapons in their hands.
Straight toward the house they went. Odysseus passed   270
Into the fruitful orchard, there to prove
His father. Going down and far within
The garden-plot, he found not Dolius there,
Nor any of the servants, nor his sons.
All were abroad, old Dolius leading them.   275
They gathered thorns to fence the garden-grounds.
There, delving in that fertile spot, around

A newly planted tree, Odysseus saw
His father only, sordidly arrayed
In a coarse tunic, patched and soiled. He wore   280
Patched greaves of bullock's hide upon his thighs,
A fence against the thorns; and on his hands
Gloves, to protect them from the prickly stems
Of bramble; and upon his head a cap
Of goatskin. There he brooded o'er his grief.   285
Him when the much-enduring chief beheld,
Wasted with age and sorrow-worn, he stopped
Beside a lofty pear-tree's stem and wept,
And pondered whether he should kiss and clasp
His father in his arms, and tell him all,   290
How he had reached his native land and home,
Or question first and prove him. Musing thus,
It pleased him to begin with sportive words;
And thus resolved, divine Odysseus drew
Near to his father stooping at his task,   295
And loosening the hard earth about a tree,
And thus the illustrious son accosted him:
"O aged man! there is no lack of skill
In tending this fair orchard, which thy care
Keeps flourishing; no growth is there of fig,   300
Vine, pear, or olive, or of plants that grow
In borders, that has missed thy friendly hand.
Yet let me say, and be thou not displeased,
Thou art ill cared for, burdened as thou art
With years, and squalid, and in mean attire.   305
It cannot be that for thy idleness
Thy master treats thee thus; nor is there seen
Aught servile in thy aspect—in thy face
Or stature; thou art rather like a king;

Thou seemest one who should enjoy the bath 310
And banquet, and lie soft—for this befits
Old men like thee. Now say, and tell me true,
Who may thy master be? whose orchard this
Which thou dost tend? And, more than this, declare,
For much I long to know, if I am come 315
To Ithaca, as I just now was told
By one who met me as I came—a man
Not overwise, who would not stop to tell
What I desired to learn, nor bear to hear
My questions, when I asked him if a guest 320
Of mine were living yet in health, or dead
And in the realm of Hades. Let me speak
Of him, and mark me well, I pray; I lodged
Once, in my native land, a man who came
Into my house, and never stranger yet 325
More welcome was than he. He was by birth
Of Ithaca, he said, Laertes' son,
And grandson of Arcesias. Him I led
Beneath my roof, and hospitably lodged,
And feasted in the plenty of my home, 330
And gave such gifts as might become a host—
Seven talents of wrought gold, a silver cup
All over rough with flowers, twelve single cloaks,
Twelve mats, twelve mantles passing beautiful,
And tunics twelve, and, chosen by himself, 335
Twelve graceful damsels, skilled in household arts."
And then his father answered, shedding tears:
"Thou art indeed, O stranger, in the land
Of which thou dost inquire, but wicked men
And lawless now possess it. Thou hast given 340
Thy generous gifts in vain; yet hadst thou found

Odysseus living yet in Ithaca,
Then would he have dismissed thee recompensed
With gifts and liberal cheer, as is the due
Of him who once has been our host. Yet say,   345
And truly say, how many years have passed
Since thou didst lodge my son, if he it was,
Thy hapless guest, whom, far away from home
And all his friends, the creatures of the deep,
And the foul birds of air, and beasts of prey,   350
Already have devoured. No mother mourned
His death and wrapped him in his shroud, nor I,
His father; nor did chaste Penelope,
His consort nobly dowered, bewail the man
She loved upon his bier with eyes dissolved   355
In tears, as fitting was—an honor due
To those who die. Now, further, truly tell,
For I would learn, what is thy name, and whence
Thou comest, from what tribe, thy city where,
And who thy parents. Where is the good ship   360
At anchor which has brought thee and thy friends?
Or hast thou landed from another's bark,
Which put thee on the shore and left the isle?"
Odysseus, the sagacious, answered thus:
"I will tell all and truly. I am come   365
From Alybas; a stately dwelling there
Is mine, Apheidas is my father, son
Of royal Polypemon, and my name
Eperitus. Some deity has warped
My course astray from the Sicanian coast,   370
And brought me hitherward against my will.
My bark lies yonder, stationed by the field
Far from the city. This is the fifth year

Since parting with me thy Odysseus left
My native land for his, ill-fated man!
Yet there were flights of birds upon the right
Of happy presage as he sailed, and I
Dismissed him cheerfully, and cheerfully
He went. We hoped that we might yet become
Each other's guests, exchanging princely gifts."
He spake, and a dark cloud of sorrow came
Over Laertes. With both hands he grasped
The yellow dust, and over his white head
Shed it with piteous groans. Odysseus felt
His heart within him melted; the hot breath
Rushed through his nostrils as he looked upon
His well-beloved father, and he sprang
And kissed and clasped him in his arms, and said:
"Nay, I am he, my father; I myself
Am he of whom thou askest. I am come
To mine own country in the twentieth year.
But calm thyself, refrain from tears, and grieve
No more, and let me tell thee, in a word,
I have slain all the suitors in my halls,
And so avenged their insolence and crimes."
And then Laertes spake again, and said:
"If now thou be Odysseus, my lost son,
Give some plain token, that I may believe."
Odysseus, the sagacious, answered thus:
"First, then, behold with thine own eyes the scar
Which once the white tusk of a forest boar
Inflicted on Parnassus, when I made
The journey thither, by thy own command,
And by my gracious mother's, to receive
Gifts which her father, King Autolycus,

375

380

385

390

395

400

405

Once promised, when he came to Ithaca.
And listen to me further; let me name
The trees which in thy well-tilled orchard grounds
Thou gavest me; I asked them all of thee,
When by thy side I trod the garden walks,   410
A little boy. We went among the trees,
And thou didst name them. Of the pear thirteen,
And of the apple ten thou gavest me,
And forty fig-trees; and thou didst engage
To give me fifty rows of vines, each row   415
Of growth to feed the winepress. Grapes are there
Of every flavor when the hours of Zeus
Shall nurse them into ripeness from on high."
He spake; a trembling seized the old man's heart
And knees, as he perceived how true were all   420
The tokens which Odysseus gave. He threw
Round his dear son his arms. The hardy chief,
Odysseus, drew him fainting to his heart.
But when the old man's strength revived, and calm
Came o'er his spirit, thus he spake again: 425
"O father Zeus, assuredly the gods
Dwell on the Olympian height, since we behold
The arrogant suitors punished for their crimes.
Yet much I fear lest all the Ithacans
Throng hither, and send messages to rouse   430
Against us all the Cephallenian states."
Odysseus, the sagacious, answered thus:
"Take courage; let no thought like that disturb
Thy mind; but let us hasten to the house.
Telemachus is there, with whom I sent   435
The herdsman and the swineherd, bidding them
Make ready with all speed our evening meal."

Thus talked the twain, and toward the dwelling took
Their way, and entering the commodious rooms
They found Telemachus, and by his side   440
The herdsman and the keeper of the swine,
Dividing for the feast the plenteous meats,
And mingling the dark wine. Then to the bath
Came the Sicilian dame, and ministered
To the large-souled Laertes, and with oil   445
Anointed him, and wrapped a sumptuous cloak
About him. Pallas gave the monarch's limbs
An ampler roundness; taller to the sight
He stood, and statelier. As he left the bath,
His son beheld with wonder in his eyes,   450
So like a god Laertes seemed, and thus
Odysseus said to him in winged words:
"Someone among the ever-living gods
Hath surely shed, O father, on thy form
And aspect all this grace and majesty."   455
The sage Laertes answered: "Father Zeus,
And Pallas and Apollo! would that I
Were now as when I took the citadel
Of Nericus, the strongly built, beside
The sea-shore of Epirus, leading on   460
My Cephallenians! With such strength as then,
Armed for the fray, I would have met and fought
The suitors in the palace yesterday,
And struck down many lifeless in the hall,
And greatly would thy spirit have rejoiced."   465
So talked they with each other. When they all
Ceased from their task, and saw their meal prepared,
They sat them down in order on the thrones
And seats, and each put forth his hand and shared

The banquet. Now approached an aged man,   470
Dolius, attended by his sons, who came
Weary with toil, for the Sicilian dame,
The nurse who reared them, went and summoned them—
She who in his late age with faithful care
Cherished the father. These, when at the board   475
They saw Odysseus, and knew who he was,
Stopped in the hall astonished. Instantly
Odysseus called to them with friendly words:
"Sit at the board, old man; let none of you
Give way to blank amazement Know that we,   480
Though keen our appetite for this repast,
Have waited long, expecting your return."
He spake, and Dolius sprang with outstretched arms
And seized Odysseus by the hand, and kissed
The wrist; and thus in winged words he spake: 485
"Dear master! since thou art returned to us,
Who longed and yet expected not to see
Thy face again—since some divinity
Has led thee hither—hail! and great may be
Thy happiness, and may the gods bestow   490
All blessings on thee! But declare, for I
Would gladly know, if sage Penelope
Have heard the tidings yet of thy return,
Or must we send them by a messenger."
Odysseus, the sagacious, answered thus: 495
"My aged friend, she knows already all.
Why wouldst thou take that care upon thyself?"
He spake, and Dolius on a polished seat
Sat down, but round the great Odysseus came
His sons, and welcomed him with loving words,   500
And hung upon his hand, and then they took

Their places by their father. So they sat
Beneath Laertes' roof, and banqueted.
Now through the city meantime swiftly ran
The rumor that the suitors all had met   505
A bloody death. No sooner had men heard
The tidings than they came with cries and moans
Before the palace, moving to and fro.
Each carried forth his dead, and gave to each
His funeral rites, except to those who came   510
From distant cities; these they put on board
Swift-sailing galleys of the fishermen,
That they might bear them home. And then they came
Sorrowing together in the market-place.
There, when the assembly now was full, arose   515
Eupeithes and addressed them. In his heart
Was sorrow, that could never be consoled,
For his slain son Antinous, who was first
To fall before Odysseus. Weeping rose
The father, and harangued the assembly thus:
"Great things, indeed, my friends, hath this man done   521
For us Achaeans. Many valiant men
He gathered in his ships and led abroad,
And lost his gallant ships, and lost his men:
And now, returning, he has put to death   525
The best of all the Cephallenian race.
Come, then, and ere he find a safe retreat
In Pylos, or in hallowed Elis, where
The Epeians rule, pursue him; endless shame
Will be our portion else, and they who live   530
In future years will hear of our disgrace.
If we avenge not on these men of blood
The murder of our sons and brothers, life

Will not be sweet to me, and I would go
At once, and gladly, down among the dead.   535
Rise, then, and fall upon them ere they flee."
So spake he, weeping; and the Greeks were moved
With pity as they heard him. Now appeared
The herald Medon and the sacred bard,
As, rising from the sleep of night, they left   540
The palace of Odysseus. They stood forth
Amid the multitude, who all beheld
With wonder. Then sagacious Medon spake:
"Give ear, ye men of Ithaca, and know
That not without the approval of the gods   545
Odysseus hath done this. I saw, myself,
One of the immortals taking part with him,
In all things like to Mentor. Now the god
Standing before Odysseus strengthened him
For combat, and now drove the routed band   550
Of suitors through the hall; in heaps they fell."
He spake, and all who heard were pale with fear.
The aged hero, Halitherses, son
Of Mastor, then came forward; he alone
Knew what was past and what was yet to come,   555
And, wisely judging, to the assembly said:
"Hear now my words, ye men of Ithaca.
Through your own wrong all this has come to pass.
To me ye would not hearken, nor obey
When Mentor, shepherd of the people, spake.   560
On the mad doings of your sons ye put
No curb, nor checked the guilty insolence
That dared to waste the substance and insult
The consort of a man of eminent worth,
Who, so they thought, would nevermore return.   565

Now be it as I counsel; let us not
Go forth to draw down evil on our heads."
He spake; but more than half the assembly rushed
Abroad with shouts; the others kept their place
Together. Ill the augur's speech had pleased   570
The most. Eupeithes had persuaded them.
They flew to arms, and when they had put on
The glittering brass, they mustered in close ranks
Before the spacious city. At their head
Eupeithes led them on, who madly deemed   575
Himself the avenger of his slaughtered son.
Yet he from that encounter nevermore
Was to return; his fate o'ertook him there.
Then Pallas thus addressed Cronus-son Zeus:
"Our Father, son of Cronus, king of kings,   580
Tell me, I pray, the purpose of thy heart
Yet unrevealed. Shall there be cruel war
And deadly combats, or wilt thou ordain
That these shall henceforth dwell in amity?"
And cloud-compelling Zeus made answer thus: 585
"My child, why ask me? Was it not with thee
A cherished purpose, that, returning home,
Odysseus amply should avenge himself
Upon the suitors? Do, then, as thou wilt.
Yet this, as the most fitting, I advise.   590
Now that the great Odysseus has avenged
His wrongs, let there be made a faithful league
With oaths, and let Odysseus ever reign;
And we will cause the living to forget
Their sons and brothers slain, and all shall dwell   595
In friendship as they heretofore have dwelt,
And there shall be prosperity and peace."

He spake, and eager as she was before,
Encouraged by his words, the goddess plunged
Down from the summits of the Olympian mount.   600
Now when they all had feasted to the full,
The much-enduring chief, Odysseus, said:
"Go, one of you, and see if they are near."
He spake; a son of Dolius at his word
Went forth, and, coming to the threshold, stopped.   605
He saw them all at hand, and instantly
Bespake Odysseus thus, with winged words:
"They are upon us; we must arm at once."
He spake; they rose, and quickly were in arms.
Four were Odysseus and his friends, and six   610
The sons of Dolius. Old Laertes then,
And Dolius, put on armor with the rest,
Gray-headed as they were, for now their aid
Was needed. When they all had clad themselves
In shining brass, they threw the portals wide   615
And sallied forth, Odysseus at their head.
Now Pallas, daughter of almighty Zeus,
Drew near them. She had taken Mentor's form
And Mentor's voice. The much-enduring chief,
Odysseus, saw her and rejoiced, and said   620
To his beloved son, Telemachus:

"Now wilt thou, of thyself, Telemachus,
Bethink thee, when thou minglest in the fray
That tries men's valor, not to cast disgrace
Upon thy forefathers—a race renowned   625
For manly daring over all the earth."
And thus discreet Telemachus replied:
"Nay, if thou wilt, my father, thou shalt see
That by no lack of valor shall I cast,

As thou hast said, dishonor on thy race."   630
Laertes heard them, and rejoiced, and said:
"O what a day for me, ye blessed gods,
Is this! With what delight I see my son
And grandson rivals on the battle-field."
And then the blue-eyed Pallas, drawing near   635
Laertes, said: "Son of Arcesias, loved
By me beyond all others of my friends,
Pray to Zeus's blue-eyed daughter, and to Zeus,
And brandish thy long spear, and send it forth."
So Pallas spake, and breathed into his frame   640
Strength irresistible. The aged chief
Prayed to the daughter of almighty Zeus,
And brandished his long spear and sent it forth.
It smote Eupeithes on the helmet's cheek.
The brass stayed not the spear, the blade passed through,   645
And heavily Eupeithes fell to earth,
His armor clashing round him as he fell.
Then rushed Odysseus and his valiant son
Forward, the foremost of their band, and smote
Their foes with swords and lances double-edged,   655
And would have struck them down to rise no more,
If Pallas, daughter of the god who bears
The aegis, had not with a mighty voice
Commanded all the combatants to cease:
"Stay, men of Ithaca; withhold your hands   655
From deadly combat. Part, and shed no blood."
So Pallas spake, and they grew pale with awe,
And fear-struck; as they heard her words they dropped
Their weapons all upon the earth. They fled
Townward as if for life, while terribly   660
The much-enduring chief Odysseus raised

His voice, and shouted after them, and sprang
Upon them as an eagle darts through air.
Then Cronus's son sent down a bolt of fire;
It fell before his blue-eyed daughter's feet,   665
And thus the goddess to Odysseus called:
"Son of Laertes, nobly born and wise,
Odysseus, hold thy hand; restrain the rage
Of deadly combat, lest the god who wields
The thunder, Cronus's son, be wroth with thee."   670
She spake, and gladly he obeyed; and then
Pallas, the child of aegis-bearing Zeus,
Plighted, in Mentor's form with Mentor's voice,
A covenant of peace between the foes.

ANSWERS TO DISCUSSION QUESTIONS

1. **Why does Homer choose to begin his epic in the final year of Odysseus's wanderings rather than with the fall of Troy?**

   As with the *Iliad*, Homer does not begin his epic *ab ovo* (Latin for "from the egg"), but plunges *in medias res* (Latin for "in the middle of things"), thus starting his epic at a moment of great tension. By holding off the beginning, Homer also gives Telemachus time to grow up—that's why Odysseus must spend seven years hidden away with Calypso (*Calypso* means "hidden" in Greek). This narrative device allows Homer to chart the dual journey and maturation process of father and son.

2. **How does the narrative structure of the *Odyssey* differ from that of the *Iliad*?**

   In a fashion that is surprisingly modern, Homer offers us parallel action in Books I-IV (the journey of Telemachus) and Books V-VIII (the journey of Odysseus). Books IX-XII are then told in flashback, narrating what happened in the nine years leading up to Book I. Because Books IX-XII are told in flashback, we get to hear Odysseus speak in first person, thus making him appear to be a real historical character.

3.   What did ancient critics say about Books I-IV?

Ancient critics considered Books I-IV to be a sort of mini-epic, focusing on the son of the great hero. They even gave that mini-epic a name: the *Telemachia*. In the third-century BC, Apollonius of Rhodes, one of the chief librarians of the Library of Alexandria, wrote his own four-book epic on Jason's Quest for the Golden Fleece, the *Argonautica* (Greek for "Voyage of the Argo," Jason's ship).

4.   Why does Telemachus have to visit Nestor and Menelaus?

The official reason why Telemachus must visit his father's comrades from the Trojan War is to obtain information from them about Odysseus's whereabouts. But there is another reason he must go. If Telemachus is to fight, and perhaps die, for his home, then he must first see what a working home looks like. The good life in the *Odyssey* is domestic rather than military, and it is vital that Telemachus see what that life can be like before he fights the suitors to attain it.

5.   How does Penelope hold off the suitors for so many years?

Though Penelope does not possess the physical strength of her husband, she shares his wit. Rather than wield a sword, she wields her feminine skill for working at the loom. She tells the suitors that she cannot marry one of them until she weaves a burial shroud for her father-in-law, Laertes. After they agree, she proceeds to weave the loom in full view of the suitors by day, but then undoes her work each night. By this stratagem, she holds them off for three years.

6. How exactly should the guest-host relationship (*xenia*) work?

According to the rules of *xenia*, when a stranger comes to your door, you must take him in and feed him *before* asking his name. Only after taking care of his needs may you ask his name and story. The guest, on the other hand, is obliged to treat his host's property with respect and not overstay his welcome. Polyphemus, the archetypal bad host, *first* asks the names of his visitors and then eats them.

7. Why does Athena, and other gods, appear in disguise most of the time?

Although the *Odyssey* is a more ethical poem than the *Iliad*, it takes place in a world where things are less certain and where treachery has grown. The gods are farther away and do not speak as directly as they did in the *Iliad*. Incidentally, Athena takes on the guise of a man named Mentor in order to guide Telemachus on his journey; it is for that reason that people today who take a young person under their wing in order to teach and direct him are called mentors.

8. What qualities does a hero need to survive and thrive in the world of the *Odyssey*?

In the *Iliad*, it is enough for a warrior to be strong and fearless. In the *Odyssey*, he must also possess a gracious tongue and be wise and discerning in his speech. Like the later knights of King Arthur, he must be both brave and courteous. In addition, he must have the ability to look through disguises and deceptions; he must not be fooled by appearances, but must persevere until the truth is revealed.

9. Can you give an example of someone holding on through disguises to reach the truth?

Menelaus shares with Telemachus an adventure he had on the coast of Egypt. In order to obtain the information he needs to get home, he is told that he must capture and hold down Proteus, the Old Man of the Sea. Menelaus is warned that when he holds down Proteus, he will change his shape from one form to another to frighten him; but that if he holds Proteus firmly until he returns to his original form, then Menelaus will be able to ask him questions and receive the answers he needs.

10. What are the two types of dangers Odysseus faces on his journeys?

The first type of danger Odysseus faces are threats to his life from savage beasts like the Cyclops, the Laestrygonians, and Scylla and Charybdis. To survive these dangers, Odysseus must draw on both his courage and his cleverness. The second type of danger is a more subtle one: that of being seduced by a false homecoming. Circe, Calypso, and Nausicaa all promise to provide the travel-weary hero with a surrogate Penelope and a new Ithaca. But Odysseus presses on through these false Penelopes until he is reunited with the real one.

11. What is the lure of the Sirens that makes them so dangerous?

In modern books and films, a Siren is usually depicted as a beautiful but cold blonde who seduces men and lures them to their doom. But the Sirens in the *Odyssey* are not beautiful; they are not even women. They have the faces and torsos of women, but the bodies of birds. It is their beautiful voices that lure sailors to the rocks; yet, even here, there is a frequent misunderstanding. Their lovely songs do not promise sex but knowledge of all things on the earth. Odysseus succeeds in hearing their voices without being killed by stuffing his men's ears with wax and having them tie him to the mast.

12. What does it mean to navigate between Scylla and Charybdis?

In the *Odyssey*, Scylla and Charybdis face each other across the narrow Strait of Messina that runs between Italy and Sicily. The former, a six-headed beast, lives in a high cave; when ships pass, she extends her doglike mouths and devours one sailor in each mouth. The latter lives in an underwater cave and periodically sucks in all the water in the strait, causing a whirlpool. To navigate between the two is to make a choice where either option threatens disaster. Scylla and Charybdis may also lie behind the phrase "caught between a rock and a hard place."

13. Why must Odysseus travel into the underworld?

According to Circe, Odysseus must travel to Hades so that he can meet the shade of the blind prophet Tiresias and receive advice that he will need to make it safely home. But there must be more to it than that, for nearly everything Tiresias tells Odysseus is later told to him again by Circe. Odysseus's descent into the underworld (*nekuia* in Greek) is meant to test the hero's courage and endurance in the face of his own mortality. So influential was this scene in western literature that the *nekuia* became a standard literary convention used by Virgil, Dante, and Milton.

14. Why does Homer give so prominent a role to Eumaeus the swineherd?

Homer was clearly fond of Eumaeus, whom he refers to as a prince among swineherds. Through his character, we see that servants can be as noble and heroic as their masters, and that loyalty is one of the greatest of virtues. Eumaeus, a curmudgeon with a heart of gold, has been a surrogate father for Telemachus in Odysseus's absence; he has steered him away from the vices of the suitors.

15. How does Penelope show her faithfulness in the Odyssey?

Penelope shows her faithfulness in two ways. First, she uses her wits to hold off the suitors, remaining loyal to her absent husband and her young son. Second, she calls for a contest and pledges to marry the winner. The reason she does this is not because she wants to marry one of the suitors (the thought disgusts her) but because she had promised Odysseus that if he did not return by the time her son had become a young man, she would marry again. By staying true to her promise, she sets in motion the contest that allows Odysseus to defeat the suitors.

16. How does Odysseus differ from and resemble the heroes of the Bible?

The heroes of the Bible begin in weakness and are made strong by God's aid; Odysseus, on the other hand, is strong and clever to begin with—traits which convince Athena to jump on his already winning team. Still, like the patriarchs of the Old Testament and the apostles of the New, Odysseus must trust for many years to the road. By doing so, he set a literary precedent that has been repeated in countless literary works: *Aeneid*, *Divine Comedy*, *Canterbury Tales*, *Don Quixote*, *Pilgrim's Progress*, *The Grapes of Wrath*, *Moby-Dick*, *The Lord of the Rings*, etc.

17. Why does Homer build a friendship between Telemachus and Peisistratus?

Though no explanation is given for why Homer matches Telemachus up with Nestor's son Peisistratus, I would give two reasons. First, Peisistratus represents, in sharp contrast to the young suitors, the right kind of friend that Telemachus needs if he is to mature into a good young man. Second, it is very possible that the *Odyssey* was put into written form under the auspices of the sixth-century BC Athenian tyrant, Peisistratus; perhaps this character was added then to flatter him.

18. How does Odysseus win back Penelope and why is that significant?

Odysseus wins back his wife by being the only person strong enough and skilled enough to string his bow and shoot an arrow through a difficult target. It is significant that the bow Odysseus strings is not one that he brought with him to Troy but which he only used for hunting on his estate. In that sense, the bow represents the domestic sphere rather than the battlefield.

19. Why is Odysseus so cruel to the maids and serving women?

Though most readers feel little remorse for the suitors slain by Odysseus and Telemachus, many are disturbed that Odysseus hangs the female lovers of the suitors. Given that Odysseus has sex with both Circe and Calypso, it might seem that he is being hypocritical in killing the maids for their illicit affairs. But his reason for doing so would be clear to Homer's audience. The maids have sullied their mistresses' home, bringing shame and scandal; as such, they are as much traitors as the suitors. That is why Eurycleia supports their execution.

20. How is Odysseus able to convince Penelope that he has truly returned home?

Afraid that she will be fooled by a false Odysseus and end up, like Helen of Troy, unfaithful to her husband, Penelope is suspicious when the beggar claims to be Odysseus. To test whether or not he is who he claims to be, she instructs the servants to drag her bed out of the bedroom so that the beggar can sleep in the hallway. Immediately, Odysseus, who carved their marriage bed out of the top of a single tree and thus knows that it cannot be moved, exclaims that such a thing would be impossible. When Penelope hears this, she knows that the man is Odysseus, for only he, a single servant, and she herself know the secret of the bed.

21. In Book XXIV, Homer gives us a final glimpse of the underworld, where we hear Agamemnon describe the funeral of Achilles and the dead suitors tell of their death at the hands of Odysseus. Why does Homer include this seemingly anti-climactic scene?

Though Homer does not give an explanation for why he includes this strange scene, I believe that he does so as a way of rounding off both the *Iliad* and *Odyssey*. Whereas Achilles achieves the good reward of the Iliadic hero (dying a soldier's death and receiving a grand funeral) and Odysseus achieves the good reward of the Odyssean hero (reunion with his family), Agamemnon (who was murdered by his wife's lover) gets neither.